**In a Land of Honor, War and Heroism,
One Powerful Samurai Would Master the
Way of the Sword . . .**

Sasaki Kojirō: The deadly samurai knew no shame or pity. He had come to Edo to make his fame and fortune—and he would kill anyone who stepped in his way . . .

Akemi: In Edo's red-light district she had known the touch of countless men. But no man could frighten her as Kojirō did—and no man could quench the flame in her heart for Musashi . . .

Zushino Kōsuke: Musashi came to him to have his sword sharpened and polished. But the old man refused, telling him, "I only polish souls . . ."

Yagyū Sekishūsai: He was the founder of the most powerful school of swordsmanship in Japan. But now he was dying, and a nation was crying out for a new master . . .

Iori: Mystical, rustic, full of the arrogance of youth, he and Musashi were bound by the earth they tilled together—and by the way that lay ahead . . .

D1293286

Books in the Musashi Saga by Eiji Yoshikawa

Book I: The Way of the Samurai
Book II: The Art of War
Book III: The Way of the Sword
Book IV: The Bushido Code

Published by POCKET BOOKS

Book V: The Way of Life and Death

Coming Soon from POCKET BOOKS

MUSASHI

BOOK IV:
THE
BUSHIDO
CODE

EIJI YOSHIKAWA

Translated from the Japanese by Charles S. Terry
Foreword by Edwin O. Reischauer

POCKET BOOKS

New York   London   Toronto   Sydney   Tokyo   Singapore

Map design by Ray Lundgren Graphics, Ltd.
Map research by Jim Moser

POCKET BOOKS, a division of Simon & Schuster Inc.
1230 Avenue of the Americas, New York, NY 10020

ISBN: 0-671-72991-8

First Pocket Books printing July 1989

10 9 8 7 6 5 4 3 2

CONTENTS

Contents

PLOT SUMMARY
Book I: *The Way of the Samurai*

Wounded in the great battle of Sekigahara, Takezō (later Musashi) and Matahachi were taken in by a beautiful girl, Akemi, and her lascivious mother, Okō. After a violent confrontation with local bandits, in which he slew the leader, Takezō left his friend with the two women and traveled back to his home province of Mimasaka. There, he was accused of having murdered Matahachi. A wild and undisciplined youth, Takezō was hunted by his own townspeople, and reacted with bitter rage—until the Buddhist town monk, Takuan Sōhō, was able to capture him without a single blow. Takuan tied Takezō up in the branches of a tall tree, but Matahachi's beloved, Otsū, took pity on him and freed him. Begging him to run away with her, she forsook Matahachi forever, but the eccentric Takuan had an even greater power over Takezō—and led him to Himeji Castle. There, by the light of a single lamp in a windowless room, Takezō began to study Suntzu's *The Art of War*, the Books of Zen, and the history of Japan. Weeks stretched into months, and gradually Takezō was transformed. When the day came for him to leave, he took the name Miyamoto Musashi and set off for Kyoto—and his first tests as a man of the sword . . .

PLOT SUMMARY
Book II: *The Art of War*

Musashi, Otsū and Takuan are in the beautiful Yagyū Valley, unaware of one another's presence, drawn by the master swordsman Sekishūsai. But a violent fight with the lords of Yagyū forces Musashi to flee—and leave Otsū behind. Outside Kyoto, Matahachi is working as a day laborer when he witnesses the brutal killing of a samurai by a crowd of workers. The dying samurai gives Matahachi a letter and a sack of gold, sending the half-starved man on a journey to Osaka, where his money is stolen from him. More destitute than ever, Matahachi learns that his former friend Takezō is traveling nearby under the name Musashi. Meanwhile, Osugi and Uncle Gon have come to Osaka, too, determined to bring back Matahachi and kill Musashi. Near the ridge of Mount Suzuka, Musashi is confronted by the brother of a man he killed years before. In Kyoto his friends, admirers and enemies are waiting for him, and so are the swordsmen of the House of Yoshioka—whom Musashi has challenged to a duel to the death . . .

PLOT SUMMARY
Book III: *The Way of the Sword*

The most powerful swordsman of the House of Yoshioka, Denshichirō, is searching for Musashi, while Musashi has fallen in with Kyoto's rich artistic crowd. Osugi and Matahachi are reunited and meet Otsū by the edge of a steep ravine. Osugi urges her son to kill the woman who betrayed him, but when he strikes out he spills the blood of the wrong person. In the company of a strange and brilliant artisan, Hon'ami Kōetsu, Musashi visits a house of pleasure, where he meets the most beautiful courtesan in Japan. But Musashi must leave her side to face Denshichirō, whom he kills in a duel. Now the Yoshiokas' very existence is threatened, and they set an extraordinary trap for Musashi. On a hill outside Kyoto he defeats their entire force, but in the process is forced to slay a young boy who is the symbolic head of the Yoshiokas. Stunned and confused, Musashi sets off for Edo. On the way he is challenged to a duel by a crude farmer and nearly loses his life. Suddenly Musashi knows his own utter fallibility—and that he has yet to learn the true essence of the samurai spirit.

CHARACTERS AND LOCALES

AKEMI, the daughter of Okō
DIAZŌ, a robber
EDO, the Shōgun's capital city
ISHIMODA GEKI, a retainer of Date Masamune
YAGYŪ HYŌGO, grandson of Yagyū Sekishūsai
TOKUGAWA IEYASU, the Shōgun, ruler of Japan
SANNOSUKE IORI, a peasant boy
JŌTARŌ, a young follower of Musashi
JŪRŌ, one of Hangawara Yajibei's thugs
OBATA KAGENORI, military instructor for the Shōgun
IWAMA KAKUBEI, a vassal of the House of Hosokawa
HON'AMI KŌETSU, an artisan
SASAKI KOJIRŌ, a young samurai
ZUSHINO KŌSUKE, a sword craftsman
KOROKU, one of Hangawara Yajibei's thugs
DATE MASAMUNE, a wealthy lord
HON'IDEN MATAHACHI, childhood friend of Musashi
YAGYŪ MUNENORI, son of Yagyū Sekishūsai and
    samurai of the Shōgun
MIYAMOTO MUSASHI, a swordsman of growing fame
HON'AMI MYŌSHŪ, the mother of Hon'ami Kōetsu
OKŌ, a lascivious woman
HON'IDEN OSUGI, the mother of Matahachi and bitter
    enemy of Musashi
OTSŪ, a young woman in love with Musashi
NAGAOKA SADO, aide to Hosokawa Tadatoshi

SEKIGAHARA, battle in which Ieyasu defeated the combined armies of the western daimyō for control of Japan

YAGYŪ SEKISHŪSAI, aging master of the Yagyū style of swordsmanship

HŌJŌ SHINZŌ, student of Obata Kagenori and son of Lord Hōjō Ujikatsu

TAKUAN SŌHŌ, an eccentric monk

KIMURA SUKEKURŌ, a swordsman of the House of Yagyū

HOSOKAWA TADATOSHI, eldest son of Lord Hosokawa Tadaoki

LORD HOSOKAWA TADAOKI, a powerful daimyō, or regional ruler

SHIMMEN TAKEZŌ, former name of Musashi

GION TŌJI, samurai of the Yoshioka school and suitor of Okō

HŌJŌ UJIKATSU, Lord of Awa and a renowned military strategist

HANGAWARA YAJIBEI, a powerful boss in Edo

OBATA YOGORŌ, son of Obata Kagenori

FOREWORD[1]
by Edwin O. Reischauer[2]

Musashi might well be called the *Gone with the Wind* of
Japan. Written by Eiji Yoshikawa (1892–1962), one of
Japan's most prolific and best-loved popular writers, it is
a long historical novel, which first appeared in serialized
form between 1935 and 1939 in the *Asahi Shimbun*,
Japan's largest and most prestigious newspaper. It has
been published in book form no less than fourteen times,
most recently in four volumes of the 53-volume complete
works of Yoshikawa issued by Kodansha. It has been
produced as a film some seven times, has been repeatedly
presented on the stage, and has often been made into
television mini-series on at least three nationwide net-
works.

Miyamoto Musashi was an actual historical person,
but through Yoshikawa's novel he and the other main
characters of the book have become part of Japan's living
folklore. They are so familiar to the public that people
will frequently be compared to them as personalities

---

[1]This foreword has been taken in its entirety from the original single-
volume American hardcover edition of *Musashi: An Epic Novel of
the Samurai Era*.
[2]Edwin O. Reischauer was born in Japan in 1910. He has been a
professor at Harvard University since 1946, and is now Professor
Emeritus. He left the university temporarily to be the United States
Ambassador to Japan from 1961 to 1966, and is one of the best-
known authorities on the country. Among his numerous works are
Japan: The Story of a Nation and *The Japanese*.

everyone knows. This gives the novel an added interest to the foreign reader. It not only provides a romanticized slice of Japanese history, but gives a view of how the Japanese see their past and themselves. But basically the novel will be enjoyed as a dashing tale of swashbuckling adventure and a subdued story of love, Japanese style.

Comparisons with James Clavell's *Shōgun* seem inevitable, because for most Americans today *Shōgun*, as a book and a television mini-series, vies with samurai movies as their chief source of knowledge about Japan's past. The two novels concern the same period of history. *Shōgun*, which takes place in the year 1600, ends with Lord Toranaga, who is the historical Tokugawa Ieyasu, soon to be the Shōgun, or military dictator of Japan, setting off for the fateful battle of Sekigahara. Yoshikawa's story begins with the youthful Takezō, later to be renamed Miyamoto Musashi, lying wounded among the corpses of the defeated army on that battlefield.

With the exception of Blackthorne, the historical Will Adams, *Shōgun* deals largely with the great lords and ladies of Japan, who appear in thin disguise under names Clavell has devised for them. *Musashi*, while mentioning many great historical figures under their true names, tells about a broader range of Japanese and particularly about the rather extensive group who lived on the ill-defined borderline between the hereditary military aristocracy and the commoners—the peasants, tradesmen and artisans. Clavell freely distorts historical fact to fit his tale and inserts a Western-type love story that not only flagrantly flouts history but is quite unimaginable in the Japan of that time. Yoshikawa remains true to history or at least to historical tradition, and his love story, which runs as a background theme in minor scale throughout the book, is very authentically Japanese.

Yoshikawa, of course, has enriched his account with much imaginative detail. There are enough strange coincidences and deeds of derring-do to delight the heart of any lover of adventure stories. But he sticks faithfully to such facts of history as are known. Not only Musashi himself but many of the other people who figure prominently in the story are real historical individuals. For example, Takuan, who serves as a guiding light and mentor to the youthful Musashi, was a famous Zen monk, calligrapher, painter, poet and tea-master of the time, who became the youngest abbot of the Daitokuji in Kyoto in 1609 and later founded a major monastery in Edo, but is best remembered today for having left his name to a popular Japanese pickle.

The historical Miyamoto Musashi, who may have been born in 1584 and died in 1645, was like his father a master swordsman and became known for his use of two swords. He was an ardent cultivator of self-discipline as the key to martial skills and the author of a famous work on swordsmanship, the *Gorin no sho*. He probably took part as a youth in the battle of Sekigahara, and his clashes with the Yoshioka school of swordsmanship in Kyoto, the warrior monks of the Hōzōin in Nara and the famed swordsman Sasaki Kojirō, all of which figure prominently in this book, actually did take place. Yoshikawa's account of him ends in 1612, when he was still a young man of about 28, but subsequently he may have fought on the losing side at the siege of Osaka castle in 1614 and participated in 1637–38 in the annihilation of the Christian peasantry of Shimabara in the western island of Kyushu, an event which marked the extirpation of that religion from Japan for the next two centuries and helped seal Japan off from the rest of the world.

Ironically, Musashi in 1640 became a retainer of the Hosokawa lords of Kumamoto, who, when they had been the lords of Kumamoto, had been the patrons of his chief rival, Sasaki Kojirō. The Hosokawas bring us back to *Shōgun*, because it was the older Hosokawa, Tadaoki, who figures quite unjustifiably as one of the main villains of that novel, and it was Tadaoki's exemplary Christian wife, Gracia, who is pictured without a shred of plausibility as Blackthorne's great love, Mariko.

The time of Musashi's life was a period of great transition in Japan. After a century of incessant warfare among petty daimyō, or feudal lords, three successive leaders had finally reunified the country through conquest. Oda Nobunaga had started the process but, before completing it, had been killed by a treacherous vassal in 1582. His ablest general, Hideyoshi, risen from the rank of common foot soldier, completed the unification of the nation but died in 1598 before he could consolidate control in behalf of his infant heir. Hideyoshi's strongest vassal, Tokugawa Ieyasu, a great daimyō who ruled much of eastern Japan from his castle at Edo, the modern Tokyo, then won supremacy by defeating a coalition of western daimyō at Sekigahara in 1600. Three years later he took the traditional title of Shōgun, signifying his military dictatorship over the whole land, theoretically in behalf of the ancient but impotent imperial line in Kyoto. Ieyasu in 1605 transferred the position of Shōgun to his son, Hidetada, but remained in actual control himself until he had destroyed the supporters of Hideyoshi's heir in sieges of Osaka castle in 1614 and 1615.

The first three Tokugawa rulers established such firm control over Japan that their rule was to last more than two and a half centuries, until it finally collapsed in 1868 in the tumultuous aftermath of the reopening of Japan to contact with the West a decade and a half earlier. The Tokugawa ruled through semi-autonomous hereditary daimyō, who numbered around 265 at the end of the period, and the daimyō in turn controlled their fiefs through their hereditary samurai retainers. The transition from constant warfare to a closely regulated peace brought the drawing of sharp class lines between the samurai, who had the privilege of wearing two swords and bearing family names, and the commoners, who though including well-to-do merchants and land owners, were in theory denied all arms and the honor of using family names.

During the years of which Yoshikawa writes, however, these class divisions were not yet sharply defined. All localities had their residue of peasant fighting men, and the country was overrun by rōnin, or masterless samurai, who were largely the remnants of the armies of the daimyō who had lost their domains as the result of the battle of Sekigahara or in earlier wars. It took a generation or two before society was fully sorted out into the strict class divisions of the Tokugawa system, and in the meantime there was considerable social ferment and mobility.

Another great transition in early seventeenth century Japan was in the nature of leadership. With peace restored and major warfare at an end, the dominant warrior class found that military prowess was less essential to successful rule than administrative talents. The samurai class started a slow transformation from being warriors of the gun and sword to being bureaucrats of the writing brush and paper. Disciplined self-control and education in a society at peace was becoming more important than skill in warfare. The Western reader may be surprised to see how widespread literacy already was at the beginning of the seventeenth century and at the constant references the Japanese made to Chinese history and literature, much as Northern Europeans of the same time continually referred to the traditions of ancient Greece and Rome.

A third major transition in the Japan of Musashi's time was in weaponry. In the second half of the sixteenth century matchlock muskets, recently introduced by the Portuguese, had become the decisive weapons of the battlefield, but in a land at peace the samurai could turn their backs on distasteful firearms and resume their traditional love affair with the sword. Schools of swordsmanship flourished. However, as the chance to use swords in actual combat diminished, martial skills were gradually becoming martial arts, and these increasingly came to emphasize the importance of inner self-control and the character-building qualities of swordsmanship rather than its untested military efficacy. A whole mystique of the sword grew up, which was more akin to philosophy than to warfare.

Yoshikawa's account of Musashi's early life illustrates all these changes going on in Japan. He was himself a typical rōnin from a mountain village and became a settled samurai retainer only late in life. He was the founder of a school of swordsmanship. Most important, he gradually transformed himself from an instinctive fighter into a man who fanatically pursued the goals of Zen-like self-discipline, complete inner mastery over oneself, and a sense of oneness with surrounding nature. Although in his early years lethal contests, reminiscent of the tournaments of medieval Europe, were still possible, Yoshikawa portrays Musashi as consciously turning his martial skills from service in warfare to a means of character building for a time of peace. Martial skills, spiritual self-discipline and aesthetic sensitivity became merged into a single indistinguishable whole. This picture of Musashi may not be far from the historical truth. Musashi is known to have been a skilled painter and an accomplished sculptor as well as a swordsman.

The Japan of the early seventeenth century which Musashi typified has lived on strongly in the Japanese consciousness. The long and relatively static rule of the Tokugawa preserved much of its forms and spirit, though in somewhat ossified form, until the middle of the nineteenth century, not much more than a century ago. Yoshikawa himself was a son of a former samurai who failed like most members of his class to make a successful economic transition to the new age. Though the samurai themselves largely sank into obscurity in the new Japan, most of the new leaders were drawn from this feudal class, and its ethos was popularized through the new compulsory educational system to become the spiritual background and ethics of the whole Japanese nation. Novels like *Musashi* and the films and plays derived from them aided in the process.

Foreword

The time of Musashi is as close and real to the modern Japanese as is the Civil War to Americans. Thus the comparison to *Gone with the Wind* is by no means far-fetched. The age of the samurai is still very much alive in Japanese minds. Contrary to the picture of the modern Japanese as merely group oriented "economic animals," many Japanese prefer to see themselves as fiercely individualistic, high-principled, self-disciplined and aesthetically sensitive modern-day Musashis. Both pictures have some validity, illustrating the complexity of the Japanese soul behind the seemingly bland and uniform exterior.

Musashi is very different from the highly psychological and often neurotic novels that have been the mainstay of translations of modern Japanese literature into English. But it is nevertheless fully in the mainstream of traditional Japanese fiction and popular Japanese thought. Its episodic presentation is not merely the result of its original appearance as a newspaper serial but is a favorite technique dating back to the beginnings of Japanese storytelling. Its romanticized view of the noble swordsman is a stereotype of the feudal past enshrined in hundreds of other stories and samurai movies. Its emphasis on the cultivation of self-control and inner personal strength through austere Zen-like self-discipline is a major feature of Japanese personality today. So also is the pervading love of nature and sense of closeness to it. *Musashi* is not just a great adventure story. Beyond that, it gives both a glimpse into Japanese history and a view into the idealized self-image of the contemporary Japanese.

January 1981

1

A One-Night Love Affair

Musashi's injury was painful, so instead of spending time in Kamisuwa to make inquiries about Otsū and Jōtarō, he went on to the hot springs at Shimosuwa. This town, on the banks of Lake Suwa, was quite a large one, with the houses of ordinary townsmen alone numbering over a thousand.

At the inn designated for use by daimyō, the bath was covered by a roof, but otherwise the pools situated along the roadside were open to the sky and available to anyone who wanted to use them.

Musashi hung his clothes and swords on a tree and eased himself into the steaming water. As he massaged the swelling on the right side of his abdomen, he rested his head against a rock on the edge of the pool, closed his eyes and savored a groggy, pleasurable sense of well-being. The sun was beginning to set, and a reddish mist rose from the surface of the lake, which he could see between the fishermen's houses along the shore.

A couple of small vegetable plots lay between the pool and the road, where people and horses were coming and going with the usual noise and bustle. At a shop selling lamp oil and sundries, a samurai was purchasing straw sandals. Having selected a suitable pair, he sat down on a stool, took off his old ones and tied the new ones on.

"You must have heard about it," he said to the shopkeeper. "It happened under the great spreading pine at Ichijōji near Kyoto. This rōnin took on the entire House of Yoshioka all by himself and fought with a spirit you rarely hear about anymore. I'm sure he passed this way. Are you certain you didn't see him?"

For all his eagerness, the samurai seemed to know little about the man he was looking for, neither his age nor how he might be dressed. Disappointed when he received a negative reply, he repeated, "I must find him somehow," two or three times while he finished tying his sandals.

The samurai, a man of about forty, was well dressed and sunburned from traveling. The hair at his temples stood out around the cords of his basket hat, and the toughness in his facial expression matched his manly build. Musashi suspected his body bore the marks and calluses that come from wearing armor. "I don't remember ever seeing him before," he thought. "But if he's going around talking about the Yoshioka School, maybe he's one of their students. The school's had so many students, a few must have some backbone. They may be hatching another plot for revenge."

When the man had completed his business and left, Musashi dried himself and put on his clothes, thinking the coast was clear. But when he walked out onto the highroad, he almost bumped into him.

The samurai bowed and, looking intently into his face, said, "Aren't you Miyamoto Musashi?"

Musashi nodded, and the samurai, ignoring the suspicion written on his face, said, "I knew it." After a short paean to his own perspicacity, he continued familiarly, "You can't know how happy I am to meet you at last. I've had the feeling I'd run into you somewhere along the way." Without pausing to give Musashi a chance to speak, he urged him to spend the night at the same inn with him. "Let me assure you," he added, "you don't have to worry about me. My status, if you'll forgive me for saying so, is such that I usually travel with a dozen attendants and a change of horses. I'm a retainer of Date Masamune, the lord of Aoba Castle in Mutsu. My name is Ishimoda Geki."

When Musashi passively accepted the invitation, Geki decided they would stay at the inn for daimyō and led him into the place.

"How about a bath?" he asked. "But of course, you've just had one. Well, make yourself comfortable while I take one. I'll be back shortly." He took off his traveling clothes, picked up a towel and left the room.

Though the man had a winning way about him, Musashi's head was full of questions. Why would this well-placed warrior be looking for him? Why was he being so friendly?

"Wouldn't you like to change into something more comfortable?" asked the maid, proffering one of the cotton-stuffed kimonos furnished to guests.

"No, thank you. I'm not sure I'll be staying."

Musashi stepped out onto the veranda. Behind him he heard the maid quietly setting the dinner trays. As he watched the ripples on the lake change from deep indigo to black, the image of Otsū's sad eyes formed in his mind. "I suppose I'm not looking in the right place," he thought. "Anyone evil enough to kidnap a woman certainly has the instinct to avoid towns." He seemed to hear Otsū calling for help. Was it really all right to take the philosophic view that all things happen as a result of heaven's will? Standing there doing nothing, he felt guilty.

Coming back from his bath, Ishimoda Geki apologized for having left him alone and sat down before his dinner tray. Noticing that Musashi still wore his own kimono, he asked, "Why don't you change?"

"I'm comfortable in what I have on. I wear this all

the time—on the road, inside the house, when I sleep on the ground under the trees."

Geki was favorably impressed. "I might have known," he said. "You want to be ready for action at any time, no matter where you are. Lord Date would admire that." He stared with unconcealed fascination at Musashi's face, which was lit from the side by the lamp. Remembering himself after a moment, he said, "Come. Sit down and have some sake." He rinsed off a cup in a bowl of water and offered it to Musashi.

Musashi seated himself and bowed. Resting his hands on his knees, he asked, "Could you tell me, sir, why you're treating me in such a friendly manner? And if you don't mind, why you were inquiring about me out on the highroad."

"I suppose it's only natural for you to wonder, but there's really very little to explain. Perhaps the simplest way to put it is that I have a sort of crush on you." He paused for a moment, laughed and went on. "Yes, it's a matter of infatuation, a case of one man being attracted to another."

Geki seemed to feel this was sufficient explanation, but Musashi was more mystified than ever. While it did not seem impossible for one man to be enamored of another, he himself had never experienced such an attachment. Takuan was too severe to inspire strong affection. Kōetsu lived in an entirely different world. Sekishūsai occupied a plane so far above Musashi's that either liking or disliking was inconceivable. Though it could be Geki's way of flattering him, a man who made such statements opened himself to the charge of insincerity. Still, Musashi doubted that this samurai was a sycophant; he was too solid, too manly in appearance, for that.

"Precisely what do you mean," Musashi asked with a sober air, "when you say you are attracted to me?"

"Perhaps I'm being presumptuous, but ever since I heard of your feat at Ichijōji, I've been convinced that you're a man I would like, and like very much."

4

"Were you in Kyoto then?"

"Yes, I arrived during the first month of the year and was staying at Lord Date's residence on Sanjō Avenue. When I happened to drop in on Lord Karasumaru Mitsuhiro the day after the fight, I heard quite a bit about you. He said he'd met you and remarked on your youth and what you'd been doing in the past. Feeling this strong attraction, I resolved that I must make an effort to meet you. On my way from Kyoto, I saw the sign you put up at Shiojiri Pass."

"Oh, you saw that?" Ironic, thought Musashi, that instead of bringing him Jōtarō, the sign had brought him someone of whose existence he had never dreamed.

But the more he considered the matter, the less he felt he deserved the esteem in which Geki seemed to hold him. Painfully conscious of his own mistakes and failures, he found Geki's adulation embarrassing.

With perfect honesty, he said, "I think you're rating me too highly."

"There are a number of outstanding samurai serving under Lord Date—his fief has an income of five million bushels, you know—and in time I've met many a skilled swordsman. But from what I've heard, it would seem that few can be compared with you. What's more, you're still very young. You have your whole future before you. And that, I suppose, is why you appeal to me. Anyway, now that I've found you, let's be friends. Have a drink, and talk about anything that interests you."

Musashi accepted the sake cup in good humor and began matching his host drink for drink. Before long, his face was bright red.

Geki, still going strong, said, "We samurai from the north can drink a lot. We do it to stay warm. Lord Date can outdrink any of us. With a strong general in the lead, it wouldn't do for the troops to fall behind."

The maid kept bringing more sake. Even after she'd trimmed the lamp wick several times, Geki showed no inclination to stop. "Let's drink all night," he suggested. "That way, we can talk all night."

"Fine," agreed Musashi. Then, with a smile: "You said you'd talked to Lord Karasumaru. Do you know him well?"

"You couldn't say we're close friends, but over the years I've been to his house any number of times on errands. He's very friendly, you know."

"Yes, I met him on the introduction of Hon'ami Kōetsu. For a nobleman, he seemed remarkably full of life."

Looking somewhat dissatisfied, Geki asked, "Is that your own impression? If you'd talked with him at any length, I'd think you'd have been struck by his intelligence and sincerity."

"Well, we were in the licensed quarter at the time."

"In that case, I suppose he refrained from revealing his true self."

"What's he really like?"

Geki settled himself in more formal fashion and in a rather grave tone said, "He's a troubled man. A man of sorrows, if you will. The shogunate's dictatorial ways disturb him greatly."

For a moment, Musashi was conscious of a lilting sound coming from the lake and the shadows cast by the white light of the lamp.

Abruptly Geki asked, "Musashi, my friend, for whose sake are you trying to perfect your swordsmanship?"

Never having considered the question, Musashi replied with guileless candor, "For my own."

"That's all right as far as it goes, but for whose sake are you trying to improve yourself? Surely your aim is not merely personal honor and glory. That's hardly sufficient for a man of your stature." By accident or design, Geki had come around to the subject he really wanted to talk about. "Now that the whole country's under Ieyasu's control," he declared, "we have a semblance of peace and prosperity. But is it real? Can the people actually live happily under the present system?

"Over the centuries, we've had the Hōjōs, the Ashikagas, Oda Nobunaga, Hideyoshi—a long string of military rulers consistently oppressing not only the people but the Emperor and the court as well. The imperial government has been taken advantage of, and the people mercilessly exploited. All the benefits have gone to the military class. This has been going on since Minamoto no Yoritomo, hasn't it? And the situation today is unchanged.

"Nobunaga seems to have had some idea of the injustice involved; at least he built a new palace for the Emperor. Hideyoshi not only honored the Emperor Go-Yōzei by requiring all the daimyō to pay obeisance to him, but even tried to provide a measure of welfare and happiness for the common people. But what of Ieyasu? To all intents and purposes, he has no interest beyond the fortunes of his own clan. So again, the happiness of the people and the well-being of the imperial family are being sacrificed to create wealth and power for a military dictatorship. We seem to be at the threshold of another age of tyranny. No one worries about this state of affairs more than Lord Date Masamune or, among the nobility, Lord Karasumaru."

Geki paused, waiting for a response, but none was forthcoming except for a barely articulate, "I see."

Like anyone else, Musashi was aware of the drastic political changes that had occurred since the Battle of Sekigahara. Yet he had never paid any attention to activities of the daimyō in the Osaka faction, or the ulterior motives of the Tokugawas, or the stands taken by powerful outside lords like Date and Shimazu. All he knew about Date was that his fief officially had an income of three million bushels per year but in fact probably yielded five million, as Geki had mentioned.

"Twice every year," Geki went on, "Lord Date sends produce from our fief to Lord Konoe in Kyoto for presentation to the Emperor. He's never failed to do this, even in times of war. That's why I was in Kyoto.

"Aoba Castle is the only one in the country to have a special room reserved for the Emperor. It's unlikely, of course, that it'll ever be used, but Lord Date set it aside for him anyway, built it out of wood taken from the old Imperial Palace when that was rebuilt. He had the wood brought from Kyoto to Sendai by boat.

"And let me tell you about the war in Korea. During the campaigns there, Katō, Konishi and other generals were competing for personal fame and triumph. Not Lord Date. Instead of his own family crest, he wore the crest of the rising sun and told everyone he'd never have led his men to Korea for the glory of his own clan or for that of Hideyoshi. He went out of love for Japan itself."

While Musashi listened attentively, Geki became absorbed in his monologue, describing his master in glowing terms and assuring Musashi that he was unexcelled in his single-minded devotion to the nation and the Emperor.

For a time he forgot about drinking but then suddenly looked down and said, "The sake's cold." Clapping his hands for the maid, he was about to order more.

Musashi hurriedly interrupted. "I've had more than enough. If you don't mind, I'd rather have some rice and tea now."

"Already?" mumbled Geki. He was obviously disappointed but, out of deference to his guest, told the girl to bring the rice.

Geki continued to talk as they ate. The impression Musashi formed of the spirit that seemed to prevail among the samurai of Lord Date's fief was that, as individuals and as a group, they were vitally concerned with the Way of the Samurai and with the problem of disciplining themselves in accordance with the Way.

This Way had existed since ancient times, when the warrior class had come into being, but its moral values and obligations were now little more than a vague memory. During the chaotic domestic strife of the fifteenth and sixteenth centuries, the ethics of the military man had been distorted, if not totally ignored, and now almost anyone who could wield a sword or shoot an arrow from a bow was regarded as a samurai, regardless of the attention—or lack of it—given to the deeper meaning of the Way.

The self-styled samurai of the day were often men of lower character and baser instincts than common peasants or townsmen. Having nothing but brawn and technique to command the respect of those beneath them, they were in the long run doomed to destruction. There were few daimyō capable of seeing this, and only a handful of the higher vassals of the Tokugawas and the Toyotomis gave any thought to establishing a new Way of the Samurai, which could become the foundation of the nation's strength and prosperity.

Musashi's thoughts returned to the years when he had been confined in Himeji Castle. Takuan, remembering that Lord Ikeda had in his library a handwritten copy of *Nichiyō Shūshin-kan* by Fushikian, had taken it out for Musashi to study. Fushikian was the literary name of the celebrated general Uesugi Kenshin; in his book, he recorded points of daily ethical training for the guidance of his chief vassals. From this, Musashi had not only learned about Kenshin's personal activities but also gained an understanding of why Kenshin's fief in Echigo had come to be known throughout the country for its wealth and military prowess.

Swayed by Geki's enthusiastic descriptions, he began to feel that Lord Date, besides equaling Kenshin in integrity, had created in his domain an atmosphere in which samurai were encouraged to develop a new Way, one that would enable them to resist even the shogunate, should that become necessary.

"You must forgive me for going on and on about matters of personal interest," said Geki. "What do you think, Musashi? Wouldn't you like to come to Sendai, see for yourself? His lordship is honest and straightforward. If you're striving to find the Way, your present status doesn't matter to him. You can talk with him as you would with any other man.

"There's a great need for samurai who will devote their lives to their country. I'll be more than happy to recommend you. If it's all right with you, we can go to Sendai together."

By this time the dinner trays had been removed, but Geki's ardor was in no way diminished. Impressed, but still cautious, Musashi replied, "I'll have to give it some thought before I can reply."

After they had said good night, Musashi went to his room, where he lay awake in the dark, his eyes glistening.

The Way of the Samurai. He concentrated on this concept as it applied to himself and to his sword.

Suddenly he saw the truth: the techniques of a swordsman were not his goal; he sought an all-embracing Way of the Sword. The sword was to be far more than a simple weapon; it had to be an answer to life's questions. The Way of Uesugi Kenshin and Date Masamune was too narrowly military, too hidebound. It would be up to him to add to his human aspect, to give it greater profundity, greater loftiness.

For the first time, he asked whether it was possible for an insignificant human being to become one with the universe.

2

A Gift of Money

Musashi's first waking thought was of Otsū and Jōtarō, and though he and Geki carried on a convivial conversation over breakfast, the problem of how to find them was very much on his mind. After emerging from the inn, he unconsciously scrutinized every face he encountered on the highroad. Once or twice he thought he saw Otsū ahead, only to find he was mistaken.

"You seem to be looking for someone," said Geki.

"I am. My companions and I got separated along the way, and I'm worried about them. I think I'd better give up the idea of going to Edo with you and search some of the other roads."

Disappointed, Geki said, "That's too bad. I was looking forward to traveling with you. I hope the fact that I talked too much last night won't change your mind about visiting Sendai."

Geki's manner, straightforward and masculine, appealed to Musashi. "That's very kind of you," he said. "I hope I have the chance someday."

"I want you to see for yourself how our samurai conduct themselves. And if you're not interested in that, then just regard it as a sightseeing trip. You can listen to the local songs and visit Matsushima. It's famous for its scenery, you know." Geki took his leave and headed briskly for Wada Pass.

Musashi turned around and went back to where the Kōshū highroad branched off from the Nakasendō. As he stood there mapping out his strategy, a group of day laborers from Suwa come up to him. Their dress suggested they were porters or grooms or bearers of the primitive palanquins used in these parts. They approached slowly, arms folded, looking like an army of crabs.

As their eyes rudely sized him up, one of them said, "Sir, you seem to be looking for someone. A beautiful lady, is it, or only a servant?"

Musashi shook his head, waved them off with a slightly disdainful gesture and turned away. He did not know whether to go east or west, but finally made up his mind to spend the day seeing what he could find out in the neighborhood. If his inquiries led nowhere, he could then proceed to the shōgun's capital with a clear conscience.

One of the laborers broke in upon his thoughts. "If you're looking for somebody, we could help you," he said. "It's better than standing around under the hot sun. What does your friend look like?"

Another added, "We won't even set a rate for our services. We'll leave it up to you."

Musashi relented to the extent of describing Otsū and Jōtarō in detail.

After consulting with his fellows, the first man said, "We haven't seen them, but if we split up we're sure to find them. The kidnappers must've taken one of the three roads between Suwa and Shiojiri. You don't know this area, but we do."

None too optimistic about his chances of success in such difficult terrain, Musashi said, "All right, go look for them."

"Done," shouted the men.

Again they huddled, ostensibly deciding who was to

go where. Then the ringleader came forward, rubbing his hands together deferentially. "There's just one little thing, sir. You see . . . I don't like to mention it, but we're just penniless laborers. Why, not one of us has had anything to eat yet today. Wonder if you couldn't advance us half a day's pay and, say, a little something extra. I guarantee we'll find your companions before sundown."

"Of course. I was planning to give you something."

The man named a figure, which Musashi found, after counting his money, was more than he had. He was not unmindful of the value of money, but being alone, with no one to support, his attitude was on the whole indifferent. Friends and admirers sometimes donated travel funds, and there were temples where he could often obtain free lodging. At other times, he slept in the open or went without ordinary food. One way or another, he had always managed to get by.

On this trip, he had left the finances to Otsū, who had received a sizable gift of travel money from Lord Karasumaru. She had been paying the bills and giving him a certain amount of spending money each morning, as any ordinary housewife might do.

Keeping only a little for himself, he distributed the rest of his money among the men, and though they'd expected more, they agreed to undertake the search as a "special favor."

"Wait for us by the two-story gate of the Suwa Myōjin Shrine," the spokesman advised. "By evening we'll be back with some news." They made off in several directions.

Rather than waste the day doing nothing, Musashi went to see Takashima Castle and the town of Shimo-suwa, stopping here and there to note features of the local topography, which might come in handy at some future date, and to observe the methods of irrigation. He asked several times whether there were any outstanding military experts in the area, but heard nothing of interest.

As sundown drew near, he went to the shrine and sat down, tired and dispirited, on the stone stairway leading up to the two-story gate. No one showed up, so he took a turn around the spacious shrine grounds. But when he returned to the gate, there was still no one there.

Though not loud, the sound of horses stamping the ground began to get on his nerves. Descending the steps, he came upon a shed, obscured by the trees, where an ancient horsekeeper was feeding the shrine's sacred white horse.

He glanced at Musashi accusingly. "Can I help you?" he asked brusquely. "Do you have some business with the shrine?"

Upon hearing why Musashi was there, he broke out in uncontrollable laughter. Musashi, seeing nothing at all funny about his predicament, made no attempt to conceal a scowl. Before he spoke, however, the old man said, "You've no business being on the road by yourself. You're too innocent. Did you really believe roadside vermin would spend the whole day looking for your friends? If you paid them in advance, you'll never see them again."

"You mean you think they were just putting on an act when they divided up and left?"

The horsekeeper's expression changed to one of sympathy. "You've been robbed!" he said. "I heard there were about ten vagrants drinking and gambling in the grove on the other side of the mountain all day today. They're most likely the ones. These things happen all the time." He went on to tell some stories of travelers being cheated out of their money by unscrupulous laborers, but concluded mildly, "That's the way the world is. You'd better be more careful from now on."

With this sage advice, he picked up his empty pail and departed, leaving Musashi feeling foolish. "It's too late to do anything now," he sighed. "I pride myself on my ability not to give my opponent any opening, and then get taken in by a gang of illiterate workmen!" This evidence of his gullibility came like a slap in the face. Such lapses could easily muddy his practice of the Art of War. How could a man so easily deceived by his inferiors effectively command an army? As he climbed slowly toward the gate, he resolved to henceforth pay more attention to the ways of the world about him.

One of the laborers was peering around in the dark, and as soon as he caught sight of Musashi, he called to him and ran partway down the steps.

"Glad I found you, sir," he said. "I've got news about one of the people you're looking for."

"Oh?" Musashi, having just reprimanded himself for his naiveté, was astonished but gratified to know that not everyone in the world was a swindler. "By one of them, do you mean the boy or the woman?"

"The boy. He's with Daizō of Narai, and I've found out where Daizō is, or at least where he's headed."

"Where might that be?"

"I didn't think that bunch I was with this morning would do what they promised. They took the day off to gamble, but I felt sorry for you. I went from Shiojiri to Seba, asking everybody I ran into. Nobody knew anything about the girl, but I heard from the maid at the inn where I ate that Daizō passed through Suwa about noon today on his way to Wada Pass. She said he had a young boy with him."

Embarrassed, Musashi said rather formally, "It was good of you to let me know." He took out his money pouch, knowing it contained only enough for his own meal. He hesitated a moment, but reflecting that honesty should not go unrewarded, gave the laborer his last bit of cash.

Pleased with the tip, the man raised the money to his forehead in a gesture of thanks and went happily on his way.

Watching his money go down the road, Musashi felt he had used it for a purpose worthier than that of filling his stomach. Perhaps the laborer, having learned that right conduct can be profitable, would go out on the road the next day and help another traveler.

It was already dark, but he decided that instead of sleeping under the eves of some peasant's house, he would cross Wada Pass. By traveling all night, he should be able to catch up with Daizō. He started off, savoring once again the satisfaction of being on a deserted road at night. Something about it appealed to his nature. Counting his footsteps, listening to the silent voice of the heavens above, he could forget everything and rejoice in his own being. When he was surrounded by crowds of busy people, his spirit often seemed sad and isolated, but now he felt alive and buoyant. He could think about life coolly and objectively, even appraise himself as he might appraise a total stranger.

A little after midnight, his musings were distracted by a light in the distance. He had been climbing steadily since crossing the bridge over the Ochiai River. One pass was behind him; the next one, at Wada, loomed up in the starry sky ahead, and beyond that the even higher crossing at Daimon. The light was in a hollow that ran parallel to the two ridges.

"It looks like a bonfire," he thought, feeling pangs of hunger for the first time in hours. "Maybe they'll let me dry off my sleeves, give me a bit of gruel or something."

As he drew near, he saw that it wasn't an outdoor fire but the light from a small roadside teahouse. There were four or five stakes for tying horses, but no horses. It seemed incredible that there would be anyone in such a place at this hour, yet he could hear the sound of raucous voices mingling with the crackling of the fire. He stood hesitantly under the eaves for a few minutes. If it had been a farmer's or a woodcutter's hut, he would have had no qualms about asking for shelter and some leftovers, but this was a place of business.

The smell of food made him hungrier than ever. The warm smoke enveloped him; he could not tear himself away. "Well, if I explain my situation to them, maybe they'll accept the statue as payment." The "statue" was the small image of Kannon he had carved from the wood of an ancient plum tree.

When he barged into the shop, the startled customers stopped talking. The interior was simple, a dirt floor with a hearth and fire hood in the middle, around which huddled three men on stools. Stewing in a pot was a mixture of boar's meat and giant radish. A jar of sake was warming in the ashes. Standing with his back to them, slicing pickles and chatting good-naturedly, was the proprietor.

"What do you want?" asked one of the customers, a keen-eyed man with long sideburns.

Too hungry to hear, Musashi passed by the men and, seating himself on the edge of a stool, said to the proprietor, "Give me something to eat, quick. Rice and pickles'll do. Anything."

The man poured some of the stew over a bowl of cold rice and set it before him. "Are you planning to cross the pass tonight?" he asked.

"Um," mumbled Musashi, who had already seized some chopsticks and was attacking the food with gusto. After his second mouthful, he asked, "Do you know if a man named Daizō—he comes from Narai—passed here this afternoon, going toward the pass? He has a young boy with him."

"I'm afraid I can't help you." Then, to the other men, "Tōji, did you or your friends see an older man traveling with a boy?"

After a bit of whispering, the three replied in the negative, shaking their heads in unison.

Musashi, filled and warmed by the hot food, began to worry about the bill. He'd hesitated discussing it with the proprietor first, due to the presence of the other men, but he didn't for a moment feel he was begging. It had simply seemed more important to tend to his stomach's needs first. He made up his mind that if the shopkeeper would not accept the statue, he'd offer him his dagger.

"I'm sorry to have to tell you this," he began, "but I don't have any cash at all. I'm not asking for a free meal, mind you. I have something here to offer in payment, if you'll take it."

With unexpected amiability, the proprietor replied, "I'm sure that'll be all right. What is it?"

"A statue of Kannon."

"A real statue?"

"Oh, it's not the work of a famous sculptor—just something I carved myself. It may not be worth even the price of a bowl of rice, but take a look at it anyway."

As he began untying the cords of his bag, the one he had carried for years, the three men left off drinking and focused their attention on his hands. Besides the statue, the bag contained a single change of underwear and a writing set. When he emptied out the contents, something fell with a clunk to the ground. The others gasped, for the object that lay at Musashi's feet was a money pouch, from which several gold and silver coins had spilled out. Musashi himself stared in speechless amazement.

"Where did that come from?" he wondered.

The other men craned their necks to gape at the treasure.

Feeling something else in the bag, Musashi pulled out a letter. It consisted of a single line, saying, "This should take care of your travel expenses for the time being," and was signed "Geki."

Musashi had a pretty clear idea of what it meant: it was Geki's way of trying to buy his services for Lord Date Masamune of Sendai and Aoba Castle. The increasing probability of a final clash between the Tokugawas and the Toyotomis made it imperative for the great daimyō to maintain sizable numbers of able fighters. A favorite method used in the cutthroat competition for the few really outstanding samurai was to attempt to get such men in debt, even for a small sum, and then forge a tacit agreement for future cooperation.

It was common knowledge that Toyotomi Hideyori was providing large sums of money to Gotō Matabei and Sanada Yukimura. Though Yukimura was ostensibly in retirement on Mount Kudo, so much gold and silver was being sent to him from Osaka Castle that Ieyasu had undertaken a full-scale investigation. Since the personal requirements of a retired general living in a hermitage were fairly modest, it was all but certain that the money was being passed on to several thousand indigent rōnin, who were idling away their time in nearby towns and cities waiting for the outbreak of hostilities.

Finding an able warrior, as Geki believed he had, and somehow enticing him into his lord's service was one of the most valuable services a retainer could perform. And it was for just this reason that Musashi had no interest in Geki's money: using it would incur an unwanted obligation. In a matter of seconds, he decided to ignore the gift, to pretend it did not exist.

Without a word he reached down, picked up the pouch and restored it to his bag. Addressing the proprietor as though nothing had happened, he said, "All right then, I'll leave the statue here in payment."

But the man balked. "I can't accept that now, sir!"

"Is there something wrong with it? I don't claim to be a sculptor, but—"

"Oh, it's not bad, and I would have taken it if you didn't have any money, like you said, but you've got plenty. Why do you throw your cash around for people to see if you want them to think you're broke?"

The other customers, sobered and thrilled by the sight of the gold, vigorously nodded their agreement. Musashi, recognizing the futility of arguing that the money was not his, took out a piece of silver and handed it to the man.

"This is far too much, sir," complained the proprietor. "Don't you have anything smaller?"

A cursory examination revealed some variation in the worth of the pieces, but nothing less valuable. "Don't worry about the change," Musashi said. "You can keep it."

No longer able to maintain the fiction that the money didn't exist, Musashi tucked the pouch into his stomach wrapper for safekeeping.

Then, despite urgings to linger awhile, he shouldered his pack and went out into the night. Having eaten and restored his strength, he calculated that he could make it to Daimon Pass by sunrise. By day, he would have seen around him an abundance of highland flowers—rhododendrons, gentians, wild chrysanthemums—but at night there in the immense sea of darkness he could see only a cottonlike mist clinging to the earth.

He was about two miles from the teahouse when one of the men he'd seen there hailed him, saying, "Wait! You forgot something." Catching up with Musashi, the man puffed, "My, you walk fast! After you left, I found this money, so I brought it to you. It must be yours."

He held out a piece of silver, which Musashi refused, saying it certainly wasn't his. The man insisted that it was. "It must have rolled into the corner when you dropped your money pouch."

Not having counted the money, Musashi was in no position to prove the man wrong. With a word of thanks, he took the silver and put it in his kimono sleeve. Yet for some reason he found himself unmoved by this display of honesty.

Though the man's errand had been completed, he fell in alongside Musashi and began making small talk.

"Perhaps I shouldn't ask, but are you studying swordsmanship under a well-known teacher?"

"No. I use my own style."

The perfunctory answer failed to discourage the man, who declared that he had been a samurai himself, adding, "But for the time being I'm reduced to living here in the mountains."

"Is that so?"

"Um. Those two back there too. We were all samurai. Now we make our living cutting trees and gathering herbs. We're like the proverbial dragon biding its time in a pond. I can't pretend to be Sano Genzaemon, but when the time comes, I'll grab my old sword and put on my threadbare armor and go fight for some famous daimyō. I'm just waiting for that day to come!"

"Are you for Osaka or Edo?"

"Doesn't matter. The main thing is to be on somebody's side, or else I'll waste my life hanging around here."

Musashi laughed politely. "Thanks for bringing the money."

Then, in an effort to lose the man, he started taking long, rapid strides. The man stayed right beside him, step for step. He also kept pressing in on Musashi's left side, an encroachment that any experienced swordsman would regard as suspicious. Rather than reveal his wariness, however, Musashi did nothing to protect his left side, leaving it wide open.

The man became increasingly friendly. "May I make a suggestion? If you'd like, why don't you come spend the night at our place? After Wada Pass, you've still got Daimon ahead of you. You might make it by morning, but it's very steep—a difficult road for a man not familiar with these parts."

"Thanks. I think I'll take you up on that."

"You should, you should. Only thing is, we don't have anything to offer in the way of food or entertainment."

"I'd be happy to have a place to lie down. Where is your house?"

"About a half mile off to the left and a little higher up."

"You really are deep in the mountains, aren't you?"

"As I said, until the proper time comes, we're lying

21

low, gathering herbs, hunting, doing things like that. I share a house with the other two men.''

"Now that you mention it, what became of them?''

"They're probably still drinking. Every time we go there, they get drunk, and I wind up lugging them home. Tonight I decided to just leave them. . . . Watch out! There's a sharp drop there—stream down below. It's dangerous.''

"Do we cross the stream?''

"Yes. It's narrow here, and there's a log across it just below us. After we cross, we turn right and climb up along the riverbank.''

Musashi sensed that the man had stopped walking, but he did not look back. He found the log and started across. A moment later, the man leaped forward and lifted the end of the log in an attempt to throw Musashi into the stream.

"What are you up to?''

The shout came from below, but the man jerked his head upward in astonishment. Musashi, having anticipated his treacherous move, had already jumped from the log and lit as lightly as a wagtail on a large rock. His startled attacker dropped the log into the stream. Before the curtain of flying water had fallen back to earth, Musashi had jumped back onto the bank, sword unsheathed, and cut his assailant down. It all happened so quickly that the man did not even see Musashi draw.

The corpse wriggled for a moment or two before subsiding into stillness. Musashi did not deign to give it a glance. He had already taken a new stance in preparation for the next attack, for he was sure there would be one. As he steeled himself for it, his hair stood up like an eagle's crown feathers.

A short silence ensued, followed by a boom loud enough to split the gorge asunder. The gunshot seemed to have come from somewhere on the other side. Musashi dodged, and the well-aimed slug hissed through the space he had been occupying, burying itself in the embankment behind him. Falling as though wounded, Musashi looked across to the opposite side, where he saw red sparks flying through the air like so many fireflies. He could just make out two figures creeping cautiously forward.

3

A Cleansing Fire

Clenching his teeth tightly on the sputtering fuse, the man made ready to fire his musket again. His confederate crouched down, and squinting into the distance, whispered, "Do you think it's safe?"

"I'm sure I got him with the first shot," came the confident reply.

The two crept cautiously forward, but no sooner had they reached the edge of the bank than Musashi jumped up. The musketeer gasped and fired but lost his balance, sending the bullet uselessly skyward. As the echo reverberated through the ravine, both men, the other two from the teahouse, fled up the path.

Suddenly one of them stopped in his tracks and roared, "Wait! What are we running for? There's two of us and only one of him. I'll take him on and you can back me up."

"I'm with you!" shouted the musketeer, letting go of the fuse and aiming the butt of his weapon at Musashi.

They were definitely a cut above ordinary hoodlums. The man Musashi took to be the leader wielded his sword with genuine finesse; nonetheless, he was a poor match for Musashi, who sent them both flying through the air with a single sword stroke. The musketeer, sliced from shoulder to waist, fell dead to the ground, his upper torso hanging over the bank as if by a thread. The other man sped up the slope, clutching a wounded forearm, with Musashi in hot pursuit. Showers of dirt and gravel rose and fell in his wake.

The ravine, Buna Valley, lay midway between Wada and Daimon passes and took its name from the beech trees that seemed to fill it. On its highest point stood an exceptionally large mountaineer's cabin surrounded by trees and itself crudely fashioned of beech logs.

Scrambling rapidly toward the tiny flame of a torch, the bandit shouted, "Douse the lights!"

Protecting the flame with an outstretched sleeve, a woman exclaimed, "Why, you— Oh! You're covered with blood!"

"Sh-shut up, you fool! Put out the lights—the ones inside too." He could hardly get the words out from panting, and with a last look behind him, he hurtled past her. The woman blew out the torch and rushed after him.

By the time Musashi arrived at the cabin, not a trace of light was visible anywhere.

"Open up!" he bellowed. He was indignant, not for being taken to be a fool, nor because of the cowardly attack, but because men like these daily inflicted great harm on innocent travelers.

He might have broken open the wooden rain shutters, but rather than make a frontal attack, which would have left his back dangerously exposed, he cautiously kept at a distance of four or five feet.

"Open up!"

Getting no answer, he picked up the largest rock he could handle and hurled it at the shutters. It struck the crack between the two panels, sending both the man and the woman reeling into the house. A sword flew out from beneath them and was followed by the man crawling on his knees. He quickly regained his feet and retreated into the house. Musashi bounded forward and seized him by the back of his kimono.

"Don't kill me! I'm sorry!" pleaded Gion Tōji, his whining tone exactly that of a petty crook.

He was soon back on his feet again, trying to find Musashi's weak point. Musashi parried each of his moves, but when he pressed forward to hem in his opponent, Tōji, mustering all his strength, pulled his short sword and made a powerful thrust. Dodging adroitly, Musashi swept him up in his arms and with a cry of contempt sent him crashing into the next room. Either an arm or a leg struck the pot hanger, for the bamboo pole from which it hung broke with a loud crack. White ashes billowed up from the hearth like a volcanic cloud.

A barrage of missiles coming through the smoke and ashes kept Musashi at bay. As the ashes settled, he saw that his adversary was no longer the bandits' chief, who was flat on his back near the wall. The woman, between curses, was throwing everything she could lay her hands on—pot lids, kindling, metal chopsticks, tea bowls.

Musashi leapt forward and quickly pinned her to the floor, but she managed to pull a bodkin from her hair and take a stab at him. When he brought his foot down on her wrist, she gnashed her teeth, then cried out in anger and disgust at the unconscious Tōji, "Haven't you any pride? How can you lose to a nobody like this?"

Hearing the voice, Musashi abruptly drew in his breath and let her go. She jumped to her feet, grabbed up the short sword and lunged at him.

"Stop it, ma'am," said Musashi.

Startled by the oddly courteous tone, she paused and gaped at him. "Why, it's . . . it's Takezō!"

His hunch was right. Apart from Osugi, the only woman who would still call him by his childhood name was Okō.

"It *is* Takezō," she exclaimed, her voice growing syrupy. "Your name's Musashi now, isn't it? You've become quite a swordsman, haven't you?"

"What are you doing in a place like this?"

"I'm ashamed to say."

"Is that man lying over there your husband?"

"You must know him. He's what's left of Gion Tōji."

"That's Tōji?" murmured Musashi. He had heard in Kyoto what a reprobate Tōji was, and how he had pocketed the money collected to enlarge the school and absconded with Okō. Still, as he looked at the human wreck by the wall, he couldn't help feeling sorry for him. "You'd better tend to him," he said. "If I'd known he was your husband, I wouldn't have been so rough with him."

"Oh, I want to crawl in a hole and hide," simpered Okō.

She went to Tōji's side, gave him some water, bound his wounds, and when he had begun to come around, told him who Musashi was.

"What?" he croaked. "Miyamoto Musashi? The one who . . . Oh, this is awful!" Placing his hands over his face, he doubled up abjectly.

Forgetting his anger, Musashi allowed himself to be treated as an honored guest. Okō swept the floor, tidied up the hearth, put on new kindling and heated some sake.

Handing him a cup, she said, in accordance with the accepted rules of etiquette, "We haven't a thing to offer, but . . ."

"I had quite enough at the teahouse," Musashi replied politely. "Please don't go to any trouble."

"Oh, I hope you can eat the food I've prepared. It's been such a long time." Having hung a pot of stew on the pot hanger, she sat down beside him and poured his sake.

"It reminds me of old times at Mount Ibuki," said Musashi amiably.

A strong wind had come up, and though the shutters were again securely in place, it came in through various cracks and teased the smoke from the hearth as it rose to the ceiling.

"Please don't remind me of that," said Okō. "But

tell me, have you heard anything of Akemi? Do you have any idea where she is?"

"I heard she spent several days at the inn on Mount Hiei. She and Matahachi were planning to go to Edo. Seems she ran away with all his money."

"Oh?" said Okō disappointedly. "Her too." She gazed at the floor, sadly comparing her daughter's life with her own.

When Tōji had recovered sufficiently, he joined them and begged Musashi's forgiveness. He had, he avowed, acted on a sudden impulse, which he now deplored. There would come a day, he assured his guest, when he would reenter society as the Gion Tōji the world had known before.

Musashi kept quiet, but he would have liked to say that there didn't seem to be much to choose from between Tōji the samurai and Tōji the bandit, but if he did return to the life of a warrior, the roads would be that much safer for travelers.

Somewhat mellowed by the sake, he said to Okō, "I think you'd be wise to give up this dangerous way of life."

"You're quite right, but of course, it's not as though I'm living this way out of choice. When we left Kyoto, we were going to try our luck in Edo. But in Suwa, Tōji got to gambling and lost everything we had—travel money, everything. I thought of the moxa business, so we started gathering herbs and selling them in the town. Oh, I've had enough of his get-rich-quick schemes to last a lifetime. After tonight, I'm through." As always, a few drinks had introduced a coquettish note into her speech. She was beginning to turn on the charm.

Okō was one of those women of indeterminate age, and she was still dangerous. A house cat will romp coyly on its master's knees so long as it is well fed and cared for, but turn it loose in the mountains, and in no time it will be prowling the night with flaming eyes, ready to feast off a corpse or tear the living flesh off travelers who have fallen sick by the wayside. Okō was very much like that.

"Tōji," she said lovingly, "according to Takezō, Akemi was headed for Edo. Couldn't we go there too and live more like human beings again? If we found Akemi, I'm sure we'd think of some profitable business to go into."

"Well, maybe," was the unenthusiastic reply. His arms were wrapped pensively around his knees; perhaps the implied idea—peddling Akemi's body—was a little raw even for him. Tōji, after living with this predatory woman, was beginning to have the same regrets as Matahachi.

To Musashi, the expression on Tōji's face seemed pathetic. It reminded him of Matahachi. With a shudder, he recalled how he himself had once been enticed by her charms.

"Okō," said Tōji, lifting his head. "It won't be long till daylight. Musashi's probably tired. Why don't you fix a place for him in the back room, so he can get some rest?"

"Yes, of course." With a tipsy sidelong glance at Musashi, she said, "You'll have to be careful, Takezō. It's dark back there."

"Thanks. I could use some sleep."

He followed her down a dark corridor to the back of the house. The room seemed to be an addition to the cabin. It was supported by logs and projected out over the valley, with a drop of about seventy feet from the outer wall to the river. The air was damp from the mist and the spray blowing in from a waterfall. Each time the groaning of the wind rose a trifle, the little room rocked like a boat.

Okō's white feet retreated across the slatted floor of the outdoor hallway to the hearth room.

"Has he gone to sleep?" asked Tōji.

"I think so," she replied, kneeling by his side. She whispered in his ear, "What are you going to do?"

29

"Go call the others."

"You're going through with it?"

"Absolutely! It's not just a matter of money. If I kill the bastard, I'll have taken revenge for the House of Yoshioka."

Tucking up the skirt of her kimono, she went outside. Under the starless sky, deep in the mountains, she sped through the black wind like a feline demon, her long hair streaming out behind.

The nooks and crevices on the mountainside were not inhabited solely by birds and beasts. As Okō raced along, she made contact with more than twenty men, all members of Tōji's band. Trained for night forays, they moved more quietly than floating leaves to a spot just in front of the cabin.

"Only one man?"

"A samurai?"

"Does he have money?"

The whispered exchanges were accompanied by explanatory gestures and eye movements. Carrying muskets and daggers and the type of lances used by boar hunters, a few of them surrounded the back room. About half went down into the valley, while a couple stopped halfway down, directly below the room.

The floor of the room was covered with reed mats. Along one wall were neat little piles of dried herbs and a collection of mortars and other tools used to make medicine. Musashi found the pleasant aroma of the herbs soothing; it seemed to beckon him to close his eyes and sleep. His body felt dull and swollen to the tips of his extremities. But he knew better than to give in to the sweet temptation.

He was aware there was something afoot. The herb gatherers of Mimasaka never had storage sheds like this; theirs were never located where dampness accumulated and were always at some distance from dense foliage. By the dim light of a small lamp resting on a mortar stand beside his pillow, he could see something else that disturbed him. The metal brackets holding the room together at the corners were surrounded by numerous nail holes. He could also discern fresh wooden surfaces that must previously have been covered by joinery. The implication was unmistakable: the room had been rebuilt, probably a number of times.

A tiny smile came to his lips, but he did not stir.

"Takezō," Okō called softly. "Are you asleep?" Gently sliding the shoji aside, she tiptoed to his pallet and placed a tray near his head. "I'll put some water here for you," she said. He gave no sign of being awake.

When she was back in the cabin itself, Tōji whispered, "Is everything all right?"

Closing her eyes for emphasis, she replied, "He's sound asleep."

With a satisfied look, Tōji hurried outside, went to the back of the cabin and waved a lighted musket fuse, whereupon the men below pulled the supports out from under the room, sending it crashing down into the valley—walls, frame, ridgepole and all.

With a triumphant roar, the others sprang from their hiding places, like hunters from behind portable blinds, and rushed down to the riverbank. The next step was to extricate the corpse and the victim's belongings from the debris. After that, it would be a simple matter to gather up the pieces and rebuild the room.

The bandits jumped into the pile of planks and posts like dogs falling on bones.

Arriving from above, others asked, "Have you found the body?"

"No, not yet."

"It's got to be here somewhere."

Tōji shouted raucously, "Maybe he struck a rock or something on the way down and bounced off to the side. Look all around."

Rocks, water, the trees and plants of the valley, were taking on a bright reddish cast. With startled exclamations, Tōji and his henchmen looked toward the sky.

Seventy feet above, bright flames spouted from the doors, windows, walls and roof of the cabin. It had turned into a huge ball of fire.

"Quick! Hur-r-ry! Get back up here!" The piercing summons came from Okō, and sounded like the howl of a woman gone mad.

By the time the men had made their way up the cliff, the flames were dancing wildly in the wind. Unprotected from the shower of sparks and embers, Okō stood tied securely to a tree trunk.

To a man, they were dumbfounded. Musashi gone? How? How could he conceivably have outwitted them all?

Tōji lost heart; he did not even send his men in pursuit. He had heard enough about Musashi to know they'd never catch him. On their own, however, the bandits quickly organized search parties and flew off in all directions.

They found no trace of Musashi.

4

Playing with Fire

Unlike the other principal routes, there were no trees lining the Kōshū highroad, which joined Shiojiri and Edo by way of Kai Province. Used for military transport during the sixteenth century, it lacked the Nakasendō's network of back roads and had only recently been upgraded to the status of a main artery.

For travelers coming from Kyoto or Osaka, its least agreeable feature was a dearth of good inns and eating places. A request for a box lunch was likely to bring forth nothing more appetizing than flat rice cakes wrapped in bamboo leaves or, even less appealing, balls of plain rice done up in dried oak leaves. Despite the primitive fare—probably not much different from that of the Fujiwara period, hundreds of years earlier—the rustic hostelries swarmed with guests, most of them bound for Edo.

A group of travelers was taking a rest above Kobotoke Pass. One of them exclaimed, "Look, there's another batch," referring to a sight he and his companions had been enjoying almost daily—a group of prostitutes on their way from Kyoto to Edo.

The girls numbered about thirty, some old, some in their twenties or early thirties, at least five in their middle teens. Together with about ten men who managed or served them, they resembled a large patriarchal family.

There were in addition several packhorses loaded down with everything from small wicker baskets to man-sized wooden chests.

The head of the "family," a man of about forty, was addressing his girls. "If your straw sandals are giving you blisters, change into zōri, but tie them tight so they don't slip around. And stop complaining that you can't walk any farther. Just look at the children on the road, the children!" It was clear from his acid tone that he was having a hard time forcing his usually sedentary charges to keep moving.

The man, whose name was Shōji Jinnai, was a native of Fushimi, a samurai by birth, who had for reasons of his own abandoned the military life to become a brothel keeper. Being both quick-witted and resourceful, he had succeeded in gaining the support of Tokugawa Ieyasu, who often took up residence at Fushimi Castle, and had not only obtained permission to move his own business to Edo but had also persuaded many of his colleagues in the trade to do likewise.

Near the crest of Kobotoke, Jinnai brought his procession to a halt, saying, "It's still a little early, but we can have our lunch now." Turning to Onao, an old woman who functioned as a sort of mother hen, he ordered her to pass out the food.

The basket containing the box lunches was duly unloaded from one of the horses and a leaf-wrapped ball of rice dealt out to each of the women, who scattered themselves about and relaxed. The dust that had yellowed their skin had also turned their black hair nearly white, though they wore broad-brimmed traveling hats or had tied hand towels around their heads. There being no tea, eating entailed a good deal of lip smacking and tooth sucking. There was no suggestion of sexual wiles or amorous thrills. "Whose arms will embrace this red, red blossom tonight?" seemed utterly beside the point.

"Oh, this is delicious!" cried one of Jinnai's younger

charges ecstatically. Her tone of voice would have brought tears to her mother's eyes.

The attention of two or three others wandered from their lunch to focus on a young samurai passing by.

"Isn't he handsome?" whispered one.

"Umm, not bad," replied another, of more worldly outlook.

A third volunteered, "Oh, I know him. He used to come to our place with men from the Yoshioka School."

"Which one are you talking about?" asked one lustful-eyed creature.

"The young one, strutting along there with the long sword on his back."

Unaware of the admiration, Sasaki Kojirō was pushing his way through a throng of porters and packhorses.

A high, flirtatious voice called, "Mr. Sasaki! Over here, Mr. Sasaki!"

Since there were lots of people named Sasaki, he didn't even turn.

"You with the forelock!"

Kojirō's eyebrows shot up, and he spun around.

"Watch your tongues!" Jinnai shouted angrily. "You're being rude." Then, glancing up from his lunch, he recognized Kojirō.

"Well, well," he said, rising quickly. "If it isn't our friend Sasaki! Where are you headed, if I may ask?"

"Why, hello. You're the master of the Sumiya, aren't you? I'm going to Edo. And what about you? You seem to be engaged in a full-scale move."

"That we are. We're moving to the new capital."

"Really? Do you think you can make a go of it there?"

"Nothing grows in stagnant waters."

"The way Edo's growing, I imagine there's plenty of work for construction workers and gunsmiths. But elegant entertainment? It seems doubtful there's much demand for it yet."

"You're wrong, though. Women made a city out of

Osaka before Hideyoshi got around to taking any notice of it."

"Maybe, but in a place as new as Edo, you probably won't even be able to find a suitable house."

"Wrong again. The government's set aside some marshland in a place called Yoshiwara for people in my business. My associates have already started filling it in, putting in streets and building houses. From all reports, I should be able to find a good street-front location fairly easily."

"You mean the Tokugawas are giving the land away? For free?"

"Of course. Who'd pay for marshland? The government's even providing some of the construction materials."

"I see. No wonder you're all abandoning the Kyoto area."

"And what about you? Or do you have some prospect of a position with a daimyō?"

"Oh, no; nothing like that. I wouldn't take one if it was offered. I just thought I'd see what's going on up there, since it's the shōgun's residence and the place where orders are going to come from in the future. Of course, if I were asked to be one of the shōgun's instructors, I might accept."

Though no judge of swordsmanship, Jinnai had a good eye for people. Thinking it just as well not to comment on Kojirō's unbridled egotism, he averted his eyes and began prodding his troop into movement. "Everybody up now! It's time we were going."

Onao, who had been counting heads, said, "We seem to be missing one girl. Which one is it, now? Kichō? Or maybe Sumizome? No; they're both over there. This is strange. Who could it be?"

Kojirō, disinclined to have a party of prostitutes for traveling companions, went on his way.

A couple of the girls who had gone back down the road to search returned to where Onao was.

Jinnai joined them. "Here, here, Onao, which one is it?"

"Ah, I know now. It was that girl named Akemi," she replied contritely, as if the fault were hers. "The one you picked up on the road in Kiso."

"She must be around here somewhere."

"We've looked everywhere. I think she must have run away."

"Well, I didn't have a written commitment from her, and I didn't lend her any 'body money.' She said she was willing, and since she was good-looking enough to be marketable, I took her on. I suppose she's cost me a bit in traveling expenses, but not enough to worry about. Never mind her. Let's get moving."

He began hustling his group along. Even if it meant traveling after sundown, he wanted to reach Hachiōji within the day. If they could get that far before stopping, they could be in Edo the next day.

A short way down the road, Akemi reappeared and fell in with them.

"Where have you been?" Onao demanded angrily. "You can't just wander off without telling anyone where you're going. Unless, of course, you're planning to leave us." The old woman went on to explain self-righteously how they had all been so worried about her.

"You don't understand," said Akemi, from whom the scolding brought nothing but giggles. "There was a man I know on the road, and I didn't want him to see me. I ran into a clump of bamboo, not knowing there was a sudden drop-off there. I slid all the way down to the bottom." She corroborated this by holding up her torn kimono and a skinned elbow. But all the time she was begging forgiveness, her face showed not the slightest sign of contrition.

From his position near the front, Jinnai caught wind of what had happened and summoned her. Sternly he said, "Your name's Akemi, isn't it? Akemi—that's hard to remember. If you're really going to succeed in this business, you'll have to find a better name. Tell me, have you really resolved to go through with this?''

"Does it require resolution to become a whore?''

"It's not something you can take up for a month or so and then quit. And if you become one of my girls, you'll have to give the customers what they ask for, like it or not. Don't make any mistake about that.''

"What difference does it make now? Men have already made a mess of my life.''

"That's not the right attitude at all. Now, you give this some careful thought. If you change your mind before we reach Edo, that's all right. I won't ask you to pay me back for your food and lodging.''

That same day, at the Yakuōin in Takao, an older man, apparently free of the pressures of business, was about to resume his leisurely journey. He, his servant and a boy of about fifteen had arrived the previous evening and requested overnight accommodations. He and the boy had been touring the temple grounds since early morning. It was now about noon.

"Use this for roof repairs, or whatever is necessary,'' he said, offering one of the priests three large gold coins.

The head priest, immediately apprised of the gift, was so overwhelmed by the donor's generosity that he personally hastened out to exchange greetings. "Perhaps you would like to leave your name,'' he said.

Another priest, saying this had already been done, showed him the entry in the temple registry, which read: "Daizō of Narai, dealer in herbs, resident at the foot of Mount Ontake in Kiso.''

The head priest apologized profusely for the poor quality of the fare served by the temple, for Daizō of Narai was known throughout the country as a lavish contributor to shrines and temples. His gifts always took the form of gold coins—in some cases, it was said, as many as several dozen. Only he himself knew whether he did this for amusement, to acquire a reputation, or out of piety.

The priest, eager to have him stay longer, begged him to inspect the temple's treasures, a privilege accorded to few.

"I'll be in Edo awhile," said Daizō. "I'll come see them another time."

"By all means, but at least let me accompany you to the outer gate," insisted the priest. "Are you planning to stop in Fuchū tonight?"

"No; Hachiōji."

"In that case, it'll be an easy trip."

"Tell me, who's the lord of Hachiōji now?"

"It's recently been put under the administration of Ōkubo Nagayasu."

"He was magistrate of Nara, wasn't he?"

"Yes, that's the man. The gold mines on Sado Island are also under his control. He's very rich."

"A very able man, it would appear."

It was still daylight when they came to the foot of the mountains and stood on the busy main street of Hachiōji, where reportedly there were no fewer than twenty-five inns.

"Well, Jōtarō, where shall we stay?"

Jōtarō, who had stuck to Daizō's side like a shadow, let it be known in no uncertain terms that he preferred "anywhere—as long as it's not a temple."

Choosing the largest and most imposing inn, Daizō entered and requested a room. His distinguished appearance, together with the elegant lacquered traveling case his servant carried on his back, made a dazzling impression on the head clerk, who said fawningly, "You're stopping quite early, aren't you?" Inns along the highroads were accustomed to having hordes of travelers tumble in at dinnertime or even later.

Daizō was shown to a large room on the first floor, but shortly after sundown, both the innkeeper and the head clerk came to Daizō's room.

"I'm sure it's a great inconvenience," the innkeeper began abjectly, "but a large party of guests has come in very suddenly. I'm afraid it'll be terribly noisy here. If you wouldn't mind moving to a room on the second floor . . ."

"Oh, that's perfectly all right," replied Daizō good-naturedly. "Glad to see your business is thriving."

Signaling Sukeichi, his servant, to take care of the luggage, Daizō proceeded upstairs. He had no sooner left the room than it was overrun by women from the Sumiya.

The inn wasn't just busy; it was frenetic. What with the hubbub downstairs, the servants did not come when called. Dinner was late, and when they had eaten, no one came to clear away the dishes. On top of that, there was the constant tramping of feet on both floors. Only Daizō's sympathy for the hired help kept him from losing his temper. Ignoring the litter in the room, he stretched out to take a nap, using his arm for a pillow. After only a few minutes, a sudden thought came to him, and he called Sukeichi.

When Sukeichi failed to materialize, Daizō opened his eyes, sat up and shouted, "Jōtarō, come here!"

But he, too, had disappeared.

Daizō got up and went to the veranda, which he saw was lined with guests, excitedly gaping with delight at the prostitutes on the first floor.

Spying Jōtarō among the spectators, Daizō swiftly yanked him back into the room. With a forbidding eye, he demanded, "What were you staring at?"

The boy's long wooden sword, which he did not take off even indoors, scraped the tatami as he sat down. "Well," he said, "everyone else is looking."

"And just what are they looking at?"

"Oh, there're a lot of women in the back room downstairs."

"Is that all?"

"Yes."

"What's so entertaining about that?" The presence

of the whores didn't bother Daizō, but for some reason he found the intense interest of the men gawking at them annoying.

"I don't know," replied Jōtarō honestly.

"I'm going for a walk around town," Daizō said. "You stay here while I'm gone."

"Can't I go with you?"

"Not at night."

"Why not?"

"As I told you before, when I go for a walk, it's not simply to amuse myself."

"Well, what's the idea, then?"

"It has to do with my religion."

"Don't you get enough of shrines and temples during the daytime? Even priests have to sleep at night."

"Religion has to do with more than shrines and temples, young man. Now go find Sukeichi for me. He has the key to my traveling case."

"He went downstairs a few minutes ago. I saw him peeking into the room where the women are."

"Him too?" exclaimed Daizō with a click of his tongue. "Go get him, and be quick about it." After Jōtarō had left, Daizō began retying his obi.

Having heard the women were Kyoto prostitutes, famous for their beauty and savoir faire, the male guests were unable to leave off feasting their eyes. Sukeichi was so absorbed with the sight that his mouth was still hanging open when Jōtarō located him.

"Come on, you've seen enough," snapped the boy, giving the servant's ear a tug.

"Ouch!" squealed Sukeichi.

"Your master's calling you."

"That's not true."

"It is too. He said he was going for a walk. He's always taking walks, isn't he?"

"Eh? Oh, all right," said Sukeichi, tearing his eyes away reluctantly.

41

The boy had turned to follow him when a voice called, "Jōtarō? You're Jōtarō, aren't you?"

The voice was that of a young woman. He looked around searchingly. The hope that he would find his lost teacher and Otsū never left him. Could it be? He peered tensely through the branches of a large evergreen shrub.

"Who is it?"

"Me."

The face that emerged from the foliage was familiar.

"Oh, it's only you."

Akemi slapped him roughly on the back. "You little monster! And it's been such a long time since I saw you. What are you doing here?"

"I could ask you the same question."

"Well, I . . . Oh, it wouldn't mean anything to you anyway."

"Are you traveling with those women?"

"I am, but I haven't made up my mind yet."

"Made up your mind about what?"

"Whether to become one of them or not," she replied with a sigh. After a long pause, she asked, "What's Musashi doing these days?"

This, Jōtarō perceived, was what she really wanted to know. He only wished he could answer the question.

"Otsū and Musashi and I . . . we got separated on the highroad."

"Otsū? Who's she?" She had hardly spoken before she remembered. "Oh, never mind; I know. Is she *still* chasing after Musashi?" Akemi was in the habit of thinking of Musashi as a dashing *shugyōsha*, wandering about as the mood suited him, living in the forest, sleeping on bare rocks. Even if she succeeded in catching him, he'd see right away how dissolute her life had become and shun her. She had long since resigned herself to the idea that her love would go unrequited.

But the mention of another woman awoke feelings of jealousy and rekindled the dying embers of her amorous instinct.

"Jōtarō," she said, "there're too many curious eyes around here. Let's go out somewhere."

They left via the garden gate. Out in the street, their eyes were regaled by the lights of Hachiōji and its twenty-five hostelries. It was the liveliest town either had seen since leaving Kyoto. To the northwest rose the dark, silent forms of the Chichibu Range and the mountains marking the boundary of Kai Province, but here the atmosphere was replete with the aroma of sake, noisy with the clicking of weavers' reeds, the shouts of market officials, the excited voices of gamblers and the dispirited whining songs of local street singers.

"I often heard Matahachi mention Otsū," Akemi lied. "What kind of person is she?"

"She's a very good person," Jōtarō said soberly. "Sweet and gentle and considerate and pretty. I really like her."

The threat Akemi felt hanging over her grew heavier, but she cloaked her feelings with a benign smile. "Is she really so wonderful?"

"Oh, yes. And she can do anything. She sings, she writes well. And she's good at playing the flute."

Now visibly ruffled, Akemi said, "I don't see what good it does a woman to be able to play the flute."

"If you don't, you don't, but everybody, even Lord Yagyū Sekishūsai, speaks highly of Otsū. There's only one little thing I don't like about her."

"All women have their faults. It's just a question of whether they honestly admit to them, the way I do, or try to hide them behind a ladylike pose."

"Otsū's not like that. It's just this one weakness of hers."

"What's that?"

"She's always breaking into tears. She's a regular crybaby."

"Oh? Why is that?"

"She cries whenever she thinks of Musashi. That makes being around her pretty gloomy, and I don't like

43

it.'' Jōtarō expressed himself with youthful abandon, heedless of the effect this might have.

Akemi's heart, her whole body, was afire with raging jealousy. It showed in the depths of her eyes, even in the color of her skin. But she continued her interrogation. "Tell me, how old is she?"

"About the same."

"You mean the same age as me?"

"Um. But she looks younger and prettier."

Akemi plunged on, hoping to turn Jōtarō against Otsū. "Musashi's more masculine than most men. He must hate having to watch a woman carry on all the time. Otsū probably thinks tears will win a man's sympathy. She's like the girls working for the Sumiya."

Jōtarō, very much irked, retorted, "That's not true at all. In the first place, Musashi likes Otsū. He never shows his feelings, but he's in love with her."

Akemi's flushed face grew bright crimson. She longed to throw herself into a river to quench the flames that were consuming her.

"Jōtarō, let's go this way." She pulled him toward a red light in a side street.

"That's a drinking place."

"Well, what of it?"

"Women have no business in a place like that. You can't go in there."

"All of a sudden I have the urge to drink, and I can't go in alone. I'd be embarrassed."

"*You'd* be embarrassed. What about me?"

"They'll have things to eat. You can have anything you want."

At first glance, the shop seemed empty. Akemi walked right in, then, facing the wall rather than the counter, said, "Bring me some sake!"

One cup after another went down as fast as was humanly possible. Jōtarō, frightened by the quantity, tried to slow her down, but she elbowed him out of the way.

"Quiet!" she yelped. "What a nuisance you are! Bring some more sake! Sake!"

Jōtarō, insinuating himself between her and the sake jar, pleaded, "You've got to stop. You can't go on drinking here like this."

"Don't worry about me," she slurred. "You're a friend of Otsū's, aren't you? I can't stand women who try to win a man with tears!"

"Well, I dislike women who get drunk."

"I'm so sorry, but how could a runt like you understand why I drink?"

"Come on, just pay the bill."

"You think I've got money?"

"Don't you?"

"No. Maybe he can collect from the Sumiya. I've already sold myself to the master anyway." Tears flooded her eyes. "I'm sorry . . . I'm really sorry."

"Weren't you the one who was making fun of Otsū for crying? Look at yourself."

"My tears aren't the same as hers. Oh, life's too much trouble. I might as well be dead."

With that, she stood up and lurched out into the street. The shopkeeper, having had other female customers like this in his time, merely laughed it off, but a rōnin who had until then been sleeping quietly in a corner opened his bleary eyes and stared at her retreating back.

Jōtarō darted after her and grabbed her around the waist, but he lost his hold. She started running down the darkened street, Jōtarō close behind.

"Stop!" he cried with alarm. "You mustn't even think of it. Come back!"

Though she seemed not to care whether she ran into something in the dark or fell into a swamp, she was fully conscious of Jōtarō's pleading. When she had plunged into the sea at Sumiyoshi, she had wanted to kill herself, but she was no longer so lacking in guile. She got a certain thrill from having Jōtarō so worried about her.

"Watch out!" he screamed, seeing that she was

headed straight toward the murky water of a moat. "Stop it! Why do you want to die? It's crazy."

As he caught her around the waist again, she wailed, "Why shouldn't I die? You think I'm wicked. So does Musashi. Everybody does. There's nothing I can do but die, embracing Musashi in my heart. Never will I let him be taken from me by a woman like that!"

"You're pretty mixed up. How did you get this way?"

"It doesn't matter. All you have to do is push me into the moat. Go ahead, Jōtarō, push." Covering her face with her hands, she burst into frenzied tears. This awakened a strange fear in Jōtarō. He, too, felt the urge to cry.

"Come on, Akemi. Let's go back."

"Oh, I yearn so to see him. Find him for me, Jōtarō. Please find Musashi for me."

"Stand still! Don't move; it's dangerous."

"Oh, Musashi!"

"Watch out!"

At that moment the rōnin from the sake shop stepped out of the darkness.

"Go away, boy," he commanded. "I'll take her back to the inn." He put his hands under Jōtarō's arms and roughly lifted him aside.

He was a tall man, thirty-four or -five years old, with deep-set eyes and a heavy beard. A crooked scar, no doubt left by a sword, ran from below his right ear to his chin. It looked like the jagged tear that appears when a peach is broken open.

Swallowing hard to overcome his fear, Jōtarō tried coaxing. "Akemi, please come with me. Everything'll be all right."

Akemi's head was now resting on the samurai's chest.

"Look," the man said, "she's gone to sleep. Off with you! I'll take her home later."

"No! Let go of her!"

When the boy refused to budge, the ronin slowly reached out with one hand and grabbed his collar.

"Hands off!" screamed Jōtarō, resisting with all his strength.

"You little bastard! How'd you like to get thrown into the moat?"

"Who's going to do it?" He wriggled loose, and as soon as he was free, his hand found the end of his wooden sword. He swung it at the man's side, but his own body did a somersault and landed on a rock by the roadside. He moaned once, then remained still.

Jōtarō had been out for some time before he began hearing voices around him.

"Wake up, there."

"What happened?"

Opening his eyes, he vaguely took in a small crowd of people.

"Are you awake?"

"Are you all right?"

Embarrassed by the attention he was attracting, he picked up his wooden sword and was trying to get away when a clerk from the inn grabbed his arm. "Wait a minute," he barked. "What happened to the woman you were with?"

Looking around, Jōtarō got the impression that the others were also from the inn, guests as well as employees. Some of the men were carrying sticks; others were holding round paper lanterns.

"A man came and said you'd been attacked and a ronin had carried the woman off. Do you know which way they went?"

Jōtarō, still dazed, shook his head.

"That's impossible. You must have some idea."

Jōtarō pointed in the first direction that came to hand. "Now I remember. It was that way." He was reluctant to say what really happened, fearing a scolding from Daizō for getting involved, but also dreading to admit in front of these people that the rōnin had thrown him.

Despite the vagueness of his reply, the crowd rushed off, and presently a cry went up: "Here she is. Over here."

The lanterns gathered in a circle around Akemi, whose disheveled form lay where she had been abandoned, on a stack of hay in a farmer's shed. Prodded back to reality by the clatter of running feet, she dragged herself to her feet. The front of her kimono was open; her obi lay on the ground. Hay clung to her hair and clothing.

"What happened?"

While the word "rape" was on the tip of everyone's tongue, no one said it. Nor did it even cross their minds to chase the villain. Whatever had happened to Akemi, they felt, she had brought on herself.

"Come on, let's go back," said one of the men, taking her hand.

Akemi pulled away quickly. Resting her face forlornly against the wall, she broke down in bitter tears.

"Seems to be drunk."

"How'd she get that way?"

Jōtarō had been watching the scene from a distance. What had befallen Akemi was not clear to him in detail, but somehow he was reminded of an experience that had nothing to do with her. The titillation of lying in the fodder shed in Koyagyū with Kocha came back to him, along with the strangely exciting fear of approaching footsteps. But his pleasure quickly evaporated. "I better get back," he said decisively.

As his pace quickened, his spirit, back from its trip to the unknown, moved him to break into song.

> "Old metal Buddha, standing in the field,
> Have you seen a girl of sixteen?
> Don't you know a girl who's strayed?
> When asked, you say 'Clang.'
> When struck, you say 'Bong.' "

5

A Cricket in the Grass

Jōtarō jogged along at a good pace, paying little attention to the road. Suddenly he halted and looked around, wondering if he'd lost his way. "I don't remember passing here before," he thought nervously.

Samurai houses fringed the remains of an old fortress. One section of the compound had been rebuilt to serve as the official residence of the recently appointed Ōkubo Nagayasu, but the rest of the area, rising like a natural mound, was covered with weeds and trees. The stone ramparts were crumbling, having been ravaged many years earlier by an invading army. The fortification looked primitive compared to the castle complexes of the last forty to fifty years. There was no moat, no bridge, nothing that could properly be described as a castle wall. It had probably belonged to one of the local gentry in the days before the great civil war daimyō incorporated their rural domains into larger feudal principalities.

On one side of the road were paddies and marshland; on the other, walls; and beyond, a cliff, atop which the fortress must once have stood.

As he tried to get his bearings, Jōtarō's eyes traveled along the cliff. Then he saw something move, stop, and move again. At first it looked like an animal, but soon the stealthily moving silhouette became the outline of a man. Jōtarō shivered but stood riveted to the spot.

The man lowered a rope with a hook attached to the top. After he had slid down the full length of the rope and found a foothold, he shook the hook loose and repeated the process. When he reached the bottom, he disappeared into a copse.

Jōtarō's curiosity was thoroughly aroused.

A few minutes later, he saw the man walking along the low rises separating the paddies and apparently heading straight for him. He nearly panicked, but relaxed when he could make out the bundle on the man's back. "What a waste of time! Nothing but a farmer stealing kindling." He thought the man must have been crazy to risk scaling the cliff for nothing more than some firewood. He was disappointed too; his mystery had become unbearably humdrum. But then came his second shock. As the man strolled up the road past the tree Jōtarō was hiding behind, the boy had to stifle a gasp. He was sure the dark figure was Daizō.

"It couldn't be," he told himself.

The man had a black cloth around his face and wore peasant's knickers, leggings and light straw sandals.

The mysterious figure turned off onto a path skirting a hill. No one with such sturdy shoulders and buoyant stride could be in his fifties, as Daizō was. Having convinced himself that he was mistaken, Jōtarō followed. He had to get back to the inn, and the man just might, unwittingly, help him find his way.

When the man came to a road marker, he set down his bundle, which appeared to be very heavy. As he leaned over to read the writing on the stone, something about him again struck Jōtarō as familiar.

While the man climbed the path up the hill, Jōtarō examined the marker, on which were carved the words "Pine Tree on Head-burying Mound—Above." This was where the local inhabitants buried the severed skulls of criminals and defeated warriors.

The branches of an immense pine were clearly visible against the night sky. By the time Jōtarō reached the top of the rise, the man had seated himself by the roots of the tree and was smoking a pipe.

Daizō! No question about it now. A peasant would never carry tobacco with him. Some had been successfully grown domestically, but on such a limited scale that it was still very expensive. Even in the relatively well-off Kansai district, it was considered a luxury. And up in Sendai, when Lord Date smoked, his scribe felt constrained to make an entry in his daily journal: "Morning, three smokes; afternoon, four smokes; bedtime, one smoke."

Financial considerations aside, most people who had a chance to try tobacco found it made them dizzy or even nauseated. Though appreciated for its flavor, it was generally regarded as a narcotic.

Jōtarō knew that smokers were few; he also knew that Daizō was one of them, for he had frequently seen him drawing on a handsomely made ceramic pipe. Not that this had ever before struck him as strange. Daizō was wealthy and a man of expensive tastes.

"What's he up to?" he thought impatiently. Accustomed now to the danger of the situation, he gradually crept closer.

Having finished his pipe, the merchant got to his feet, removed his black kerchief and tucked it into his waist. Then slowly he walked around the pine. The next thing Jōtarō knew, he was holding a shovel in his hands. Where had that come from? Leaning on the shovel, Daizō looked around at the night scenery for a moment, apparently fixing the location in his mind.

Seemingly satisfied, Daizō rolled aside a large rock on the north side of the tree and began digging energetically, looking neither right nor left. Jōtarō watched the hole grow nearly deep enough for a man to stand in. Finally, Daizō stopped and wiped the sweat from his face with his kerchief. Jōtarō remained as still as a rock and totally baffled.

"This'll do," the merchant murmured softly, as he finished trampling down the soft dirt at the bottom of the hole. For an instant, Jōtarō had a peculiar impulse to call out and warn him not to bury himself, but he held back.

Jumping up to the surface, Daizō proceeded to drag the heavy bundle from the tree to the edge of the hole and undo the hempen cord around the top. At first Jōtarō thought the sack was made of cloth, but now he could see that it was a heavy leather cloak, of the sort generals wore over their armor. Inside was another sack, made of tenting or some similar fabric. When this was opened, the top of an incredible stack of gold came into view—semi-cylindrical ingots made by pouring the molten metal into half sections of bamboo, split lengthwise.

There was more to come. Loosening his obi, Daizō unburdened himself of several dozen large, newly minted gold pieces, which had been stuffed into his stomach wrapper, the back of his kimono and other parts of his clothing. Having placed these neatly on top of the ingots, he tied both containers securely and dropped the bundle into the pit, as he might have dumped the carcass of a dog. He then shoveled the dirt back in, stamped on it with his feet, and replaced the rock. He finished off by scattering dry grass and twigs around the rock.

Then he set about transforming himself back into the well-known Daizō of Narai, affluent dealer in herbs. The peasant's garb, wrapped around the shovel, went into a thicket not likely to be explored by passersby. He donned his traveling cloak and hung his money pouch around his neck in the manner of itinerant priests. As he slipped his feet into his zōri, he mumbled with satisfaction, "Quite a night's work."

When Daizō was out of hearing range, Jōtarō emerged from his hiding place and went to the rock. Though he scrutinized the spot carefully, he could discern no trace of what he had just witnessed. He stared at the ground as if at a magician's empty palm.

"I'd better get moving," he thought suddenly. "If I'm not there when he gets back to the inn, he'll be suspicious." Since the lights of the town were now visible beneath him, he had no trouble setting his course. Running like the wind, he somehow contrived to stay on back roads and keep well out of Daizō's path.

It was with an expression of perfect innocence that he climbed the stairs at the inn and entered their room. He was in luck; Sukeichi was slumped against the lacquered traveling case, alone and sound asleep. A thin trickle of saliva ran down his chin.

"Hey, Sukeichi, you'll catch cold there." Purposely Jōtarō shook him to wake him up.

"Oh, it's you, is it?" drawled Sukeichi, rubbing his eyes. "What were you doing out this late without telling the master?"

"Are you crazy? I've been back for hours. If you'd been awake, you'd have known that."

"Don't try to fool me. I know you went out with that woman from the Sumiya. If you're running around after a whore now, I hate to think what you'll be acting like when you grow up."

Just then, Daizō open the shoji. "I'm back," was all he said.

An early morning start was necessary in order to make Edo before nightfall. Jinnai had his troupe, Akemi restored to it, on the road well before sunrise. Daizō, Sukeichi and Jōtarō, however, took their time over breakfast and were not ready to leave until the sun was fairly high in the sky.

Daizō led the way, as usual, but Jōtarō trailed behind with Sukeichi, which was unusual.

Finally Daizō stopped, asking, "What's the matter with you this morning?"

"Pardon?" Jōtarō did his best to appear nonchalant.

"Is something wrong?"

"No, nothing at all. Why do you ask?"

"You look glum. Not like you."

"It's nothing, sir. I was just thinking. If I stay with you, I don't know whether I'll ever find my teacher or not. I'd like to go and look for him on my own, if it's all right with you."

Without a moment's hesitation, Daizō replied, "It isn't!"

Jōtarō had sidled up and started to take hold of the man's arm, but now he withdrew his hand and asked nervously, "Why not?"

"Let's rest here awhile," said Daizō, lowering himself onto the grassy plain for which the province of Musashi was famous. Once seated, he gestured to Sukeichi to go on ahead.

"But I have to find my teacher—as soon as possible," pleaded Jōtarō.

"I told you, you're not going off by yourself." Looking very stern. Daizō put his ceramic pipe to his lips and took a puff. "As of today, you're my son."

He sounded serious. Jōtarō swallowed hard, but then Daizō laughed, and the boy, assuming it was all a joke, said, "I couldn't do that. I don't want to be your son."

"What?"

"You're a merchant. I want to be a samurai."

"I'm sure you'll find that Daizō of Narai is no ordinary townsman, without honor or background. Become my adopted son, and I'll make a real samurai out of you."

Jōtarō realized with dismay that he meant what he was saying. "May I ask why you decided this so suddenly?" the boy asked.

In a trice, Daizō seized him and pinioned him to his side. Putting his mouth to the boy's ear, he whispered, "You saw me, didn't you, you little bastard?"

"Saw you?"

"Yes; you were watching, weren't you?"

"I don't know what you're talking about. Watching what?"

"What I did last night."

Jōtarō tried his best to stay calm.

"Why did you do that?"

The boy's defenses were close to collapse.

"Why were you prying into my private affairs?"

"I'm sorry!" blurted Jōtarō. "I'm really sorry. I won't tell a soul."

"Keep your voice down! I'm not going to punish you, but in return, you're going to become my adopted son. If you refuse, you give me no choice but to kill you. Now, don't force me to do that. I think you're a fine boy, very likable."

For the first time in his life, Jōtarō began to feel real fear. "I'm sorry," he repeated fervently. "Don't kill me. I don't want to die!" Like a captured skylark, he wriggled timidly in Daizō's arms, afraid that if he really struggled, the hand of death would descend on him forthwith.

Although the boy felt his grip to be viselike, Daizō was not holding him tightly at all. In fact, when he pulled the boy onto his lap, his touch was almost tender. "Then you'll be my son, won't you?" His stubbly chin scratched Jōtarō's cheek.

Though he couldn't have identified it, what fettered Jōtarō was an adult, masculine scent. He was like an infant on Daizō's knee, unable to resist, unable even to speak.

"It's for you to decide. Will you let me adopt you, or will you die? Answer me, now!"

With a wail, the boy burst into tears. He rubbed his face with dirty fingers until muddy little puddles formed on both sides of his nose.

"Why cry? You're lucky to have such an opportunity. I guarantee you'll be a great samurai when I finish with you."

"But . . ."

"What is it?"

"You're . . . you're . . ."

"Yes?"

"I can't say it."

"Out with it. Speak. A man should state his thoughts simply and clearly."

"You're . . . well, your business is stealing." Had it not been for the hands resting lightly on him, Jōtarō would have been off like a gazelle. But Daizō's lap was a deep pit, the walls of which prevented him from moving.

"Ha, ha," chortled Daizō, giving him a playful slap on the back. "Is that all that's bothering you?"

"Y-y-yes."

The big man's shoulders shook with laughter. "I might be the sort of person who'd steal the whole country, but a common burglar or highwayman I am not. Look at Ieyasu or Hideyoshi or Nobunaga—they're all warriors who stole or tried to steal the whole nation, aren't they? Just stick with me, and one of these days you'll understand."

"Then you're not a thief?"

"I wouldn't bother with a business that's so unprofitable." Lifting the boy off his knee, he said, "Now stop blubbering, and let's be on our way. From this moment on, you're my son. I'll be a good father to you. Your end of the bargain is that you never breathe a word to anyone about what you think you saw last night. If you do, I'll wring your neck."

Jōtarō believed him.

6

The Pioneers

On the day near the end of the fifth month when Osugi arrived in Edo, the air was steamingly sultry, the way it was only when the rainy season failed to bring rain. In the nearly two months since she had left Kyoto, she had traveled at a leisurely pace, taking time to pamper her aches and pains or to visit shrines and temples.

Her first impression of the shōgun's capital was distasteful. "Why build houses in a swamp like this?" she remarked disdainfully. "The weeds and rushes haven't even been cleared away yet."

Because of the unseasonable drought, a pall of dust hung over the Takanawa highroad, with its newly planted trees and recently erected milestones. The stretch from Shioiri to Nihombashi was crowded with oxcarts loaded with rocks or lumber. All along the way, new houses were going up at a furious clip.

"Of all the—!" gasped Osugi, looking up angrily at a half-finished house. A gob of wet clay from a plasterer's trowel had accidentally landed on her kimono.

The workmen exploded with laughter.

"How dare you throw mud on people and then stand there laughing? You should be on your knees, apologizing!"

Back in Miyamoto, a few sharp words from her

would have had her tenants or any of the other villagers cowering. These laborers, among the thousands of newcomers from all over the country, barely looked up from their work.

"What's the old hag babbling about?" a worker asked.

Osugi, incensed, shouted, "Who said that? Why, you . . ."

The more she sputtered, the harder they laughed. Spectators began to gather, asking each other why the old woman wasn't acting her age and taking the matter in stride.

Storming into the house, Osugi seized the end of the plank the plasterers were standing on and yanked it off its supports. Men and buckets full of wet clay clattered to the floor.

"You old bitch!"

Jumping to their feet, they surrounded her threateningly.

Osugi did not flinch. "Come outside!" she commanded grimly as she placed her hand on her short sword.

The workmen had second thoughts. The way she looked and carried on, she had to be from a samurai family; they might get into trouble if they weren't careful. Their manner softened noticeably.

Observing the change, Osugi declared grandly, "Henceforward, I'll not countenance rudeness from the likes of you." With a look of satisfaction on her face, she went out and started up the road again, leaving the spectators to gape at her stubborn, straight back.

She was hardly on her way again before an apprentice, his muddy feet grotesquely covered with shavings and sawdust, ran up behind her, carrying a bucket of mucky clay.

Shouting, "How do you like this, you old witch?" he slung the contents of his pail at her back.

"O-w-w-w!" The howl did credit to Osugi's lungs,

but before she could turn around, the apprentice had vanished. When she realized the extent of the damage, she scowled bitterly and tears of sheer vexation filled her eyes.

The merriment was general.

"What're you nincompoops laughing at?" raged Osugi, baring her teeth. "What's so funny about an old woman being splattered with grime? Is this the way you welcome elderly people to Edo? You're not even human! Just remember, you'll all be old one day."

This outburst attracted even more onlookers.

"Edo, indeed!" she snorted. "To hear people talk, you'd think it was the greatest city in the whole country. And what is it? A place full of dirt and filth, where everybody's pulling down hills and filling in swamps and digging ditches and piling up sand from the seaside. Not only that, it's full of riffraff, like you'd never find in Kyoto or anywhere in the west." Having got that off her chest, she turned her back on the sniggering crowd and went rapidly on her way.

To be sure, the city's newness was its most remarkable feature. The wood and plaster of the houses was all bright and fresh, many building sites were only partially filled in, and ox and horse dung assailed the eyes and nostrils.

Not so long ago, this road had been a mere footpath through the rice paddies between the villages of Hibiya and Chiyoda. Had Osugi gone a little to the west, nearer Edo Castle, she would have found an older and more sedate district, where daimyō and vassals of the shōgun had begun building residences soon after Tokugawa Ieyasu occupied Edo in 1590.

As it was, absolutely nothing appealed to her. She felt ancient. Everyone she saw—shopkeepers, officials on horseback, samurai striding by in basket hats—all were young, as were laborers, craftsmen, vendors, soldiers, even generals.

The front of one house, where plasterers were still at

work, bore a shop sign, behind which sat a heavily powdered woman, brushing her eyebrows as she awaited customers. In other half-finished buildings, people were selling sake, setting up displays of dry goods, laying in supplies of dried fish. One man was hanging out a sign advertising medicine.

"If I weren't looking for someone," Osugi mumbled sourly, "I wouldn't stay in this garbage dump a single night."

Coming to a hill of excavated dirt blocking the road, she halted. At the foot of a bridge crossing the as yet waterless moat stood a shanty. Its walls consisted of reed matting held in place by strips of bamboo, but a banner proclaimed that this was a public bath. Osugi handed over a copper coin and went in to wash her kimono. After cleaning it as well as she could, she borrowed a drying pole and hung the garment up by the side of the shanty. Clothed in her underwear, with a light bathrobe draped over her back, she squatted in the shadow of the bathhouse and gazed absently at the road.

Across the street, half a dozen men stood in a circle, haggling in voices loud enough for Osugi to hear what they were saying.

"How many square feet is it? I wouldn't mind considering it if the price is right."

"There's two thirds of an acre. The price is what I mentioned before. I can't come down from that."

"It's too much. You must know that yourself."

"Not at all. It costs a lot of money to fill in land. And don't forget, there's no more available around here."

"Oh, there must be. They're filling in everywhere."

"Already sold. People are snatching it up as it is, swamp and all. You won't find three hundred square feet for sale. Of course, if you're willing to go way over toward the Sumida River, you might be able to get something cheaper."

"Do you guarantee there's two thirds of an acre?"

"You don't have to take my word for it. Get a rope and measure it off yourself."

Osugi was astounded; the figure quoted for a hundred square feet would have been sufficient for tens of acres of good rice land. But essentially the same conversation was taking place all over the city, for many a merchant speculated in land. Osugi was also mystified. "Why would anybody want land here? It's no good for rice, and you can't call this place a city."

By and by the deal across the street was sealed with a ritual hand clapping intended to bring good luck to all concerned.

As she idly watched the departing shadows, Osugi became conscious of a hand on the back of her obi. "Thief!" she shrieked as she made a grab for the pickpocket's wrist. But her coin purse had already been removed, and the thief was already in the street.

"Thief!" Osugi screamed again. Flying after the man, she managed to throw her arms around his waist. "Help! Thief!"

The pickpocket struggled, striking her several times in the face without being able to break her grip. "Let go of me, you cow!" he shouted, kicking her in the ribs. With a loud grunt, Osugi fell down, but she had her short sword out and slashed at the man's ankle.

"Ow!" Blood pouring from the wound, he limped a few steps, then flopped down on the ground.

Startled by the commotion, the land dealers turned around, and one of them exclaimed, "Hey, isn't that that good-for-nothing from Kōshū?" The speaker was Hangawara Yajibei, master of a large gang of construction workers.

"Looks like him," agreed one of his henchmen. "What's that in his hand? Looks like a purse."

"It does, doesn't it? And somebody just yelled thief. Look! There's an old woman sprawled out on the ground. Go see what's the matter with her. I'll take care of him."

The pickpocket was on his feet and running again,

but Yajibei caught up with him and slapped him to the ground as he might have swatted a grasshopper.

Returning to his boss, the henchman reported, "Just as we thought. He stole the old lady's purse."

"I have it here. How is she?"

"Not hurt bad. She fainted, but came to screaming bloody murder."

"She's still sitting there. Can't she stand up?"

"I guess not. He kicked her in the ribs."

"You son of a bitch!" Still glaring at the pickpocket, Yajibei issued a command to his underling. "Ushi, put up a stake."

The words set the thief to trembling as though the point of a knife were being pressed against his throat. "Not that," he pleaded, groveling in the dirt at Yajibei's feet. "Let me off just this once. I promise I won't do it again."

Yajibei shook his head. "No. You'll get what you deserve."

Ushi, who had been named after the zodiac sign under which he was born, a not uncommon practice among farmers, returned with two workmen from the nearby bridge site.

"Over there," he said, pointing toward the middle of a vacant lot.

After the workmen had driven a heavy post into the ground, one of them asked, "This good enough?"

"That's fine," said Yajibei. "Now tie him to it, and nail a board above his head."

When this had been done, Yajibei borrowed a carpenter's ink pot and brush and wrote on the board: "This man is a thief. Until recently, he worked for me, but he has committed a crime for which he must be punished. He is to be tied here, exposed to rain and sun, for seven days and seven nights. By order of Yajibei of Bakurō-chō."

"Thanks," he said, returning the ink pot. "Now, if it's not too much trouble, give him a bit to eat every once in a while. Just enough to keep him from starving. Anything left over from your lunch will do."

The two workmen, along with others who had congregated in the meantime, signified their assent. Some of the laborers promised that they would see to it that the thief got his share of ridicule. It wasn't just samurai who feared public exposure of their misdeeds or weaknesses. Even for ordinary townspeople in these times, to be laughed at was the worst of all punishments.

Punishing criminals without reference to law was a firmly established practice. In the days when the warriors were too busy with warfare to maintain order, townsmen had, for the sake of their own safety, taken it upon themselves to deal with miscreants. Though Edo now had an official magistrate and a system was developing whereby leading citizens in each district functioned as government representatives, the summary administration of justice still occurred. With conditions still being a bit chaotic, the authorities saw little reason to interfere.

"Ushi," said Yajibei, "take the old lady her purse. Too bad this had to happen to somebody her age. She seems to be all alone. What happened to her kimono?"

"She says she washed it and hung it up to dry."

"Go get it for her, then bring her along. We might as well take her home with us. There's little point in punishing the thief if we're going to leave her here for some other ruffian to prey on."

Moments later, Yajibei strode away. Ushi was close behind, the kimono over his arm and Osugi on his back.

They soon reached Nihombashi, the "Bridge of Japan" from which all distances along the roads leading out of Edo were now measured. Stone parapets supported the wooden arch, and since the bridge had been constructed only about a year before, the railings still preserved a feeling of newness. Boats from Kamakura and Odawara were moored along one riverbank. On the other was the city's fish market.

"Oh, my side hurts," Osugi said with a loud groan.

The fishmongers looked up to see what was going on.

Being gaped at was not to Yajibei's liking. Glancing back at Osugi, he said, "We'll be there soon. Try to hold on. Your life's not in danger."

Osugi laid her head on Ushi's back and became as quiet as a baby.

In the downtown area, tradesmen and artisans had formed their own neighborhoods. There was a blacksmiths' district, one for lance-makers, others for dyers, tatami weavers, and so on. Yajibei's house stood out prominently from those of the other carpenters because the front half of the roof was covered with tiles; all the other houses had board roofs. Until a fire a couple of years before, nearly all the roofs had been made of thatch. As it happened, Yajibei had acquired what passed for his surname from his roof, Hangawara meaning "half tiled."

He had come to Edo as a rōnin, but being both clever and warmhearted, he had proved to be a skillful manager of men. Before long he set himself up as a contractor employing a sizable crew of carpenters, roofers and unskilled workers. From building projects carried out for various daimyō, he acquired enough capital to branch out into the real estate business as well. Too affluent now to have to work with his own hands, he played the role of local boss. Among Edo's numerous self-appointed bosses, Yajibei was one of the best known and most highly respected.

The townspeople looked up to the bosses as well as to the warriors, but of the two, the bosses were the more highly admired, because they usually stood up for the common people. Although those of Edo had a style and spirit of their own, the bosses were not unique to the new capital. Their history went back to the troubled latter days of the Ashikaga shogunate, when gangs of thugs roamed the countryside like prides of lions, pillaging at will and submitting to no restraints.

According to a writer of that era, they wore little more than vermilion loincloths and wide stomach wrappers. Their long swords were very long—nearly four feet—and even their short swords were more than two feet in length. Many used other weapons, of a cruder type, such as battle-axes and "iron rakes." They let their hair grow wild, using thick strips of rope for headbands, and leather leggings often covered their calves.

Having no fixed loyalties, they operated as mercenaries, and after peace was restored, were ostracized by both farmers and samurai alike. By the Edo era, those not content with being bandits or highwaymen often sought their fortunes in the new capital. More than a few succeeded, and this breed of leaders was once described as having "righteousness for bones, love of the people for flesh and gallantry for skin." In short, they were popular heroes par excellence.

7

Slaughter by the Riverside

Life under Yajibei's half-tiled roof agreed so much with Osugi that a year and a half later she was still there. After the first few weeks, during which she rested and recovered her health, hardly a day passed without her telling herself she should be on her way.

Whenever she broached the subject to Yajibei, whom she didn't see often, he urged her to stay on. "What's the hurry?" he would ask. "There's no reason for you to go anywhere. Bide your time until we find Musashi. Then we can serve as your seconds." Yajibei knew nothing of Osugi's enemy except what she herself had told him—that he was, in so many words, the blackest of blackguards—but since the day of her arrival, all of his men had been under instructions to report immediately anything they heard or saw of Musashi.

After initially detesting Edo, Osugi had mellowed in attitude to the point where she was willing to admit that the people were "friendly, carefree and really very kind at heart."

The Hangawara household was a particularly easy-going place and something of a haven for social misfits; country boys too lazy to farm, displaced rōnin, profligates who had run through their parents' money and tattooed ex-convicts made up a coarse and motley crew,

whose unifying esprit de corps curiously resembled that
of a well-run school for warriors. The ideal here, however, was blustering masculinity rather than spiritual
manliness; it was really a "dōjō" for thugs.

As in the martial arts dōjō, there was a rigid class
structure. Under the boss, who was the ultimate temporal
and spiritual authority, came a group of seniors, usually
referred to as the "elder brothers." Below them were the
ordinary henchmen—the *kobun*—whose ranking was determined largely by length of service. There was also a
special class of "guests"; their status depended on such
factors as their ability with weapons. Bolstering the hier-
archical organization was a code of etiquette, of uncertain
origin but strictly adhered to.

At one point, Yajibei, thinking Osugi might be bored,
suggested that she take care of the younger men. Since
then, her days had been fully occupied with sewing,
mending, washing and straightening up after the *kobun*,
whose slovenliness gave her plenty of work.

For all their lack of breeding, the *kobun* recognized
quality when they saw it. They admired both Osugi's
spartan habits and the efficiency with which she went
about her chores. "She's a real samurai lady," they were
wont to say. "The House of Hon'iden must have very
good blood in it."

Osugi's unlikely host treated her with consideration
and had even built her separate living quarters on the
vacant lot behind his house. And whenever he was at
home, he went to pay his respects each morning and
evening. When asked by one of his underlings why he
displayed such deference toward a stranger, Yajibei con-
fessed that he had acted very badly toward his own father
and mother while they were still alive. "At my age," he
said, "I feel I have a filial duty to all older people."

Spring came, and the wild plum blossoms fell, but
the city itself had as yet almost no cherry blossoms.
Apart from a few trees in the sparsely settled hills to the
west, there were only the saplings that Buddhists had

planted along the road leading to the Sensōji, in Asakusa. Rumor had it that this year they were sprouting buds and would blossom for the first time.

One day Yajibei came to Osugi's room and said, "I'm going to the Sensōji. Do you feel like coming along?"

"I'd love to. That temple's dedicated to Kanzeon, and I'm a great believer in her powers. She's the same bodhisattva as the Kannon I prayed to at Kiyomizudera in Kyoto."

With Yajibei and Osugi went two of the *kobun*, Jūrō and Koroku. Jūrō bore the nickname "Reed Mat," for reasons no one knew, but it was obvious why Koroku was called the "Acolyte." He was a small, compact man with a distinctly benign face, if one overlooked the three ugly scars on his forehead, evidence of a proclivity for street brawls.

They first made their way to the moat at Kyōbashi, where boats were available for hire. After Koroku had skillfully sculled them out of the moat and into the Sumida River, Yajibei ordered the box lunches opened.

"I'm going to the temple today," he explained, "because it's the anniversary of my mother's death. I really should go back home and visit her grave, but it's too far, so I compromise by going to the Sensōji and making a donation. But that's neither here nor there; just think of it as a picnic." He reached over the side of the boat, rinsed off a sake cup and offered it to Osugi.

"It's very fine of you to remember your mother," she said as she accepted the cup, all the while wondering fretfully if Matahachi would do the same when she was gone. "I wonder, though, is drinking sake on the anniversary of your poor mother's passing the thing to do?"

"Well, I'd rather do that than hold some pompous ceremony. Anyway, I believe in the Buddha; that's all that counts for ignorant louts like me. You know the saying, don't you? 'He who has faith need have no knowledge.' "

Osugi, letting it go at that, proceeded to have several refills. After a time she remarked, "I haven't drunk like this for ages. I feel like I'm floating on air."

"Drink up," urged Yajibei. "It's good sake, isn't it? Don't worry about being out on the water. We're here to take care of you."

The river, flowing south from the town of Sumida, was broad and placid. On the Shimōsa side, the east bank opposite Edo, stood a luxuriant forest. Tree roots jutting into the water formed nests holding limpid pools, which shone like sapphires in the sunlight.

"Oh," said Osugi. "Listen to the nightingales!"

"When the rainy season comes, you can hear cuckoos all day long."

"Let me pour for you. I hope you don't mind my joining in your celebration."

"I like to see you having a good time."

From the stern, Koroku called out lustily, "Say, boss, how about passing the sake around?"

"Just pay attention to your work. If you start now, we'll all drown. On the way back you can have all you want."

"If you say so. But I just want you to know the whole river's beginning to look like sake."

"Stop thinking about it. Here, pull over to that boat next to the bank so we can buy some fresh fish."

Koroku did as he was told. After a bit of haggling, the fisherman, flashing a happy smile, lifted the cover off a tank built into the deck and told them to take anything they wanted. Osugi had never seen anything like it. The tank was full to the brim with wriggling, flapping fish, some from the sea, some from the river. Carp, prawns, catfish, black porgies, gobies. Even trout and sea bass.

Yajibei sprinkled soy sauce on some whitebait and began eating it raw. He offered some to Osugi, but she declined, with a look of dread on her face.

When they drew up on the west side of the river and disembarked, Osugi seemed a little wobbly on her feet.

"Be careful," warned Yajibei. "Here, take my hand."

"No, thank you. I don't need any help." She waved her own hand before her face indignantly.

After Jūrō and Koroku had moored the boat, the four of them crossed a broad expanse of stones and puddles to get to the riverbank proper.

A group of small children were busily turning over stones, but seeing the unusual foursome, they stopped and flocked around, chattering excitedly.

"Buy some, sir. Please."

"Won't you buy some, Granny?"

Yajibei seemed to like children; at least, he showed no signs of annoyance. "What have you got there—crabs?"

"Not crabs; arrowheads," they cried, producing handfuls of them from their kimonos.

"Arrowheads?"

"That's right. A lot of men and horses are buried in a mound by the temple. People coming here buy arrowheads to offer to the dead. You should too."

"I don't think I want any arrowheads, but I'll give you some money. How'll that do?"

That, it appeared, would do admirably, and as soon as Yajibei had passed out a few coins, the children ran off to resume their digging. But even as he watched, a man emerged from a thatched-roof house nearby, took the coins away from them and went back inside. Yajibei clicked his tongue and turned away in disgust.

Osugi was gazing out over the river, fascination in her eyes. "If there are a lot of arrowheads lying around," she observed, "there must have been a big battle."

"I don't really know, but it seems there were quite a few battles here in the days when Edo was only a provincial estate. That was four or five hundred years ago. I've heard that Minamoto no Yoritomo came up here from Izu to organize troops in the twelfth century. When the Imperial Court was divided—when was that, fourteenth century?—Lord Nitta of Musashi was defeated by the Ashikagas somewhere in the neighborhood. Just in the last couple of centuries, Ōta Dōkan and other local generals are said to have fought many battles not far up the river."

While they were talking, Jūrō and Koroku went on ahead to make a place for them to sit on the veranda of the temple.

The Sensōji turned out to be a terrible disappointment to Osugi. In her eyes it was nothing more than a large, run-down house, the priest's residence a mere shack. "Is this it?" she wanted to know, with more than a hint of deprecation. "After all I've heard about the Sensōji . . ."

The setting was a splendidly primeval forest of large, ancient trees, but not only did the Kanzeon hall look shabby; when the river flooded, the water came through the woods right up to the veranda. Even at other times, small tributaries washed over the grounds.

"Welcome. Good to see you again."

Glancing up in surprise, Osugi saw a priest kneeling on the roof.

"Working on the roof?" asked Yajibei amiably.

"Have to, because of the birds. The oftener I mend it, the oftener they steal the thatch to make nests with. There's always a leak somewhere. Make yourselves comfortable. I'll be down shortly."

Yajibei and Osugi picked up votive candles and went into the dim interior. "No wonder it leaks," she thought, looking at the starlike holes above her.

Kneeling beside Yajibei, she took out her prayer beads and with a dreamy look in her eye chanted the Vow of Kanzeon from the Lotus Sutra.

> "You will reside in the air like the sun.
> And if you are pursued by evil men
> And pushed off the Diamond Mountain,
> Reflect on the power of Kanzeon

And you will not lose a hair from your head.
And if bandits surround you
And threaten you with swords,
If you reflect on the power of Kanzeon,
The bandits will take pity on you.
And if the king sentences you to death
And the sword is about to behead you,
Reflect on the power of Kanzeon.
The sword will break into pieces."

She recited softly at first, but as she became oblivious to the presence of Yajibei, Jūrō and Koroku, her voice rose and grew resonant; a rapt expression came to her face.

"The eighty-four thousand sentient beings
Began to aspire in their hearts
For *anuttara-samyak-sambodhi*,
The unsurpassed Wisdom of the Buddhas."

Prayer beads trembling in her fingers, Osugi went without a break from the recitation into a personal supplication of her own.

"Hail to Kanzeon, World-Honored One!
Hail to the Bodhisattva of Infinite Mercy and
Infinite Compassion!
Look favorably on this old woman's one wish.
Let me strike Musashi down, and very soon!
Let me strike him down!
Let me strike him down!"

Abruptly lowering her voice, she bowed to the floor. "And make Matahachi a good boy! Cause the House of Hon'iden to prosper!"

After the long prayer ended, there was a moment's silence before the priest invited them outside to have some tea. Yajibei and the two younger men, who had knelt in proper fashion throughout the invocation, got up rubbing their tingly legs and went out on the veranda.

"I can have some sake now, can't I?" Jūrō asked eagerly. Permission having been granted, he hastened to the priest's house and arranged their lunch on the porch. By the time the others joined him, he was sipping sake with one hand and broiling the fish they had bought with the other. "Who cares if there aren't any cherry blossoms?" he remarked. "Feels just like a flower-viewing picnic anyway."

Yajibei handed the priest an offering, delicately wrapped in paper, and told him to use it for the roof repairs. As he did so, he happened to notice a row of wooden plaques on which were written donors' names, together with the amounts they had contributed. Nearly all were about the same as Yajibei's, some less, but one stood out conspicuously. "Ten gold coins, Daizō of Narai, Province of Shinano."

Turning to the priest, Yajibei remarked, somewhat diffidently, "Perhaps it's crass of me to say so, but ten gold coins is a considerable sum. Is this Daizō of Narai as rich as all that?"

"I really couldn't say. He appeared out of the blue one day toward the end of last year and said it was a disgrace that the most famous temple in the Kanto district was in such bad shape. He told me the money should be added to our fund for buying lumber."

"Sounds like an admirable sort of man."

"He also donated three gold coins to Yushima Shrine and no fewer than twenty to Kanda Myōjin Shrine. He wanted the latter to be kept in good condition because it enshrines the spirit of Taira no Masakado. Daizō insists that Masakado was not a rebel. He thinks he should be revered as the pioneer who opened up the eastern part of the country. You'll find there are some very unusual donors in this world."

Hardly had he finished speaking when a crowd of children came running helter-skelter toward them.

"What're you doing here?" shouted the priest sternly. "If you want to play, go down by the river. You mustn't run wild in the temple grounds."

But the children swept on like a school of minnows until they reached the veranda.

"Come quick," cried one. "It's awful!"

"There's a samurai down there. He's fighting."

"One man against four."

"Real swords!"

"Praise to Buddha, not again!" lamented the priest as he hurriedly slipped on his sandals. Before running off, he took a moment to explain. "Forgive me. I'll have to leave you for a while. The riverbank is a favorite place for fights. Every time I turn around, somebody's down there cutting people to pieces or beating them to a pulp. Then men from the magistrate's office come to me for a written report. I'll have to go see what it is this time."

"A fight?" chorused Yajibei and his men, and off they raced. Osugi followed but was so much slower on her feet that by the time she got there the fight was over. The children and some onlookers from a nearby fishing village all stood around in silence, swallowing hard and looking pale.

At first Osugi thought the silence strange, but then she, too, caught her breath, and her eyes opened wide. Across the ground flitted the shadow of a swallow. Walking toward them was a young, smug-faced samurai clad in a purplish-red warrior's cloak. Whether or not he noticed the spectators, he paid them no heed.

Osugi's gaze shifted to four bodies lying in a tangle some twenty paces behind the samurai.

The victor paused. As he did so, a low gasp went up from several lips, for one of the vanquished had moved. Struggling to his feet, he cried, "Wait! You can't run away."

The samurai assumed a waiting stance while the wounded man ran forward, gasping, "This . . . fight's . . . not over yet."

When he leapt weakly to the attack, the samurai retreated a step, allowing the man to stumble forward. Then he struck. The man's head split in two.

"Now is it over?" he shouted viciously.

No one had even seen the Drying Pole drawn.

Having wiped off his blade, he stooped to wash his hands in the river. Though the villagers were accustomed to fights, they were astonished at the samurai's sangfroid. The last man's death had been not only instantaneous but inhumanly cruel. Not a word was uttered.

The samurai stood up and stretched. "It's just like the Iwakuni River," he said. "Reminds me of home." For a few moments he gazed idly at the wide stream and a flock of white-bellied swallows swooping and skimming the water. Then he turned and walked rapidly downstream.

He made straight for Yajibei's boat, but as he began untying it, Jūrō and Koroku came running out of the forest.

"Wait! What do you think you're doing?" shouted Jūrō, who was now close enough to see the blood on the samurai's *hakama* and sandal thongs but took no notice of it.

Dropping the rope, the samurai grinned and asked, "Can't I use the boat?"

"Of course not," snapped Jūrō.

"Suppose I paid to use it?"

"Don't talk nonsense." The voice brusquely refusing the samurai's request was Jūrō's, but in a sense, it was the whole brash new city of Edo speaking fearlessly through his mouth.

The samurai did not apologize, but neither did he resort to force. He turned and walked off without another word.

"Kojirō! Kojirō! Wait!" Osugi called at the top of her lungs.

When Kojirō saw who it was, the grimness vanished from his face and he broke into a friendly smile. "Why, what are you doing here? I've been wondering what happened to you."

"I'm here to pay my respects to Kanzeon. I came with Hangawara Yajibei and these two young men. Yajibei's letting me stay at his house in Bakurōchō."

"When was it I saw you last? Let's see—Mount Hiei. You said then you were going to Edo, so I thought I might run into you. I hardly expected it to be here." He glanced at Jūrō and Koroku, who were in a state of shock. "You mean those two there?"

"Oh, they're just a couple of ruffians, but their boss is a very fine man."

Yajibei was just as thunderstruck as everybody else to see his guest chatting amiably with the awesome samurai. He was on the spot in no time, bowing to Kojirō and saying, "I'm afraid my boys spoke very rudely to you, sir. I hope you'll forgive them. We're just ready to leave. Perhaps you'd like to ride downstream with us."

8

Shavings

Like most people thrown together by circumstance, who ordinarily have little or nothing in common, the samurai and his host soon found mutual ground. The supply of sake was plentiful, the fish fresh, and Osugi and Kojirō had an odd spiritual kinship that kept the atmosphere from getting stickily formal. It was with genuine concern that she inquired about his career as a *shugyōsha* and he about her progress in achieving her "great ambition."

When she told him she'd had no word of Musashi's whereabouts for a long time, Kojirō offered a ray of hope. "I heard a rumor that he visited two or three prominent warriors last fall and winter. I have a hunch he's still in Edo."

Yajibei wasn't so sure, of course, and told Kojirō that his men had learned absolutely nothing. After they had discussed Osugi's predicament from every angle, Yajibei said, "I hope we can count on your continued friendship."

Kojirō responded in the same vein and made rather a display of rinsing out his cup and offering it not only to Yajibei but to his two minions, for each of whom he poured a drink.

Osugi was positively exhilarated. "They say," she observed gravely, "that good is to be found wherever one

77

looks. Even so, I'm exceptionally lucky! To think that I have two strong men like you on my side! I'm sure the great Kanzeon is looking after me." She made no attempt to conceal her sniffling or the tears that came to her eyes.

Not wanting the conversation to get maudlin, Yajibei said, "Tell me, Kojirō, who were the four men you cut down back there?"

This seemed to be the opportunity Kojirō had been waiting for, for his agile tongue set to work without delay. "Oh, them!" he began with a nonchalant laugh. "Just some rōnin from Obata's school. I went there five or six times to discuss military matters with Obata, and those fellows kept butting in with impertinent remarks. They even had the nerve to spout off on the subject of swordsmanship, so I told them that if they'd come to the banks of the Sumida, I'd give them a lesson in the secrets of the Ganryū Style, along with a demonstration of the Drying Pole's cutting edge. I let them know I didn't care how many of them came.

"When I got there, there were five of them, but the minute I took a stance, one turned tail and ran. I must say, Edo has no shortage of men who talk better than they fight." He laughed again, this time boisterously.

"Obata?"

"You don't know him? Obata Kagenori. He comes from the lineage of Obata Nichijō, who served the Takeda family of Kai. Ieyasu took him on, and now he's a lecturer in military science to the shōgun, Hidetada. He also has his own school."

"Oh, yes, I remember now." Yajibei was surprised and impressed by Kojirō's apparent familiarity with such a celebrated person. "The young man still has his forelock," he marveled to himself, "but he must be somebody if he associates with samurai of that rank." The carpenter boss was, after all, a simple soul, and the quality he most admired in his fellow man was clearly brute strength. His admiration for Kojirō intensified.

Leaning toward the samurai, he said, "Let me make

you a proposition. I've always got forty or fifty young
louts lying around my house. How would it be if I built a
dōjō for you and asked you to train them?''

"Well, I wouldn't mind giving them lessons, but you
must understand that so many daimyō are tugging at my
sleeve with offers—two, three thousand bushels—that I
don't know what to do. Frankly, I wouldn't seriously
consider going into anyone's service for less than five
thousand. Also, I'm rather obligated, just for the sake of
courtesy, to stay where I'm living now. Still, I've no
objection to coming to your place.''

With a low bow, Yajibei said, "I'd greatly appreciate
that.''

Osugi chimed in, "We'll be expecting you.''

Jūrō and Koroku, far too naive to recognize the
condescension and self-serving propaganda lacing Kojirō's speech, were bowled over by the great man's lar-
gesse.

When the boat rounded the turn into the Kyōbashi
moat, Kojirō said, "I'll be getting off here.'' He then
leapt onto the bank and in a matter of seconds was lost in
the dust hovering over the street.

"Very impressive young man,'' said Yajibei, still
under the spell.

"Yes,'' Osugi agreed with conviction. "He's a real
warrior. I'm sure plenty of daimyō would pay him a
handsome stipend.'' After a moment's pause, she added
wistfully, "If only Matahachi were like that.''

About five days later, Kojirō breezed into Yajibei's
establishment and was ushered into the guest room.
There, the forty or fifty henchmen on hand paid their
respects, one by one. Kojirō, delighted, remarked to
Yajibei that he seemed to lead a very interesting life.

Pursuing his earlier idea, Yajibei said, "As I told
you, I'd like to build a dōjō. Would you care to take a
look at the property?''

The field in back of the house measured nearly two

acres. Freshly dyed cloth hung in one corner, but Yajibei assured Kojirō the dyer he had rented the plot to could easily be evicted.

"You don't really need a dōjō," observed Kojirō. "The area's not open to the street; no one's likely to intrude."

"Whatever you say, but what about rainy days?"

"I won't come if the weather's bad. I should warn you, though: the practice sessions will be rougher than the ones held by the Yagyū or other schools around town. If your men aren't careful, they might wind up crippled, or worse. You'd better make that clear to them."

"There'll be no misunderstanding about that. Feel free to conduct classes as you see fit."

They agreed on having lessons three times a month, on the third, the thirteenth and the twenty-third, weather permitting.

Kojirō's appearances in Bakurōchō were a source of endless gossip. One neighbor was heard to say, "Now they've got a show-off over there worse than all the others put together." His boyish forelock also came in for considerable comment, the general opinion being that since he must be in his early twenties, it was high time he conformed to the samurai practice of shaving his pate. But only those inside the Hangawara household were treated to the sight of Kojirō's brightly embroidered underrobe, which they got to see every time he bared his shoulder to give his arm free play.

Kojirō's demeanor was quite what might be expected. Though this was practice and many of his students were inexperienced, he gave no quarter. By the third session, the casualties already included one man permanently deformed, plus four or five suffering from lesser injuries. The wounded were not far off; their moans could be heard coming from the back of the house.

"Next!" shouted Kojirō, brandishing a long sword made of loquat wood. At the beginning he had told them that a blow struck with a loquat sword "will rot your flesh to the bone."

"Ready to quit? If you're not, come forward. If you are, I'm going home," he taunted contemptuously.

Out of pure chagrin, one man said, "All right, I'll give it a try." He disengaged himself from the group, walked toward Kojirō, then leaned over to pick up a wooden sword. With a sharp crack, Kojirō flattened him.

"That," he declared, "is a lesson in why not to leave yourself open. It's the worst thing you can do." With obvious self-satisfaction, he looked around at the faces of the others, thirty to forty in number, most of them all but visibly trembling.

The latest victim was carried to the well, where water was poured over him. He did not come to.

"Poor guy's done for."

"You mean . . . he's dead?"

"He's not breathing."

Others ran up to stare at their slain comrade. Some were angry, some resigned, but Kojirō didn't give the corpse a second glance.

"If something like this frightens you," he said menacingly, "you'd better forget about the sword. When I think that any one of you would be itching to fight if somebody on the street called you a thug or a braggart . . ." He didn't finish the sentence, but as he walked across the field in his leather socks, he continued his lecture. "Give the matter some thought, my fine hoodlums. You're ready to draw the minute a stranger steps on your toes or brushes against your scabbard, but you're tied up in knots when the time comes for a real bout. You'll throw your lives away cheerfully over a woman or your own petty pride, but you haven't the guts to sacrifice yourself in a worthy cause. You're emotional, you're moved only by vanity. That's not enough, nowhere near enough."

Throwing his chest out, he concluded, "The truth is simple. The only real bravery, the only genuine self-confidence, comes from training and self-discipline. I dare any one of you: stand up and fight me like a man."

One student, hoping to make him eat his words, attacked from behind. Kojirō bent double, almost touching the ground, and the assailant flew over his head and landed in front of him. The next instant, there was the loud crack of Kojirō's loquat sword against the man's hipbone.

"That'll be all for today," he said, tossing the sword aside and going to the well to wash his hands. The corpse was lying in a flaccid heap beside the sink. Kojirō dipped his hands in the water and splashed some on his face without a word of sympathy.

Slipping his arm back into his sleeve, he said, "I hear a lot of people go to this place called Yoshiwara. You men must know the district pretty well. Wouldn't you like to show me around?" Bluntly announcing that he wanted to have a good time or go drinking was a habit of Kojirō's, but it was a matter of conjecture whether he was being deliberately impudent or disarmingly candid.

Yajibei chose the more charitable interpretation. "Haven't you been to Yoshiwara yet?" he asked with surprise. "We'll have to do something about that. I'd go with you myself, but, well, I have to be here this evening for the wake and so on."

He singled out Jūrō and Koroku and gave them some money. Also a warning, "Remember, you two—I'm not sending you out to play around. You're only going along to take care of your teacher and see that he has a good time."

Kojirō, a few steps in front of the other two, soon found he had trouble staying on the road, for at night most of Edo was pitch black, to an extent unimaginable in cities like Kyoto, Nara and Osaka.

"This road's terrible," he said. "We should have brought a lantern."

"People'd laugh if you went around the licensed

quarter carrying a lantern," said Jūrō. "Watch out, sir. That pile of dirt you're on came out of the new moat. You'd better come down before you fall in."

Presently the water in the moat took on a reddish cast, as did the sky beyond the Sumida River. A late spring moon hung like a flat white cake above the roofs of Yoshiwara.

"That's it over there, across the bridge," said Jūrō. "Shall I lend you a hand towel?"

"What for?"

"To hide your face a little—like this." Jūrō and Koroku both drew red cloths from their obi and tied them kerchief-fashion over their heads. Kojirō followed suit, using a piece of russet silk crepe.

"That's the way," said Jūrō. "Stylish like."

"Looks very good on you."

Kojirō and his guides fell in with the bandannaed throng sauntering from house to house. Like Yanagimachi in Kyoto, Yoshiwara was brightly lit. The entrances to the houses were gaily decorated with curtains of red or pale yellow; some had bells at the bottom to let the girls know when customers entered.

After they had been in and out of two or three houses, Jūrō said leeringly to Kojirō, "There's no use trying to hide it, sir."

"Hide what?"

"You said you'd never been here before, but a girl in the last house recognized you. The minute we went in, she gave a little cry and hid behind a screen. Your secret's out, sir."

"I've never been here before. Who're you talking about?"

"Don't play innocent, sir. Let's go back. I'll show you."

They reentered the house, whose curtain bore a crest shaped like a bitter buckbean leaf, split in three. "Sumiya" was written in rather small characters to the left.

The house's heavy beams and stately corridors were

reminiscent of Kyoto temple architecture, but the garish newness nullified the attempt to create an aura of tradition and dignity. Kojirō strongly suspected that swamp plants still thrived beneath the floor.

The large parlor they were shown to upstairs had not been straightened up after the last customers. Both table and floor were strewn with bits of food, tissue paper, toothpicks and whatnot. The maid who came to clean up performed her chore with all the finesse of a day laborer.

When Onao arrived to take their orders, she made a point of letting them know how busy she was. She claimed that she hardly had time to sleep and another three years of this hectic pace would put her in her grave. The better houses of Kyoto contrived to maintain the fiction that their raison d'être was to entertain and please their customers. Here the aim was obviously to relieve men of their money as quickly as possible.

"So this is Edo's pleasure quarter," sniffed Kojirō, with a critical glance at the knotholes in the ceiling. "Pretty shoddy, I'd say."

"Oh, this is only temporary," Onao protested. "The building we're putting up now will be finer than anything you'd see in Kyoto or Fushimi." She stared at Kojirō a moment. "You know, sir, I've seen you somewhere before. Ah, yes! It was last year on the Kōshū highroad."

Kojirō had forgotten the chance meeting, but reminded of it, he said with a spark of interest, "Why, yes, I guess our fates must be entwined."

"I should say they are," Jūrō said, laughing, "if there's a girl here who remembers you." While teasing Kojirō about his past, he described the girl's face and clothing and asked Onao to go find her.

"I know the one you mean," said Onao, and went to fetch her.

When some time had passed and she still hadn't come back, Jūrō and Koroku went out in the hall and clapped their hands to summon her. They had to clap several more times before she finally reappeared.

"She's not here, the one you asked for," said Onao.

"She was here only a few minutes ago."

"It's strange, just as I was saying to the master. We were at Kobotoke Pass and that samurai you're with came walking along the road, and she went off by herself that time too."

Behind the Sumiya stood the frame of the new building, roof partly finished, no walls.

"Hanagiri! Hanagiri!"

This was the name they had given Akemi, who was hiding between a stack of lumber and a small mountain of shavings. Several times the searchers had passed so close she had had to hold her breath.

"How disgusting!" she thought. For the first few minutes her wrath had been directed at Kojirō alone. By now it had expanded to embrace every member of the masculine sex—Kojirō, Seijūrō, the samurai at Hachiōji, the customers who manhandled her nightly at the Sumiya. All men were her enemies, all abominable.

Except one. The right one. The one who would be like Musashi. The one she had sought incessantly. Having given up on the real Musashi, she had now persuaded herself that it would be comforting to pretend to be in love with someone similar to him. Much to her chagrin, she found no one remotely like him.

"Ha-na-gi-ri!" It was Shōji Jinnai himself, first shouting from the back of the house, now drawing closer to her hiding place.

He was accompanied by Kojirō and the other two men. They had complained at tiresome length, making Jinnai repeat his apologies over and over, but finally they went off toward the street.

Akemi, seeing them go, breathed a sigh of relief and waited until Jinnai went back inside, then ran straight to the kitchen door.

"Why, Hanagiri, were you out there all the time?" the kitchen maid asked hysterically.

"Shh! Be quiet, and give me some sake."

"Sake? Now?"

"Yes, sake!" Since coming to Edo, the times when Akemi had sought solace in sake had become more and more frequent.

The frightened maid poured her a large cupful. Shutting her eyes, Akemi drained the vessel dry, her powdered face tilted back until it was almost parallel with the white bottom of the cup.

As she turned away from the door, the maid cried in alarm, "Where're you off to now?"

"Shut up. I'll just wash my feet, then go back inside."

Taking her at her word, the maid shut the door and returned to her work.

Akemi slipped her feet into the first pair of zōri she saw and walked somewhat unsteadily to the street. "How good to be out in the open!" was her first reaction, but this was followed very closely by revulsion. She spat in the general direction of the pleasure-seekers strolling along the brightly lit road and took to her heels.

Coming to a place where stars were reflected in a moat, she stopped to look. She heard running feet behind her. "Oh, oh! Lanterns this time. And they're from the Sumiya. Animals! Can't they even let a girl have a few minutes' peace? No. Find her! Put her back to making money! Turning flesh and blood into a little lumber for their new house—that's the only thing that'll satisfy them. Well, they won't get me back!"

The curled wood shavings hanging loosely in her hair bobbed up and down as she ran as fast as her legs would carry her into the darkness. She had no idea where she was going, and couldn't have cared less, so long as it was away, far away.

9

The Owl

When they finally forsook the teahouse, Kojirō was barely able to stand.

"Shoulder . . . shoulder," he gurgled, grabbing onto both Jūrō and Koroku for support.

The three lumbered uncertainly down the dark, deserted street.

Jūrō said, "Sir, I told you we should spend the night."

"In that dive? Not on your life! I'd rather go back to the Sumiya."

"I wouldn't, sir."

"Why not?"

"That girl, she ran away from you. If they find her, she could be forced to go to bed with you, but for what? You wouldn't enjoy it then."

"Umm. Maybe you're right."

"Do you want her?"

"Nah."

"But you can't quite get her out of your mind, can you?"

"I've never fallen in love in my life. I'm not the type. I've got more important things to do."

"What, sir?"

"Obvious, my boy. I'm going to be the best, most

famous swordsman ever, and the quickest way to do that is to be the shōgun's teacher.''

"But he already has the House of Yagyū to teach him. And I hear he recently hired Ono Jirōemon.''

"Ono Jirōemon! Who gives a fart about him? The Yagyūs don't impress me much either. You watch me. One of these days . . .''

They had reached the stretch of road along which the new moat was being dug, and soft dirt was piled halfway up the willow trees.

"Watch out, sir; it's very slippery,'' said Jūrō as he and Koroku tried to help their teacher down from the pile of dirt.

"Hold it!'' Kojirō shouted, abruptly shoving the two men away. He slid rapidly down the dirt pile. "Who's there?''

The man who had just lunged at Kojirō's back lost his balance and tumbled headfirst into the moat.

"Have you forgotten, Sasaki?''

"You killed four of our comrades!''

Kojirō jumped to the top of the dirt pile, from where he could see that there were at least ten men among the trees, partly hidden by rushes. Swords pointed at him, they slowly began closing in.

"So you're from the Obata School, are you?'' he said in a contemptuous tone. The sudden action had sobered him completely. "Last time, you lost four men out of five. How many of you came tonight? How many want to die? Just give me the number, and I'll oblige. Cowards! Attack if you dare!'' His hand went deftly over his shoulder to the hilt of the Drying Pole.

Obata Nichijō, before taking the tonsure, had been one of the most celebrated warriors in Kai, a province famous for its heroic samurai. After the defeat of the House of Takeda by Tokugawa Ieyasu, the Obata family had lived in obscurity until Kagenori distinguished himself at the Battle of Sekigahara. He had subsequently been summoned into service by Ieyasu himself and had gained fame as a teacher of military science. He had, however, refused the shogunate's offer of a choice plot of land in central Edo with the plea that a country warrior like himself would feel out of place there. He preferred a wooded lot adjoining Hirakawa Tenjin Shrine, where he had established his school in an ancient thatched farmhouse to which had been added a new lecture hall and a rather imposing entrance.

Now advanced in years and suffering from a neural disorder, Kagenori had been confined to his sickroom in recent months, appearing only rarely in the lecture hall. The woods were full of owls, and he had taken to signing his name as "Old Man Owl." Sometimes he'd smile weakly and say, "I'm an owl, like the others."

Not infrequently, the pain from the waist up was agonizing. Tonight had been one of those times.

"Feel a little better? Would you like some water?" The speaker was Hōjō Shinzō, son of Hōjō Ujikatsu, the celebrated military strategist.

"I'm much more comfortable now," said Kagenori. "Why don't you go to bed? It'll soon be light." The invalid's hair was white, his frame as skinny and angular as an aged plum tree.

"Don't worry about me. I get plenty of sleep during the day."

"You can't have much time left for sleeping when you spend your days taking over my lectures. You're the only one who can do that."

"Sleeping too much isn't good discipline."

Noticing that the lamp was about to go out, Shinzō stopped rubbing the old man's back and went to fetch some oil. When he returned, Kagenori, still lying on his stomach, had raised his bony face from the pillow. The light was reflected eerily in his eyes.

"What is it, sir?"

"Don't you hear it? It sounds like splashing water."

"It seems to be coming from the well."

"Who would it be at this hour? Do you suppose some of the men have been out drinking again?"

"That's probably it, but I'll take a look anyhow."

"Give them a good scolding while you're at it."

"Yes, sir. You'd better go to sleep. You must be tired."

When Kagenori's pain had subsided and he had dropped off to sleep, Shinzō carefully tucked the covers up around his shoulders and went to the back door. Two students were leaning over the well bucket, washing blood off their faces and hands.

He ran toward them with a scowl on his face. "You went, didn't you?" he said curtly. "After I pleaded with you not to!" The exasperation in his voice faded when he saw a third man lying in the shadow of the well. From the way he was groaning, it sounded as if he might die from his wounds at any moment.

Like little boys begging for help from an older brother, both men, their faces oddly twisted, sobbed uncontrollably.

"Fools!" Shinzō had to restrain himself from giving them a thrashing. "How many times did I warn you you were no match for him? Why didn't you listen?"

"After he dragged our master's name through the mud? After he killed four of our men? You keep saying we're not being reasonable. Aren't you the one who's lost his reason? Controlling your temper, holding yourself back, bearing insults in silence! Is that what you call reasonable? That's not the Way of the Samurai."

"Isn't it? If confronting Sasaki Kojirō was the thing to do, I'd have challenged him myself. He went out of his way to insult our teacher and commit other outrages against us, but that's no excuse for losing our sense of proportion. I'm not afraid to die, but Kojirō is not worth risking my life or anybody else's over."

"That's not the way most people see it. They think we're afraid of him. Afraid to stand up for our honor. Kojirō's been maligning Kagenori all over Edo."

"If he wants to run off at the mouth, let him. Do you think anybody who knows Kagenori is going to believe he lost an argument to that conceited novice?"

"Do as you please, Shinzō. The rest of us are not going to sit by and do nothing."

"Just exactly what do you have in mind?"

"Only one thing. Kill him!"

"You think you can? I told you not to go to the Sensōji. You wouldn't listen. Four men died. You've just returned after being defeated by him again. Isn't that piling shame on dishonor? It's not Kojirō who's destroying Kagenori's reputation, it's you. I have one question. Did you kill him?"

There was no answer.

"Of course not. I'll bet anything he doesn't have a scratch on him. The trouble with you is you don't have enough sense to avoid meeting him on his own terms. You don't understand his strength. True, he's young, he's of low character, he's coarse, he's arrogant. But he's an outstanding swordsman. How he learned his skill, I don't know, but there's no denying he has it. You underestimate him. That's your first mistake."

One man pressed in on Shinzō as though ready to attack him physically. "You're saying that whatever the bastard does, there's nothing we can do about it."

Shinzō nodded defiantly. "Exactly. There's nothing we can do. We're not swordsmen; we're students of military science. If you think my attitude is cowardly, then I'll just have to put up with being called a coward."

The wounded man at their feet moaned. "Water . . . water . . . please."

His two comrades knelt and propped him into a sitting position.

Seeing they were about to give him some water, Shinzō cried in alarm, "Stop! If he drinks water, it'll kill him!"

As they hesitated, the man put his mouth to the

bucket. One swallow and his head collapsed into it, bringing the night's death toll to five.

While the owls hooted at the morning moon, Shinzō silently returned to the sickroom. Kagenori was still asleep, breathing deeply. Reassured, Shinzō went to his own cubicle.

Works on military science lay open on his desk, books he had begun reading but had had no time to finish. Though well born, as a child he had done his share of splitting firewood, carrying water and studying long hours by candlelight. His father, a great samurai, did not believe that young men of his class should be pampered. Shinzō had entered the Obata School with the ultimate aim of strengthening military skills in his family's fief, and though one of the younger students, he ranked highest in his teacher's estimation.

These days, caring for his ailing master kept him awake most of the night. He sat now with his arms folded and heaved a deep sigh. Who would look after Kagenori if he were not there? All the other students living at the school were of an uncouth type typically attracted to military matters. The men who came to the school only for classes were even worse. They blustered about, voicing opinions on the masculine subjects that samurai habitually discussed; none of them really understood the spirit of the lonely man of reason who was their teacher. The finer points of military science went over their heads. Far more comprehensible was any kind of slur, either real or fancied, against their pride or their ability as samurai. Insulted, they became mindless instruments of vengeance.

Shinzō had been away on a trip when Kojirō arrived at the school. Since Kojirō had claimed that he wanted to ask some questions about military textbooks, his interest seemed genuine and he had been introduced to the master. But then, without asking a single question, he began arguing with Kagenori presumptuously and arrogantly, which suggested that his real purpose was to humiliate the old man. When some students finally got him into another room and demanded an explanation, he reacted with a flood of invective and an offer to fight any of them at any time.

Kojirō had then spread allegations that Obata's military studies were superficial, that they were no more than a rehash of the Kusunoki Style or the ancient Chinese military text known as the *Six Secrets,* and that they were spurious and unreliable. When his malicious pronouncements got back to the ears of the students, they vowed to make him pay with his life.

Shinzō's opposition—the problem was trivial, their master ought not to be disturbed by matters of this sort, Kojirō was not a serious student of military science—had proved futile, though he had also pointed out that before any decisive step was taken, Kagenori's son Yogorō, who was away on a long journey, should be consulted.

"Can't they see how much useless trouble they're causing?" lamented Shinzō. The fading light of the lamp dimly illuminated his troubled face. Still racking his brain for a solution, he laid his arms across the open books and dozed off.

He awoke to the murmur of indistinct voices.

Going first to the lecture hall and finding it empty, he slipped on a pair of zōri and went outside. In a bamboo grove that was part of the sacred compound of the Hirakawa Tenjin Shrine, he saw what he had expected: a large group of students holding an emotion-charged council of war. The two wounded men, their faces ashen, their arms suspended in white slings, stood side by side, describing the night's disaster.

One man asked indignantly, "Are you saying ten of you went and half were killed by this one man?"

"I'm afraid so. We couldn't even get close to him."

"Murata and Ayabe were supposed to be our best swordsmen."

"They were the first to go. Yosobei managed by

sheer guts to get back here, but he made the mistake of drinking some water before we could stop him."

A grim silence descended over the group. As students of military science, they were concerned with problems of logistics, strategy, communications, intelligence and so on, not with the techniques of hand-to-hand combat. Most of them believed, as they had been taught, that swordsmanship was a matter for ordinary soldiers, not generals. Yet their samurai pride stood in the way of their accepting the logical corollary, which was that they were helpless against an expert swordsman like Sasaki Kojirō.

"What can we do?" asked a mournful voice. For a time the only answer was the hooting of the owls.

Then one student said brightly, "I have a cousin in the House of Yagyū. Maybe through him we could get them to help us."

"Don't be stupid!" shouted several others.

"We can't ask for outside help. It'd only bring more shame on our teacher. It'd be an admission of weakness."

"Well, what can we do?"

"The only way is to confront Kojirō again. But if we do it on a dark road again, it'll only do more damage to the school's reputation. If we die in open battle, we die. At least we won't be thought of as cowards."

"Should we send him a formal challenge?"

"Yes, and we have to keep at it, no matter how many times we lose."

"I think you're right, but Shinzō isn't going to like this."

"He doesn't have to know about it, nor does our master. Remember that, all of you. We can borrow brush and ink from the priest."

They started quietly for the priest's house. Before they had gone ten paces, the man in the lead gasped and stepped back. The others instantly came to a dead halt, their eyes riveted on the back veranda of the timeworn shrine building. There, against a backdrop formed by the shadow of a plum tree laden with green fruit, stood Kojirō, one foot propped on the railing and a malevolent grin on his face. To a man, the students turned pale; some had trouble breathing.

Kojirō's voice was venomous. "I gather from your discussion that you still haven't learned, that you've decided to write a letter of challenge and have it delivered to me. Well, I've saved you the trouble. I'm here, ready to fight.

"Last night, before I'd even washed the blood off my hands, I came to the conclusion there'd be a sequel, so I followed you sniveling cowards home."

He paused to let this sink in, then continued in an ironic tone. "I was wondering how you decide on the time and place to challenge an enemy. Do you consult a horoscope to pick the most propitious day? Or do you consider it wiser not to draw your swords until there comes a dark night when your opponent is drunk and on his way home from the licensed quarter?"

He paused again, as though waiting for an answer.

"Have you nothing to say? Isn't there a single red-blooded man among you? If you're so eager to fight me, come on. One at a time, or all at once—it's all the same to me! I wouldn't run from the likes of you if you were in full armor and marching to the beat of drums!"

No sound came from the cowed men.

"What's the matter with you?" The pauses grew longer. "Have you decided not to challenge me? . . . Isn't there even one among you with some backbone?

"All right, it's time now to open your stupid ears and listen.

"I am Sasaki Kojirō. I learned the art of the sword indirectly from the great Toda Seigen after his death. I know the secrets of unsheathing invented by Katayama Hisayasu, and I have myself created the Ganryū Style. I'm not like those who deal in theory, who read books and listen to lectures on Sun-tzu or the *Six Secrets*. In spirit, in will, you and I have nothing in common.

"I don't know the details of your daily study, but I'm showing you now what the science of fighting is all about in real life. I'm not bragging. Think! When a man is set upon in the dark as I was last night, if he has the good fortune to win, what does he do? If he's an ordinary man, he goes as quickly as he can to a safe place. Once there, he thinks back over the incident and congratulates himself on having survived. Isn't that right? Isn't that what you would do?

"But did I do that? No! Not only did I cut down half of your men, I followed the stragglers home and waited here, right under your noses. I listened while you tried to make up your weak minds, and I took you completely by surprise. If I wanted to, I could attack now and smash you to bits. That's what it means to be a military man! That's the secret of military science!

"Some of you have said Sasaki Kojirō is just a swordsman, that he had no business coming to a military school and shooting off his mouth. How far do I have to go to convince you how wrong you are? Perhaps today I'll also prove to you that I'm not only the greatest swordsman in the country but also a master of tactics!

"Ha, ha! This is turning into quite a little lecture, isn't it? I'm afraid if I continue to pour out my fund of knowledge, poor Obata Kagenori may find himself out of a stipend. That wouldn't do, would it?

"Oh, I'm thirsty, Koroku! Jūrō! Get me some water!"

"Right away, sir!" they replied in unison from beside the shrine, where they had been watching in rapt admiration.

Having brought him a large earthen cup of water, Jūrō asked eagerly, "What are you going to do, sir?"

"Ask them!" Kojirō sneered. "Your answer's in those weaselly, empty faces."

"Did you ever see men look so stupid?" Koroku laughed.

"What a gutless bunch," said Jūrō. "Come on, sir, let's go. They're not going to stand up to you."

While the three of them swaggered through the shrine gate, Shinzō, concealed among the trees, muttered through clenched teeth, "I'll get you for this."

The students were despondent. Kojirō had outwitted and defeated them; then he'd gloated, leaving them frightened and humiliated.

The silence was broken by a student running up and asking in a bewildered tone, "Did we order coffins?" When no one replied, he said, "The coffin-maker's just arrived with five coffins. He's waiting."

Finally, one of the group answered dispiritedly, "The bodies have been sent for. They haven't arrived yet. I'm not sure, but I think we'll need one more coffin. Ask him to make it, and put the ones he brought in the storehouse."

That night a wake was held in the lecture hall. Though everything was done quietly, in the hope that Kagenori would not hear, he was able to guess more or less what had occurred. He refrained from asking questions, nor did Shinzō make any comment.

From that day, the stigma of defeat hung over the school. Only Shinzō, who had urged restraint and been accused of cowardice, kept alive the desire for revenge. His eyes harbored a glint that none of the others could fathom.

In early fall, Kagenori's illness worsened. Visible from his bedside was an owl perched on a limb of a large zelkova tree, staring, never moving, hooting at the moon in the daytime. Shinzō now heard in the owl's hoot the message that his master's end was near.

Then a letter arrived from Yogorō, saying he had heard about Kojirō and was on his way home. For the next few days, Shinzō wondered which would come first, the arrival of the son or the death of the father. In either case, the day for which he was waiting, the day of his release from his obligations, was at hand.

On the evening before Yogorō was expected, Shinzō left a farewell letter on his desk and took his leave of the Obata School. From the woods near the shrine, he faced Kagenori's sickroom and said softly, "Forgive me for leaving without your permission. Rest at ease, good master. Yogorō will be home tomorrow. I don't know if I can present Kojirō's head to you before you die, but I must try. If I should die trying, I shall await you in the land of the dead."

10

A Plate of Loaches

Musashi had been roaming the countryside, devoting himself to ascetic practices, punishing his body to perfect his soul. He was more resolved than ever to go it alone: if that meant being hungry, sleeping out in the open in cold and rain and walking about in filthy rags, then so be it. In his heart was a dream that would never be satisfied by taking a position in Lord Date's employ, even if his lordship were to offer him his entire three-million-bushel fief.

After the long trip up the Nakasendō, he had spent only a few nights in Edo before taking to the road again, this time north to Sendai. The money given him by Ishimoda Geki had been a burden on his conscience; from the moment he'd discovered it, he'd known he'd find no peace until it was returned.

Now, a year and a half later, he found himself on Hōtengahara, a plain in Shimōsa Province, east of Edo, little changed since the rebellious Taira no Masakado and his troops had rampaged through the area in the tenth century. The plain was a dismal place still, sparsely settled and growing nothing of value, only weeds, a few trees and some scrubby bamboo and rushes. The sun, low on the horizon, reddened the pools of stagnant water but left the grass and brush colorless and indistinct.

"What now?" Musashi mumbled, resting his weary legs at a crossroads. His body felt listless and still water-logged from the cloudburst he'd been caught in a few days earlier at Toshigi Pass. The raw evening damp made him eager to find human habitation. For the past two nights he'd slept under the stars, but now he longed for the warmth of a hearth and some real food, even simple peasant fare such as millet boiled with rice.

A touch of saltiness in the breeze suggested that the sea was near. If he headed toward it, he reasoned, he just might find a house, perhaps even a fishing village or small port. If not, then he'd have to resign himself to yet another night in the autumn grasses, under the great autumn moon.

He realized with no small hint of irony that were he a more poetic type, he might savor these moments in a poignantly lonely landscape. As it was, he wanted only to escape it, to be with people, to have some decent food and get some rest. Yet the incessant buzzing of the insects seemed to be reciting a litany to his solitary wandering.

Musashi stopped on a dirt-covered bridge. A definite splashing noise seemed to rise above the peaceful rippling of the narrow river. An otter? In the fading daylight, he strained his eyes until he could just make out a figure kneeling in the hollow by the water's edge. He chuckled to note that the face of the young boy peering up at him was distinctly otter-like.

"What are you up to down there?" Musashi called in a friendly voice.

"Loaches," was the laconic reply. The boy was shaking a wicker basket in the water to clean the mud and sand off his wriggling catch.

"Catch many?" Musashi inquired, loath to sever this newly found bond with another human.

"Aren't many around. It's already fall."

"How about letting me have some?"

"My loaches?"

"Yes, just a handful. I'll pay you for them."

"Sorry. These are for my father." Hugging the basket, he leapt nimbly up the bank and was off like a shot into the darkness.

"Speedy little devil, I must say." Musashi, alone once again, laughed. He was reminded of his own childhood and of Jōtarō. "I wonder what's become of him," he mused. Jōtarō had been fourteen when Musashi had last seen him. Soon he would be sixteen. "Poor boy. He accepted me as his teacher, loved me as his teacher, served me as his teacher, and what did I do for him? Nothing."

Absorbed in his memories, he forgot his fatigue. He stopped and stood still. The moon had risen, bright and full. It was on nights like this that Otsū liked to play the flute. In the insects' voices he heard the sound of laughter, Otsū's and Jōtarō's together.

Turning his head to one side, he spotted a light. He turned the rest of his body in the same direction and made straight for it.

Lespedeza grew all around the isolated shack, almost as high as the lopsided roof. The walls were covered with calabash vines, the blossoms looking from a distance like enormous dewdrops. As he drew nearer, he was startled by the great angry snort of an unsaddled horse tied up beside the hovel.

"Who's there?"

Musashi recognized the voice coming from the shack as that of the boy with the loaches. Smiling, he called, "How about putting me up for the night? I'll leave first thing in the morning."

The boy came to the door and looked Musashi over carefully. After a moment, he said, "All right. Come in."

The house was as rickety as any Musashi had ever seen. Moonlight poured through cracks in the walls and roof. After removing his cloak, he couldn't find even a peg to hang it on. Wind from below made the floor drafty, despite the reed mat covering it.

The boy knelt before his guest in formal fashion and

said, "Back there at the river you said you wanted some loaches, didn't you? Do you like loaches?"

In these surroundings, the boy's formality so surprised Musashi that he merely stared.

"What are you looking at?"

"How old are you?"

"Twelve."

Musashi was impressed by his face. It was as dirty as a lotus root just pulled out of the ground, and his hair looked and smelled like a bird's nest. Yet there was character in his expression. His cheeks were chubby, and his eyes, shining like beads through the encircling grime, were magnificent.

"I have a little millet and rice," said the boy hospitably. "And now that I've given some to my father, you can have the rest of the loaches, if you want them."

"Thanks."

"I suppose you'd like some tea too."

"Yes, if it's not too much trouble."

"Wait here." He pushed open a screechy door and went into the next room.

Musashi heard him breaking firewood, then fanning the flame in an earthen hibachi. Before long, the smoke filling the shack drove a host of insects outdoors.

The boy came back with a tray, which he placed on the floor in front of Musashi. Falling to immediately, Musashi devoured the salty broiled loaches, the millet and rice and the sweetish black bean paste in record time.

"That was good," he said gratefully.

"Was it really?" The boy seemed to take pleasure in another person's happiness.

A well-behaved lad, thought Musashi. "I'd like to express my thanks to the head of the house. Has he gone to bed?"

"No, he's right in front of you." The boy pointed at his own nose.

"Are you here all alone?"

"Yes."

"Oh, I see." There was an awkward pause. "And what do you do for a living?" Musashi asked.

"I rent out the horse and go along as a groom. We used to farm a little too. . . . Oh, we've run out of lamp oil. You must be ready for bed anyway, aren't you?"

Musashi agreed that he was and lay down on a worn straw pallet spread next to the wall. The hum of the insects was soothing. He fell asleep, but perhaps because of his physical exhaustion, he broke into a sweat. Then he dreamed he heard rain falling.

The sound in his dream made him sit up with a start. No mistake about it. What he heard now was a knife or sword being honed. As he reached reflexively for his sword, the boy called in to him, "Can't you sleep?"

How had he known that? Amazed, Musashi said, "What are you doing sharpening a blade at this hour?" The question was uttered so tensely that it sounded more like the counterblow of a sword than an inquiry.

The boy broke into laughter. "Did I scare you? You look too strong and brave to be frightened so easily."

Musashi was silent. He wondered if he had come upon an all-seeing demon in the guise of a peasant boy.

When the scraping of the blade on the whetstone began again, Musashi went to the door. Through a crack, he could see that the other room was a kitchen with a small sleeping space at one end. The boy was kneeling in the moonlight next to the window with a large jug of water at his side. The sword he was sharpening was of a type farmers used.

"What do you intend to do with that?" asked Musashi.

The boy glanced toward the door but continued with his work. After a few more minutes, he wiped the blade, which was about a foot and a half long, and held it up to inspect it. It glistened brightly in the moonlight.

"Look," he said, "do you think I can cut a man in half with this?"

"Depends on whether you know how."

"Oh, I'm sure I do."

"Do you have someone particular in mind?"

"My father."

"Your *father?*" Musashi pushed open the door. "I hope that's not your idea of a joke."

"I'm not joking."

"You can't mean you intend to kill your father. Even the rats and wasps in this forsaken wilderness have better sense than to kill their parents."

"But if I don't cut him in two, I can't carry him."

"Carry him where?"

"I have to take him to the burial ground."

"You mean he's dead?"

"Yes."

Musashi looked again at the far wall. It had not occurred to him that the bulky shape he had seen there might be a body. Now he saw that it was indeed the corpse of an old man, laid out straight, with a pillow under its head and a kimono draped over it. By its side was a bowl of rice, a cup of water and a helping of broiled loaches on a wooden plate.

Recalling how he had unwittingly asked the boy to share the loaches intended as an offering to the dead man's spirit, Musashi felt a twinge of embarrassment. At the same time, he admired the boy for having the coolness to conceive of cutting the body into pieces so as to be able to carry it. His eyes riveted on the boy's face, for a few moments he said nothing.

"When did he die?"

"This morning."

"How far away is the graveyard?"

"It's up in the hills."

"Couldn't you have got somebody to take him there for you?"

"I don't have any money."

"Let me give you some."

The boy shook his head. "No. My father didn't like

to accept gifts. He didn't like to go to the temple either. I can manage, thank you."

From the boy's spirit and courage, his stoic yet practical manner, Musashi suspected that his father had not been born an ordinary peasant. There had to be something to explain the son's remarkable self-sufficiency.

In deference to the dead man's wishes, Musashi kept his money and instead offered to contribute the strength needed to transport the body in one piece. The boy agreed, and together they loaded the corpse on the horse. When the road got steep, they took it off the horse, and Musashi carried it on his back. The graveyard turned out to be a small clearing under a chestnut tree, where a solitary round stone served as a marker.

After the burial, the boy placed some flowers on the grave and said, "My grandfather, grandmother and mother are buried here too." He folded his hands in prayer. Musashi joined him in silent supplication for the family's repose.

"The gravestone doesn't seem to be very old," he remarked. "When did your family settle here?"

"During my grandfather's time."

"Where were they before that?"

"My grandfather was a samurai in the Mogami clan, but after his lord's defeat, he burned our genealogy and everything else. There was nothing left."

"I don't see his name carved on the stone. There's not even a family crest or a date."

"When he died, he ordered that nothing appear on the stone. He was very strict. One time some men came from the Gamō fief, another time from the Date fief, and offered him a position, but he refused. He said a samurai shouldn't serve more than one master. That was the way he was about the stone too. Since he'd become a farmer, he said putting his name on it would reflect shame on his dead lord."

"Do you know your grandfather's name?"

"Yes. It was Misawa Iori. My father, since he was only a farmer, dropped the surname and just called himself San'emon."

"And your name?"

"Sannosuke."

"Do you have any relatives?"

"An older sister, but she went away a long time ago. I don't know where she is."

"No one else?"

"No."

"How do you plan to make your living now?"

"Same as before, I guess." But then he added hurriedly, "Look, you're a *shugyōsha*, aren't you? You must travel around just about everywhere. Take me with you. You can ride my horse and I'll be your groom."

As Musashi turned the boy's request over in his mind, he gazed out upon the land below them. Since it was fertile enough to support a plethora of weeds, he could not understand why it was not cultivated. It was certainly not because the people hereabouts were well off; he had seen evidence of poverty everywhere.

Civilization, Musashi was thinking, does not flourish until men have learned to exercise control over the forces of nature. He wondered why the people here in the center of the Kanto Plain were so powerless, why they allowed themselves to be oppressed by nature. As the sun rose, Musashi caught glimpses of small animals and birds reveling in the riches that man had not yet learned to harvest. Or so it seemed.

He was soon reminded that Sannosuke, despite his courage and independence, was still a child. By the time the sunlight made the dewy foliage glisten and they were ready to start back, the boy was no longer sad, seemed in fact to have put all thoughts of his father completely out of mind.

Halfway down the hill, he began badgering Musashi for an answer to his proposal. "I'm ready to start today," he declared. "Just think, anywhere you go, you'll be able to ride the horse, and I'll be there to wait on you."

This elicited a noncommittal grunt. While Sannosuke had much to recommend him, Musashi questioned whether he should again put himself in the position of being responsible for a boy's future. Jōtarō—he had natural ability, but how had he benefited by attaching himself to Musashi? And now that he had disappeared to heaven knew where, Musashi felt his responsibility even more keenly. Still, Musashi thought, if a man dwells only on the dangers ahead, he cannot advance a single step, let alone make his way through life successfully. Furthermore, in the case of a child, no one, not even his parents, can actually guarantee his future. "Is it really possible to decide objectively what's good for a child and what's not?" he asked himself. "If it's a matter of developing Sannosuke's talents and guiding him in the right direction, I can do that. I guess that's about as much as anyone can do."

"Promise, won't you? Please," the boy insisted.

"Sannosuke, do you want to be a groom all your life?"

"Of course not. I want to be a samurai."

"That's what I thought. But if you come with me and become my pupil, you'll be in for a lot of rough times, you know."

The boy threw down the rope and, before Musashi knew what he was up to, knelt on the ground below the horse's head. Bowing deeply, he said, "I beg you, sir, make a samurai of me. That's what my father wanted, but there was no one we could ask for help."

Musashi dismounted, looked around for a moment, then picked up a stick and handed it to Sannosuke. He found another one for himself and said, "I want you to strike me with that stick. After I've seen how you handle it, I can decide whether you have the talent to be a samurai.''

"If I hit you, will you say yes?"

"Try it and see." Musashi laughed.

Sannosuke took a firm grip on his weapon and rushed forward as if possessed. Musashi showed no mercy. Time and again the boy was struck—on the shoulders, in the face, on the arms. After each setback, he staggered away but always came back to the attack.

"Pretty soon he'll be in tears," thought Musashi.

But Sannosuke would not give up. When his stick broke in two, he charged empty-handed.

"What do you think you're doing, you runt?" Musashi snapped with deliberate meanness. He seized the boy by his obi and threw him flat on the ground.

"You big bastard!" shouted Sannosuke, already on his feet and attacking again.

Musashi caught him by the waist and held him up in the air. "Had enough?"

"No!" he shouted defiantly, though the sun was in his eyes and he was reduced to uselessly waving his arms and legs.

"I'm going to throw you against that rock over there. It'll kill you. Ready to give up?"

"No!"

"Stubborn, aren't you? Can't you see you're beaten?"

"Not as long as I'm alive I'm not! You'll see. I'll win in the end."

"How do you expect to do that?"

"I'll practice, I'll discipline myself."

"But while you're practicing for ten years, I'll be doing the same thing."

"Yes, but you're a lot older than I am. You'll die first."

"Hmm."

"And when they put you in a coffin, I'll strike the final blow and win!"

"Fool!" shouted Musashi, tossing the boy to the ground.

When Sannosuke stood up, Musashi looked at his face for a moment, laughed and clapped his hands together once. "Good. You can be my pupil."

11

Like Teacher, Like Pupil

On the short journey back to the shack, Sannosuke rattled on and on about his dreams for the future.

But that night, when Musashi told him he should be ready to bid farewell to the only home he had ever known, he became wistful. They sat up late and Sannosuke, misty-eyed and speaking in a soft voice, shared his memories of parents and grandparents.

In the morning, while they were preparing to move out, Musashi announced that henceforth he would call Sannosuke Iori. "If you're going to become a samurai," he explained, "it's only proper that you take your grandfather's name." The boy was not yet old enough for his coming-of-age ceremony, when he would normally have been given his adult name; Musashi thought taking his grandfather's name would give him something to live up to.

Later, when the boy seemed to be lingering inside the house, Musashi said quietly but firmly, "Iori, hurry up. There's nothing in there you need. You don't want reminders of the past."

Iori came flying out in a kimono barely covering his thighs, a groom's straw sandals on his feet and a cloth wrapper containing a box lunch of millet and rice in his hand. He looked like a little frog, but he was ready and eager for a new life.

"Pick a tree away from the house and tie the horse up," Musashi commanded.

"You may as well mount it now."

"Do as I say."

"Yes, sir."

Musashi noted the politeness; it was a small but encouraging sign of the boy's readiness to adopt the ways of the samurai in place of the slovenly speech of peasants.

Iori tied up the horse and came back to where Musashi was standing under the eaves of the old shack, gazing at the surrounding plain. "What's he waiting for?" wondered the boy.

Putting his hand on Iori's head, Musashi said, "This is where you were born and where you acquired your determination to win."

Iori nodded.

"Rather than serve a second lord, your grandfather withdrew from the warrior class. Your father, true to your grandfather's dying wish, contented himself with being a mere farmer. His death left you alone in the world, so the time has come for you to stand on your own feet."

"Yes, sir."

"You must become a great man!"

"I'll try." Tears sprang to his eyes.

"For three generations this house sheltered your family from wind and rain. Say your thanks to it, then say good-bye, once and for all, and have no regrets."

Musashi went inside and set fire to the hovel.

When he came out, Iori was blinking back his tears.

"If we left the house standing," said Musashi, "it'd only become a hideout for highwaymen or common thieves. I'm burning it to keep men like that from desecrating the memory of your father and grandfather."

"I'm grateful."

The shack turned into a small mountain of fire, then collapsed.

"Let's go," said Iori, no longer concerned with relics of the past.

"Not yet."

"There's nothing else to do here, is there?"

Musashi laughed. "We're going to build a new house on that knoll over there."

"New house? What for? You just burned the old one down."

"That belonged to your father and grandfather. The one we build will be for us."

"You mean we're going to stay here?"

"That's right."

"We're not going away somewhere and train and discipline ourselves?"

"We'll do that here."

"What can we train ourselves for here?"

"To be swordsmen, to be samurai. We'll discipline our spirits and work hard to make ourselves into real human beings. Come with me, and bring that ax with you." He pointed to a clump of grass where he had put the farm tools.

Shouldering the ax, Iori followed Musashi to the knoll, where there were a few chestnut trees, pines and cryptomerias.

Musashi, stripping to the waist, took the ax and went to work. Soon he was sending up a veritable shower of white chips of raw wood.

Iori watched, thinking: "Maybe he's going to build a dōjō. Or are we going to practice out in the open?"

One tree fell, then another and another. Sweat poured down Musashi's ruddy cheeks, washing away the lethargy and loneliness of the past few days.

He had conceived of his present plan while standing by the farmer's fresh grave in the tiny burial ground. "I'll lay down my sword for a time," he had decided, "and work with a hoe instead." Zen, calligraphy, the art of tea, painting pictures and carving statues were all useful in perfecting one's swordsmanship. Couldn't tilling a field also contribute to his training? Wasn't this broad tract of earth, waiting for someone to bring it under cultivation, a perfect training hall? By changing inhospitable flatlands into farmlands, he would also be promoting the welfare of future generations.

He'd lived his whole life like a mendicant Zen priest—on the receiving end, so to speak, depending on other people for food, shelter and donations. He wanted to make a change, a radical one, since he'd long suspected that only those who had actually grown their own grain and vegetables really understood how sacred and valuable they were. Those who hadn't were like priests who did not practice what they preached or swordsmen who learned combat techniques but knew nothing of the Way.

As a boy, he had been taken by his mother into the fields and had worked alongside the tenants and villagers. His purpose now, however, was more than just to produce food for his daily meals; he sought nourishment for his soul. He wanted to learn what it meant to work for a living, rather than beg for one. He also wanted to implant his own way of thinking among the people of the district. As he saw it, by surrendering the land to weeds and thistles and giving in to storms and floods, they were passing on their hand-to-mouth existence from generation to generation without ever opening their eyes to their own potentialities and those of the land around them.

"Iori," he called, "get some rope and tie up this timber. Then drag it down to the riverbank."

When that was done, Musashi propped his ax against a tree and wiped the sweat off his forehead with his elbow. He then went down and stripped the bark off the trees with a hatchet. When darkness fell, they built a bonfire with the scraps and found blocks of wood to use as pillows.

"Interesting work, isn't it?" said Musashi.

With perfect honesty, Iori answered, "I don't think it's interesting at all. I didn't have to become your pupil to learn how to do this."

"You'll like it better as time goes on."

As autumn waned, the insect voices faded into silence. Leaves withered and fell. Musashi and Iori finished their cabin and addressed themselves to the task of making the land ready for planting.

One day while he was surveying the land, Musashi suddenly found himself thinking it was like a diagram of the social unrest that lasted for a century after the Ōnin War. Such thoughts aside, it was not an encouraging picture.

Unknown to Musashi, Hōtengahara had over the centuries been buried many times by volcanic ash from Mount Fuji, and the Tone River had repeatedly flooded the flatlands. When the weather was fair, the land became bone dry, but whenever there were heavy rains, the water carved out new channels, carrying great quantities of dirt and rock along with it. There was no principal stream into which the smaller ones flowed naturally, the nearest thing to this being a wide basin that lacked sufficient capacity to either water or drain the area as a whole. The most urgent need was obvious: to bring the water under control.

Still, the more he had looked, the more he had questioned why the area was undeveloped. "It won't be easy," he thought, excited by the challenge it posed. Joining water and earth to create productive fields was not much different from leading men and women in such a way that civilization might bloom. To Musashi it seemed that his goal was in complete agreement with his ideals of swordsmanship.

He had come to see the Way of the Sword in a new light. A year or two earlier, he had wanted only to conquer all rivals, but now the idea that the sword existed for the purpose of giving him power over other people was unsatisfying. To cut people down, to triumph over them, to display the limits of one's strength, seemed increasingly vain. He wanted to conquer himself, to make life itself submit to him, to cause people to live rather than die. The Way of the Sword should not be used merely for his own perfection. It should be a source of strength for governing people and leading them to peace and happiness.

He realized his grand ideals were no more than dreams, and would remain so as long as he lacked the political authority to implement them. But here in this wasteland, he needed neither rank nor power. He plunged into the struggle with joy and enthusiasm.

Day in and day out, stumps were uprooted, gravel sifted, land leveled, soil and rocks made into dikes. Musashi and Iori worked from before dawn until after the stars were shining bright in the sky.

Their relentless toil attracted attention. Villagers passing by often stopped, stared, and commented.

"What do they think they're doing?"

"How can they live in a place like that?"

"Isn't the boy old San'emon's son?"

Everyone laughed, but not all let it go at that. One man came out of genuine kindness and said, "I hate to tell you this, but you're wasting your time. You can break your backs making a field here, but one storm and it'll be gone overnight."

When he saw they were still at it several days later, he seemed a bit offended. "All you're doing here, I tell you, is making a lot of water holes where they won't do any good."

A few days later he concluded that the strange samurai was short on brains. "Fools!" he shouted in disgust.

The next day brought a whole group to heckle.

"If anything could grow here, we wouldn't sweat under the blazing sun working our own fields, poor as they are. We'd sit home and play the flute."

"And there wouldn't be any famines."

"You're digging up the place for nothing."

"Got the sense of a pile of manure."

Still hoeing, Musashi kept his eyes on the ground and grinned.

Iori was less complacent, though Musashi had earlier scolded him for taking the peasants seriously. "Sir"—he pouted—"they all say the same thing."

"Pay no attention."

"I can't help it," he cried, seizing a rock to throw at their tormentors.

An angry glare from Musashi stopped him. "Now, what good do you think that would do? If you don't behave yourself, I'm not going to have you as my pupil."

Iori's ears burned at the rebuke, but instead of dropping the rock, he cursed and hurled it at a boulder. The rock gave off sparks as it cracked in two. Iori tossed his hoe aside and began to weep.

Musashi ignored him, though he wasn't unmoved. "He's all alone, just as I am," he thought.

As though in sympathy with the boy's grief, a twilight breeze swept over the plain, setting everything astir. The sky darkened and raindrops fell.

"Come on, Iori, let's go in," called Musashi. "Looks like we're in for a squall." Hurriedly collecting his tools, he ran for the house. By the time he was inside, the rain was coming down in gray sheets.

"Iori," he shouted, surprised that the boy had not come with him. He went to the window and strained his eyes toward the field. Rain spattered from the sill into his face. A streak of lightning split the air and struck the earth. As he shut his eyes and put his hands over his ears, he felt the force of the thunder.

In the wind and rain, Musashi saw the cryptomeria tree at the Shippōji and heard the stern voice of Takuan. He felt that whatever he had gained since then he owed to them. He wanted to possess the tree's immense strength as well as Takuan's icy, unwavering compassion.

If he could be to Iori what the old cryptomeria had been to him, he would feel he'd succeeded in repaying a part of his debt to the monk.

"Iori! . . . Iori!"

There was no answer, only thunder and the rain pounding on the roof.

"Where could he have gone?" he wondered, still unwilling to venture outside.

When the rain slackened to a drizzle, he did go out. Iori had not moved an inch. With his clothing clinging to his body and his face still screwed up in an angry frown, he looked rather like a scarecrow. How could a child be so stubborn?

"Idiot!" Musashi chided. "Get back into the house. Being drenched like that's not exactly good for you. Hurry up, before rivers start forming. Then you won't be able to get back."

Iori turned, as though trying to locate Musashi's voice, then started laughing. "Something bothering you? This kind of rain doesn't last. See, the clouds are breaking up already."

Musashi, not expecting to receive a lesson from his pupil, was more than a little put out, but Iori didn't give the matter a second thought. "Come on," the boy said, picking up his hoe. "We can still get quite a bit done before the sun's gone."

For the next five days, bulbuls and shrikes conversed hoarsely under a cloudless blue sky, and great cracks grew in the earth as it caked around the roots of the rushes. On the sixth day, a cluster of small black clouds appeared on the horizon and rapidly spread across the heavens until the whole plain seemed to be under an eclipse.

Iori studied the sky briefly and said in a worried tone, "This time it's the real thing." Even as he spoke, an inky wind swirled around them. Leaves shook and little birds dropped to the earth as if felled by a silent and invisible horde of hunters.

"Another shower?" Musashi asked.

"Not with the sky like that. I'd better go to the village. And you'd better gather up the tools and get inside as fast as you can." Before Musashi could ask why, Iori took off across the flatlands and was quickly lost in a sea of high grass.

Again, Iori's weather sense was accurate. The sudden downpour, driven by a raging, gusty wind, that sent Musashi scurrying for shelter developed its own distinctive rhythms. The rain fell in unbelievable quantity for a time, stopped suddenly, then recommenced with even greater fury. Night came, but the storm continued unabated. It began to seem as though the heavens were set on making the entire earth into an ocean. Several times Musashi feared that the wind would rip off the roof; the floor was already littered with shingles torn off its underside.

Morning came, gray and formless and with no sign of Iori. Musashi stood by the window, and his heart sank; he could do nothing. Here and there a tree or a clump of grass was visible; all else was a vast muddy swamp. Luckily, the cabin was still above water level, but in what had been a dry riverbed immediately below it, there was now a rushing torrent, carrying along everything in its path.

Not knowing for sure that Iori hadn't fallen into the water and drowned, Musashi felt time drag on, until finally he thought he heard Iori's voice calling, *"Sensei! Here!"* He was some distance beyond the river, riding a bullock, with a great bundle tied behind him.

Musashi watched in consternation as Iori rode straight into the muddy flow, which seemed about to suck him under at every step.

When he gained the other bank, he was quaking from the cold and wet, but he calmly guided the bullock to the side of the cabin.

"Where have you been?" demanded Musashi, his voice both angry and relieved.

"To the village, of course. I brought back lots of food. It'll rain half a year's worth before this storm's over, and when it is, we'll be trapped by the floodwaters."

After they had taken the straw bundle inside, Iori untied it and removed the items one by one from the inner wrapping of oiled paper. "Here are some chestnuts . . . lentil beans . . . salted fish. . . . We shouldn't run out of food even if it takes a month or two for the water to go down."

Musashi's eyes misted over with gratitude, but he said nothing. He was too abashed at his own lack of common sense. How could he guide humanity if he was careless about his own survival? Were it not for Iori, he would now be facing starvation. And the boy, having been raised in a remote rural area, must have known about laying in supplies since he was two years old.

It struck Musashi as odd that the villagers had agreed to furnish all this food. They couldn't have had very much for themselves. When he recovered his voice and raised the question, Iori replied, "I left my money pouch in hock and borrowed from the Tokuganji."

"And what's the Tokuganji?"

"It's the temple about two miles from here. My father told me there was some powdered gold in the pouch. He said if I got into difficulty, I should use it a little at a time. Yesterday, when the weather turned bad, I remembered what he said." Iori wore a smile of triumph.

"Isn't the pouch a keepsake from your father?"

"Yes. Now that we've burned the old house down, that and the sword are the only things left." He rubbed the hilt of the short weapon in his obi. Though the tang bore no craftsman's signature, Musashi had noted when he'd examined the blade earlier that it was of excellent quality. He also had the feeling that the inherited pouch had some significance beyond that of the powdered gold it contained.

"You shouldn't hand keepsakes over to other people. One of these days, I'll get it back for you, but after that you must promise not to let go of it."

"Yes, sir."

"Where did you spend the night?"

"The priest told me I'd better wait there till morning."

"Have you eaten?"

"No. You haven't either, have you?"

"No, but there's no firewood, is there?"

"Oh, there's plenty." He pointed downward, indicating the space under the cabin, where he'd stored a good supply of sticks and roots and bamboo picked up while he worked in the fields.

Holding a piece of straw matting over his head, Musashi crawled under the cabin and again marveled at the boy's good sense. In an environment like this, survival depended on foresight and a small mistake could spell the difference between life and death.

When they had finished eating, Iori brought out a book. Then, kneeling formally before his teacher, he said, "While we're waiting for the water to go down so we can work, would you teach me some reading and writing?"

Musashi agreed. On such a dismal stormy day, it was a good way to pass the time. The book was a volume of the *Analects of Confucius*. Iori said it had been given to him at the temple.

"Do you really want to study?"

"Yes."

"Have you done much reading?"

"No; only a little."

"Who taught you?"

"My father."

"What have you read?"

"The Lesser Learning."

"Did you enjoy it?"

"Yes, very much," he said eagerly, his eyes brightening.

"All right then. I'll teach you all I know. Later on, you can find somebody better educated to teach you what I don't know."

They devoted the rest of the day to a study session, the boy reading aloud, Musashi stopping him to correct him or explain words he did not understand. They sat in utter concentration, oblivious of the storm.

The deluge lasted two more days, by which time there was no land visible anywhere.

On the following day, it was still raining. Iori, delighted, took out the book again and said, "Shall we begin?"

"Not today. You've had enough of reading for a while."

"Why?"

"If you do nothing but read, you'll lose sight of the reality around you. Why don't you take the day off and play? I'm going to relax too."

"But I can't go outside."

"Then just do like me," said Musashi, sprawling on his back and crossing his arms under his head.

"Do I have to lie down?"

"Do what you want. Lie down, stand up, sit—whatever's comfortable."

"Then what?"

"I'll tell you a story."

"I'd like that," said Iori, flopping down on his stomach and wiggling his legs in the air. "What kind of story?"

"Let me see," said Musashi, going over the tales he had liked to hear as a child. He chose the one about the battles between the Genji and the Heike. All boys loved that.

Iori proved to be no exception. When Musashi came to the part about the Genji being defeated and the Heike taking over the country, the boy's face became gloomy.

He had to blink to keep from crying over Lady Tokiwa's sad fate. But his spirits rose as he heard about Minamoto no Yoshitsune learning swordsmanship from the "long-nosed goblins" on Mount Kurama and later making his escape from Kyoto.

"I like Yoshitsune," he said, sitting up. "Are there really goblins on Mount Kurama?"

"Maybe. Anyway, there're people in this world who might as well be goblins. But the ones who taught Yoshitsune weren't real goblins."

"What were they?"

"Loyal vassals of the defeated Genji. They couldn't come out in the open while the Heike were in power, so they stayed hidden in the mountains until their chance came."

"Like my grandfather?"

"Yes, except he waited all his life, and his chance never came. After Yoshitsune grew up, the faithful Genji followers who had looked after him during his childhood got the opportunity they had prayed for."

"I'll have a chance to make up for my grandfather, won't I?"

"Hmm. I think it's possible. Yes, I really think so."

He pulled Iori to him, lifted him up and balanced him on his hands and feet like a ball. "Now try being a great man!" He laughed.

Iori giggled, and stammered, "You . . . you're a gob-goblin too! Stop . . . it. I'll fa-fall." He reached down and pinched Musashi's nose.

On the eleventh day, it finally stopped raining. Musashi chafed to be out in the open, but it was another week before they were able to return to work under a bright sun. The field they had so arduously carved out of the wilderness had disappeared without a trace; in its place were rocks, and a river where none had been before. The water seemed to mock them just as the villagers had.

Iori, seeing no way to reclaim their loss, looked up and said, "This place is beyond hope. Let's look for better land somewhere else."

"No," Musashi said firmly. "With the water drained off, this would make excellent farmland. I examined the location from every angle before I chose it."

"What if we have another heavy rain?"

"We'll fix it so the water doesn't come this way. We'll lay a dam from here all the way to that hill over there."

"That's an awful lot of work."

"You seem to forget that this is our dōjō. I'm not giving up a foot of this land until I see barley growing on it."

Musashi carried on his stubborn struggle throughout the winter, into the second month of the new year. It took several weeks of strenuous labor to dig ditches, drain the water off, pile dirt for a dike and then cover it with heavy rocks.

Three weeks later everything was again washed away.

"Look," Iori said, "we're wasting our energy on something impossible. Is that the Way of the Sword?" The question struck close to the bone, but Musashi would not give in.

Only a month passed before the next disaster, a heavy snowfall followed by a quick thaw. Iori, on his return from trips to the temple for food, inevitably wore a long face, for the people there rode him mercilessly about Musashi's failure. And finally Musashi himself began to lose heart.

For two full days and on into a third, he sat silently brooding and staring at his field.

Then it dawned on him suddenly. Unconsciously, he had been trying to create a neat, square field like those common in other parts of the Kanto Plain, but this was not what the terrain called for. Here, despite the general flatness, there were slight variations in the lay of the land

and the quality of the soil that argued for an irregular shape.

"What a fool I've been," he exclaimed aloud. "I tried to make the water flow where I thought it should and force the dirt to stay where I thought it ought to be. But it didn't work. How could it? Water's water, dirt's dirt. I can't change their nature. What I've got to do is learn to be a servant to the water and a protector of the land."

In his own way, he had submitted to the attitude of the peasants. On that day he became nature's manservant. He ceased trying to impose his will on nature and let nature lead the way, while at the same time seeking out possibilities beyond the grasp of other inhabitants of the plain.

The snow came again, and another thaw; the muddy water oozed slowly over the plain. But Musashi had had time to work out his new approach, and his field remained intact.

"The same rules must apply to governing people," he said to himself. In his notebook, he wrote: "Do not attempt to oppose the way of the universe. But first make sure you know the way of the universe."

12

Mountain Devils

"Let me make myself clear. I don't want you to go to any trouble on my account. Your hospitality, which I appreciate greatly, is quite sufficient."

"Yes, sir. That's very considerate of you, sir," replied the priest.

"I'd just like to relax. That's all."

"By all means."

"Now I hope you'll forgive my rudeness," said the samurai, stretching out casually on his side and propping his graying head on his forearm.

The guest who'd just arrived at the Tokuganji was Nagaoka Sado, a high-ranking vassal of Lord Hosokawa Tadaoki of Buzen. He had little time for personal matters, but he invariably came on such occasions as the anniversary of his father's death, usually staying overnight, since the temple was some twenty miles from Edo. For a man of his rank, he traveled unostentatiously, accompanied this time by only two samurai and one young personal attendant.

To get away from the Hosokawa establishment even for a short time, he had had to trump up an excuse. He rarely had the chance to do as he pleased, and now that he did, he was fully enjoying the local sake while listening to the croaking of frogs. Briefly he could forget about everything—the problems of administration and the constant need to be attuned to the nuances of daily affairs.

After dinner, the priest quickly cleared the dishes and left. Sado was chatting idly with his attendants, who were seated next to the wall, only their faces showing in the light of the lamp.

"I could just lie here forever and enter Nirvana, like the Buddha," Sado said lazily.

"Careful you don't catch cold. The night air is damp."

"Oh, leave me alone. This body's survived a few battles. It can hold its own against a sneeze or two. But just smell those ripe blossoms! Nice fragrance, isn't it?"

"I don't smell anything."

"Don't you? If your sense of smell is that poor . . . you sure you don't have a cold yourself?"

They were engrossed in this kind of seemingly light banter when suddenly the frogs fell silent, and a loud voice shouted, "You devil! What're you doing here, staring into the guest room?"

Sado's bodyguards were on their feet instantly.

"What is it?"

"Who's out there?"

As their cautious eyes scanned the garden, the clatter of small feet receded in the direction of the kitchen.

A priest looked in from the veranda, bowed and said, "Sorry for the disturbance. It's only one of the local children. There's nothing to worry about."

"Are you sure?"

"Yes, of course. He lives a couple of miles from here. His father worked as a groom, until he died recently, but his grandfather is said to have been a samurai, and every time he sees one, he stops and stares—with his finger in his mouth."

Sado sat up. "You mustn't be too hard on him. If he wants to be a samurai, bring him in. We'll have some sweets and talk it over."

By now Iori had reached the kitchen. "Hey,

Granny,'' he shouted. ''I've run out of millet. Fill this up for me, will you?'' The sack he thrust out to the wrinkled old woman who worked in the kitchen would have held half a bushel.

She shouted right back. ''Watch your tongue, you beggar! You talk as if we owe you something.''

''You've got a lot of nerve to begin with!'' said a priest who was washing dishes. ''The head priest took pity on you, so we're giving you food, but don't be insolent. When you're asking a favor, do it politely.''

''I'm not begging. I gave the priest the pouch my father left me. There's money in it, plenty of money.''

''And how much could a groom living out in the sticks leave his son?''

''Are you going to give me the millet? Yes or no?''

''There you go again. Just look at yourself. You're crazy, taking orders from that fool rōnin. Where did he come from anyway? Who is he? Why should he be eating your food?''

''None of your business.''

''Hmph. Digging around in that barren plain where there's never going to be a field or garden or anything else! The whole village is laughing at you.''

''Who asked for your advice?''

''Whatever's wrong with that rōnin's head must be catching. What do you expect to find up there—a pot of gold, like in a fairy tale? You're not even dry behind the ears, and you're already digging your own grave.''

''Shut up and give me the millet. The millet! Now.''

The priest was still teasing Iori a couple of minutes later when something cold and slimy hit his face. His eyes popped, then he saw what it was—a warty toad. He screamed and lunged for Iori, but just as he collared him, another priest arrived to announce that the boy was wanted in the samurai's room.

The head priest had also heard the commotion, and rushed to the kitchen. ''Did he do something to upset our guest?'' he asked worriedly.

"No. Sado just said he'd like to talk to him. He'd like to give him some sweets too."

The head priest hurriedly took Iori by the hand and delivered him personally to Sado's room.

As Iori timidly sat down beside the priest, Sado asked, "How old are you?"

"Thirteen."

"And you want to become a samurai?"

"That's right," replied Iori, nodding vigorously.

"Well, well. Why don't you come and live with me, then? You'd have to help with the housework at the beginning, but later I'd make you one of the apprentice samurai."

Iori shook his head silently. Sado, taking this for bashfulness, assured him that the offer was serious.

Iori, flashing an angry look, said, "I heard you wanted to give me some sweets. Where are they?"

Paling, the head priest slapped him on the wrist.

"Don't scold him," Sado said reprovingly. He liked children and tended to indulge them. "He's right. A man should keep his word. Have the sweets brought in."

When they arrived, Iori began stuffing them into his kimono.

Sado, a little taken aback, asked, "Aren't you going to eat them here?"

"No. My teacher's waiting for me at home."

"Oh? You have a teacher?"

Without bothering to explain himself, Iori bolted from the room and disappeared through the garden.

Sado thought his behavior highly amusing. Not so the head priest, who bowed to the floor two or three times before going to the kitchen in pursuit of Iori.

"Where is that insolent brat?"

"He picked up his sack of millet and left."

They listened for a moment but heard only a discordant screeching. Iori had plucked a leaf from a tree and was trying to improvise a tune. None of the few songs he knew seemed to work. The grooms' chantey was too slow, the *Bon* festival songs too complicated. Finally, he settled on a melody resembling the sacred dance music at the local shrine. This suited him well enough, for he liked the dances, which his father had sometimes taken him to see.

About halfway to Hōtengahara, at a point where two streams joined to make a river, he gave a sudden start. The leaf flew from his mouth, along with a spray of saliva, and he leapt into the bamboo beside the road.

Standing on a crude bridge were three or four men, engaged in a furtive conversation. "It's them," Iori exclaimed softly.

A remembered threat rang in his frightened ears. When mothers in this region scolded their children, they were apt to say, "If you're not good, the mountain devils will come down and get you." The last time they had actually come had been in the fall of the year before last.

Twenty miles or so from here, in the mountains of Hitachi, there was a shrine dedicated to a mountain deity. Centuries earlier, the people had so feared this god that the villages had taken turns making annual offerings of grain and women to him. When a community's turn came, the inhabitants had assembled their tribute and gone in a torchlight procession to the shrine. As time went on and it became evident that the god was really only a man, they became lax in making their offerings.

During the period of the civil wars, the so-called mountain god had taken to having his tribute collected by force. Every two or three years, a pack of brigands, armed with halberds, hunting spears, axes—anything to strike terror into the hearts of peaceful citizens—would descend on first one community, then the next, carrying away everything that caught their fancy, including wives and daughters. If their victims put up any resistance, the plundering was accompanied by slaughter.

Their last raid still vivid in his memory, Iori cringed in the underbrush. A group of five shadows came running across the field to the bridge. Then, through the night mist, another small band, and still another, until the bandits numbered between forty and fifty.

Iori held his breath and stared while they debated a course of action. They soon reached a decision. Their leader issued a command and pointed toward the village. The men rushed off like a swarm of locusts.

Before long, the mist was rent by a great cacophony—birds, cattle, horses, the wailing of people young and old.

Iori quickly made up his mind to get help from the samurai at the Tokuganji, but the minute he left the shelter of the bamboo, a shout came from the bridge: "Who's there?" He had not seen the two men left behind to stand guard. Swallowing hard, he ran for all he was worth, but his short legs were no match for those of grown men.

"Where do you think you're going?" shouted the man who got hold of him first.

"Who are you?"

Instead of crying like a baby, which might have thrown the men off guard, Iori scratched and fought against the brawny arms imprisoning him.

"He saw all of us together. He was going to tell somebody."

"Let's beat him up and dump him in a rice field."

"I've got a better idea."

They carred Iori to the river, threw him down the bank and, jumping down after him, tied him to one of the bridge posts.

"There, that takes care of him." The two ruffians climbed back up to their station on the bridge.

The temple bell tolled in the distance. Iori watched horrified as the flames rising from the village dyed the river a bloody red. The sound of babies crying and women wailing came closer and closer. Then wheels rumbled onto the bridge. Half a dozen of the bandits were leading oxcarts and horses loaded with loot.

"Filthy scum!" screamed a masculine voice.

"Give me back my wife!"

The scuffle on the bridge was brief but fierce. Men shouted, metal clanged, a shriek went up, and a bloody corpse landed at Iori's feet. A second body splashed into the river, spraying his face with blood and water. One by one farmers fell from the bridge, six of them in all. The bodies rose to the surface and floated slowly downstream, but one man, not quite dead, grasped at the reeds and clawed the earth until he had pulled himself halfway out of the water.

"You!" cried Iori. "Untie this rope. I'll go for help. I'll see that you get your revenge." Then his voice rose to a bellow. "Come on. Untie me. I've got to save the village."

The man lay motionless.

Straining at his bonds with all his might, Iori finally loosened them enough to squirm down and kick the man in the shoulder.

The face that turned toward his was blotched with mud and gore, the eyes dull and uncomprehending.

The man crawled painfully closer; with his last ounce of strength, he undid the knots. As the rope fell loose, he collapsed and died.

Iori looked cautiously up at the bridge and bit his lip. There were more bodies up there. But luck was with him. A cartwheel had broken through a rotten plank. The thieves, hurrying to pull it out, didn't notice his escape.

Realizing he couldn't make it to the temple, Iori tiptoed along in the shadows until he reached a place shallow enough to cross. When he gained the other bank, he was on the edge of Hōtengahara. He covered the remaining mile to the cabin as though lightning was nipping at his heels.

As he neared the knoll where the cabin stood, he saw that Musashi was standing outside, looking at the sky. "Come quick!" he shouted.

"What happened?"

"We have to go to the village."

"Is that where the fire is?"

"Yes. The mountain devils have come again."

"Devils? . . . Bandits?"

"Yes, at least forty of them. Please hurry. We have to rescue the villagers."

Musashi ducked into the cabin and emerged with his swords. While he was tying his sandals, Iori said, "Follow me. I'll show you the way."

"No. You stay here."

Iori couldn't believe his ears.

"It's too dangerous."

"I'm not scared."

"You'd be in the way."

"You don't even know the shortest way there!"

"The fire's all the guide I need. Now just be a good boy and stay right here."

"Yes, sir." Iori nodded obediently, but with deep misgivings. He turned his head toward the village and watched somberly as Musashi streaked off in the direction of the red glow.

The bandits had tied their female captives, moaning and screaming, in a row and were pulling them mercilessly toward the bridge.

"Stop your squawking!" shouted one bandit.

"You act like you don't know how to walk. Move!"

When the women held back, the ruffians lashed them with whips. One woman fell, dragging down others. Seizing the rope and forcing them back on their feet, one man snarled, "Stubborn bitches! What have you got to groan about? Stay here and you work like slaves the rest of your lives, all for a bit of millet. Look at you, nothing but skin and bones! You'll be a lot better off having fun with us."

Picking one of the healthier-looking animals, which were all heavily loaded with booty, they tied the rope to it and gave it a sharp slap on the rump. The slack in the rope was snapped up suddenly and fresh shrieks rent the air as the women were yanked forward again. Those who fell were dragged along, with their faces scraping the ground.

"Stop!" screamed one. "My arms're coming off!"

A wave of raucous laughter swept through the brigands.

At that moment, horse and women came to a dead halt.

"What's going on? . . . Somebody's up ahead!"

All eyes strained to see.

"Who's there?" roared one bandit.

The silent shadow walking toward them carried a white blade. The bandits, trained to be sensitive to odors, instantly recognized the one they smelled now—blood dripping from the sword.

As the men in front fell back clumsily, Musashi sized up the enemy force. He counted twelve men, all hard-muscled and brutish-looking. Recovering from the initial shock, they readied their weapons and took defensive stances. One ran forward with an ax. Another, carrying a hunter's spear, approached diagonally, keeping his body low and aiming at Musashi's ribs. The man with the ax was the first to go.

"A-w-w-k!" Sounding as though he'd bitten his own tongue off, he weaved crazily and collapsed in a heap.

"Don't you know me?" Musashi's voice rang out sharply. "I am the protector of the people, a messenger from the god who watches over this village." In the same breath, he seized the spear pointed at him, wrested it from its owner's hands and threw it violently to the ground.

Moving swiftly into the band of ruffians, he was kept busy countering thrusts from all sides. But after the first surge, made while they still fought with confidence, he had a good idea of what lay ahead. It was a matter not of numbers but of the opposition's cohesiveness and self-control.

Seeing one man after another turned into a blood-spurting missile, the bandits were soon falling back to ever greater distances, until finally they panicked and lost all semblance of organization.

Musashi was learning even as he fought, acquiring experience that would lead him to specific methods to be used by a smaller force against a larger one. This was a valuable lesson and couldn't be learned in a fight with a single enemy.

His two swords were in their scabbards. For years, he'd practiced to master the art of seizing his opponent's weapon and turning it against him. Now he'd put study into practice, taking the sword away from the first man he'd encountered. His reason wasn't that his own sword, which he thought of as his soul, was too pure to be sullied by the blood of common brigands. He was being practical; against such a motley array of weapons, a blade might get chipped, or even broken.

When the five or six survivors fled toward the village, Musashi took a minute or two to relax and catch his breath, fully expecting them to return with reinforcements. Then he freed the women and ordered those who could stand to take care of the others.

After some words of comfort and encouragement, he told them it was up to them to save their parents and children and husbands.

"You'd be miserable if you survived and they perished, wouldn't you?" he asked.

There was a murmur of agreement.

"You yourselves have the strength to protect yourselves and save the others. But you don't know how to use that strength. That's why you're at the mercy of outlaws. We're going to change that. I'm going to help you by showing you how to use the power you have. The first thing to do is arm yourselves."

He had them collect the weapons lying about and distributed one to each of the women.

"Now follow me and do just as I say. You mustn't

be afraid. Try to believe that the god of this district is on your side."

As he led the women toward the burning village, other victims emerged from the shadows and joined them. Soon the group had grown into a small army of nearly a hundred people. Women tearfully hugged loved ones: daughters were reunited with parents, wives with husbands, mothers with children.

At first, as the women described how Musashi had dealt with the bandits, the men listened with shocked expressions on their faces, not believing that this could be the idiot rōnin of Hōtengahara. When they did accept it, their gratitude was obvious, despite the barrier imposed by their dialect.

Turning to the men, Musashi told them to find weapons. "Anything'll do, even a good heavy stick or a length of fresh bamboo."

No one disobeyed, or even questioned his orders.

Musashi asked, "How many bandits are there in all?"

"About fifty."

"How many houses in the village?"

"Seventy."

Musashi calculated that there was probably a total of seven or eight hundred people. Even allowing for old people and children, the brigands would still be outnumbered by as much as ten to one.

He smiled grimly at the thought that these peaceful villagers had believed they had no recourse but to throw up their hands in despair. He knew that if something was not done, the atrocity would be repeated. Tonight he wanted to accomplish two things: show the villagers how to protect themselves and see that the brigands were banished forever.

"Sir," cried a man who had just come from the village. "They're on their way here."

Though the villagers were armed now, the news

made them uneasy. They showed signs of breaking and running.

To restore confidence, Musashi said loudly, "There's nothing to be alarmed about. I was expecting this. I want you to hide on both sides of the road, but first listen to my instructions." He talked rapidly but calmly, briefly repeating points of emphasis. "When they get here, I'll let them attack me. Then I'll pretend to run away. They'll follow me. You—all of you—stay where you are. I won't need any help.

"After a time, they'll come back. When they do, attack. Make lots of noise; take them by surprise. Strike at their sides, legs, chests—any area that's unguarded. When you've taken care of the first bunch, hide again and wait for the next one. Keep doing this until they're all dead."

He barely had time to finish and the peasants to disperse before the marauders appeared. From their dress and lack of coordination, Musashi guessed that theirs was a primitive fighting force, of a sort that might have been common long ago, when men hunted and fished for sustenance. The name Tokugawa meant nothing to them, no more than did Toyotomi. The mountains were their tribal home; the villagers existed to provide them with food and supplies.

"Stop!" ordered the man at the head of the pack. There were about twenty of them, some with crude swords, some with lances, one with a battle-ax, another with a rusty spear. Silhouetted against the glow of the fire, their bodies looked like demonic, jet-black shadows.

"Is he the one?"

"Yeah, that's him, all right."

Some sixty feet ahead of them, Musashi stood his ground, blocking the road. Disconcerted, they began to doubt their own strength, and for a short time none of them moved.

But only for a moment. Then Musashi's blazing eyes started to pull them inexorably toward him.

"You the son of a bitch trying to get in our way?"

"Right!" roared Musashi, raising his sword and tearing into them. There was a loud reverberation, followed by a whirlwind fray in which it was impossible to make out individual movements. It was like a spinning swarm of winged ants.

The rice fields on one side of the road and the embankment lined with trees and bushes on the other were ideal for Musashi, since they provided a measure of cover, but after the first skirmish, he executed a strategic withdrawal.

"See that?"

"The bastard's running away!"

"After him!"

They pursued him to a far corner of the nearest field, where he turned and faced them. With nothing behind him, his position seemed worse, but he kept his opponents at bay by moving swiftly to right and left. Then the moment one of them made a false move, Musashi struck.

His dark form seemed to flit from place to place, a geyser of blood rising before him each time he paused. The bandits who were not killed were soon too dazed to fight, while Musashi grew sharper with every strike. It was a different sort of battle from the one at Ichijōji. He did not have the feeling of standing on the border between life and death, but he had reached a plane of selflessness, body and sword performing without the need of conscious thought. His attackers fled in complete disarray.

A whisper went along the line of villagers. "They're coming." Then a group of them jumped out of hiding and fell upon the first two or three bandits, killing them almost effortlessly. The farmers melted into the darkness again, and the process was repeated until all the bandits had been ambushed and slain.

Counting the corpses bolstered the villagers' confidence.

"They're not so strong after all," gloated one man.

"Wait! Here comes another one."

"Get him!"

"No, don't attack. It's the rōnin."

With a minimum of confusion, they lined up along the road like soldiers being reviewed by their general. All eyes were fixed on Musashi's bloody clothing and dripping sword, whose blade was chipped in a dozen places. He threw it away and picked up a lance.

"Our work's not done," he said. "Get yourselves some weapons and follow me. By combining your strength, you can drive the marauders out of the village and rescue your families."

Not one man hesitated. The women and children also found weapons and followed along.

The damage to the village was not as extensive as they had feared, because the dwellings were set well apart. But the terrified farm animals were raising a great ruckus, and somewhere a baby was crying its lungs out. Loud popping noises came from the roadside, where the fire had spread to a grove of green bamboo.

The bandits were nowhere in sight.

"Where are they?" asked Musashi. "I seem to smell sake. Where would there be a lot of sake in one place?"

The villagers were so absorbed in gaping at the fires that nobody had noticed the smell, but one of them said, "Must be the village headman's house. He's got barrels of sake."

"Then that's where we'll find them," said Musashi.

As they advanced, more men came out of hiding and joined their ranks. Musashi was gratified by the growing spirit of unity.

"That's it, there," said one man, pointing out a large house surrounded by an earthen wall.

While the peasants were getting themselves organized, Musashi scaled the wall and invaded the bandits' stronghold. The leader and his chief lieutenants were ensconced in a large dirt-floored room, swilling sake and forcing their attentions on young girls they were holding captive.

"Don't get excited!" the leader shouted angrily in a rough, mountain dialect. "He's only one man. I shouldn't have to do anything myself. The rest of you take care of him." He was upbraiding an underling who had rushed in with the news of the defeat outside the village.

As their chief fell silent, the others became aware of the hum of angry voices beyond the wall and stirred uneasily. Dropping half-eaten chickens and sake cups, they jumped to their feet and instinctively reached for their weapons. Then they stood there, staring at the entrance to the room.

Musashi, using his lance as a pole, vaulted through a high side window, landing directly behind the chief. The man whirled around, only to be impaled on the lance. Letting out a fearsome "A-w-r-g," he grabbed with both hands the lance lodged in his chest. Musashi calmly let go of the lance, and the man toppled face down on the ground, the blade and most of the shaft projecting from his back.

The second man to attack Musashi was relieved of his sword. Musashi sliced him through, brought the blade down on the head of a third man, and thrust it into the chest of a fourth. The others made helter-skelter for the door. Musashi hurled the sword at them and in a continuation of the same motion extricated the lance from the chief's body.

"Don't move!" he bellowed. He charged with the lance held horizontally, parting the bandits like water struck with a pole. This gave him enough room to make effective use of the long weapon, which he now swung with a deftness that tested the very resiliency of its black oak shaft, striking sideways, slicing downward, thrusting viciously forward.

The bandits attempting to get out the gate found their way blocked by the armed villagers. Some climbed the wall. When they hit the ground, most were slaughtered on the spot. Of the few who succeeded in escaping, nearly all received crippling wounds.

For a time the air was filled with shouts of triumph from young and old, male and female, and as the first flush of victory subsided, man and wife, parents and children, hugged each other and shed tears of joy.

In the midst of this ecstatic scene, someone asked, "What if they come back?"

There was a moment of sudden, anxious stillness.

"They won't be back," Musashi said firmly. "Not to this village. But don't be overconfident. Your business is using plows, not swords. If you grow too proud of your fighting ability, the punishment heaven will mete out to you will be worse than any raid by mountain devils."

"Did you find out what happened?" Nagaoka Sado asked his two samurai when they got back to the Tokuganji. In the distance, across field and swamp, he could see that the light of the fires in the village was fading.

"Everything's quieted down now."

"Did you chase the bandits away? How much damage was done in the village?"

"The villagers killed all but a few of them before we got there. The others got away."

"Well, that's odd." He looked surprised, for if this was true, he had some thinking to do about the way of governing in his own lord's district.

On leaving the temple the following day, he directed his horse toward the village, saying, "It's out of the way, but let's have a look."

A priest came along to show them the way, and while they rode, Sado observed, "Those bodies along the roadside don't look to me as though they were cut down by farmers," and asked his samurai for more details.

The villagers, forgoing sleep, were hard at work, burying corpses and cleaning up debris from the conflagration. But when they saw Sado and the samurai, they ran inside their houses and hid.

"Get one of the villagers to come here, and let's find out exactly what happened," he said to the priest.

The man who came back with the priest gave them a fairly detailed account of the night's events.

"Now it begins to make sense," Sado said, nodding. "What's this rōnin's name?"

The peasant, never having heard Musashi's name, cocked his head to one side. When Sado insisted on knowing it, the priest asked about for a time and came up with the required information.

"Miyamoto Musashi?" Sado said thoughtfully. "Is he the man the boy spoke of as his teacher?"

"That's right. From the way he's been trying to develop a piece of waste land on Hōtengahara, the villagers thought he was a little soft in the head."

"I'd like to meet him," said Sado, but then he remembered the work waiting for him in Edo. "Never mind; I'll talk to him the next time I come out here." He turned his horse around and left the peasant standing by the road.

A few minutes later he reined up in front of the village headman's gate. There, written in shiny ink on a fresh board, hung a sign: "Reminder for the People of the Village: Your plow is your sword. Your sword is your plow. Working in the fields, don't forget the invasion. Thinking of the invasion, don't forget your fields. All things must be balanced and integrated. Most important, do not oppose the Way of successive generations."

"Hmm. Who wrote this?"

The headman had finally come out and was now bowing on the ground before Sado. "Musashi," he answered.

Turning to the priest, Sado said, "Thank you for bringing us here. It's too bad I couldn't meet this Musashi, but just now I don't have the time. I'll be back this way before long."

13

First Planting

The management of the palatial Hosokawa residence in Edo, as well as the performance of the fief's duties to the shōgun, was entrusted to a man still in his early twenties, Tadatoshi, the eldest son of the diamyō, Hosokawa Tadaoki. The father, a celebrated general who also enjoyed a reputation as a poet and master of the tea ceremony, preferred to live at the large Kokura fief in Buzen Province on the island of Kyushu.

Though Nagaoka Sado and a number of other trusted retainers were assigned to assist the young man, this was not because he was in any way incompetent. He was not only accepted as a peer by the powerful vassals closest to the shōgun but had distinguished himself as an energetic and farsighted administrator. In fact, he seemed more in tune with the peace and prosperity of the times than the older lords, who had been nurtured on constant warfare.

At the moment, Sado was walking in the general direction of the riding ground. "Have you seen the Young Lord?" he asked of an apprentice samurai coming toward him.

"I believe he's at the archery range."

As Sado threaded his way down a narrow path, he heard a voice asking, "May I have a word with you?"

Sado stopped, and Iwama Kakubei, a vassal respected for his shrewdness and practicality, came up to him. "You're going to talk with his lordship?" he asked.

"Yes."

"If you're not in a hurry, there's a little matter I'd like to consult with you about. Why don't we sit down over there?" As they walked the few steps to a rustic arbor, Kakubei said, "I have a favor to ask. If you have a chance during your talk, there's a man I'd like to recommend to the Young Lord."

"Someone wanting to serve the House of Hosokawa?"

"Yes. I know all sorts of people come to you with the same request, but this man's very unusual."

"Is he one of those men interested only in security and a stipend?"

"Definitely not. He's related to my wife. He's been living with us since he came up from Iwakuni a couple of years ago, so I know him quite well."

"Iwakuni? The House of Kikkawa held Suō Province before the Battle of Sekigahara. Is he one of their rōnin?"

"No. He's the son of a rural samurai. His name's Sasaki Kojirō. He's still young, but he was trained in the Tomita Style of Kanemaki Jisai, and he learned the techniques of drawing a sword with lightning swiftness from Lord Katayama Hisayasu of Hōki. He's even created a style of his own, which he calls Ganryū." Kakubei went on, listing in detail Kojirō's various exploits and accomplishments.

Sado was not really listening. His mind had gone back to his last visit to the Tokuganji. Though he was sure, even from the little he'd seen and heard, that Musashi was the right sort of man for the House of Hosokawa, he had intended to meet him personally before recommending him to his master. In the meantime, a year and a half had slipped by without his finding an opportunity to visit Hōtengahara.

When Kakubei finished, Sado said, "I'll do what I can for you," and continued on to the archery range.

Tadatoshi was engaged in a contest with some vassals of his own age, none of whom was remotely a match for him. His shots, unerringly on target, were executed with flawless style. A number of retainers had chided him for taking archery so seriously, arguing that in an age of gun and lance, neither sword nor bow was any longer of much use in actual combat. To this he had replied cryptically, "My arrows are aimed at the spirit."

The Hosokawa retainers had the highest respect for Tadatoshi, and would have served under him with enthusiasm even if his father, to whom they were also devoted, had not been a man of substantial accomplishments. At the moment, Sado regretted the promise he'd just made to Kakubei. Tadatoshi was not a man to whom one lightly recommended prospective retainers.

Wiping the sweat off his face, Tadatoshi walked past several young samurai with whom he'd been talking and laughing. Catching sight of Sado, he called, "How about it, Ancient One? Have a shot?"

"I make it a rule to compete only against adults," Sado replied.

"So you still think of us as little boys with our hair tied up on our heads?"

"Have you forgotten the Battle of Yamazaki? Nirayama Castle? I have been commended for my performance on the battlefield, you know. Besides, I go in for real archery, not—"

"Ha, ha. Sorry I mentioned it. I didn't mean to get you started again." The others joined in the laughter. Slipping his arm out of his sleeve, Tadatoshi became serious and asked, "Did you come to discuss something?"

After going over a number of routine matters, Sado said, "Kakubei says he has a samurai to recommend to you."

For a moment there was a faraway look in Tadatoshi's eyes. "I suppose he's talking about Sasaki Kojirō. He's been mentioned several times."

"Why don't you call him in and have a look at him?"

"Is he really good?"

"Shouldn't you see for yourself?"

Tadatoshi put on his glove and accepted an arrow from an attendant. "I'll take a look at Kakubei's man," he said. "I'd also like to see that rōnin you mentioned. Miyamoto Musashi, was it?"

"Oh, you remember?"

"I do. You're the one who seems to have forgotten."

"Not at all. But being so busy, I haven't had a chance to go out to Shimōsa."

"If you think you've found someone, you should take the time. I'm surprised at you, Sado, letting something so important wait until you've got other business to take you out there. It's not like you."

"I'm sorry. There's always too many men looking for positions. I thought you'd forgotten about it. I suppose I should have brought it up again."

"Indeed you should have. I don't necessarily accept other people's recommendations, but I'm eager to see anyone old Sado considers suitable. Understand?"

Sado apologized again before taking his leave. He went directly to his own house and without further ado had a fresh horse saddled and set out for Hōtengahara.

"Isn't this Hōtengahara?"

Satō Genzō, Sado's attendant, said, "That's what I thought, but this is no wilderness. There're rice fields all over. The place they were trying to develop must be nearer the mountains."

They had already gone a good distance beyond the Tokuganji and would soon be on the highroad to Hitachi. It was late afternoon, and the white herons splashing about in the paddies made the water seem like powder. Along the riverbank and in the shadows of hillocks grew patches of hemp and waving stalks of barley.

"Look over there, sir," said Genzō.

"What is it?"

"There's a group of farmers."

"So there is. They seem to be bowing to the ground, one by one, don't they?"

"It looks like some sort of religious ceremony."

With a snap of the reins, Genzō forded the river first, making sure it was safe for Sado to follow.

"You, there!" called Genzō.

The farmers, looking surprised, spread out from their circle to face the visitors. They were standing in front of a small cabin, and Sado could see that the object they'd been bowing before was a tiny wooden shrine, no larger than a birdcage. There were about fifty of them, on their way home from work, it appeared, for their tools had all been washed.

A priest came forward, saying, "Why, it's Nagaoka Sado, isn't it? What a pleasant surprise!"

"And you're from the Tokuganji, aren't you? I believe you're the one who guided me to the village after the bandit raid."

"That's right. Have you come to pay a call at the temple?"

"No, not this time. I'll be going back right away. Could you tell me where I might find that rōnin named Miyamoto Musashi?"

"He's not here anymore. He left very suddenly."

"Left suddenly? Why should he do that?"

"One day last month, the villagers decided to take a day off and celebrate the progress that's been made here. You can see for yourself how green it is now. Well, the morning after that, Musashi and the boy, Iori, were gone." The priest looked around, as though half expecting Musashi to materialize out of the air.

In response to Sado's prompting, the priest filled in the details of his story. After the village had strengthened its defenses under Musashi's leadership, the farmers were so thankful for the prospect of living in peace that they practically deified him. Even the ones who had ridiculed him most cruelly had come forward to help with the development project.

Musashi treated them all fairly and equally, first convincing them that it was pointless to live like animals. He then tried to impress upon them the importance of exerting a little extra effort so as to give their children a chance for a better life. To be real human beings, he told them they must work for the sake of posterity.

With forty or fifty villagers pitching in to help each day, by fall they were able to keep the floodwaters under control. When winter came, they plowed. And in the spring, they drew water from the new irrigation ditches and transplanted the rice seedlings. By early summer the rice was thriving, while in the dry fields, hemp and barley were already a foot high. In another year, the crop would double; the year after that, triple.

Villagers began to drop in at the cabin to pay their respects, thanking Musashi from the bottom of their hearts, the women bearing gifts of vegetables. On the day of the celebration, the men arrived with great jars of sake, and all took part in performing a sacred dance, accompanied by drums and flutes.

With the villagers gathered around him, Musashi had assured them that it was not his strength, but theirs. "All I did was show you how to use the energy you possess."

Then he had taken the priest aside to tell him that he was concerned about their relying on a vagabond like him. "Even without me," he said, "they should have confidence in themselves and maintain solidarity." He had then taken out a statue of Kannon he'd carved and given it to the priest.

The morning after the celebration, the village was in an uproar.

"He's gone!"

"He can't be."

"Yes, he's disappeared. The cabin's empty."

Grief-stricken, none of the farmers went near the fields that day.

When he heard about it, the priest reproached them sharply for their ingratitude, urging them to remember what they'd been taught and subtly coaxing them to carry on the work that had been started.

Later, the villagers had built the tiny shrine and placed the treasured image of Kannon in it. They paid their respects to Musashi morning and evening, on their way to and from the fields.

Sado thanked the priest for the information, concealing the fact that he was disconsolate as only a man of his position could do.

As his horse made its way back through the evening mist of late spring, he thought uneasily: "I shouldn't have put off coming. I was derelict in my duty, and now I've failed my lord."

14

The Flies

On the east bank of the Sumida River where the road from Shimōsa converged with a branch of the Ōshū highroad rose a great barrier with an imposing gate, ample evidence of the firm rule of Aoyama Tadanari, the new magistrate of Edo.

Musashi stood in line, idly waiting his turn, Iori at his side. When he had passed through Edo three years earlier, entering and leaving the city had been a simple matter. Even at this distance, he could see that there were far more houses than before, fewer open spaces.

"You there, rōnin. You're next."

Two officials in leather *hakama* began frisking Musashi with great thoroughness, while a third glared at him and asked questions.

"What business do you have in the capital?"

"Nothing specific."

"No special business, eh?"

"Well, I am a *shugyōsha*. I suppose it could be said that studying to be a samurai is my business."

The man was silent. Musashi grinned.

"Where were you born?"

"In the village of Miyamoto, district of Yoshino, Mimasaka Province."

"Your master?"

"I have none."

"Who furnishes your travel money?"

"No one. I carve statues and draw pictures. Sometimes I can exchange them for food and lodging. Often I stay at temples. Occasionally I give lessons in the sword. One way or another, I manage."

"Where are you coming from?"

"For the past two years, I've been farming in Hōtengahara in Shimōsa. I decided I didn't want to do that for the rest of my life, so I've come here."

"Do you have a place to stay in Edo? No one can enter the city unless he has relatives or a place to live."

"Yes," replied Musashi on the spur of the moment. He saw that if he tried to stick to the truth, there was going to be no end to it.

"Well?"

"Yagyū Munenori, Lord of Tajima."

The official's mouth dropped open.

Musashi, amused at the man's reaction, congratulated himself. The risk of being caught in a lie did not trouble him greatly. He felt that the Yagyūs must have heard about him from Takuan. It seemed unlikely they would deny all acquaintance with him if questioned. It might even be that Takuan was in Edo now. If so, Musashi had his means of introduction. It was too late to have a bout with Sekishūsai, but he longed to have one with Munenori, his father's successor in the Yagyū Style and a personal tutor of the shōgun.

The name acted like magic. "Well, well," said the official amiably. "If you're connected with the House of Yagyū, I'm sorry to have troubled you. As you must realize, there are all sorts of samurai on the road. We have to be particularly careful about anyone who appears to be a rōnin. Orders, you know." After a few more questions for the sake of form or face, he said, "You can go now," and personally escorted Musashi to the gate.

"Sir," Iori asked when they were on the other side, "why are they so careful about rōnin and nobody else?"

"They're on the lookout for enemy spies."

"What spy would be stupid enough to come here looking like a rōnin? The officials are pretty dumb—them and their stupid questions! They made us miss the ferry!"

"Shh. They'll hear you. Don't worry about the ferry. You can look at Mount Fuji while we're waiting for the next one. Did you know you could see it from here?"

"So what? We could see it from Hōtengahara too."

"Yes, but it's different here."

"How?"

"Fuji's never the same. It varies from day to day, hour to hour."

"Looks the same to me."

"It's not, though. It changes—time, weather, season, the place you're looking at it from. It differs, too, according to the person who's looking at it, according to his heart."

Unimpressed, Iori picked up a flat stone and sent it skimming across the water. After amusing himself in this fashion for a few minutes, he came back to Musashi and asked, "Are we really going to Lord Yagyū's house?"

"I'll have to think about that."

"Isn't that what you told the guard?"

"Yes. I intend to go, but it's not all that simple. He's a daimyō, you know."

"He must be awfully important. That's what I want to be when I grow up."

"Important?"

"Umm."

"You shouldn't aim so low."

"What do you mean?"

"Look at Mount Fuji."

"I'll never be like Mount Fuji."

"Instead of wanting to be like this or that, make yourself into a silent, immovable giant. That's what the mountain is. Don't waste your time trying to impress people. If you become the sort of man people can respect, they'll respect you, without your doing anything."

Musashi's words didn't have time to sink in, for just then Iori shouted, "Look, here comes the ferry," and ran ahead to be the first one on board.

The Sumida River was a study in contrasts, wide in places, narrow in others, shallow here and deep there. At high tide, the waves washing the banks took on a muddy hue. Sometimes the estuary swelled to twice its normal width. At the point where the ferry crossed, it was virtually an inlet of the bay.

The sky was clear, the water transparent. Looking over the side, Iori could see schools of countless tiny fish racing about. Among the rocks he also spotted the rusty remains of an old helmet. He had no ears for the conversation going on around him.

"What do you think? Is it going to stay peaceful, the way it is now?"

"I doubt it."

"You're probably right. Sooner or later, there'll be fighting. I hope not, but what else can you expect?"

Other passengers kept their thoughts to themselves and stared dourly at the water, afraid an official, possibly in disguise, might overhear and connect them with the speakers. Those who did take the risk seemed to enjoy flirting with the ubiquitous eyes and ears of the law.

"You can tell from the way they're checking everybody that we're heading for war. It's only very recently they've been clamping down like that. And there're a lot of rumors about spies from Osaka."

"You also hear about burglars breaking into daimyō's houses, though they try to hush it up. It must be embarrassing being robbed when you're supposed to be the enforcers of law and order."

"You'd have to be after more than money to take that kind of risk. It's got to be spies. No ordinary crook would have the nerve."

As he looked around, it occurred to Musashi that the ferry was transporting a fair cross section of Edo society. A lumberman with sawdust clinging to his work clothes, a couple of cheap geisha who might have come from Kyoto, a broad-shouldered roughneck or two, a group of well-diggers, two openly coquettish whores, a priest, a beggar monk, another rōnin like himself.

When the boat reached the Edo side and they all piled out, a short, heavyset man called to Musashi, "Hey, you. The rōnin. You forgot something." He held out a reddish brocade pouch, so old that the dirt seemed to shine more brightly than the few gold threads left in it.

Musashi, shaking his head, said, "It's not mine. It must belong to one of the other passengers."

Iori piped up, "It's mine," snatched the pouch from the man's hand and stuffed it into his kimono.

The man was indignant. "What're you doing, grabbing like that! Give it here! Then you're going to bow three times before you get it back. If you don't, you're going to get thrown in the river!"

Musashi intervened, asking the man to excuse Iori's rudeness because of his age.

"What are you?" the man asked roughly. "Brother? Master? What's your name!"

"Miyamoto Musashi."

"What!" exclaimed the ruffian, staring hard at Musashi's face. After a moment he said to Iori, "You'd better be more careful from now on." Then, as though eager to escape, he turned away.

"Just a moment," said Musashi. The gentleness of his tone took the man completely by surprise.

He whirled around, his hand going to his sword. "What do you want?"

"What's your name?"

"What's it to you?"

"You asked mine. As a matter of courtesy, you should tell me yours."

"I'm one of Hangawara's men. My name's Jūrō."

"All right. You can go," said Musashi, pushing him away.

"I won't forget that!" Jūrō stumbled a few steps before he found his feet and fled.

"Serves him right, the coward," said Iori. Satisfied that he'd been vindicated, he looked up worshipfully at Musashi's face and moved closer to him.

As they walked into the city, Musashi said, "Iori, you have to realize that living here is not like being out in the country. There, we had only foxes and squirrels for neighbors. Here, there're lots of people. You'll have to be more careful about your manners."

"Yes, sir."

"When people live together in harmony, the earth is a paradise," Musashi went on gravely. "But every man has a bad side as well as a good side. There are times when only the bad comes out. Then the world's not paradise, but hell. Do you understand what I'm saying?"

"Yes, I think so," said Iori, more subdued now.

"There's a reason we have manners and etiquette. They keep us from letting the bad side take over. This promotes social order, which is the objective of the government's laws." Musashi paused. "The way you acted . . . It was a trivial matter, but your attitude couldn't help but make the man angry. I'm not at all happy about it."

"Yes, sir."

"I don't know where we'll be going from here. But wherever we are, you'd better follow the rules and act courteously."

The boy bobbed his head a couple of times and made a small, stiff bow. They walked on in silence for a short while.

"Sir, would you carry my pouch for me? I don't want to lose it again."

Accepting the small brocade bag, Musashi inspected it closely before tucking it into his kimono. "Is this the one your father left you?"

"Yes, sir. I got it back from the Tokuganji at the

beginning of the year. The priest didn't take any of the money. You can use some of it if you need to."

"Thanks," Musashi said lightly. "I'll take good care of it."

"He has a talent I don't have," mused Musashi, thinking ruefully of his own indifference to personal finances. The boy's innate prudence had taught Musashi the meaning of economics. He appreciated the boy's trust and was growing fonder of him by the day. He looked forward with enthusiasm to the task of helping him develop his native intelligence.

"Where would you like to stay tonight?" he asked.

Iori, who had been looking at his new surroundings with great curiosity, remarked, "I see lots of horses over there. It looks like a marketplace, right here in town." He spoke as though he had run across a long-lost friend in a strange country.

They had reached Bakurōchō, where there was a large and diverse selection of tea shops and hostelries catering to the equine professions—sellers, buyers, draymen, grooms, a variety of lesser factotums. Men in small groups haggled and babbled in a welter of dialects, the most prominent being the tangy, irate-sounding speech of Edo.

Among the rabble was a well-groomed samurai, searching for good horses. With a disgruntled look, he said, "Let's go home. There's nothing here but nags, nothing worth recommending to his lordship."

Striding briskly between the animals, he came face to face with Musashi, blinked, and stepped back in surprise. "You're Miyamoto Musashi, aren't you?"

Musashi looked at the man for an instant, then broke into a grin. It was Kimura Sukekurō. Although the two men had come within inches of locking swords at Koyagyū Castle, Sukekurō's manner was cordial. He seemed to bear no lingering rancor from that encounter.

"I certainly didn't expect to see you here," he said. "Have you been in Edo long?"

"I've just come from Shimōsa," replied Musashi. "How's your master? Is he still in good health?"

"Yes, thank you, but of course at Sekishūsai's age . . . I'm staying with Lord Munenori. You must come to visit; I'd be glad to introduce you. Oh, there's something else, too." He flashed a meaningful look and smiled. "We have a beautiful treasure that belongs to you. You must come as soon as you can."

Before Musashi could inquire what the "beautiful treasure" might be, Sukekurō made a slight bow and walked rapidly away, his attendant trailing along behind.

The guests staying at the inexpensive inns of Baku-rōchō were mostly horse traders in from the provinces. Musashi decided to take a room there rather than in another part of town, where the rates would most likely be higher. Like the other inns, the one he chose had a large stable, so large in fact that the rooms themselves seemed rather like an annex. But after the rigors of Hōtengahara, even this third-rate hostelry seemed luxurious.

Despite his feeling of well-being, Musashi found the horseflies annoying and began grumbling.

The proprietress heard him. "I'll change your room," she offered solicitously. "The flies aren't so bad on the second floor."

Once resettled, Musashi found himself exposed to the full strength of the western sun and felt like grumbling again. Only a few days ago, the afternoon sun would have been a source of cheer, a bright ray of hope shedding nourishing warmth on the rice plants and portending good weather for the morrow. As for the flies, when his sweat had attracted them while he worked in the fields, he had taken the view that they were only going about their chores, just as he was going about his. He had even regarded them as fellow creatures. Now, having crossed one wide river and entered the maze of the city, he found the heat of the sun anything but comforting, the flies only an irritation.

His appetite took his mind off the inconveniences. He glanced at Iori, and saw symptoms of lassitude and gluttony in his face too. Small wonder, for a party in the next room had ordered a great pot of steaming food and was now attacking it ravenously, amid much talk, laughter and drinking.

Buckwheat noodles—*soba*—that's what he wanted! In the country, if a man wanted *soba*, he planted buckwheat in the early spring, watched it flower in the summer, dried the grain in the fall, ground the flour in the winter. Then he could make *soba*. Here it required no more effort than clapping one's hands for service.

"Iori, shall we order some *soba*?"

"Yes," came the eager reply.

The proprietress came and took their order. While they waited, Musashi propped his elbows on the windowsill and shaded his eyes. Diagonally across the way was a signboard reading: "Souls polished here. Zushino Kōsuke, Master in the Hon'ami Style."

Iori had noticed it too. After staring for a moment in bewilderment, he said, "That sign says 'Souls polished.' What sort of business is that?"

"Well, it also says the man works in the Hon'ami Style, so I suppose he's a sword polisher. Come to think of it, I ought to have my sword worked on."

The *soba* was slow to arrive, so Musashi stretched out on the tatami for a nap. But the voices in the next room had risen several decibels and became quarrelsome. "Iori," he said, opening one eye, "will you ask the people next door to be a little quieter?"

Only shoji separated the two rooms, but instead of opening them, Iori went out into the hall. The door to the other room was open. "Don't make so much noise," he shouted. "My teacher's trying to sleep."

"Hunh!" The squabble came to an abrupt halt. The men turned and stared angrily at him.

"You say something, shrimp?"

Pouting at the epithet, Iori said, "We came upstairs because of the flies. Now you're yelling so much he can't rest."

"Is this your idea, or did your master send you?"

"He sent me."

"Did he? Well, I'm not wasting my time talking to a little turd like you. Go tell your master Kumagorō of Chichibu will give him his answer later. Now beat it!"

Kumagorō was a great brute of a man, and the two or three others in the room were not much smaller. Cowed by the menace in their eyes, Iori quickly retreated. Musashi had dropped off to sleep; not wanting to disturb him, Iori sat down by the window.

Presently, one of the horse traders opened the shoji a crack and peeked in at Musashi. There followed much laughter, accompanied by loud and insulting remarks.

"Who does he think he is, butting into our party? Dumb rōnin! No telling where he comes from. Just barges in and starts acting like he owns the place."

"We'll have to show him what's what."

"Yeah, we'll make sure he knows what the horse traders of Edo are made of."

"Talking's not going to show him. Let's haul him out back and throw a bucket of horse piss in his face."

Kumagorō spoke up. "Hold on, now. Let me handle this. Either I'll get an apology in writing or we'll wash his face with horse piss. Enjoy your sake. Leave everything to me."

"This should be good," said one man, as Kumagorō, with a confident smirk, tightened his obi.

"I beg your pardon," said Kumagorō, sliding the shoji open. Without standing up, he shuffled into Musashi's room on his knees.

The *soba*, six helpings in a lacquered box, had finally arrived. Musashi was sitting up now, addressing his chopsticks to his first helping.

"Look, they're coming in," said Iori under his breath, moving slightly to get out of the way.

Kumagorō seated himself behind and to Iori's left, legs crossed, elbows resting on his knees. With a fierce scowl, he said, "You can eat later. Don't try to hide the fact that you're scared by sitting there playing with your food."

Though he was grinning, Musashi gave no indication that he was listening. He stirred the *soba* with his chopsticks to separate the strands, lifted a mouthful and swallowed with a joyous slurp.

The veins in Kumagorō's forehead nearly popped. "Put that bowl down," he said angrily.

"And who are you?" Musashi asked mildly, making no move to comply.

"You don't know who I am? The only people in Bakurōchō who haven't heard my name are good-for-nothings and deaf-mutes."

"I'm a little hard of hearing myself. Speak up, tell me who you are and where you come from."

"I'm Kumagorō from Chichibu, the best horse trader in Edo. When children see me coming, they get so scared they can't even cry."

"I see. Then you're in the horse business?"

"You bet I am. I sell to the samurai. You'd better remember that when you're dealing with me."

"In what way am I dealing with you?"

"You sent that runt there to complain about the noise. Where do you think you are? This is no fancy inn for daimyō, nice and quiet and all. We horse traders like noise."

"I gathered that."

"Then why were you trying to bust up our party? I demand an apology."

"Apology?"

"Yes, in writing. You can address it to Kumagorō and his friends. If we don't get one we'll take you outside and teach you a thing or two."

"What you say is interesting."

"Hunh!"

"I mean your way of speaking is interesting."

"Cut out the nonsense! Do we get the apology or don't we? Well?" Kumagorō's voice had gone from a growl to a roar, and the sweat on his crimson forehead glistened in the evening sun. Looking ready to explode, he bared his hairy chest and took a dagger from his stomach wrapper.

"Make up your mind! If I don't hear your answer soon, you're in big trouble." He uncrossed his legs and held the dagger vertically beside the lacquered box, its point touching the floor.

Musashi, restraining his mirth, said, "Well, now how should I respond to that?"

Lowering his bowl, he reached out with his chopsticks, removed a dark speck from the *soba* in the box and threw it out the window. Still silent, he reached out again and picked off another dark speck, then another.

Kumagorō's eyes bugged; his breath halted.

"There's no end to them, is there?" remarked Musashi casually. "Here, Iori, go give these chopsticks a good washing."

As Iori went out, Kumagorō faded silently back into his own room and in a hushed voice told his companions of the incredible sight he had just witnessed. After first mistaking the black spots on the *soba* for dirt, he had realized they were live flies, plucked so deftly they had had no time to escape. Within minutes, he and his fellows transferred their little party to a more remote quarter, and silence reigned.

"That's better, isn't it?" said Musashi to Iori. The two of them grinned at one another.

By the time they'd finished their meal, the sun was down, and the moon was shining wanly above the roof of the "soul polisher's" shop.

Musashi stood up and straightened his kimono. "I

think I'll see about having my sword taken care of," he said.

He picked up the weapon and was about to leave when the proprietress came halfway up the blackened staircase and called, "A letter's come for you."

Puzzled that anyone should know his whereabouts so soon, Musashi went down, accepted the missive and asked, "Is the messenger still here?"

"No, he left immediately."

The outside of the letter bore only the word "Suke," which Musashi took to stand for Kimura Sukekurō. Unfolding it, he read: "I informed Lord Munenori that I saw you this morning. He seemed happy to receive word of you after all this time. He instructed me to write and ask when you will be able to visit us."

Musashi descended the remaining steps and went to the office, where he borrowed ink and brush. Seating himself in a corner, he wrote on the back of Sukekurō's letter: "I shall be happy to visit Lord Munenori whenever he wishes to have a bout with me. As a warrior, I have no other purpose in calling on him." He signed the note "Masana," a formal name he seldom used.

"Iori," he called from the bottom of the stairs. "I want you to run an errand for me."

"Yes, sir."

"I want you to deliver a letter to Lord Yagyū Munenori."

"Yes, sir."

According to the proprietress, everybody knew where Lord Munenori lived, but she offered directions anyway. "Go down the main street until you come to the highroad. Go straight along that as far as Nihombashi. Then bear to the left and go along the river until you get to Kobikichō. That's where it is; you can't miss it."

"Thanks," said Iori, who already had his sandals on. "I'm sure I can find it." He was delighted at the opportunity to go out, particularly since his destination was the home of an important daimyō. Giving no thought to the hour, he walked away quickly, swinging his arms and holding his head up proudly.

As Musashi watched him turn the corner, he thought: "He's a little too self-confident for his own good."

15

The Soul Polisher

"Good evening," called Musashi.

Nothing about Zushino Kōsuke's house suggested it was a place of business. It lacked the grilled front of most shops, and there was no merchandise on display. Musashi stood in the dirt-floored passageway running down the left side of the house. To his right was a raised section, floored with tatami and screened off from the room beyond it.

The man sleeping on the tatami with his arms resting on a strongbox resembled a Taoist sage Musashi had once seen in a painting. The long, thin face was the grayish color of clay. Musashi could detect in it none of the keenness he associated with sword craftsmen.

"Good evening," Musashi repeated, a little louder.

When his voice penetrated Kōsuke's torpor, the craftsman raised his head very slowly; he might have been awakening from centuries of slumber.

Wiping the saliva from his chin and sitting up straight, he asked lackadaisically, "Can I help you?" Musashi's impression was that a man like this might make swords, as well as souls, duller, but he nevertheless held out his own weapon and explained why he was there.

"Let me take a look at it." Kōsuke's shoulders perked up smartly. Placing his left hand on his knee, he reached out with his right to take the sword, simultaneously bowing his head toward it.

"Strange creature," thought Musashi. "He barely acknowledges the presence of a human being but bows politely to a sword."

Holding a piece of paper in his mouth, Kōsuke quietly slid the blade out of the scabbard. He stood it vertically in front of him and examined it from hilt to tip. His eyes took on a bright glitter, reminding Musashi of glass eyes in a wooden Buddhist statue.

Snapping the weapon back into its scabbard, Kōsuke looked up inquiringly at Musashi. "Come, have a seat," he said, moving back to make room and offering Musashi a cushion.

Musashi removed his sandals and stepped up into the room.

"Has the sword been in your family for some generations?"

"Oh, no," said Musashi. "It's not the work of a famous swordsmith, nothing like that."

"Have you used it in battle, or do you carry it for the usual purposes?"

"I haven't used it on the battlefield. There's nothing special about it. The best you could say is that it's better than nothing."

"Mm." Looking directly into Musashi's eyes, Kōsuke then asked, "How do you want it polished?"

"How do I want it polished? What do you mean?"

"Do you want it sharpened so it'll cut well?"

"Well, it is a sword. The cleaner it cuts, the better."

"I suppose so," agreed Kōsuke with a defeated sigh.

"What's wrong with that? Isn't it the business of a craftsman to sharpen swords so they'll cut properly?" As Musashi spoke, he squinted curiously into Kōsuke's face.

The self-proclaimed polisher of souls shoved the weapon toward Musashi and said, "I can't do anything for you. Take it to somebody else."

Strange, indeed, thought Musashi. He could not disguise a certain vexation, but he said nothing. Kōsuke, his lips tightly set, made no attempt to explain.

While they sat silently staring at each other, a man from the neighborhood stuck his head in the door. "Kōsuke, have you got a fishing pole? It's high tide, and the fish are jumping. If you'll lend me a pole, I'll divide my catch with you."

Kōsuke plainly regarded the man as one more burden he ought not to have to bear. "Borrow one somewhere else," he rasped. "I don't believe in killing, and I don't keep instruments for murder in my house."

The man went quickly away, leaving Kōsuke looking grumpier than ever.

Another man might have become discouraged and left, but Musashi's curiosity held him there. There was something appealing about this man—not wit nor intelligence, but a rough natural goodness like that of a Karatsu sake jar or a tea bowl by Nonkō. Just as pottery often has a blemish evocative of its closeness to the earth, Kōsuke had, in a semi-bald spot on his temple, a lesion of some sort, which he'd covered with salve.

While attempting to conceal his growing fascination, Musashi said, "What is there to keep you from polishing my sword? Is it of such poor quality you can't put a good edge on it?"

"Of course not. You're the owner. You know as well as I do it's a perfectly good Bizen sword. I also know you want it sharpened for the purpose of cutting people."

"Is there anything wrong with that?"

"That's what they all say—what's wrong with wanting me to fix a sword so it'll cut better? If the sword cuts, they're happy."

"But a man bringing in a sword to be polished naturally wants—"

"Just a minute." Kōsuke raised his hand. "I'll take some time to explain. First, I'd like you to take another look at the sign on the front of my shop."

"It says 'Souls polished,' or at least I think so. Is there any other way of reading the characters?"

"No. You'll notice it doesn't say a word about polishing swords. My business is polishing the souls of the samurai who come in, not their weapons. People don't understand, but that's what I was taught when I studied sword polishing."

"I see," said Musashi, although he didn't really.

"Since I try to abide by my master's teachings, I refuse to polish the swords of samurai who take pleasure in killing people."

"Well, you have a point there. But tell me, who was this master of yours?"

"That's written on the sign too. I studied in the House of Hon'ami, under Hon'ami Kōetsu himself." Kōsuke squared his shoulders proudly as he uttered his master's name.

"That's interesting. I happen to have made the acquaintance of your master and his excellent mother, Myōshū." Musashi went on to tell how he had met them in the field near the Rendaiji and later spent a few days at their house.

Kōsuke, astonished, scrutinized him closely for a moment. "Are you by any chance the man who caused a great stir in Kyoto some years ago by defeating the Yoshioka School at Ichijōji? Miyamoto Musashi was the name, I believe."

"That is my name." Musashi's face reddened slightly.

Kōsuke moved back a bit and bowed deferentially, saying, "Forgive me. I shouldn't have been lecturing you. I had no idea I was talking to the famous Miyamoto Musashi."

"Don't give it a second thought. Your words were very instructive. Kōetsu's character comes through in the lessons he teaches his disciples."

"As I'm sure you know, the Hon'ami family served the Ashikaga shōguns. From time to time they've also been called upon to polish the Emperor's swords. Kōetsu was always saying that Japanese swords were created not to kill or injure poeple but to maintain the imperial rule and protect the nation, to subdue devils and drive out evil. The sword *is* the samurai's soul; he carries it for no other purpose than to maintain his own integrity. It is an ever-present admonition to the man who rules over other men and seeks in doing so to follow the Way of Life. It's only natural that the craftsman who polishes the sword must also polish the swordsman's spirit."

"How true," agreed Musashi.

"Kōetsu said that to see a good sword is to see the sacred light, the spirit of the nation's peace and tranquillity. He hated touching a bad sword. Even being near one used to nauseate him."

"I see. Are you saying you sensed something evil in my sword?"

"No, not in the least. I just felt a little depressed. Since coming to Edo, I've worked on any number of weapons, but none of their owners seem to have an inkling of the sword's true meaning. I sometimes doubt they have souls to polish. All they care about is quartering a man or splitting his head open—helmet and all. It got so tiresome. That's why I put up a new sign a few days ago. It doesn't seem to have had much effect, though."

"And I came in asking for the same thing, didn't I? I understand how you feel."

"Well, that's a beginning. Things may turn out a little differently with you. But frankly, when I saw that blade of yours, I was shocked. All those nicks and stains, stains made by human flesh. I thought you were just one more senseless rōnin, proud of himself for committing a number of meaningless murders."

Musashi bowed his head. It was the voice of Kōetsu, coming from Kōsuke's mouth. "I'm grateful for this lesson," he said. "I've carried a sword since I was a boy, but I've never really given sufficient thought to the spirit that resides in it. In the future, I'll pay heed to what you've said."

Kōsuke appeared vastly relieved. "In that case, I'll polish the sword for you. Or perhaps I should say I consider it a privilege for one in my profession to be able to polish the soul of a samurai like yourself."

Twilight had faded, and the lights had been lit. Musashi decided it was time to go.

"Wait," said Kōsuke. "Do you have another sword to carry while I'm working on this one?"

"No; I have only the one long sword."

"In that case, why don't you pick out a replacement? None of the swords I have here now are very good, I'm afraid, but come and take a look."

He guided Musashi into the back room, where he took several swords out of a cabinet and lined them up on the tatami. "You can take any one of these," he offered.

Despite the craftsman's modest disavowal, they were all weapons of excellent quality. Musashi had difficulty choosing from the dazzling display, but finally he selected one and immediately fell in love with it. Just holding it in his hands, he sensed its maker's dedication. Drawing the blade from the scabbard confirmed his impression; it was indeed a beautiful piece of workmanship, probably dating from the Yoshino period in the fourteenth century. Nagged by the doubt that it was too elegant for him, once he had brought it close to the light and examined it, he found his hands reluctant to let it go.

"May I take this one?" he asked. He could not bring himself to use the word "borrow."

"You have the eye of an expert," observed Kōsuke, as he put away the other swords.

For once in his life, Musashi was swamped by covetousness. He knew it was futile to mention buying the sword outright; the price would be far beyond his means. But he couldn't help himself.

"I don't suppose you'd consider selling me this sword, would you?" he asked.

"Why not?"

"How much are you asking for it?"

"I'll let you have it for what I paid for it."

"How much was that?"

"Twenty pieces of gold."

An almost inconceivable sum to Musashi. "I'd better give it back," he said hesitantly.

"Why?" asked Kōsuke with a puzzled look. "I'll lend it to you for as long as you wish. Go on, take it."

"No; that'd make me feel even worse. Wanting it the way I do is bad enough. If I wore it for a while, it would be torture to part with it."

"Are you really so attached to it?" Kōsuke looked at the sword, then at Musashi. "All right then, I'll give it to you—in wedlock, as it were. But I expect an appropriate gift in exchange."

Musashi was baffled; he had absolutely nothing to offer.

"I heard from Kōetsu that you carve statues. I'd be honored if you'd make me an image of Kannon. That would be sufficient payment."

The last Kannon Musashi had carved was the one he'd left in Hōtengahara. "I have nothing on hand," he said. "But in the next few days, I can carve something for you. May I have the sword then?"

"Certainly. I didn't mean to imply I expected it this minute. By the way, instead of putting up at that inn, why don't you come and stay with us? We have a room we're not using."

"That would be perfect," said Musashi. "If I moved in tomorrow, I could start on the statue right away."

"Come and take a look at it," urged Kōsuke, who was also happy and excited.

Musashi followed him down the outside passageway, at the end of which was a flight of half a dozen steps. Tucked in between the first and second floors, not quite belonging to either, was an eight-mat room. Through the window Musashi could see the dew-laden leaves of an apricot tree.

Pointing at a roof covered with oyster shells, Kōsuke said, ''That's my workshop there.''

The craftsman's wife, as if summoned by a secret signal, arrived with sake and some tidbits. When the two men sat down, the distinction between host and guest seemed to evaporate. They relaxed, legs stretched out, and opened their hearts to each other, oblivious of the restraints normally imposed by etiquette. The talk, of course, turned to their favorite subject.

''Everybody pays lip service to the importance of the sword,'' said Kōsuke. ''Anybody'll tell you the sword's the 'soul of the samurai' and that a sword is one of the country's three sacred treasures. But the way people actually treat swords is scandalous. And I include samurai and priests, as well as townsmen. I took it upon myself at one time to go around to shrines and old hous' . where there were once whole collections of beautiful swords, and I can tell you the situation is shocking.''

Kōsuke's pale cheeks were ruddy now. His eyes burned with enthusiasm, and the saliva that gathered at the corners of his mouth occasionally flew in a spray right into his companion's face.

''Almost none of the famous swords from the past are being properly taken care of. At Suwa Shrine in Shinano Province there are more than three hundred swords. They could be classed as heirlooms, but I found only five that weren't rusted. Ōmishima Shrine in Iyo is famous for its collection—three thousand swords dating back many centuries. But after spending a whole month there, I found only ten that were in good condition. It's disgusting!'' Kōsuke caught his breath and continued. ''The problem seems to be that the older and more famous the sword is, the more the owner is inclined to make sure it's stored in a safe place. But then nobody can get at it to take care of it, and the blade gets rustier and rustier.

"The owners are like parents who protect their children so jealously that the children grow up to be fools. In the case of children, more are being born all the time—doesn't make any difference if a few are stupid. But swords . . ."

Pausing to suck in the spit, he raised his thin shoulders even higher and with a gleam in his eyes declared, "We already have all the good swords there'll ever be. During the civil wars, the swordsmiths got careless—no, downright sloppy! They forgot their techniques, and swords have been deteriorating ever since.

"The only thing to do is to take better care of the swords from the earlier periods. The craftsmen today may try to imitate the older swords, but they'll never turn out anything as good. Doesn't it make you angry to think about it?"

Abruptly he stood up and said, "Just look at this." Bringing out a sword of awesome length, he laid it down for his guest to inspect. "It's a splendid weapon, but it's covered with the worst kind of rust."

Musashi's heart skipped a beat. The sword was without doubt Sasaki Kojirō's Drying Pole. A flood of memories came rushing back.

Controlling his emotions, he said calmly, "That's really a long one, isn't it? Must take quite a samurai to handle it."

"I imagine so," agreed Kōsuke. "There aren't many like it." Taking the blade out, he turned the back toward Musashi and handed it to him by the hilt. "See," he said. "It's rusted badly—here and here and here. But he's used it anyway."

"I see."

"This is a rare piece of workmanship, probably forged in the Kamakura period. It'll take a lot of work, but I can probably fix it up. On these ancient swords, the rust is only a relatively thin film. If this were a new blade,

I'd never be able to get the stains off. On new swords, rust spots are like malignant sores; they eat right into the heart of the metal.''

Reversing the sword's position so that the back of the blade was toward Kōsuke, Musashi said, "Tell me, did the owner of this sword bring it in himself?"

"No. I was at Lord Hosokawa's on business, and one of the older retainers, Iwama Kakubei, asked me to drop in at his house on the way back. I did, and he gave it to me to work on. Said it belonged to a guest of his.''

"The fittings are good too," remarked Musashi, his eyes still focused on the weapon.

"It's a battle sword. The man's been carrying it on his back up till now, but he wants to carry it at his side, so I've been asked to refit the scabbard. He must be a very large man. Either that or he has a very practiced arm.''

Kōsuke had begun to feel his sake. His tongue was becoming a little thick. Musashi concluded it was time to take his leave, which he did with a minimum of ceremony.

It was much later than he thought. There were no lights in the neighborhood.

Once inside the inn, he groped through the darkness to the stairway and up to the second floor. Two pallets had been spread, but both were empty. Iori's absence made him uncomfortable, for he suspected the boy was wandering about lost on the streets of this great unfamiliar city.

Going back downstairs, he shook the night watchman awake. "Isn't he back yet?" asked the man, who seemed more surprised than Musashi. "I thought he was with you.''

Knowing he would only stare at the ceiling until Iori came back, Musashi went out into the black-lacquer night again and stood with arms crossed under the eaves.

16

The Fox

"Is this Kobikichō?"

In spite of repeated assurances that it was, Iori still had his doubts. The only lights visible on the broad expanse of land belonged to the makeshift huts of woodworkers and stonemasons, and these were few and far between. Beyond them, in the distance, he could just make out the foaming white waves of the bay.

Near the river were piles of rocks and stacks of lumber, and although Iori knew that buildings were going up at a furious pace all over Edo, it struck him as unlikely that Lord Yagyū would build his residence in an area like this.

"Where to next?" he thought dejectedly as he sat down on some lumber. His feet were tired and burning. To cool them he wiggled his toes in the dewy grass. Soon his tension ebbed away and the sweat dried, but his spirits remained decidedly damp.

"It's all the fault of that old woman at the inn," he muttered to himself. "She didn't know what she was talking about." The time he himself had spent gawking at the sights in the theater district at Sakaichō conveniently slipped his mind.

The hour was late, and there was no one around from whom he could ask directions. Yet the idea of spending the night in these unfamiliar surroundings made him uneasy. He had to complete his errand and return to the inn before daybreak, even if it meant waking up one of the workers.

As he approached the nearest shack where a light showed, he saw a woman with a strip of matting tied over her head like a shawl.

"Good evening, auntie," he said innocently.

Mistaking him for the helper at a nearby sake shop, the woman glared and sniffed, "You, is it? You threw a rock at me and ran away, didn't you, you little brat?"

"Not me," protested Iori. "I've never seen you before!"

The woman came hesitantly toward him, then burst out laughing. "No," she said, "you're not the one. What's a cute little boy like you doing wandering around here at this time of night?"

"I was sent on an errand, but I can't find the house I'm looking for."

"Whose house is it?"

"Lord Yagyū of Tajima's."

"Are you joking?" She laughed. "Lord Yagyū is a diamyō, and a teacher to the shōgun. Do you think he'd open his gate to *you*?" She laughed again. "You know somebody in the servants' quarters perhaps?"

"I've brought a letter."

"Who to?"

"A samurai named Kimura Sukekurō."

"Must be one of his retainers. But you, you're so funny—throwing Lord Yagyū's name around like you knew him."

"I just want to deliver this letter. If you know where the house is, tell me."

"It's on the other side of the moat. If you cross that bridge over there, you'll be in front of Lord Kii's house. The next one is Lord Kyōgoku, then Lord Katō, then Lord Matsudaira of Suō." Holding up her fingers, she

counted off the sturdy storehouses on the opposite bank.
"I'm sure the one after that is the one you want."

"If I cross the moat, will I still be in Kobikichō?"

"Of course."

"Of all the stupid—"

"Here now, that's no way to talk. Hmm, you seem
such a nice boy, I'll come along and show you Lord
Yagyū's place."

Walking in front of him with the matting on her head,
she looked to Iori rather like a ghost.

They were in the middle of the bridge when a man
coming toward them brushed against her sleeve and whis-
tled. He reeked of sake. Before Iori knew what was going
on, the woman turned and made for the drunk. "I know
you," she warbled. "Don't just pass me by like that. It
isn't nice." She grabbed his sleeve and started toward a
place from which they could go below the bridge.

"Let go," he said.

"Wouldn't you like to go with me?"

"No money."

"Oh, I don't care." Latching on to him like a leech, she
looked back at Iori's startled face and said, "Run
along now. I've got business with this gentleman."

Iori watched in bewilderment as the two of them
tugged back and forth. After a few moments, the woman
appeared to get the upper hand, and they disappeared
below the bridge. Still puzzled, Iori went to the railing
and looked over at the grassy riverbank.

Glancing up, the woman shouted, "Nitwit!" and
picked up a rock.

Swallowing hard, Iori dodged the missile and made
for the far end of the bridge. In all his years on the barren
plain of Hōtengahara, he had never seen anything so
frightening as the woman's angry white face in the dark.

On the other side of the river, he found himself
before a storehouse. Next to that was a fence, then
another storehouse, then another fence, and so on down
the street. "This must be it," he said when he came to

the fifth building. On the gleaming white plaster wall was a crest in the form of a two-tiered woman's hat. This, Iori knew from the words of a popular song, was the Yagyū family crest.

"Who's there?" demanded a voice from inside the gate.

Speaking as loudly as he dared, Iori announced, "I'm the pupil of Miyamoto Musashi. I've brought a letter."

The sentry said a few words Iori could not catch. In the gate was a small door, through which people could be let in and out without opening the great gate itself. After a few seconds, the door slowly opened, and the man asked suspiciously, "What are you doing here at this hour?"

Iori thrust the letter at the guard's face. "Please deliver this for me. If there's an answer, I'll take it back."

"Hmm," mused the man, taking the letter. "This is for Kimura Sukekurō, is it?"

"Yes, sir."

"He's not here."

"Where is he?"

"He's at the house in Higakubo."

"Huh? Everybody told me Lord Yagyū's house was in Kobikichō."

"People say that, but there's only storehouses here—rice, lumber and a few other things."

"Lord Yagyū doesn't live here?"

"That's right."

"How far is it to the other place—Higakubo?"

"Pretty far."

"Just where is it?"

"In the hills outside the city, in Azabu Village."

"Never heard of it." Iori sighed disappointedly, but his sense of responsibility prevented him from giving up. "Sir, would you draw me a map?"

"Don't be silly. Even if you knew the way, it'd take you all night to get there."

"I don't mind."

"Lot of foxes in Azabu. You don't want to be bewitched by a fox, do you?"

"No."

"Do you know Sukekurō well?"

"My teacher does."

"I'll tell you what. Since it's so late, why don't you catch some sleep over there in the granary, and go in the morning?"

"Where am I?" exclaimed Iori, rubbing his eyes. He jumped up and ran outside. The afternoon sun made him dizzy. Squinting his eyes against the glare, he went to the gatehouse, where the guard was eating his lunch.

"So you're finally up."

"Yes, sir. Could you draw me that map now?"

"You in a hurry, Sleepyhead? Here, you'd better have something to eat first. There's enough for both of us."

While the boy chewed and gulped, the guard sketched a rough map and explained how to get to Higakubo. They finished simultaneously, and Iori, fired up with the importance of his mission, set off at a run, never thinking that Musashi might be worried about his failure to return to the inn.

He made good time through the busy thoroughfares until he reached the vicinity of Edo Castle, where the imposing houses of the leading daimyō stood on the land built up between the crisscross system of moats. As he looked around, his pace slowed. The waterways were jammed with cargo boats. The stone ramparts of the castle itself were half covered with log scaffolding, which from a distance resembled the bamboo trellises used for growing morning glories.

He dawdled again in a broad, flat area called Hibiya, where the scraping of chisels and the thud of axes raised a dissonant hymn to the power of the new shogunate.

Iori stopped. He was mesmerized by the spectacle of

the construction work: the laborers hauling huge rocks, the carpenters with their planes and saws and the samurai, the dashing samurai, who stood proudly supervising it all. How he wanted to grow up and be like them!

A lusty song rose from the throats of the men hauling rocks:

> "We'll pluck the flowers
> In the fields of Musashi—
> The gentians, the bellflowers,
> Wild blossoms splashed
> In confusing disarray.
> And that lovely girl,
> The flower unpluckable,
> Moistened by the dew—
> 'Twill only dampen your sleeve,
>   like falling tears."

He stood enchanted. Before he realized it, the water in the moats was taking on a reddish cast and the evening voices of crows reached his ears.

"Oh, no, it's nearly sundown," he chastised himself. He sped away and for a time moved along at full speed, paying attention to nothing save the map the guard had drawn for him. Before he knew it, he was climbing the path up Azabu Hill, which was so thickly overhung with trees it might as well have been midnight. Once he reached the top, however, he could see the sun was still in the sky, though low on the horizon.

There were almost no houses on the hill itself, Azabu Village being a mere scattering of fields and farm dwellings in the valley below. Standing in a sea of grass and ancient trees, listening to the brooks gurgling down the hillside, Iori felt his fatigue give way to a strange refreshment. He was vaguely aware that the spot where he was standing was historic, although he didn't know why. In fact it was the very place that had given birth to the great warrior clans of the past, both the Taira and the Minamoto.

He heard the loud booming of a drum being beaten, the kind often used at Shinto festivals. Down the hill, visible in the forest, were the sturdy cross-logs atop the ridgepole of a religious sanctuary. Had Iori but known, it was the Great Shrine of Iigura he'd studied about, the famous edifice sacred to the sun goddess of Ise.

The shrine was a far cry from the enormous castle he had just seen, even from the stately gates of the daimyō. In its simplicity it was almost indistinguishable from the farmhouses around it, and Iori thought it puzzling that people talked more reverently about the Tokugawa family than they did about the most sacred of deities. Did that mean the Tokugawas were greater than the sun goddess? he wondered. "I'll have to ask Musashi about that when I get back."

Taking out his map, he pored over it, looked about him and stared at it again. Still there was no sign of the Yagyū mansion.

The evening mist spreading over the ground gave him an eerie feeling. He'd felt something similar before, when in a room with the shoji shut the setting sun's light played on the rice paper so that the interior seemed to grow lighter as the outside darkened. Of course, such a twilight illusion is just that, but he felt it so strongly, in several flashes, that he rubbed his eyes as if to erase his lightheadedness. He knew he wasn't dreaming and looked around suspiciously.

"Why, you sneaky bastard," he cried, jumping forward and whipping out his sword. In the same motion he cut through a clump of tall grass in front of him.

With a yelp of pain, a fox leapt from its hiding place and streaked off, its tail glistening with blood from a cut on its hindquarters.

"Devilish beast!" Iori set off in hot pursuit, and though the fox was fast, Iori was too. When the limping creature stumbled, Iori lunged, confident of victory. The fox, however, slipped nimbly away, to surge ahead several yards, and no matter how fast Iori attacked, the animal managed to get away each time.

On his mother's knee, Iori had heard countless tales proving beyond a shadow of a doubt that foxes had the power to bewitch and possess human beings. He was fond of most other animals, even wild boar and noisome possums, but foxes he hated. He was also afraid of them. To his way of thinking, coming across this wily creature lurking in the grass could mean only one thing—it was to blame for his not finding his way. He was convinced it was a treacherous and evil being that had been following him since the night before and had, just moments before, cast its malevolent spell over him. If he didn't slay it now, it was sure to hex him again. Iori was prepared to pursue his quarry to the end of the earth, but the fox, bounding over the edge of a drop, was lost to sight in a thicket.

Dew glistened on the flowers of the dog nettle and spiderwort. Exhausted and parched, Iori sank down and licked the moisture from a mint leaf. Shoulders heaving, he finally caught his breath, whereupon sweat poured copiously from his forehead. His heart thumped violently. "Where did it go?" he asked, his voice halfway between a scream and a choke.

If the fox had really gone, so much the better, but Iori didn't know what to believe. Since he had injured the animal, he felt it was certain to take revenge, one way or another. Resigning himself, he sat still and waited.

Just as he was beginning to feel calmer, an eerie sound floated to his ears. Wide-eyed, he looked around. "It's the fox, for sure," he said, steeling himself against being bewitched. Rising quickly, he moistened his eyebrows with saliva—a trick thought to ward off the influence of foxes.

A short distance away, a woman came floating through the evening mist, her face half hidden by a veil of silk gauze. She was riding a horse sidesaddle, the reins lying loosely across the low pommel. The saddle was made of lacquered wood with mother-of-pearl inlay.

"It's changed into a woman," thought Iori. This vision in a veil, playing a flute and silhouetted against the thin rays of the evening sun, could by no stretch of the imagination be a creature of this world.

As he squatted in the grass like a frog, Iori heard an otherworldly voice call, "Otsū!" and was sure it had come from one of the fox's companions.

The rider had nearly reached a turnoff, where a road diverged to the south, and the upper part of her body glowed reddish. The sun, sinking behind the hills of Shibuya, was fringed by clouds.

If he killed her, he could expose her true fox form. Iori tightened his grip on the sword and braced himself, thinking: "Lucky it doesn't know I'm hiding here." Like all those acquainted with the truth about foxes, he knew the animal's spirit would be situated a few feet behind its human form. He swallowed hard in anticipation, while waiting for the vision to proceed and make the turn to the south.

But when the horse reached the turnoff, the woman stopped playing, put her flute in a cloth wrapper and tucked it into her obi. Lifting her veil, she peered about with searching eyes.

"Otsū!" the voice called again.

A pleasant smile came to her face as she called back, "Here I am, Hyōgo. Up here."

Iori watched as a samurai came up the road from the valley. "Oh, oh!" he gasped when he noticed that the man walked with a slight limp. *This* was the fox he had wounded; no doubt about it! Disguised not as a beautiful temptress but as a handsome samurai. The apparition terrified Iori. He shivered violently and wet himself.

After the woman and the samurai had exchanged a few words, the samurai took hold of the horse's bit and led it right past the place where Iori was hiding.

"Now's the time," he decided, but his body would not respond.

The samurai noticed a slight motion and looked around, his gaze falling squarely on Iori's petrified face. The light from the samurai's eyes seemed more brilliant than the edge of the setting sun. Iori prostrated himself and buried his face in the grass. Never in his entire fourteen years had he experienced such terror.

Hyōgo, seeing nothing alarming about the boy, walked on. The slope was steep, and he had to lean back to keep the horse in check. Looking over his shoulder at Otsū, he asked gently, "Why are you so late? You've been gone a long time just to have ridden to the shrine and back. My uncle got worried and sent me to look for you."

Without answering, Otsū jumped down from the horse.

Hyōgo stopped. "Why are you getting off? Something wrong?"

"No, but it's not fitting for a woman to ride when a man's walking. Let's walk together. We can both hold the bit." She took her place on the other side of the horse.

They descended into the darkening valley and passed a sign reading: "Sendan'en Academy for Priests of the Sōdō Zen Sect." The sky was filling with stars, and the Shibuya River could be heard in the distance. The river divided the valley into North Higakubo and South Higakubo. Since the school, established by the monk Rintatsu, lay on the north slope, the priests were casually referred to as the "fellows of the north." The "fellows of the south" were the men studying swordsmanship under Yagyū Munenori, whose establishment was directly across the valley.

As Yagyū Sekishūsai's favorite among his sons and grandsons, Yagyū Hyōgo enjoyed a special status among the "fellows of the south." He had also distinguished himself in his own right. At the age of twenty, he had been summoned by the famous general Katō Kiyomasa and given a position at Kumamoto Castle in Higo Province at a stipend of fifteen thousand bushels. This was unheard of for a man so young, but after the Battle of Sekigahara, Hyōgo began to have second thoughts about his status, because of the danger inherent in having to side with either the Tokugawas or the Osaka faction. Three years earlier, using his grandfather's illness as a pretext, he had taken a leave of absence from Kumamoto and returned to Yamato. After that, saying he needed more training, he had traveled about the countryside for a time.

He and Otsū had been thrown together by chance the previous year, when he had come to stay with his uncle. For more than three years prior to that, Otsū had led a precarious existence, never quite able to escape from Matahachi, who had dragged her along everywhere, glibly telling prospective employers that she was his wife. He had been willing to work as an apprentice to a carpenter or a plasterer or a stonemason, he could have found employment on the day they arrived in Edo, but he preferred to imagine they could work together at softer jobs, she as a domestic servant perhaps, he as a clerk or accountant.

Finding no takers for his services, they had managed to survive by doing odd jobs. And as the months passed, Otsū, hoping to lull her tormentor into complacency, had given in to him in every way short of surrendering her body.

Then one day they had been walking along the street when they encountered a diamyō's procession. Along with everyone else, they moved to the side of the road and assumed a properly respectful attitude.

The palanquins and lacquered strongboxes bore the Yagyū crest. Otsū had raised her eyes enough to see this, and memories of Sekishūsai and the happy days at Ko-yagyū Castle flooded her heart. If only she were back in that peaceful land of Yamato now! With Matahachi at her

side, she could only stare blankly after the passing retinue.

"Otsū, isn't that you?" The conical sedge hat came
low over the samurai's face, but as he drew closer, Otsū
had seen that it was Kimura Sukekurō, a man she remembered with affection and respect. She couldn't have been
more amazed or thankful if he had been the Buddha
himself, surrounded by the wondrous light of infinite
compassion. Slipping away from Matahachi's side, she
had hurried to Sukekurō, who promptly offered to take
her home with him.

When Matahachi had opened his mouth to protest,
Sukekurō said peremptorily, "If you have anything to
say, come to Higakubo and say it there."

Powerless before the prestigious House of Yagyū,
Matahachi held his tongue, biting his lower lip in angry
frustration as he sullenly watched his precious treasure
escape from him.

17

An Urgent Letter

At thirty-eight, Yagyū Munenori was regarded as the best swordsman of them all. This hadn't kept his father from constantly worrying about his fifth son. "If only he can control that little quirk of his," he often said to himself. Or: "Can anybody that self-willed manage to keep a high position?"

It was now fourteen years since Tokugawa Ieyasu had commanded Sekishūsai to provide a tutor for Hidetada. Sekishūsai had passed over his other sons, grandsons and nephews. Munenori was neither particularly brilliant nor heroically masculine, but he was a man of good, solid judgment, a practical man not likely to get lost in the clouds. He possessed neither his father's towering stature nor Hyōgo's genius, but he was reliable, and most important, he understood the cardinal principle of the Yagyū Style, namely that the true value of the Art of War lay in its application to government.

Sekishūsai had not misinterpreted Ieyasu's wishes; the conquering general had no use for a swordsman to teach his heir only technical skills. Some years before Sekigahara, Ieyasu himself had studied under a master swordsman named Okuyama, his objective being, as he himself frequently expressed it, "to acquire the eye needed to oversee the country."

Still, Hidetada was now shōgun, and it would not do for the shōgun's instructor to be a man who lost in actual combat. A samurai in Munenori's position was expected to excel over all challengers and to demonstrate that Yagyū swordsmanship was second to none. Munenori felt he was constantly being scrutinized and tested, and while others might regard him as lucky to have been singled out for this distinguished appointment, he himself often envied Hyōgo and wished he could live the way his nephew did.

Hyōgo, as it happened, was now walking down the outside passageway leading to his uncle's room. The house, though large and sprawling, was neither stately in appearance nor lavish in its appointments. Instead of employing carpenters from Kyoto to create an elegant, graceful dwelling, Munenori had deliberately entrusted the work to local builders, men accustomed to the sturdy, spartan warrior style of Kamakura. Though the trees were relatively sparse, and the hills of no great height, Munenori had chosen the solid rustic style of architecture exemplified by the old Main House at Koyagyū.

"Uncle," called Hyōgo softly and politely, as he knelt on the veranda outside Munenori's room.

"Is that you, Hyōgo?" asked Munenori without removing his eyes from the garden.

"May I come in?"

Having received permission to enter, Hyōgo made his way into the room on his knees. He had taken quite a few liberties with his grandfather, who was inclined to spoil him, but he knew better than to do that with his uncle. Munenori, though no martinet, was a stickler for etiquette. Now, as always, he was seated in strict formal fashion. At times Hyōgo felt sorry for him.

"Otsū?" asked Munenori, as though reminded of her by Hyōgo's arrival.

"She's back. She'd only gone to Hikawa Shrine, the way she often does. On the way back, she let her horse wander around for a while."

"You went looking for her?"

"Yes, sir."

Munenori remained silent for a few moments. The lamplight accented his tight-lipped profile. "It worries me to have a young woman living here indefinitely. You never know what might happen. I've told Sukekurō to look for an opportunity to suggest she go elsewhere."

His tone slightly plaintive, Hyōgo said, "I'm told she has no place to go." His uncle's change of attitude surprised him, for when Sukekurō had brought Otsū home and introduced her as a woman who had served Sekishūsai well, Munenori had welcomed her cordially and said she was free to stay as long as she wished. "Don't you feel sorry for her?" he asked.

"Yes, but there's a limit to what you can do for people."

"I thought you yourself thought well of her."

"It has nothing to do with that. When a young woman comes to live in a house full of young men, tongues are apt to wag. And it's difficult for the men. One of them might do something rash."

This time Hyōgo was silent, but not because he took his uncle's remarks personally. He was thirty and, like the other young samurai, single, but he firmly believed his own feelings toward Otsū were too pure to raise doubts about his intentions. He had been careful to allay his uncle's misgivings by making no secret of his fondness for her, while at the same time not once letting on that his feelings went beyond friendship.

Hyōgo felt that the problem might lie with his uncle. Munenori's wife came from a highly respected and well-placed family, of the sort whose daughters were delivered to their husbands on their wedding day in curtained palanquins lest they be seen by outsiders. Her chambers, together with those of the other women, were well removed from the more public parts of the house, so virtually no one knew whether relations between the master and his wife were harmonious. It was not difficult to imagine that the lady of the house might take a dim view of beautiful and eligible young women in such proximity to her husband.

Hyōgo broke the silence, saying, "Leave the matter to Sukekurō and me. We'll work out some solution that won't be too hard on Otsū."

Munenori nodded, saying, "The sooner the better."

Sukekurō entered the anteroom just then, and placing a letter box on the tatami, knelt and bowed. "Your lordship," he said respectfully.

Turning his eyes toward the anteroom, Munenori asked, "What is it?"

Sukekurō moved forward on his knees.

"A courier from Koyagyū has just arrived by fast horse."

"Fast horse?" said Munenori quickly, but without surprise.

Hyōgo accepted the box from Sukekurō and handed it to his uncle. Munenori opened the letter, which was from Shōda Kizaemon. Written in haste, it said: "The Old Lord has had another spell, worse than any previous. We fear he may not last long. He stoutly insists his illness is not sufficient reason for you to leave your duties. However, after discussing the matter among ourselves, we retainers decided to write and inform you of the situation."

"His condition is critical," said Munenori.

Hyōgo admired his uncle's ability to remain calm. He surmised that Munenori knew exactly what was to be done and had already made the necessary decisions.

After some minutes of silence, Munenori said, "Hyōgo, will you go to Koyagyū in my stead?"

"Of course, sir."

"I want you to assure my father there's nothing to worry about in Edo. And I want you to look after him personally."

"Yes, sir."

"I suppose it's all in the hands of the gods and the

Buddha now. All you can do is hurry and try to get there before it's too late."

"I'll leave tonight."

From Lord Munenori's room, Hyōgo went immediately to his own. During the short time it took him to lay out the few things he would need, the bad news spread to every corner of the house.

Otsū quietly went to Hyōgo's room, dressed, to his surprise, for traveling. Her eyes were moist. "Please take me with you," she pleaded. "I can never hope to repay Lord Sekishūsai for taking me into his home, but I'd like to be with him and see if I can be of some assistance. I hope you won't refuse."

Hyōgo considered it possible that his uncle might have refused her, but he himself did not have the heart to. Perhaps it was a blessing that this opportunity to take her away from the house in Edo had presented itself.

"All right," he agreed, "but it'll have to be a fast journey."

"I promise I won't slow you down." Drying her tears, she helped him finish packing and then went to pay her respects to Lord Munenori.

"Oh, are you going to accompany Hyōgo?" he said, mildly surprised. "That's very kind of you. I'm sure my father will be pleased to see you." He made a point of giving her ample travel money and a new kimono as a going-away present. Despite his conviction that it was for the best, her departure saddened him.

She bowed herself out of his presence. "Take good care of yourself," he said with feeling, as she reached the anteroom.

The vassals and servants lined up along the path to the gate to see them off, and with a simple "Farewell" from Hyōgo, they were on their way.

Otsū had folded her kimono up under her obi, so the hem reached only five or six inches below her knees. On her head was a broad-brimmed lacquered traveling hat and in her right hand she carried a stick. Had her shoulders been draped with blossoms, she would have been the image of the Wisteria Girl so often seen in woodblock prints.

Since Hyōgo had decided to hire conveyances at the stations along the highroad, their goal tonight was the inn town of Sangen'ya, south of Shibuya. From there, his plan was to proceed along the Ōyama highroad to the Tama River, take the ferry across, and follow the Tōkaidō to Kyoto.

In the night mist, it was not long before Otsū's lacquered hat glistened with moisture. After walking through a grassy river valley, they came to a rather wide road, which since the Kamakura period had been one of the most important in the Kantō district. At night it was lonely and deserted, with trees growing thickly on both sides.

"Gloomy, isn't it?" said Hyōgo with a smile, again slowing down his naturally long strides to let Otsū catch up with him. "This is Dōgen Slope. There used to be bandits around here," he added.

"Bandits?" There was just enough alarm in her voice to make him laugh.

"That was a long time ago, though. A man by the name of Dōgen Tarō, who was related to the rebel Wada Yoshimori, is supposed to have been the head of a band of thieves who lived in the caves around here."

"Let's not talk about things like that."

Hyōgo's laughter echoed through the dark, and hearing it made him feel guilty for acting frivolous. He couldn't help himself, however. Though sad, he looked forward with pleasure to being with Otsū these next few days.

"Oh!" cried Otsū, taking a couple of steps backward.

"What's the matter?" Instinctively, Hyōgo's arm went around her shoulders.

"There's somebody over there."

"Where?"

"It's a child, sitting there by the side of the road, talking to himself and crying. The poor thing!"

When Hyōgo got close enough, he recognized the boy he had seen earlier that evening, hiding in the grass in Azabu.

Iori leaped to his feet with a gasp. An instant later, he uttered an oath and pointed his sword at Hyōgo. "Fox!" he cried. "That's what you are, a fox!"

Otsū caught her breath and stifled a scream. The look on Iori's face was wild, almost demonic, as if he were possessed by an evil spirit. Even Hyōgo drew back cautiously.

"Foxes!" Iori shouted again. "I'll take care of you!" His voice cracked hoarsely, like an old woman's. Hyōgo stared at him in puzzlement but was careful to steer clear of his blade.

"How's this?" shouted Iori, whacking off the top of a tall shrub not far from Hyōgo's side. Then he sank to the ground, exhausted by his effort. Breathing hard, he asked, "What did you think of that, fox?"

Turning to Otsū, Hyōgo said with a grin, "Poor little fellow. He seems to be possessed by a fox."

"Maybe you're right. His eyes are ferocious."

"Just like a fox's."

"Isn't there something we can do to help him?"

"Well, they say there's no cure for either madness or stupidity, but I suspect there's a remedy for his ailment." He walked up to Iori and glared sternly at him.

Glancing up, the boy hastily gripped his sword again. "Still here, are you?" he cried. But before he could get to his feet, his ears were assailed by a fierce roar coming from the pit of Hyōgo's stomach.

"Y-a-a-w-r!"

Iori was scared witless. Hyōgo picked him up by the waist, and holding him horizontally, strode back down the hill to the bridge. He turned the boy upside down, grasped him by the ankles and held him out over the railing.

"Help! Mother! Help, help! *Sensei*! Save me!" The screams gradually changed to a wail.

Otsū hastened to the rescue. "Stop that, Hyōgo. Let him go. You shouldn't be so cruel."

"I guess that's enough," said Hyōgo, setting the boy down gently on the bridge.

Iori was in a terrible state, bawling and choking, convinced there was not a soul on earth who could help him. Otsū went to his side and put her arm affectionately around his drooping shoulders. "Where do you live, child?" she asked softly.

Between sobs, Iori stammered, "O-over th-th-that way," and pointed.

"What do you mean, 'that way'?"

"Ba-ba-bakurōchō."

"Why, that's miles away. How did you get all the way out here?"

"I came on an errand. I got lost."

"When was that?"

"I left Bakurōchō yesterday."

"And you've been wandering around all night and all day?" Iori half shook his head, but didn't say anything. "Why, that's terrible. Tell me, where were you supposed to go?"

A little calmer now, he replied promptly, as though he'd been waiting for the question. "To the residence of Lord Yagyū Munenori of Tajima." After feeling around under his obi, he clutched the crumpled letter and waved it proudly in front of his face. Bringing it close to his eyes, he said, "It's for Kimura Sukekurō. I'm to deliver it and wait for an answer."

Otsū saw that Iori took his mission very seriously and was ready to guard the missive with his life. Iori, for his part, was determined to show the letter to no one before he reached his destination. Neither had any inkling of the irony of the situation—a missed chance, a happening rarer than the coming together across the River of Heaven of the Herdboy and the Spinning Maiden.

Turning to Hyōgo, Otsū said, "He seems to have a letter for Sukekurō."

"He's wandered off in the wrong direction, hasn't he? Fortunately, it's not very far." Calling Iori to him, he gave him directions. "Go along this river to the first crossroads, then go left and up the hill. When you get to a place where three roads come together, you'll see a pair of large pine trees off to the right. The house is to the left, across the road."

"And watch out you don't get possessed by a fox again," added Otsū.

Iori had regained his confidence. "Thanks," he called back, already running along the river. When he reached the crossroads, he half turned and shouted, "To the left here?"

"That's it," answered Hyōgo. "The road's dark, so be careful." He and Otsū stood watching from the bridge for a minute or two. "What a strange child," he said.

"Yes, but he seems rather bright." In her mind she was comparing him with Jōtarō, who had been only a little bigger than Iori when she had last seen him. Jōtarō, she reflected, must be seventeen now. She wondered what he was like and felt an inevitable pang of yearning for Musashi. So many years since she'd had any word of him! Though now accustomed to living with the suffering that love entails, she dared hope that leaving Edo might bring her closer to him, that she might even meet him somewhere along the road.

"Let's get on," Hyōgo said brusquely, to himself as much as to Otsū. "There's nothing to be done about tonight, but we'll have to be careful not to waste any more time."

18

Filial Piety

"What're you doing, Granny, practicing your handwriting?" Jūrō the Reed Mat's expression was ambiguous; it might have been admiration, or simply shock.

"Oh, it's you," said Osugi with a trace of annoyance.

Sitting down beside her, Jūrō mumbled, "Copying a Buddhist sutra, are you?" This elicited no reply. "Aren't you old enough so you don't have to practice your writing anymore? Or are you thinking of becoming a calligraphy teacher in the next world?"

"Be quiet. To copy the holy scriptures, one has to achieve a state of selflessness. Solitude is best for that. Why don't you go away?"

"After I hurried home just to tell you what happened to me today?"

"It can wait."

"When will you be finished?"

"I have to put the spirit of the Buddha's enlightenment into each character I write. It takes me three days to make one copy."

"You've got a lot of patience."

"Three days is nothing. This summer I'm going to make dozens of copies. I've made a vow to make a thousand before I die. I'll leave them to people who don't have a proper love for their parents.''

"A thousand copies? That's a lot.''

"It's my sacred vow.''

"Well, I'm not very proud of it, but I guess I've been disrespectful to my parents, like the rest of these louts around here. They forgot about them a long time ago. The only one who cares for his mother and father is the boss.''

"It's a sad world we live in.''

"Ha, ha. If it upsets you that much, you must have a good-for-nothing son too.''

"I'm sorry to say, mine has caused me a lot of grief. That's why I took the vow. This is the *Sutra on the Great Love of Parents*. Everyone who doesn't treat his mother or father right should be forced to read it.''

"You're really giving a copy of whatever-you-call-it to a thousand people?''

"They say that by planting one seed of enlightenment you can convert a hundred people, and if one sprout of enlightenment grows in a hundred hearts, ten million souls can be saved.'' Laying down her brush, she took a finished copy and handed it to Jūrō. "Here, you can have this. See that you read it when you have time.''

She looked so pious Jūrō nearly burst out laughing, but he managed to contain himself. Overcoming his urge to stuff it into his kimono like so much tissue paper, he lifted it respectfully to his forehead and placed it on his lap.

"Say, Granny, you sure you wouldn't like to know what happened today? Maybe your faith in the Buddha gets results. I ran into somebody pretty special.''

"Who might that be?''

"Miyamoto Musashi. I saw him down at the Sumida River, getting off the ferry.''

"You saw Musashi? Why didn't you say so!'' She pushed the writing table away with a grunt. "Are you sure? Where is he now?''

"There, now, take it easy. Your old Jūrō doesn't do things halfway. After I found out who he was, I followed him without him knowing it. He went to an inn in Baku-rōchō."

"He's staying near here?"

"Well, it's not all that close."

"It may not seem that way to you, but it does to me. I've been all over the country looking for him." Springing to her feet, she went to her clothes cabinet and took out the short sword that had been in her family for generations.

"Take me there," she ordered.

"Now?"

"Of course now."

"I thought you had a lot of patience, but . . . Why do you have to go now?"

"I'm always ready to meet Musashi, even on a moment's notice. If I get killed, you can send my body back to my family in Mimasaka."

"Couldn't you wait until the boss comes home? If we go off like this, all I'll get for finding Musashi is a bawling out."

"But there's no telling when Musashi might go some-where else."

"Don't worry about that. I sent a man to keep an eye on the place."

"Can you guarantee Musashi won't get away?"

"What? I do you a favor, and you want to tie me up with obligations! Oh, all right. I guarantee it. Absolutely. Look, Granny, now's the time when you should be taking it easy, sitting down copying sutras or something like that."

"Where is Yajibei?"

"He's on a trip to Chichibu with his religious group. I don't know exactly when he'll be back."

"I can't afford to wait."

"If that's the way it is, why don't we get Sasaki Kojirō to come over? You can talk to him about it."

* * *

The next morning, after contacting his spy, Jūrō informed Osugi that Musashi had moved from the inn to the house of a sword polisher.

"See? I told you," declared Osugi. "You can't expect him to sit still in one place forever. The next thing you know, he'll be gone again." She was seated at her writing table but hadn't written a word all morning.

"Musashi hasn't got wings," Jūrō assured her. "Just be calm. Koroku's going to see Kojirō today."

"Today? Didn't you send somebody last night? Tell me where he lives. I'll go myself."

She started getting ready to go out, but Jūrō suddenly disappeared and she had to ask a couple of the other henchmen for directions. Having seldom left the house during her more than two years in Edo, she was quite unfamiliar with the city.

"Kojirō's living with Iwama Kakubei," she was told.

"Kakubei's a vassal of the Hosokawas, but his own house is on the Takanawa highroad."

"It's about halfway up Isarago Hill. Anybody can tell you where that is."

"If you have any difficulty, ask for Tsukinomisaki. That's another name for Isarago Hill."

"The house is easy to recognize, because the gate is painted bright red. It's the only place around there with a red gate."

"All right, I understand," said Osugi impatiently, resenting the implication that she was senile, or stupid. "It doesn't sound difficult, so I'll just be on my way. Take care of things while I'm out. Be careful about fire. We don't want the place to burn down while Yajibei's away." Having put on her zōri, she checked to make sure her short sword was at her side, took a firm grip on her staff and marched off.

A few minutes later, Jūrō reappeared and asked where she was.

197

"She asked us how to get to Kakubei's house and went out by herself."

"Oh, well, what can you do with a pigheaded old woman?" Then he shouted in the direction of the men's quarters, "Koroku!"

The Acolyte abandoned his gambling and answered the summons posthaste.

"You were going to see Kojirō last night, then you put it off. Now look what's happened. The old woman's gone by herself."

"So?"

"When the boss gets back, she'll blab to him."

"You're right. And with that tongue of hers, she'll make us look real bad."

"Yeah. If she could only walk as well as she talks, but she's thin as a grasshopper. If she gets run into by a horse, that'll be the end of her. I hate to ask you, but you better go after her and see she gets there in one piece."

Koroku ran off, and Jūrō, ruminating on the absurdity of it all, appropriated a corner of the young men's room. It was a big room, perhaps thirty by forty feet. The floor was covered with thin, finely woven matting, and a wide variety of swords and other weapons were lying about. Hanging from nails were hand towels, kimono, underwear, fire hats and other items of the sort a band of ne'er-do-wells might require. There were two incongruous articles. One was a woman's kimono, in bright colors with a red silk lining; the other was the gold-lacquered mirror stand over which it was suspended. They had been placed there on the instructions of Kojirō, who explained to Yajibei, somewhat mysteriously, that if a group of men lived together in one room with no feminine touch, they were apt to get out of hand and fight each other, rather than save their energies for meaningful battles.

"You're cheating, you son of a bitch!"

"Who's cheating? You're nuts."

Jūrō cast a disdainful look at the gamblers and lay down with his legs crossed comfortably. With all the rumpus going on, sleep was out of the question, but he wasn't going to demean himself by joining one of the card or dice games. No competition, as he saw it.

As he closed his eyes, he heard a dejected voice say, "It's no good today—no luck at all." The loser, with the sad eyes of the utterly defeated, dropped a pillow on the floor and stretched out beside Jūrō. They were joined by another, then another and another.

"What's this?" asked one of them, reaching out for the sheet of paper that had fallen from Jūrō's kimono. "Well, I'll be—it's a sutra. Now, what would a mean cuss like you be carrying a sutra for?"

"Jūrō opened one sleepy eye and said lazily, "Oh, that? It's something the old woman copied. She said she'd sworn to make a thousand of them."

"Let me see it," said another man, making a grab for it. "What do you know? It's written out nice and clear. Why, anybody could read it."

"Does that mean you think *you* can read it?"

"Of course. It's child's play."

"All right then, let's hear some of it. Put a nice tune to it. Chant it like a priest."

"Are you joking? It's not a popular song."

"What difference does that make? A long time ago they used to sing sutras. That's how Buddhist hymns got started. You know a hymn when you hear one, don't you?"

"You can't chant these words to the tune of a hymn."

"Well, use any tune you like."

"You sing, Jūrō."

Encouraged by the enthusiasm of the others, Jūrō, still lying on his back, opened the sutra above his face and began:

"The Sutra on the Great Love of Parents.

> Thus have I heard.
> Once when the Buddha was on the Sacred
>   Vulture Peak
> In the City of Royal Palaces,
> Preaching to bodhisattvas and disciples,
> There gathered a multitude of monks and nuns
>   and lay believers, both male and female,
> All the people of all the heavens, dragon gods
>   and demons,
> To hear the Sacred Law.
> Around the jeweled throne they gathered
> And gazed, with unwavering eyes,
> At the holy face—"

"What's all that mean?"

"When it says 'nuns,' does it mean the girls we call nuns? You know, I heard some of the nuns from Yoshiwara have started powdering their faces gray and will give it to you for less than in the whorehouses—"

"Quiet!"

> "At this time the Buddha
> Preached the Law as follows:
> 'All ye good men and good women,
> Acknowledge your debt for your father's
>   compassion
> Acknowledge your debt for your mother's mercy.
> For the life of a human being in this world
> Has karma as its basic cause,
> But parents as its immediate means of origin.' "

"It's just talking about being good to your mama and daddy. You've already heard it a million times."

"Shh!"

"Sing some more. We'll be quiet."

" 'Without a father, the child is not born.
　　Without a mother, the child is not nourished.
　　The spirit comes from the father's seed;
　　The body grows within the mother's womb.' "

Jūrō paused to rearrange himself and pick his nose, then resumed.

" 'Because of these relationships,
　　The concern of a mother for her child
　　Is without comparison in this world. . . .' "

Noticing how silent the others were, Jūrō asked, "Are you listening?"
"Yes. Go on."

" 'From the time when she receives the child in
　　　her womb,
　　During the passage of nine months,
　　Going, coming, sitting, sleeping,
　　She is visited by suffering.
　　She ceases to have her customary love for
　　　food or drink or clothing
　　And worries solely about a safe delivery.' "

"I'm tired," complained Jūrō. "That's enough, isn't it?"
"No. Keep singing. We're listening."

" 'The months are full, and the days sufficient.
　　At the time of birth, the winds of karma
　　　hasten it on,
　　Her bones are racked with pain.
　　The father, too, trembles and is afraid.
　　Relatives and servants worry and are
　　　distressed.

When the child is born and dropped upon
    the grass,
The boundless joy of the father and mother
Match that of a penurious woman
Who has found the omnipotent magic jewel.
When the child utters its first sounds,
The mother feels that she herself is born
    anew.
Her chest becomes the child's place of rest;
Her knees, its playground,
Her breasts, its source of food.
Her love, its very life.
Without its mother, the child cannot dress or
    undress.
Though the mother hungers,
She takes the food from her own mouth and
    gives it to her child.
Without the mother, the child cannot be
    nourished . . .' "

"What's the matter? Why'd you stop?"
"Wait a minute, will you?"
"Will you look at that? He's crying like a baby."
"Aw, shut up!"
It had all begun as an idle way to pass the time,
almost a joke, but the meaning of the words of the sutra
was sinking in. Three or four others besides the reader
had unsmiling faces, their eyes a faraway look.

" 'The mother goes to the neighboring village
    to work.
She draws water, builds the fire,
Pounds the grain, makes the flour.
At night when she returns,
Before she reaches the house,
She hears the baby's crying
And is filled with love.

Her chest heaves, her heart cries out,
The milk flows forth, she cannot bear it.
She runs to the house.
The baby, seeing its mother approach from
    afar,
Works its brain, shakes its head,
And wails for her.
She bends her body,
Takes the child's two hands,
Places her lips upon its lips.
There is no greater love than this.
When the child is two,
He leaves the mother's breast.
But without his father, he would not know
    that fire can burn.
Without his mother, he would not know that
    a knife can cut off fingers.
When he is three, he is weaned and learns to
    eat.
Without his father, he would not know that
    poison can kill.
Without his mother, he would not know that
    medicine cures.
When the parents go to other houses
And are presented with marvelous
    delicacies,
They do not eat but put the food in their
    pockets
And take it home for the child, to make him
    rejoice. . . .' "

"You blubbering again?"
"I can't help it. I just remembered something."
"Cut it out. You'll have me doing it too."
Sentimentality with regard to parents was strictly
taboo among these denizens of society's outer edge, for

to express filial affection was to invite charges of weakness, effeminacy or worse. But it would have done Osugi's aging heart good to see them now. The sutra reading, possibly because of the simplicity of the language, had reached the core of their being.

"Is that all? Isn't there any more?"

"There's lots more."

"Well?"

"Wait a minute, will you?" Jūrō stood up, blew his nose loudly and sat down to intone the rest.

" 'The child grows.
   The father brings cloth to clothe him.
   The mother combs his locks.
   The parents give every beautiful thing they
      possess to him,
   Keeping for themselves only that which is
      old and worn.
   The child takes a bride
   And brings this stranger into the house.
   The parents become more distant.
   The new husband and wife are intimate with
      each other.
   They stay in their own room, talking happily
      with each other.' "

"That's the way it works, all right," broke in a voice.

" 'The parents grow old.
   Their spirits weaken, their strength diminishes.
   They have only the child to depend on,
   Only his wife to do things for them.
   But the child no longer comes to them,
   Neither at night nor in the daytime.
   Their room is cold.
   There is no more pleasant talk.
   They are like lonely guests at an inn.

A crisis arises, and they call their child.
Nine times in ten, he comes not,
Nor does he serve them.
He grows angry and reviles them,
Saying it would be better to die
Than to linger on unwanted in this world.
The parents listen, and their hearts are filled
    with rage.
Weeping, they say, "When you were young,
Without us, you would not have been born,
Without us, you could not have grown.
Ah! How we—" ' "

Juro broke off abruptly and threw the text aside. "I
. . . I can't. Somebody else read it."

But there was no one to take his place. Lying on
their backs, sprawled out on their bellies, sitting with
their legs crossed and their heads drooping between their
knees, they were as tearful as lost children.

Into the middle of this unlikely scene walked Sasaki
Kojirō.

19

Spring Shower in Red

"Isn't Yajibei here?" Kojirō asked loudly.

The gamblers were so absorbed in their play, and the weepers in their memories of childhood, that no one replied.

Going over to Jūrō, who was lying on his back with his arms over his eyes, Kojirō said, "May I ask what's going on?"

"Oh, I didn't know it was you, sir." There was a hasty wiping of eyes and blowing of noses as Jūrō and the others pulled themselves to their feet and bowed sheepishly to their sword instructor.

"Are you crying?" he asked.

"Unh, yes. I mean, no."

"You're an odd one."

While the others drifted off, Jūrō began telling about his chance encounter with Musashi, happy to have a subject that might distract Kojirō's attention from the state of the young men's room. "Since the boss is away," he said, "we didn't know what to do, so Osugi decided to go and talk to you."

Kojirō's eyes flared brightly. "Musashi's putting up at an inn in Bakurōchō?"

"He was, but now he's staying at Zushino Kōsuke's house."

"That's an interesting coincidence."

"Is it?"

"It just happens I sent my Drying Pole to Zushino to work on. As a matter of fact, it should be ready now. I came this way today to pick it up."

"You've been there already?"

"Not yet. I thought I'd drop in here for a few minutes first."

"That's lucky. If you'd showed up suddenly, Musashi might have attacked you."

"I'm not afraid of him. But how can I confer with the old lady when she's not here?"

"I don't imagine she's reached Isarago yet. I'll send a good runner to bring her back."

At the council of war held that evening, Kojirō expressed the opinion that there was no reason to wait for Yajibei's return. He himself would serve as Osugi's second, so that she might, at long last, take her proper revenge. Jūrō and Koroku asked to go along too, more for the honor than to help. Though aware of Musashi's reputation as a fighter, they never imagined he might be a match for their brilliant instructor.

Nothing could be done tonight, however. For all her enthusiasm, Osugi was dead tired and complained of a backache. They decided they would carry out their plan the following night.

The next afternoon, Osugi bathed under cold water, blackened her teeth and dyed her hair. At twilight, she made her preparations for battle, first donning a white underrobe she had bought to be buried in and had carried around with her for years. She had had it stamped for good luck at every shrine and temple she visited—Sumiyoshi Shrine in Osaka, Oyama Hachiman Shrine and Kiyomizudera in Kyoto, the Kannon Temple in Asakusa, and dozens of less prominent religious establishments in various parts of the country. The sacred imprints made the robe resemble a tie-dyed kimono; Osugi felt safer than she would have in a suit of mail.

She carefully tucked a letter to Matahachi into the sash under her obi, together with a copy of the *Sutra on the Great Love of Parents*. There was also a second letter, which she always carried in a small money pouch; this said: "Though I am old, it has become my lot to wander about the country in an effort to realize one great hope. There is no way of knowing but that I may be slain by my sworn enemy or die of illness by the wayside. Should this be my fate, I ask the officials and people of goodwill to use the money in this purse to send my body home. Sugi, widow of Hon'iden, Yoshino Village, Mimasaka Province."

With her sword in place, her shins wrapped in white leggings, fingerless gloves on her hands and a blind-stitched obi snugly holding her sleeveless kimono in place, her preparations were nearly complete. Placing a bowl of water on her writing table, she knelt before it and said, "I'm going now." She then closed her eyes and sat motionless, addressing her thoughts to Uncle Gon.

Jūrō opened the shoji a crack and peeked in. "Are you ready?" he asked. "It's about time we were leaving. Kojirō's waiting."

"I'm ready."

Joining the others, she went to the place of honor they had left open for her before the alcove. The Acolyte took a cup from the table, put it in Osugi's hand and carefully poured her a cupful of sake. Then he did the same for Kojirō and Jūrō. When each of the four had drunk, they extinguished the lamp and set forth.

Quite a few of the Hangawara men clamored to be taken along, but Kojirō refused, since a large group would not only attract attention but encumber them in a fight.

As they were going out the gate, one young man called to them to wait. He then struck sparks from a flint to wish them luck. Outside, under a sky murky with rain clouds, nightingales were singing.

As they made their way through the dark, silent streets, dogs started barking, set off, perhaps, by some instinctive sense that these four human beings were on a sinister mission.

"What's that?" Koroku asked, staring back along a narrow lane.

"Did you see something?"

"Somebody's following us."

"Probably one of the fellows from the house," said Kojirō. "They were all so eager to come with us."

"They'd rather brawl than eat."

They turned a corner, and Kojirō stopped under the eaves of a house, saying, "Kōsuke's shop's around here, isn't it?" Their voices dropped to whispers.

"Down the street, there, on the other side."

"What do we do now?" asked Koroku.

"Proceed according to plan. The three of you hide in the shadows. I'll go to the shop."

"What if Musashi tries to sneak out the back door?"

"Don't worry. He's no more likely to run away from me than I am from him. If he ran away, he'd be finished as a swordsman."

"Maybe we should position ourselves on opposite sides of the house anyway—just in case."

"All right. Now, as we agreed, I'll bring Musashi outside and walk along with him. When we get near Osugi, I'll draw my sword and take him by surprise. That's the time for her to come out and strike."

Osugi was beside herself with gratitude. "Thank you, Kojirō. You're so good to me. You must be an incarnation of the great Hachiman." She clasped her hands and bowed, as if before the god of war himself.

In his heart, Kojirō was thoroughly convinced that he was doing the right thing. Indeed, it is doubtful that ordinary mortals could imagine the vastness of his self-righteousness at the moment he stepped up to Kōsuke's door.

At the beginning, when Musashi and Kojirō had been

very young, full of spirit and eager to demonstrate their superiority, there had existed no deep-seated cause for enmity between them. There had been rivalry, to be sure, but only the friction that normally arose between two strong and almost equally matched fighters. What had subsequently rankled with Kojirō was seeing Musashi gradually gaining fame as a swordsman. Musashi, for his part, respected Kojirō's extraordinary skill, if not his character, and always treated him with a certain amount of caution. As the years passed, however, they found themselves at odds over various matters—the House of Yoshioka, the fate of Akemi, the affair of the Hon'iden dowager. Conciliation was by now out of the question.

And now that Kojirō had taken it upon himself to become Osugi's protector, the trend of events bore the unmistakable seal of fate.

"Kōsuke!" Kojirō rapped lightly on the door. "Are you awake?" Light seeped through a crack, but there was no other sign of life inside.

After a few moments, a voice asked, "Who's there?"

"Iwama Kakubei gave you my sword to work on. I've come for it."

"The great long one—is that the one?"

"Open up and let me in."

"Just a moment."

The door slid open, and the two men eyed each other. Blocking the way, Kōsuke said curtly, "The sword's not ready yet."

"I see." Kojirō brushed past Kōsuke and seated himself on the step leading up to the shop. "When will it be ready?"

"Well, let's see. . . ." Kōsuke rubbed his chin, pulling the corners of his eyes down and making his long face seem even longer.

Kojirō had the feeling he was being made fun of. "Don't you think it's taking an awful long time?"

"I told Kakubei very clearly I couldn't promise when I'd finish."

"I can't do without it much longer."

"In that case, take it back."

"What's this?" Kojirō was taken aback. Artisans didn't talk that way to samurai. But instead of trying to ascertain what might be behind the man's attitude, he jumped to the conclusion that his visit had been anticipated. Thinking it best to act quickly, he said, "By the way, I heard Miyamoto Musashi, from Mimasaka, is staying here with you."

"Where did you hear that?" Kōsuke said, looking anxious. "As it happens, he is staying with us."

"Would you mind calling him? I haven't seen him for a long time, since we were both in Kyoto."

"What's your name?"

"Sasaki Kojirō. He'll know who I am."

"I'll tell him you're here, but I don't know whether he can see you or not."

"Just a moment."

"Yes?"

"Perhaps I'd better explain. I happened to hear at Lord Hosokawa's house that a man of Musashi's description was living here. I came with the idea of inviting Musashi out to drink a little and talk a little."

"I see." Kōsuke turned and went toward the back of the house.

Kojirō mulled over what to do if Musashi smelled a rat and refused to see him. Two or three stratagems came to mind, but before he had come to a decision, he was startled by a horrendous howling scream.

He jumped like a man who had been savagely kicked. He had miscalculated. His strategy had been seen through—not only seen through but turned against him. Musashi must have sneaked out the back door, gone around to the front and attacked. But who had screamed? Osugi? Jūrō? Koroku?

"If that's the way it is . . . ." thought Kojirō grimly,

as he ran out into the street. Muscles taut, blood racing, in an instant he was ready for anything. "I have to fight him sooner or later anyway," he thought. He had known this since that day at the pass on Mount Hiei. The time had come! If Osugi had already been struck down, Kojirō swore that Musashi's blood would become an offering for the eternal peace of her soul.

He had covered about ten paces when he heard his name called from the side of the road. The painfully forced voice seemed to clutch at his running footsteps.

"Koroku, is that you?"

"I-I-I've b-been h-h-hit."

"Jūrō! Where's Jūrō?"

"H-him too."

"Where is he?" Before the answer came, Kojirō spotted Jūrō's blood-soaked form about thirty feet away. His entire body bristling with vigilance for his own safety, he thundered, "Koroku! Which way did Musashi go?"

"No . . . not . . . Musashi." Koroku, unable to lift his head, rolled it from side to side.

"What are you saying? Are you telling me it wasn't Musashi who attacked you?"

"Not . . . Not . . . Musa—"

"Who was it?"

It was a question Koroku would never answer.

His thoughts in a turmoil, Kojirō ran to Jūrō and pulled him up by the red sticky collar of his kimono. "Jūrō, tell me. Who did it? Which way did he go?"

But Jūrō, instead of answering, used his last tearful breath to say, "Mother . . . sorry . . . shouldn't have . . ."

"What are you talking about?" snorted Kojirō, letting go of the bloody garment.

"Kojirō! Kojirō, is that you?"

Running in the direction of Osugi's voice, he saw the old woman lying helpless in a ditch, straw and vegetable peelings clinging to her face and hair. "Get me out of here," she pleaded.

"What are you doing in that filthy water?"

Kojirō, sounding more angry than sympathetic, yanked her unceremoniously out onto the road, where she collapsed like a rag.

"Where did the man go?" she asked, taking the words out of his mouth.

"What man? Who attacked you?"

"I don't know exactly what happened, but I'm sure it was the man who was following us."

"Did he attack suddenly?"

"Yes! Out of nowhere, like a gust of wind. There was no time to speak. He jumped out of the shadows and got Jūrō first. By the time Koroku drew his sword, he was wounded too."

"Which way did he go?"

"He shoved me aside, so I didn't even see him, but the footsteps went that way." She pointed toward the river.

Running across a vacant lot where the horse market was held, Kojirō came to the dike at Yanagihara and stopped to look around. Some distance away, he could see piles of lumber, lights and people.

When he got closer, he saw they were palanquin bearers. "My two companions have been struck down in a side street near here," he said. "I want you to pick them up and take them to the house of Hangawara Yajibei in the carpenters' district. You'll find an old woman with them. Take her too."

"Were they attacked by robbers?"

"Are there robbers around here?"

"Packs of them. Even we have to be careful."

"Whoever it was must have come running out from that corner over there. Didn't you see anyone?"

"Just now, you mean?"

"Yes."

"I'm leaving," said the bearer. He and the others picked up three palanquins and prepared to depart.

"What about the fare?" asked one.

"Collect it when you get there."

Kojirō made a quick search of the riverbank and around the stacks of lumber, deciding as he did so that he'd do just as well to go back to Yajibei's house. There was little point in meeting Musashi without Osugi; it also seemed unwise to face the man in his present state of mind.

Starting back, he came to a firebreak, along one side of which grew a row of paulownia trees. He looked at it for a minute, then as he turned away, he saw the glint of a blade among the trees. Before he knew it, half a dozen leaves fell. The sword had been aimed at his head.

"Yellow-livered coward!" he shouted.

"Not me!" came the reply as the sword struck out a second time from the darkness.

Kojirō whirled and jumped back a full seven feet. "If you're Musashi, why don't you use the proper—" Before he could finish, the sword was at him again. "Who are you?" he shouted. "Aren't you making a mistake?"

He dodged a third stroke successfully, and the attacker, badly winded, realized before attempting a fourth that he was wasting his effort. Changing tactics, he began inching forward with his blade extended before him. His eyes were shooting fire. "Silence," he growled. "There's no mistake at all. Perhaps it'll refresh your memory if you know my name. I'm Hōjō Shinzō."

"You're one of Obata's students, aren't you?"

"You insulted my master and killed several of my comrades."

"By the warrior's code, you're free to challenge me openly at any time. Sasaki Kojirō doesn't play hide-and-seek."

"I'll kill you."

"Go ahead and try."

As Kojirō watched him close the distance—twelve feet, eleven, ten—he quietly loosened the upper part of his kimono and placed his right hand on his sword. "Come on!" he cried.

The challenge caused an involuntary hesitation on Shinzō's part, a momentary wavering. Kojirō's body bent forward, his arm snapped like a bow, and there was a metallic ring. The next instant, his sword clicked sharply back into its scabbard. There had been only a thin flashing thread of light.

Shinzō was still standing, his legs spread apart. There was no sign of blood yet, but it was plain that he'd been wounded. Though his sword was still stretched out at eye level, his left hand had gone reflexively to his neck.

"Oh!" Gasps went up on both sides of Shinzō at the same time—from Kojirō and from a man running up behind Shinzō. The sound of footsteps, together with the voice, sent Kojirō off into the darkness.

"What happened?" cried Kōsuke. He reached out to support Shinzō, only to have the full weight of the other man's body fall into his arms. "Oh, this looks bad!" cried Kōsuke. "Help! Help, somebody!"

A piece of flesh no larger than a clamshell fell from Shinzō's neck. The blood gushing out soaked first Shinzō's arm, then the skirts of his kimono all the way to his feet.

20

A Block of Wood

Plunk. Another green plum fell from the tree in the dark garden outside. Musashi ignored it, if he heard it at all. In the bright but unsteady lamplight, his disheveled hair appeared heavy and bristly, lacking in natural oil and reddish in color.

"What a difficult child!" his mother had often complained. The stubborn disposition that had so often reduced her to tears was still with him, as enduring as the scar on his head left by a large carbuncle during childhood.

Memories of his mother now floated through his mind; at times the face he was carving closely resembled hers.

A few minutes earlier Kōsuke had come to the door, hesitated and called in: "Are you still working? A man named Sasaki Kojirō says he'd like to see you. He's waiting downstairs. Do you want to speak to him, or shall I tell him you've already gone to bed?"

Musashi had the vague impression Kōsuke had repeated the message but wasn't sure whether he himself had answered.

The small table, Musashi's knees and the floor immediately around him were littered with wood chips. He was trying to finish the image of Kannon he had promised

216

Kōsuke in exchange for the sword. His task had been made even more challenging because of a special request by Kōsuke, a man of pronounced likes and dislikes.

When Kōsuke had first taken the ten-inch block out of a cupboard and very gently handed it to him, Musashi saw that it must have been six or seven hundred years old. Kōsuke treated it like an heirloom, for it had come from an eighth-century temple at the tomb of Prince Shōtoku in Shinaga. "I was on a trip there," he explained, "and they were repairing the old buildings. Some stupid priests and carpenters were axing up the old beams for firewood. I couldn't stand seeing the wood wasted that way, so I got them to cut off this block for me."

The grain was good, as was the feel of the wood to the knife, but thinking of how highly Kōsuke valued his treasure made Musashi nervous. If he made a slip, he would ruin an irreplaceable piece of material.

He heard a bang, which sounded like the wind blowing open the gate in the garden hedge. Looking up from his work, for almost the first time since he had begun carving, he thought: "Could that be Iori?" and cocked his head, waiting for confirmation.

"What're you standing there gaping for?" Kōsuke shouted at his wife. "Can't you see the man's badly wounded? It doesn't make any difference which room!"

Behind Kōsuke, the men carrying Shinzō excitedly offered to help.

"Any spirits to wash the wound with? If there aren't, I'll go home for some."

"I'll fetch the doctor."

After the commotion died down a bit, Kōsuke said, "I want to thank all of you. I think we saved his life; no more need to worry." He bowed deeply to each man as he left the house.

Finally it penetrated Musashi's consciousness that something had happened and Kōsuke was involved. Brushing the chips from his knees, he descended the staircase formed by the tops of tiered storage chests and went to the room where Kōsuke and his wife stood staring down at the wounded man.

"Oh, are you still awake?" asked the sword polisher, moving over to make a place for Musashi.

Sitting down near the man's pillow, Musashi looked closely at his face and inquired, "Who is he?"

"I couldn't have been more surprised. I didn't recognize him until we got him back here, but it's Hōjō Shinzō, the son of Lord Hōjō of Awa. He's a very dedicated young man who's been studying under Obata Kagenori for several years."

Musashi carefully lifted the edge of the white bandage around Shinzō's neck and examined the wound, which had been cauterized, then washed with alcohol. The clam-sized piece of flesh had been sliced out cleanly, exposing the pulsating carotid artery. Death had come that close. "Who?" Musashi wondered. From the shape of the wound, it seemed probable the sword had been on the upswing of a swallow-flight stroke.

Swallow-flight stroke? Kojirō's specialty.

"Do you know what happened?" Musashi asked.

"Not yet."

"Neither do I, of course, but I can tell you this much." He nodded his head confidently. "It's the work of Sasaki Kojirō."

Back in his own room, Musashi lay down on the tatami with his hands under his head, ignoring the mess around him. His pallet had been spread, but he ignored that too, despite his fatigue.

He had been working on the statue for nearly forty-eight hours straight. Not being a sculptor, he lacked the technical skills necessary to solve difficult problems, nor could he execute the deft strokes that would cover up a mistake. He had nothing to go on but the image of Kannon he carried in his heart, and his sole technique was to clear his mind of extraneous thoughts and do his best to faithfully transfer this image to the wood.

He would think for a time that the sculpture was

taking form, but then somehow it would go wrong, some slip would occur between the image in his mind and the hand working with the dagger. Just as he felt he was making progress again, the carving would get out of hand again. After many false starts, the ancient piece of wood had shrunk to a length of no more than four inches.

He heard a nightingale call twice, then dropped off to sleep for perhaps an hour. When he awoke, his strong body was surging with energy, his mind perfectly clear. As he arose, he thought: "I'll make it this time." Going to the well behind the house, he washed his face and swilled water through his teeth. Refreshed, he sat down by the lamp again and took up his work with renewed vigor.

The knife had a different feel to it now. In the grain of the wood he sensed the centuries of history contained within the block. He knew that if he did not carve skillfully this time, there would be nothing left but a pile of useless chips. For the next few hours, he concentrated with feverish intensity. Not once did his back unbend, nor did he stop for a drink of water. The sky grew light, the birds began to sing, all the doors in the house save his were thrown open for the morning's cleaning. Still, his attention remained focused on the tip of his knife.

"Musashi, are you all right?" asked his host in a worried tone, as he slid open the shoji and entered the room.

"It's no good," Musashi sighed. He straightened up and tossed his dagger aside. The block of wood was no larger than a man's thumb. The wood around his legs lay like fallen snow.

"No good?"

"No good."

"How about the wood?"

"Gone . . . I couldn't get the bodhisattva's form to emerge." Placing his hands behind his head, he felt himself returning to earth after having been suspended for an indeterminate length of time between delusion and enlightenment. "No good at all. It's time to forget and to meditate."

He lay on his back. When he closed his eyes, distractions seemed to fade away, to be replaced by a blinding mist. Gradually, his mind filled with the single idea of the infinite void.

Most of the guests leaving the inn that morning were horse traders, going home after the four-day market that had ended the day before. For the next few weeks, the inn would see few customers.

Catching sight of Iori going up the stairs, the proprietess called out to him from the office.

"What do you want?" asked Iori. From his vantage point, he could see the woman's artfully disguised bald spot.

"Where do you think you're going?"

"Upstairs, where my teacher is. Something wrong?"

"More than you know," replied the woman with an exasperated glance. "Just when did you leave here?"

Counting on his fingers, Iori answered, "The day before the day before yesterday, I think."

"Three days ago, wasn't it?"

"That's right."

"You certainly took your time, didn't you? What happened? Did a fox bewitch you or something?"

"How'd you know? You must be a fox yourself." Giggling at his own riposte, he started for the top of the stairs again.

"Your teacher's not here anymore."

"I don't believe you." He ran up the stairs, but soon came back with a dismayed look on his face. "Has he changed rooms?"

"What's the matter with you? I told you he left."

"Really gone?" There was alarm in the boy's voice.

"If you don't believe me, look at the account book. See?"

"But why? Why would he leave before I got back?"

"Because you were gone too long."

"But . . . but . . ." Iori burst into tears. "Where did he go? Please tell me."

"He didn't tell me where he was going. I imagine he left you behind because you're so useless."

His color changing, Iori charged out into the street. He looked east, west, then he gazed up at the sky. Tears poured down his cheeks.

Scratching the bald spot with a comb, the woman broke into raucous laughter. "Stop your bawling," she called. "I was only fooling. Your teacher's staying at the sword polisher's, over there." She had barely finished speaking when a straw horseshoe came sailing into the office.

Meekly, Iori sat down in formal fashion at Musashi's feet and in a subdued voice announced, "I'm back."

He'd already noticed the atmosphere of gloom hanging over the house. The wood chips had not been cleaned up, and the burned-out lamp was still sitting where it had been the night before.

"I'm back," Iori repeated, no more loudly than before.

"Who is it?" mumbled Musashi, slowly opening his eyes.

"Iori."

Musashi sat up quickly. Although relieved to see the boy back safe, his only greeting was: "Oh, it's you."

"I'm sorry I took so long." This met with silence. "Forgive me." Neither his apology nor a polite bow elicited a response.

Musashi tightened his obi and said, "Open the windows and tidy up the room."

He was out the door before Iori had time to say, "Yes, sir."

Musashi went to the room downstairs at the back and asked Kōsuke how the invalid was this morning.

"He seems to be resting better."

221

"You must be tired. Shall I come back after breakfast so you can have a rest?"

Kōsuke answered that there was no need. "There is one thing I would like to see done," he added. "I think we should let the Obata School know about this, but I don't have anybody to send."

Having offered to either go himself or send Iori, Musashi went back to his own room, which was now in good order. As he sat down, he said, "Iori, was there an answer to my letter?"

Relieved at not being scolded, the boy broke into a smile. "Yes, I brought a reply. It's right here." With a look of triumph, he fished the letter from his kimono.

"Let me have it."

Iori advanced on his knees and placed the folded paper in Musashi's outstretched hand. "I am sorry to say," Sukekurō had written, "that Lord Munenori, as tutor to the shōgun, cannot engage in a bout with you, as you requested. If, however, you should visit us for some other purpose, there is a possibility that his lordship may greet you in the dōjō. If you still feel strongly about trying your hand against the Yagyū Style, the best plan, I think, would be for you to confront Yagyū Hyōgo. I regret to say, however, that he left yesterday for Yamato to be at the bedside of Lord Sekishūsai, who is gravely ill. Such being the case, I must ask you to postpone your visit until a later day. I shall be happy to make arrangements at that time."

As he slowly refolded the lengthy scroll, Musashi smiled. Iori, feeling more secure, extended his legs comfortably and said, "The house is not in Kobikichō; it's at a place called Higakubo. It's very large, very splendid, and Kimura Sukekurō gave me lots of good things to eat—"

His eyebrows arching in disapproval at this display of familiarity, Musashi said gravely, "Iori."

The boy's legs quickly shot back to their proper place under him. "Yes, sir."

"Even if you did get lost, don't you think three days is a rather long time? What happened?"

"I was bewitched by a fox."

"A fox?"

"Yes, sir, a fox."

"How could a boy like you, born and raised in the country, be bewitched by a fox?"

"I don't know, but afterward I couldn't remember where I'd been for half a day and half a night."

"Hmm. Very strange."

"Yes, sir. I thought so myself. Maybe foxes in Edo have it in for people more than the ones in the country do."

"I suspect that's true." Taking into account the boy's seriousness, Musashi did not have the heart to scold him, but he did feel it necessary to pursue his point. "I also suspect," he continued, "you were up to something you shouldn't have been up to."

"Well, the fox was following me, and to keep it from bewitching me, I cut it with my sword. Then the fox punished me for that."

"No, it didn't."

"Didn't it?"

"No. It wasn't the fox punishing you; it was your own conscience, which is invisible. Now, you sit there and think about that for a while. When I come back, you can tell me what you think it means."

"Yes, sir. Are you going somewhere?"

"Yes; to a place near the Hirakawa Shrine in Kōjimachi."

"You'll be back by evening, won't you?"

"Ha, ha. I should be, unless a fox gets me."

Musashi departed, leaving Iori to ponder his conscience. Outside, the sky was obscured by the dull, sullen clouds of the summer rainy season.

21

The Deserted Prophet

The forest around the Hirakawa Tenjin Shrine was alive with the hum of cicadas. An owl hooted as Musashi walked from the gate to the entrance hall of the Obata house.

"Good day!" he called, but his greeting echoed back as though from an empty cavern.

After a time, he heard footsteps. The young samurai who emerged wearing his two swords was clearly no mere underling assigned to answer the door.

Without bothering to kneel, he said, "May I ask your name?" Though no more than twenty-four or -five, he gave the impression of being someone to be reckoned with.

My name is Miyamoto Musashi. Am I correct in thinking this is Obata Kagenori's academy of military science?"

"That's right," came the reply, in clipped tones. From the samurai's manner, it was evident he expected Musashi to explain how he was traveling around to perfect his knowledge of the martial arts, and so on.

"One of the students from your school has been wounded in a fight," said Musashi. "He's now being cared for by the sword polisher Zushino Kōsuke, whom I believe you know. I came at Kōsuke's request."

"It must be Shinzō!" There were fleeting signs of severe shock, but the youth recovered immediately. "Forgive me. I'm Kagenori's only son, Yogorō. Thank you for taking the trouble to come and tell us. Is Shinzō's life in danger?"

"He seemed better this morning, but it's still too early for him to be moved. I think it'd be wise to let him stay at Kōsuke's house for the time being."

"I hope you'll convey our thanks to Kōsuke."

"I'd be happy to."

"To tell the truth, since my father is bedridden, Shinzō was lecturing in his stead until last fall when he suddenly left. As you can see, there's almost nobody here now. I regret we're not able to receive you properly."

"Of course; but tell me, is there a feud going on between your school and Sasaki Kojirō?"

"Yes. I was away when it started, so I don't know all the details, but apparently Kojirō insulted my father, which of course incited the students. They took it upon themselves to punish Kojirō, but he killed several of them. As I understand it, Shinzō left because he finally came to the conclusion that he himself should take revenge."

"I see. It's beginning to make sense. I'd like to give you a bit of advice. Don't fight Kojirō. He can't be beaten by ordinary sword techniques, and he's even less vulnerable to clever strategy. As a fighter, as a speaker, as a strategist, he's without rival, even among the greatest masters alive today."

This assessment brought a burst of angry fire from Yogorō's eyes. Observing this, Musashi felt it prudent to repeat his warning. "Let the proud have their day," he added. "It's senseless to risk disaster over a trivial grievance. Don't entertain the idea that Shinzō's defeat makes it necessary for you to settle the score. If you do, you'll simply follow in his footsteps. That would be foolish, very foolish."

After Musashi was out of sight, Yogorō leaned against the wall with his arms folded. Softly, in a faintly tremulous voice, he muttered, "To think it's come to this. Even Shinzō has failed!" Gazing vacantly at the ceiling, he thought of the letter Shinzō had left for him, in which he'd said that his purpose in leaving was to kill Kojirō and that if he did not succeed, Yogorō would probably never see him alive again.

That Shinzō was not dead did not make his defeat any less humiliating. With the school forced to suspend operations, the public in general had concluded that Kojirō was right: the Obata Academy was a school for cowards, or at best for theoreticians devoid of practical ability. This had led to the desertion of some of the students. Others, apprehensive over Kagenori's illness or the apparent decline of the Kōshū Style, had switched to the rival Naganuma Style. Only two or three were still in residence.

Yogorō decided not to tell his father about Shinzō. It seemed that the only course open to him was to nurse the old man as best he could, although the doctor's opinion was that recovery was out of the question.

"Yogorō, where are you?"

It was a source of constant amazement to Yogorō that although Kagenori was at death's door, when an impulse moved him to summon his son, his voice became that of a perfectly healthy man.

"Coming." He ran to the sickroom, fell to his knees and said, "You called?"

As he often did when he was tired of lying flat on his back, Kagenori had propped himself up by the window, using his pillow as an armrest. "Who was the samurai who just went out the gate?" he asked.

"Huh," said Yogorō, somewhat flustered. "Oh, him. Nobody in particular. He was just a messenger."

"Messenger from where?"

"Well, it seems Shinzō has had an accident. The

226

samurai came to tell us. He gave his name as Miyamoto
Musashi.''

"Mm. He wasn't born in Edo, was he?''

"No. I've heard he's from Mimasaka. He's a rōnin.
Did you think you recognized him?''

"No.'' Kagenori replied with a vigorous shake of his
thin gray beard. ''I don't recall ever having seen or heard
of him. But there's something about him. . . . I've met a
lot of people during my lifetime, you know, on the
battlefield as well as in ordinary life. Some were very
good people, people I valued greatly. But the ones I could
consider to be genuine samurai, in every sense of the
term, were very few. This Man—Musashi, did you say?—
appealed to me. I'd like to meet him, talk to him a little.
Go bring him back.''

"Yes, sir,'' Yogorō answered obediently, but before
getting to his feet, he continued in a slightly puzzled tone:
"What was it you noticed about him? You only saw him
from a distance.''

"You wouldn't understand. When you do, you'll be
old and withered like me.''

"But there must have been something.''

"I admired his alertness. He wasn't taking any
chances, even on a sick old man like me. When he came
through the gate, he paused and looked around—at the
layout of the house, at the windows, whether they were
open or closed, at the path to the garden—everything.
He took it all in at a single glance. There was nothing
unnatural about it. Anyone would have assumed he was
simply halting for a moment as a sign of deference. I was
amazed.''

"Then you believe he's a samurai of real merit?''

"Perhaps. I'm sure he'd be a fascinating man to talk
to. Call him back.''

"Aren't you afraid it'll be bad for you?'' Kagenori
had become quite excited, and Yogorō was reminded of
the doctor's warning that his father shouldn't talk for any
length of time.

"Don't worry your head about my health. I've been waiting for years to meet a man like that. I didn't study military science all this time to teach it to children. I grant that my theories of military science are called the Kōshū Style, but they're not simply an extension of the formulas used by the famous Kōshū warriors. My ideas differ from those of Takeda Shingen, or Uesugi Kenshin, or Oda Nobunaga, or the other generals who were fighting for control of the country. The purpose of military science has changed since then. My theory is directed toward the achievement of peace and stability. You know some of these things, but the question is, whom can I entrust my ideas to?"

Yogorō was silent.

"My son, while there are many things I want to pass on to you, you're still immature, too immature to recognize the remarkable qualities of the man you just met."

Yogorō dropped his eyes but endured the criticism in silence.

"If even I, inclined as I am to look favorably on everything you do, see you as immature, then there's no doubt in my mind. You're not yet the person who can carry on my work, so I must find the right man and entrust your future to him. I've been waiting for the right person to come along. Remember, when the cherry blossom falls, it must rely on the wind to spread its pollen."

"You mustn't fall, Father. You must try to live."

The old man glared and raised his head. "Talk like that proves you're still a child! Now go quickly and find the samurai!"

"Yes, sir!"

"Don't push him. Just tell him roughly what I've told you, and bring him back with you."

"Right away, Father."

Yogorō departed on the run. Once outside, he first tried the direction he'd seen Musashi take. Then he looked all over the shrine grounds, even went out to the main street running through Kōjimachi, but to no avail.

He was not unduly disturbed, for he was not as thoroughly convinced as his father of Musashi's superiority, nor was he grateful for Musashi's warning. The talk about Kojirō's unusual ability, about the folly of "risking disaster over a trivial grievance" had stuck in his craw. It was as though Musashi's visit had been for the express purpose of singing Kojirō's praises.

Even while listening submissively to his father, he had been thinking to himself: "I'm not as young and immature as you say." And the truth was that just then, he really couldn't have cared less what Musashi thought.

They were about the same age. Even if Musashi's talent was exceptional, there were limits to what he could know and what he could do. In the past, Yogorō had gone away for a year, two years, even three, to lead the life of the ascetic *shugyōsha*. He had lived and studied for a while at the school of another military expert, and he had studied Zen under a strict master. Yet his father, after merely catching a glimpse of the man, had not only formed what Yogorō suspected was an exaggerated opinion of the unknown rōnin's worth but had gone so far as to suggest that Yogorō take Musashi as a model.

"May as well go back," he thought sadly. "I suppose there's no way to convince a parent that his son is no longer a child." He longed desperately for the day when Kagenori would look at him and suddenly see that he was both a grown man and a brave samurai. It pained him to think that his father might die before that day arrived.

"Hey, Yogorō! It is Yogorō, isn't it?"

Yogorō turned on his heel and saw that the voice belonged to Nakatogawa Handayū, a samurai from the House of Hosokawa. They had not seen each other recently, but there had been a time when Handayū had attended Kagenori's lectures regularly.

"How's our revered teacher's health? Official duties keep me so busy I haven't had time to call."

"He's about the same, thanks."

"Say, I hear Hōjō Shinzō attacked Sasaki Kojirō and was beaten."

"You've heard that already?"

"Yes; they were talking about it at Lord Hosokawa's this morning."

"It only happened last night."

"Kojirō's a guest of Iwama Kakubei. Kakubei must have passed the word around. Even Lord Tadatoshi knew about it."

Yogorō was too young to listen with detachment, yet he was loath to reveal his anger by some involuntary twitch. Taking leave of Handayū as quickly as possible, he hurried home.

His mind was made up.

22

The Talk of the Town

Kōsuke's wife was in the kitchen making gruel for Shinzō when Iori came in.

"The plums are turning yellow," he said.

"If they're almost ripe, that means the cicadas will be singing soon," she answered absently.

"Don't you pickle the plums?"

"No. There aren't many of us here, and pickling all those plums would take several pounds of salt."

"The salt wouldn't go to waste, but the plums will if you don't pickle them. And if there was a war or a flood, they'd come in handy, wouldn't they? Since you're busy taking care of the wounded man, I'll be happy to pickle them for you."

"My, what a funny child you are, worrying about floods and such. You think like an old man."

Iori was already getting an empty wooden bucket out of the closet. With this in hand, he sauntered out into the garden and looked up at the plum tree. Alas, though sufficiently grown up to worry about the future, he was still young enough to be easily distracted by the sight of a buzzing cicada. Sneaking closer, he captured it and held it in his cupped hands, making it screech like a terrified hag.

Peeking between his thumbs, Iori experienced a

strange sensation. Insects were supposed to be bloodless, he thought, but the cicada felt warm. Perhaps even cicadas when faced with the peril of death gave off body heat. Suddenly he was seized by a mixture of fear and pity. Spreading his palms, he tossed the cicada into the air and watched it fly off toward the street.

The plum tree, which was quite large, was the home of a sizable community—fat caterpillars with surprisingly beautiful fur, ladybirds, tiny blue frogs clinging to the underside of leaves, small sleeping butterflies, dancing gadflies. Gazing in fascination at this little corner of the animal kingdom, he thought it would be inhuman to throw these ladies and gentlemen into consternation by shaking a branch. Carefully, he reached out, picked a plum and bit into it. Then he shook the nearest branch gently and was surprised when the fruit did not fall off. Reaching out, he picked a few plums and dropped them into the bucket below.

"Son of a bitch!" shouted Iori, abruptly firing three or four plums into the narrow lane next to the house. The clothes-drying pole between the house and the fence fell to the ground with a clatter, and footsteps hastily retreated from the lane into the street.

Kōsuke's face appeared at the bamboo grille of his workroom window. "What was that noise?" he asked, his eyes wide with astonishment.

Jumping down from the tree, Iori cried, "Another strange man was hiding in the shadows, squatting right there in the lane. I threw some plums at him, and he ran away."

The sword polisher came outside, wiping his hands on a towel. "What sort of man?"

"A thug."

"One of Hangawara's men?"

"I don't know. Why do those men come snooping around here?"

"They're looking for a chance to get back at Shinzō."

Iori looked toward the back room, where the injured man was just finishing his gruel. His wound had healed to the extent that the bandage was no longer necessary.

"Kōsuke," called Shinzō.

The craftsman walked to the edge of the veranda and asked, "How are you feeling?"

Pushing his tray aside, Shinzō reseated himself more formally. "I want to apologize for causing you so much trouble."

"Don't mention it. I'm sorry I've been too busy to do more for you."

"I notice that besides worrying about me, you're being annoyed by those Hangawara hoodlums. The longer I stay, the more danger there is that they'll come to regard you as an enemy too. I think I should be leaving."

"Don't give it a thought."

"I'm much better now, as you can see. I'm ready to go home."

"Today?"

"Yes."

"Don't be in such a hurry. At least wait until Musashi comes back."

"I'd rather not, but please thank him for me. He's been very kind to me too. I can walk all right now."

"You don't seem to understand. Hangawara's men are watching this house day and night. They'll pounce on you the minute you step outside. I can't possibly let you leave alone."

"I had a good reason for killing Jūrō and Koroku. Kojirō started all this, not me. But if they want to attack me, let them attack."

Shinzō was on his feet and ready to go. Sensing there was no way of holding him back, Kōsuke and his wife went to the front of the shop to see him off.

Musashi appeared at the door just then, his sunburned forehead moist with sweat. "Going out?" he asked. "Going home? . . . Well, I'm glad to see you feel well enough, but it'd be dangerous to go alone. I'll go with you."

Shinzō tried to refuse, but Musashi insisted. Minutes later, they set off together.

"It must be difficult to walk after being in bed so long."

"Somehow the ground seems higher than it really is."

"It's a long way to Hirakawa Tenjin. Why don't we hire a palanquin for you?"

"I suppose I ought to have mentioned it before. I'm not going back to the school."

"Oh? Where then?"

Casting his eyes downward, Shinzō answered, "It's rather humiliating, but I think I'll go to my father's house for a while. It's in Ushigome."

Musashi stopped a palanquin and virtually forced Shinzō into it. Despite the insistence of the bearers, Musashi refused one for himself—to the disappointment of the Hangawara men watching from around the next corner.

"Look, he put Shinzō into a palanquin."

"I saw him glance this way."

"It's too early to do anything yet."

After the palanquin turned right by the outer moat, they hitched up their skirts, pulled back their sleeves, and followed along behind, their glittering eyes seemingly ready to pop out and shoot toward Musashi's back.

Musashi and Shinzō had reached the neighborhood of Ushigafuchi when a small rock glanced off the palanquin pole. At the same time, the gang started shouting and moved in to surround its prey.

"Wait!" called one of them.

"Just stay where you are, you bastard!"

The bearers, terrified, dropped the palanquin and fled. Shinzō crawled out of the palanquin, hand on sword. Pulling himself to his feet, he assumed a stance and cried, "Is it me you're telling to wait?"

Musashi jumped in front of him and shouted, "State your business!"

The hoodlums inched closer, cautiously, as though feeling their way through shallow water.

"You know what we want!" spat one of them. "Turn over that yellowbelly you're protecting. And don't try anything funny, or you'll be dead too."

Encouraged by this bravado, they seethed with bloodthirsty fury, but none advanced to strike with his sword. The fire in Musashi's eyes was sufficient to hold them at bay. They howled and cursed, from a safe distance.

Musashi and Shinzō glared at them in silence. Moments passed before Musashi took them unawares by shouting, "If Hangawara Yajibei is among you, let him come forward."

"The boss isn't here. But if you have anything to say, speak to me, Nembutsu Tazaemon, and I'll do you the favor of listening." The elderly man who stepped forward wore a white hemp kimono and had Buddhist prayer beads hung around his neck.

"What do you have against Hōjō Shinzō?"

Squaring his shoulders, Tazaemon replied, "He slaughtered two of our men."

"According to Shinzō, your two louts helped Kojirō kill a number of Obata's students."

"That was one thing. This is another. If we don't settle our score with Shinzō, we'll be laughed off the streets."

"That may be the way things are done in the world you live in," Musashi said in a conciliatory tone. "But it's different in the world of the samurai. Among warriors, you can't fault a man for seeking and taking his proper revenge. A samurai may take revenge for the sake of justice or to defend his honor, but not to satisfy a personal grudge. It's not manly. And what you're trying to do right now isn't manly."

"Not manly? You're accusing us of being unmanly?"

"If Kojirō came forward and challenged us in his own name, that'd be all right. But we can't get involved in a squabble raised by Kojirō's minions."

"There you go, preaching self-righteously, just like any other samurai. Say what you please. We still have to protect our name."

"If samurai and outlaws fight over whose rules are to prevail, the streets will be filled with blood. The only place to settle this is at the magistrate's office. How about it, Nembutsu?"

"Horse manure. If it was something the magistrate could settle, we wouldn't be here to begin with."

"Listen, how old are you?"

"What business is it of yours?"

"I'd say you look old enough to know you shouldn't be leading a group of young men to a meaningless death."

"Ah, keep your smart talk to yourself. I'm not too old for a fight!" Tazaemon drew his sword, and the hoodlums moved forward, jostling and shouting.

Musashi dodged Tazaemon's thrust and grabbed him by the back of his gray head. Covering the ten paces or so to the moat in great strides, he summarily dumped him over the edge. Then, as the mob closed in, he dashed back, picked Shinzō up by the waist and made off with him.

He ran across a field, toward the middle reaches of a hill. Below them a stream flowed into the moat and a bluish marsh was visible at the bottom of the slope. Halfway up, Musashi stopped and stood Shinzō on his feet. "Now," he said, "let's run." Shinzō hesitated, but Musashi prodded him into motion.

The hoodlums, having recovered from their shock, were giving chase.

"Catch him!"

"No pride!"

"*That's* a samurai?"

"He can't throw Tazaemon in the moat and get away with it!"

Ignoring the taunts and slurs, Musashi said to Shinzō, "Don't even consider getting involved with them. Run! It's the only thing to do in a case like this." With a grin, he added, "It's not so easy to make good time on this terrain, is it?" They were passing through what would someday be known as Ushigafuchi and Kudan Hill, but now the area was heavily wooded.

By the time they lost their pursuers, Shinzō's face was deathly pale.

"Worn out?" Musashi asked solicitously.

"It's . . . It's not so bad."

"I suppose you don't like the idea of letting them insult us like that without fighting back."

"Well . . . "

"Ha, ha! Think about it quietly and calmly, and you'll see why. There're times when it makes you feel better to run away. There's a stream over there. Rinse your mouth out, and then I'll take you to your father's house."

In a few minutes, the forest around the Akagi Myōjin Shrine came into view. Lord Hōjō's house was just below.

"I hope you'll come in and meet my father," Shinzō said when they came to the earthen wall surrounding the house.

"Some other time. Get plenty of rest and take care of yourself." With that, he was off.

After this incident, Musashi's name was heard quite frequently in the streets of Edo, far more frequently than he would have wished. People were calling him "a fake," "the coward to end all cowards," and saying, "shameless . . . a disgrace to the samurai class. If a fraud like that defeated the Yoshiokas in Kyoto, they must have been hopelessly weak. He must have challenged them knowing they couldn't protect themselves. And then he probably ran away before he was in any real danger. All that phony wants to do is sell his name to people who don't know swordsmanship." Before long, it was impossible to find anyone who would put in a good word for him.

The crowning insult was signs posted all over Edo: "Here's a word to Miyamoto Musashi, who turned tail and ran. The Hon'iden dowager is eager for revenge. We, too, would like to see your face instead of your back for a change. If you are a samurai, come out and fight. The Hangawara Association."

23

A Chat with the Men

Before having breakfast, Lord Hosokawa Tadatoshi began his day with the study of the Confucian classics. Official duties, which often required his attendance at Edo Castle, consumed most of his time, but when he could fit it into his schedule, he practiced the martial arts. Evenings, whenever possible, he liked to spend in the company of the young samurai in his service.

The atmosphere was rather like that of a harmonious family seated around its patriarch, not completely informal, to be sure, for the idea that his lordship was just one of the boys was not encouraged, but the usually rigorous etiquette was relaxed a bit. Tadatoshi, lounging in a lightweight hemp kimono, encouraged an exchange of views, which often included the latest gossip.

"Okatani," said his lordship, singling out one of the more robust men.

"Yes, sir."

"I hear you're pretty good with the lance now."

"That's right. Very good, in fact."

"Ha, ha. You certainly don't suffer from false modesty."

"Well, sir, with everybody else saying so, why should I deny it?"

"One of these days I'll find out for myself how advanced your technique really is."

"I've been looking forward to that day, but it never seems to come."

"You're lucky it doesn't."

"Tell me, sir, have you heard the song everybody's singing?"

"What's that?"

"It goes like this:

> "There're lancers and lancers,
> All sorts of lancers,
> But the greatest one of all is
> Okatani Gorōji—"

Tadatoshi laughed. "You can't take me in that easily. That song's about Nagoya Sanzō."

The others joined in the laughter.

"Oh, you knew?"

"You'd be surprised at what I know." He was on the verge of giving further evidence of this but thought better of it. He enjoyed hearing what his men were thinking and talking about and considered it his duty to keep himself well informed, but it would hardly do to reveal just how much he actually knew. Instead he asked, "How many of you are specializing in the lance, how many in the sword?"

Out of seven, five were studying the lance, only two the sword.

"Why do so many of you prefer the lance?" asked Tadatoshi.

The consensus among the lancers was that it was more effective in battle.

"And what do the swordsmen think about that?"

One of the two replied, "The sword is better. Swordsmanship prepares you for peace as well as for war."

This was a perennial subject for discussion and the debate was usually lively.

One of the lancers asserted, "The longer the lance is, the better, provided it's not too long to handle efficiently. The lance can be used for striking, thrusting or slicing, and if you fail with it, you can always fall back on your sword. If you have only a sword and it gets broken, that's it."

"That may be true," rejoined an exponent of sword fighting, "but a samurai's work isn't limited to the battlefield. The sword is his soul. To practice its art is to refine and discipline your spirit. In the broadest sense, the sword is the basis for all military training, whatever drawbacks it may have in battle. If you master the inner meaning of the Way of the Samurai, the discipline can be applied to the use of the lance, or even guns. If you know the sword, you don't make silly mistakes or get taken unawares. Swordsmanship is an art with universal applications."

The argument might have gone on indefinitely, had not Tadatoshi, who had been listening without taking sides, said, "Mainosuke, what you just said sounds to me like something you heard somebody else say."

Matsushita Mainosuke grew defensive. "No, sir. That's my own opinion."

"Come now, be honest."

"Well, to tell the truth, I heard something similar when I was visiting Kakubei recently. Sasaki Kojirō said about the same thing. But it fitted in so well with my own idea . . . I wasn't trying to deceive anyone. Sasaki just put it into words better than I could."

"I thought as much," said Tadatoshi with a knowing smile. The mention of Kojirō's name reminded him that he had not yet made a decision as to whether to accept Kakubei's recommendation.

Kakubei had suggested that since Kojirō was not very old, he might be offered a thousand bushels or so. But much more than the matter of the stipend was involved. Tadatoshi had been told by his father many times that it was of prime importance to first exercise good judgment in hiring samurai and then to treat them well. Before accepting a candidate, it was imperative to assess not only his skills but also his character. No matter how desirable a man might seem to be, if he could not work together with the retainers who had made the House of Hosokawa what it was today, he would be virtually useless.

A fief, the elder Hosokawa had advised, was like a castle wall built of many rocks. A rock that could not be cut to fit in comfortably with the others would weaken the whole structure, even though the rock itself might be of admirable size and quality. The daimyō of the new age left the unsuitable rocks in the mountains and fields, for there was an abundance of them. The great challenge was to find one great rock that would make an outstanding contribution to one's own wall. Thought of in this way, Tadatoshi felt, Kojirō's youth was in his favor. He was still in his formative years and consequently susceptible to a certain amount of molding.

Tadatoshi was also reminded of the other rōnin. Nagaoka Sado had first mentioned Musashi at one of these evening get-togethers. Though Sado had allowed Musashi to slip through his fingers, Tadatoshi had not forgotten him. If Sado's information was accurate, Musashi was both a better fighter than Kojirō and a man of sufficient breadth to be valuable in government.

As he compared the two, he had to admit that most daimyō would prefer Kojirō. He came from a good family and had studied the Art of War thoroughly. Despite his youth, he had developed a formidable style of his own, and he had gained considerable fame as a fighter. The story of his "brilliant" defeat of the men from the Obata Academy on the banks of the Sumida River and again at the dike on the Kanda River was already well known.

Nothing had been heard of Musashi for some time. His victory at Ichijōji had made his reputation. But that had been years ago, and soon afterward word had spread that the story was exaggerated, that Musashi was a seeker after fame who had trumped up the fight, made a flashy attack and then fled to Mount Hiei. Every time Musashi did something praiseworthy, a spate of rumors followed, denigrating his character and ability. It had reached the point where even the mention of his name usually met with critical remarks. Or else people ignored him entirely. As the son of a nameless warrior in the mountains of Mimasaka, his lineage was insignificant. Though other men of humble origin—most notably Toyotomi Hideyoshi, who came from Nakamura in Owari Province—had risen to glory in recent memory, people were on the whole class-conscious and not given to paying much heed to a man of Musashi's background.

As Tadatoshi mulled over the question, he looked around and asked, "Do any of you know of a samurai named Miyamoto Musashi?"

"Musashi?" replied a surprised voice. "It'd be impossible not to hear of him. His name's all over town." It was evident that they were all familiar with the name.

"Why is that?" A look of anticipation came over Tadatoshi's face.

"There are signs up about him," offered one young man, with a slight air of reticence.

Another man, whose name was Mori, chimed in, "People were copying the signs, so I did too. I've got it with me now. Shall I read it?"

"Please do."

"Ah, here it is," said Mori, unfolding a crumpled scrap of paper. " 'Here's a word to Miyamoto Musashi, who turned tail and ran—' "

Eyebrows were raised and smiles began to appear, but Tadatoshi's face was grave. "Is that all?"

"No." He read the rest of it and said, "The signs were put up by a gang from the carpenters' district. People find it amusing because it's a case of street ruffians tweaking the nose of a samurai."

Tadatoshi frowned slightly, feeling that the words maligning Musashi called his own judgment into question. This was a far cry from the image he had formed of Musashi. Still, he was not ready to accept what he had heard at face value. "Hmm," he murmured. "I wonder if Musashi is really that sort of man."

"I gather he's a worthless lout," volunteered Mori, whose opinion was shared by the others. "Or at least a coward. If he wasn't, why would he allow his name to be dragged through the mud?"

The clock struck, and the men departed, but Tadatoshi sat on, thinking: "There's something interesting about this man." Not one to be swayed by the prevailing opinion, he was curious to know Musashi's side of the story.

The next morning, after listening to a lecture on the Chinese classics, he emerged from his study onto the veranda and caught sight of Sado in the garden. "Good morning, my elderly friend," he said.

Sado turned and politely bowed his morning greeting.

"Are you still on the lookout?" asked Tadatoshi.

Puzzled by the question, Sado merely stared back.

"I mean, are you still keeping an eye out for Miyamoto Musashi?"

"Yes, my lord." Sado lowered his eyes.

"If you do find him, bring him here. I want to see what he's like."

Shortly after noon on the same day, Kakubei approached Tadatoshi at the archery range and pressed his recommendation of Kojirō.

As he picked up his bow, the Young Lord said quietly, "Sorry, I'd forgotten. Bring him any time you wish. I'd like to have a look at him. Whether he becomes a retainer or not is another matter, as you well know."

24

Buzzing Insects

Seated in a back room of the small house Kakubei had lent him, Kojirō was examining the Drying Pole. After the incident with Hōjō Shinzō, he had requested Kakubei to press the craftsman for the return of the weapon. It had come back this morning.

"It won't be polished, of course," Kojirō had predicted, but in fact the sword had been worked on with an attention and care that were beyond his wildest hopes. From the blue-black metal, rippling like the current of a deep-running stream, there now sprang a brilliant white glow, the light of centuries past. The rust spots, which had seemed like leprous blemishes, were gone; the wavy tempering pattern between the blade's edge and the ridge line, hitherto smudged with bloodstains, was now serenely beautiful as a misty moon floating in the sky.

"It's like seeing it for the first time," marveled Kojirō. Unable to take his eyes from the sword, he didn't hear the visitor calling from the front of the house: "Are you here? . . . Kojirō?"

This part of the hill had been given the name Tsuki-nomisaki because of the magnificent view it afforded of the rising moon. From his sitting room, Kojirō could see the stretch of bay from Shiba to Shinagawa. Across the bay, frothy clouds appeared to be on a level with his eyes. At this moment, the white of the distant hills and the greenish blue of the water seemed fused with the blade.

"Kojirō! Isn't anybody here?" This time the voice came from the grass-woven side gate.

Coming out of his reverie, he shouted, "Who is it?" and returned the sword to its scabbard. "I'm in the back. If you want to see me, come around to the veranda."

"Oh, here you are," said Osugi, walking around to where she could see into the house.

"Well, this is a surprise," said Kojirō cordially. "What brings you out on a hot day like this?"

"Just a minute. Let me wash my feet. Then we can talk."

"The well's over there. Be careful. It's quite deep. You, boy—go with her and see she doesn't fall in." The man addressed as "boy" was a low-ranking member of Hangawara's gang who had been sent along to guide Osugi.

After washing her sweaty face and rinsing her feet, Osugi entered the house and exchanged a few words of greeting. Noticing the pleasant breeze coming off the bay, she squinted and said, "The house is nice and cool. Aren't you afraid you'll get lazy, staying in a comfortable place like this?"

Kojirō laughed. "I'm not like Matahachi."

The old woman blinked her eyes sadly but ignored the barb. "Sorry I didn't bring you a real gift," she said. "In place of one I'll give you a sutra I copied." As she handed him the *Sutra on the Great Love of Parents*, she added, "Please read it when you have time."

After a perfunctory glance at her handiwork, Kojirō turned to her guide and said, "That reminds me. Did you put up the signs I wrote for you?"

"The ones telling Musashi to come out of hiding?"

"Yes, those."

"It took us two whole days, but we put one up at almost every important intersection."

Osugi said, "We passed some on the way here. Everywhere they're posted, people are standing around gossiping. It made me feel good to hear the things they're saying about Musashi."

"If he doesn't answer the challenge, he's finished as a samurai. The whole country'll be laughing at him. That should be ample revenge for you, Granny."

"Not on your life. Being laughed at isn't going to get through to him. He's shameless. And it won't satisfy me either. I want to see him punished once and for all."

"Ha, ha," laughed Kojirō, amused by her tenacity. "You get older, but you never give up, do you? By the way, did you come about anything in particular?"

The old lady rearranged herself and explained that after more than two years with Hangawara she felt she should be moving on. It was not right for her to live on Yajibei's hospitality indefinitely; besides, she was tired of mothering a houseful of roughnecks. She had seen a nice little place for rent in the vicinity of Yoroi Ferry.

"What do you think?" Her face was serious, questioning. "It doesn't look like I'll find Musashi soon. And I have a feeling Matahachi's somewhere in Edo. I think I should have some money sent from home and stay on for a while. But by myself, as I said."

There being no reason for Kojirō to object, he quickly agreed with her. His own connection with the Hangawara ménage, entertaining and useful at the beginning, was now a little embarrassing. It was certainly no asset to a rōnin looking for a master. He had already decided to discontinue the practice sessions.

Kojirō summoned one of Kakubei's subordinates and had him bring a watermelon from the patch behind the house. They chatted while it was being cut and served, but before long he showed his guest out, his manner rather suggesting he preferred to have her out of the way before sundown.

When they had left, he himself swept his rooms and sprinkled the garden with well water. The morning glory and yam vines growing on the fence had reached the top and returned to the ground again, threatening to ensnare the foot of the stone water basin. Their white flowers waved in the evening breeze.

In his room again, he lay down and wondered idly if his host would be on duty that night at the Hosokawa house. The lamp, which would probably have been blown out by the wind anyway, was unlit. The light of the moon, rising beyond the bay, was already on his face.

At the bottom of the hill, a young samurai was breaking through the cemetery fence.

Kakubei stabled the horse he rode to and from the Hosokawa mansion at a florist's shop at the foot of Isarago Hill.

This evening, curiously enough, there was no sign of the florist, who always came out promptly to take charge of the animal. Not seeing him inside the shop, Kakubei went around to the back and started to tether his horse to a tree. As he did so, the florist came running out from behind the temple.

Taking the reins from Kakubei's hands, he panted, "Sorry, sir. There was a strange man in the cemetery, on his way up the hill. I shouted, told him there was no pathway there. He turned and stared at me—angry he was—then disappeared." He paused for a moment, peered up into the dark trees and added worriedly, "Do you think he could be a burglar? They say a lot of daimyō houses have been broken into recently."

Kakubei had heard the rumors, but he replied with a short laugh, "That's all talk, nothing more. If the man you saw was a burglar, I daresay he was a petty thief or one of the rōnin who waylay people on the streets."

"Well, we're right here at the entrance to the Tōkaidō, and lots of travelers have been attacked by men fleeing to other provinces. It makes me nervous when I see suspicious-looking men around at night."

"If anything happens, run up the hill and knock at

my gate. The man staying with me is chafing at the bit, always complaining there's never any action around here."

"You mean Sasaki Kojirō? He's got quite a reputation as a swordsman here in the neighborhood."

Hearing this did Kakubei's self-esteem no harm. Apart from liking young people, he knew quite well that it was regarded as both admirable and wise for established samurai like himself to take on promising younger men as protégés. Should an emergency arise, there could be no more persuasive proof of his loyalty than to be able to furnish his lord with good fighters. And if one of them turned out to be outstanding, due credit would be given to the retainer who had recommended him. One of Kakubei's beliefs was that self-interest was an undesirable trait in a vassal; nevertheless, he was realistic. In a large fief, there were few retainers willing to disregard their own interests entirely.

Despite the fact that he held his position through heredity, Kakubei was as loyal to Lord Tadatoshi as the other retainers, without being the sort who would strive to outdo others in demonstrating his fealty. For purposes of routine administration, men of his type were on the whole much more satisfactory than the firebrands who sought to perform spectacular feats.

"I'm back," he called on entering the gate to his house. The hill was quite steep, and he was always a little winded when he reached this point. Since he had left his wife in the country and the house was populated mostly by men, with only a few woman servants, feminine touches tended to be lacking. Yet on evenings when he had no night duty, he invariably found the stone path from the red gate to the entrance inviting, for it had been freshly watered down in anticipation of his return. And no matter how late the hour, someone always came to the front door to greet him.

"Is Kojirō here?" he asked.

"He's been in all day," replied the servant. "He's lying down in his room, enjoying the breeze."

"Good. Get some sake ready and ask him to come in to see me."

While preparations were being made, Kakubei took off his sweaty clothes and relaxed in the bath. Then, donning a light kimono, he entered his sitting room, where Kojirō sat waving a fan.

The sake was brought in. Kakubei poured, saying, "I called you because something encouraging happened today that I wanted to tell you about."

"Good news?"

"Since I mentioned your name to Lord Tadatoshi, he seems to have heard of you from other sources as well. Today he told me to bring you to see him some time soon. As you know, it's not easy to arrange these matters. There are dozens of retainers with someone they want to suggest." His expectation that Kojirō would be immensely pleased showed clearly in his tone and manner.

Kojirō put his cup to his lips and drank. When he did speak, his expression was unchanged and he said only, "Let me pour you one now."

Kakubei, far from being put out, admired the young man for being able to conceal his emotions. "This means I've been successful in carrying out what you requested of me. I think that calls for a celebration. Have another."

Kojirō bowed his head slightly and mumbled, "I'm grateful for your kindness."

"I was only doing my duty, of course," Kakubei replied modestly. "When a man is as capable and talented as you, I owe it to my lord to see that you're given consideration."

"Please don't overestimate me. And let me reemphasize one point. It's not the stipend I'm interested in. I simply think the House of Hosokawa is a very good one for a samurai to serve. It's had three outstanding men in a row." The three men were Tadatoshi and his father and grandfather, Sansai and Yūsai.

"You needn't think I've talked you up to the high heavens. I didn't have to. The name Sasaki Kojirō is known throughout the capital."

"How could I be famous when all I do is loaf around here all day long? I don't see that I'm outstanding in any way. It's just that there are so many fakes around."

"I was told that I could bring you anytime. When would you like to go?"

"Any time suits me too."

"How about tomorrow?"

"That's all right with me." His face revealed no eagerness, no anxiety, only calm self-confidence.

Kakubei, even more impressed at his sangfroid, chose this time to say matter-of-factly, "You understand, of course, his lordship won't be able to make a final decision until he's seen you. You needn't let that worry you. It's only a matter of form. I have no doubt but what the position will be offered."

Kojirō set his cup down on the table and stared straight into Kakubei's face. Then, very coldly and defiantly, he said, "I've changed my mind. Sorry to have put you to so much trouble." Blood seemed about to burst from his earlobes, already bright red from the drink.

"Wh-what?" stammered Kakubei. "You mean you're giving up the chance for a position with the House of Hosokawa?"

"I don't like the idea," answered his guest curtly, offering no further explanation. His pride told him there was no reason for him to submit to an inspection; dozens of other daimyō would snap him up sight unseen for fifteen hundred, even twenty-five hundred, bushels.

Kakubei's puzzled disappointment seemed to make no impression on him whatsoever, nor did it matter that he would be regarded as a willful ingrate. Without the least suggestion of doubt or repentance, he finished off his food in silence and returned to his own quarters.

The moonlight fell softly on the tatami. Stretching out drunkenly on the floor, arms under his head, he began to laugh quietly to himself. "Honest man, that Kakubei. Good, old, honest Kakubei." He knew his host would be at a loss to explain this sudden shift to Tadatoshi, but he knew also that Kakubei would not be angry at him for very long, no matter how outrageously he behaved.

While he had piously denied interest in the stipend, he was in fact consumed with ambition. He wanted a stipend and much more—every ounce of fame and success he could possibly achieve. Otherwise, what would be the purpose of persevering through years of arduous training?

Kojirō's ambition was different from that of other men only by dint of its magnitude. He wanted to be known throughout the country as a great and successful man, to bring glory to his home in Iwakuni, to enjoy every one of the benefits that can possibly derive from being born human. The quickest road to fame and riches was to excel in the martial arts. He was fortunate in having a natural talent for the sword; he knew this and derived no small measure of self-satisfaction from it. He had planned his course intelligently and with remarkable foresight. Every action of his was calculated to put him closer to his goal. To his way of thinking, Kakubei, though his senior, was naive and a little sentimental.

He fell asleep dreaming of his brilliant future.

Later, when the moonlight had edged a foot across the tatami, a voice no louder than the breeze whispering through the bamboo said, "Now." A shadowy form, crouching among the mosquitoes, crept forward like a frog to the eaves of the unlighted house.

The mysterious man seen earlier at the foot of the hill advanced slowly, silently, until he reached the veranda, where he stopped and peered into the room. Stooping in the shadows, out of the moonlight, he might have remained undiscovered indefinitely had he himself made no sound.

Kojirō snored on. The soft hum of insects, briefly interrupted as the man moved into position, came again across the dew-covered grass.

Minutes passed. Then the silence was broken by the clatter the man made as he whipped out his sword and jumped up onto the veranda.

He leapt toward Kojirō and cried, "Arrgh!" an instant before he clenched his teeth and struck.

There was a sharp hissing as a long black object descended heavily on his wrist, but the original force of his strike had been powerful. Instead of falling from his hand, his sword sank into the tatami, where Kojirō's body had been.

Like a fish darting away from a pole striking water, the intended victim had streaked to the wall. He now stood facing the intruder, the Drying Pole in one hand, its scabbard in the other.

"Who are you?" Kojirō's breath was calm. Alert as always to the sounds of nature's creatures, to the falling of a dewdrop, he was unperturbed.

"I-it-it's me!"

" 'Me' doesn't tell my anything. I know you're a coward, attacking a man in his sleep. What's your name?"

"I am Yogorō, the only son of Obata Kagenori. You took advantage of my father when he was sick. And you spread gossip about him all over the city."

"I wasn't the one who spread the gossip. It was the gossipers—the people of Edo."

"Who was it who lured his students into a fight and killed them?"

"I did that, no doubt about it. I, Sasaki Kojirō. How can I help it if I'm better than they? Stronger. Braver. More knowledgeable in the Art of War."

"How can you have the gall to say that when you called on Hangawara's vermin to help you?"

With a snarl of disgust, Kojirō took a step forward. "If you want to hate me, go ahead! But any man who carries a personal grudge into a test of strength in the Art of War isn't even a coward. He's worse than that, more pitiable, more laughable. So once again I have to take the life of an Obata man. Are you resigned to that?"

No answer.

"I said, are you resigned to your fate?" He moved another step forward. As he did so, the light of the moon reflecting off the newly polished blade of his sword blinded Yogorō.

Kojirō stared at his prey as a starving man stares at a feast.

25

The Eagle

Kakubei regretted having allowed himself to be used shabbily and vowed to have nothing more to do with Kojirō. Yet deep down, he liked the man. What he didn't like was being caught between his master and his protégé. Then he began to rethink the matter.

"Maybe Kojirō's reaction proves how exceptional he is. The ordinary samurai would have jumped at the chance to be interviewed." The more he reflected on Kojirō's fit of pique, the more the rōnin's independent spirit appealed to him.

For the next three days Kakubei was on night duty. He did not see Kojirō until the morning of the fourth day, when he walked casually over to the young man's quarters.

After a short but awkward silence, he said, "I want to talk to you for a minute, Kojirō. Yesterday, when I was leaving, Lord Tadatoshi asked me about you. He said he'd see you. Why don't you drop in at the archery range and have a look at the Hosokawa technique?"

When Kojirō grinned without replying, Kakubei added, "I don't know why you insist on thinking it's demeaning. It's usual to interview a man before offering him an official position."

"I know, but supposing he rejects me, then what?

I'd be a castoff, wouldn't I? I'm not so hard up that I have to go around peddling myself to the highest bidder."

"Then the fault is mine. I put it the wrong way. His lordship never meant to imply any such thing."

"Well, what answer did you give him?"

"None yet. But he seems a little impatient."

"Ha, ha. You've been very thoughtful, very helpful. I suppose I shouldn't put you in such a difficult position."

"Wouldn't you reconsider—go and call on him, just once?"

"All right, if it means so much to you," Kojirō said patronizingly, but Kakubei was nonetheless pleased.

"How about today?"

"So soon?"

"Yes."

"What time?"

"How about a little after noon? That's when he practices archery."

"All right, I'll be there."

Kojirō set about making elaborate preparations for the meeting. The kimono he chose was of excellent quality, and the *hakama* was made of imported fabric. Over the kimono he wore a formal vestlike garment of sheer silk, sleeveless but with stiff flaring shoulders. To complement his finery, he had the servants provide him with a new zōri and a new basket hat.

"Is there a horse I can use?" he inquired.

"Yes. The master's spare horse, the white one, is at the shop at the bottom of the hill."

Failing to find the florist, Kojirō glanced toward the temple compound across the way, where a group of people were gathering around a corpse covered with reed matting. He went over to have a look.

They were discussing plans for burial with the local priest. The victim had no identifying possessions on him; no one knew who he was, only that he was young and of the samurai class. The blood around the deep gash ex-

tending from the tip of one shoulder to his waist was
dried and black.

"I've seen him before. About four days ago, in the
evening," said the florist, who went on talking excitedly
until he felt a hand on his shoulder.

When he looked to see who it was, Kojirō said, "I'm
told Kakubei's horse is kept at your place. Get him ready
for me, please."

Bowing hastily, the florist asked perfunctorily, "Are
you going out?" and hurried off.

He patted the dappled-gray steed on the neck as he
led it out of his stable.

"Quite a good horse," Kojirō remarked.

"Yes, indeed. A fine animal."

Once Kojirō was in the saddle, the florist beamed
and said, "It's a good match."

Taking some money from his purse, Kojirō threw it
to the man. "Use this for flowers and incense."

"Huh? Who for?"

"The dead man over there."

Beyond the temple gate, Kojirō cleared his throat
and spat, as if to eject the bitter taste left by the sight of
the corpse. But he was pursued by the feeling that the
youth he had cut down with the Drying Pole had thrown
aside the reed matting and was following him. "I did
nothing he could hate me for," he told himself, and felt
better for the thought.

As horse and rider moved along the Takanawa highroad under the boiling sun, townsmen and samurai alike
stood aside to make way. Heads turned in admiration.
Even on the streets of Edo, Kojirō cut an impressive
figure, causing people to wonder who he was and where
he came from.

At the Hosokawa residence, he turned the horse over
to a servant and entered the house. Kakubei rushed to
meet him. "My thanks for coming. It's just the right time
too," he said, as though Kojirō were doing him a great
personal favor. "Rest awhile. I'll tell his lordship you're

here." Before doing so, he made sure the guest was provided with cool water, barley tea and a tobacco tray.

When a retainer came to show him to the archery range, Kojirō handed over his beloved Drying Pole and followed along wearing only his short sword.

Lord Tadatoshi had resolved to shoot a hundred arrows a day during the summer months. A number of close retainers were always there, watching each shot with bated breath and making themselves useful retrieving arrows.

"Give me a towel," his lordship commanded, standing his bow beside him.

Kneeling, Kakubei asked, "May I trouble you, sir?"

"What is it?"

"Sasaki Kojirō is here. I would appreciate your seeing him."

"Sasaki? Oh, yes."

He fitted an arrow to the bowstring, took an open stance, and raised his shooting arm above his eyebrows. Neither he nor any of the others so much as glanced in Kojirō's direction until the hundred shots were finished.

With a sigh Tadatoshi said, "Water. Bring me some water."

An attendant brought some from the well and poured it into a large wooden tub at Tadatoshi's feet. Letting the upper part of his kimono hang loose, he wiped off his chest and washed his feet. His men assisted by holding his sleeves, running to fetch more water and wiping off his back. There was nothing formal in their manner, nothing to suggest to an observer that this was a daimyō and his retinue.

Kojirō had supposed that Tadatoshi, a poet and an aesthete, the son of Lord Sansai and the grandson of Lord Yūsai, would be a man of aristocratic bearing, as refined in his conduct as the elegant courtiers of Kyoto. But his surprise did not show in his eyes as he watched.

Slipping his still damp feet into his zōri, Tadatoshi looked at Kakubei, who was waiting off to one side. With the air of one who has suddenly recalled a promise, he said, "Now, Kakubei, I'll see your man." He had a stool brought and placed in the shade of a tent, where he sat down in front of a banner bearing his crest, a circle surrounded by eight smaller circles, representing the sun, moon and seven planets.

Beckoned by Kakubei, Kojirō came forward and knelt before Lord Tadatoshi. As soon as the formal greeting was completed, Tadatoshi invited Kojirō to sit on a stool, thus signifying that he was an honored guest.

"By your leave," said Kojirō, as he rose and took a seat facing Tadatoshi.

"I've heard about you from Kakubei. I believe you were born in Iwakuni, weren't you?"

"That is correct, sir."

"Lord Kikkawa Hiroie of Iwakuni was well known as a wise and noble ruler. Were your ancestors retainers of his?"

"No, we never served the House of Kikkawa. I've been told we're descended from the Sasakis of Ōmi Province. After the fall of the last Ashikaga shōgun, my father seems to have retired to my mother's village."

After a few more questions concerning family and lineage, Lord Tadatoshi asked, "Will you be going into service for the first time?"

"I do not yet know whether I am going into service."

"I gathered from Kakubei you wish to serve the House of Hosokawa. What are your reasons?"

"I believe it is a house I would be willing to live and die for."

Tadatoshi seemed pleased with this answer. "And your style of fighting?"

"I call it the Ganryū Style."

" 'Ganryū'?"

"It's a style I invented myself."

"Presumably it has antecedents."

"I studied the Tomita Style, and I had the benefit of lessons from Lord Katayama Hisayasu of Hōki, who in his old age retired to Iwakuni. I've also mastered many techniques on my own. I used to practice cutting down swallows on the wing."

"I see. I suppose the name Ganryū comes from the name of that river near where you were born?"

"Yes, sir."

"I'd like to see a demonstration." Tadatoshi looked around at the faces of his samurai. "Which one of you would like to take this man on?"

They had been watching the interview in silence, thinking that Kojirō was remarkably young to have acquired the reputation he had. Now all looked first at each other, then at Kojirō, whose flushed cheeks proclaimed his willingness to face any challenger.

"How about you, Okatani?"

"Yes, sir."

"You're always claiming the lance is superior to the sword. Now's your chance to prove it."

"I shall be glad to, if Sasaki is willing."

"By all means," Kojirō answered with alacrity. In his tone, which was polite but extremely cool, there was a hint of cruelty.

The samurai who had been sweeping the sand on the archery range and putting away the equipment assembled behind their master. Although weapons were as familiar to them as chopsticks, their experience had been primarily in the dōjō. The chance to witness, much less have, a real bout would occur only a few times throughout their lives. They would readily agree that a man-to-man fight was a greater challenge than going out on the battlefield, where it was sometimes possible for a man to pause and get his wind while his comrades fought on. In hand-to-hand combat, he had only himself to rely on, only his own alertness and strength from beginning to end. Either he won, or he was killed or maimed.

They watched Okatani Gorōji solemnly. Even among the lowest-ranking foot soldiers there were quite a few who were adept with the lance; Gorōji was generally conceded to be the best. He had not only been in battle but had practiced diligently and devised techniques of his own.

"Give me a few minutes," said Gorōji, bowing toward Tadatoshi and Kojirō before withdrawing to make his preparations. It pleased him that today, as on other days, he had on spotless underwear, in the tradition of the good samurai, who started each day with a smile and an uncertainty: by evening he might be a corpse.

After borrowing a three-foot wooden sword, Kojirō selected the ground for the match. His body seemed relaxed and open, the more so since he didn't hitch up his pleated *hakama*. His appearance was formidable; even his enemies would have had to admit that. There was an eaglelike air of valor about him, and his handsome profile was serenely confident.

Worried eyes began to turn toward the canopy behind which Gorōji was adjusting his clothing and equipment.

"What's taking him so long?" someone asked.

Gorōji was calmly wrapping a piece of damp cloth around the point of his lance, a weapon he had used to excellent effect on the battlefield. The shaft was nine feet long, and the tapering blade alone, at eight or nine inches, was the equivalent of a short sword.

"What are you doing?" called Kojirō. "If you're worried about hurting me, save yourself the trouble." Again, though the words were courteous, the implication was arrogant. "I don't mind if you leave it unwrapped."

Looking sharply at him, Gorōji said, "Are you sure?"

"Perfectly."

Though neither Lord Tadatoshi nor his men spoke, their piercing eyes told Gorōji to go ahead. If the stranger had the gall to ask for it, why not run him through?

"In that case . . ." Gorōji tore off the wrapping and advanced holding the lance midway along the shaft. "I'm

261

happy to comply, but if I use a naked blade, I want you to use a real sword."

"This wooden one's fine."

"No; I can't agree to that."

"Certainly you wouldn't expect me, an outsider, to have the audacity to employ a real sword in the presence of his lordship."

"But—"

With a touch of impatience, Lord Tadatoshi said, "Go ahead, Okatani. Nobody will consider you cowardly for complying with the man's request." It was obvious Kojirō's attitude had affected him.

The two men, faces flushed with determination, exchanged greetings with their eyes. Gorōji made the first move, leaping to the side, but Kojirō, like a bird stuck to a limed fowling pole, slipped under the lance and struck directly at his chest. Lacking time to thrust, the lancer whirled sideways and tried to jab the nape of Kojirō's neck with the butt of his weapon. With a resounding crack, the lance flew back up into the air, as Kojirō's sword bit into Gorōji's ribs, which had been exposed by the momentum of the rising lance. Gorōji slid to one side, then leapt away, but the attack continued without letup. With no time to catch his breath, he jumped aside again, then again and again. The first few dodges were successful, but he was like a peregrine falcon trying to fend off an eagle. Hounded by the raging sword, the lance shaft snapped in two. At the same instant, Gorōji emitted a cry; it sounded as though his soul was being torn from his body.

The brief battle was ended. Kojirō had hoped to take on four or five men, but Tadatoshi said that he had seen enough.

When Kakubei came home that evening, Kojirō asked him, "Did I go a little too far? In front of his lordship, I mean."

"No, it was a magnificent performance." Kakubei

felt rather ill at ease. Now that he could assess the full extent of Kojirō's ability, he felt like a man who had hugged a tiny bird to his chest, only to see it grow up to be an eagle.

"Did Lord Tadatoshi say anything?"

"Nothing in particular."

"Come now, he must have said something."

"No; he left the archery range without a word."

"Hmm." Kojirō looked disappointed but said, "Oh, it doesn't matter. He impressed me as a greater man than he's usually made out to be. I was thinking if I had to serve anyone, it might as well be him. But of course I have no control over how things turn out." He didn't reveal how carefully he had thought about the situation. After the Date, Kuroda, Shimazu and Mōri clans, the Hosokawa was the most prestigious and secure. He felt sure this would continue to be true so long as Lord Sansai held the Buzen fief. And sooner or later, Edo and Osaka would clash once and for all. There was no way of predicting the outcome; a samurai who had chosen the wrong master might easily find himself a rōnin again, his whole life sacrificed for a few months' stipend.

The day after the bout, word came that Gorōji had survived, though his pelvis or left thighbone had been smashed. Kojirō accepted the news calmly, telling himself that even if he did not receive a position, he had given a good enough account of himself.

A few days later he abruptly announced he was going to pay a call on Gorōji. Offering no explanation for this sudden display of kindness, he set out alone and on foot for Gorōji's house near Tokiwa Bridge.

The unexpected visitor was received cordially by the injured man.

"A match is a match," said Gorōji, a smile on his lips and moistness in his eyes. "I may deplore my own lack of skill, but I certainly hold nothing against you. It was good of you to come to see me. Thank you."

After Kojirō left, Gorōji remarked to a friend, "Now,

there's a samurai I can admire. I thought he was an arrogant son of a bitch, but he turns out to be both friendly and polite."

This was precisely the reaction Kojirō had hoped for. It was part of his plan; other visitors would hear him praised by the defeated man himself. Calling once every two or three days, he made three more visits to Gorōji's house. On one occasion he had a live fish delivered from the fish market as a get-well present.

26

Green Persimmons

In the dog days after the summer rainy season, the land crabs crawled sluggishly in the parched street, and the signs taunting Musashi to "come out and fight" were no longer visible. The few that hadn't fallen in the rain-softened earth or been stolen for firewood were obscured by weeds and tall grass.

"There must be something somewhere," thought Kojirō, looking around for a place to eat. But this was Edo, not Kyoto, and the cheap rice-and-tea shops so common in the older city had not yet made their appearance here. The only likely place stood in a vacant lot, screened off with reed blinds. Smoke rose lazily from behind the blinds, and on a vertical banner was the word "Donjiki." The word immediately reminded him of *tonjiki*, which in the distant past had meant the rice balls used as military rations.

As he approached, he heard a masculine voice ask for a cup of tea. Inside, two samurai were energetically gobbling rice, one from an ordinary rice bowl, the other from a sake bowl.

Kojirō seated himself on the edge of a bench across from them and asked the proprietor, "What do you have?"

"Rice dishes. I also have sake."

"On the banner it says 'Donjiki.' What does that mean?"

"As a matter of fact, I don't know."

"Didn't you write it?"

"No. It was written by a retired merchant who stopped in to rest."

"I see. Good calligraphy, I must say."

"He said he was on a religious pilgrimage, said he'd visited Hirakawa Tenjin Shrine, Hikawa Shrine, Kanda Myōjin, all sorts of places, making big contributions to each of them. Very pious and generous, he seemed."

"Do you know his name?"

"He told me it was Daizō of Narai."

"I've heard the name."

"Donjiki—well, I don't understand it. But I figured if a fine man like him wrote it, it might help keep the god of poverty away." He laughed.

After a look into several large china bowls, Kojirō took some rice and fish, poured tea over the rice, brushed a fly away with his chopsticks and began eating.

One of the other customers stood up and peered through a broken slat in the blind. "Take a look out there, Hamada," he said to his companion. "Isn't that the watermelon vendor?"

The other man went quickly to the blind and looked out. "Yeah, that's him all right."

The vendor, shouldering a pole with baskets at either end, was walking languidly past the Donjiki. The two samurai ran out of the shop and caught up with him. Drawing their swords, they cut the ropes supporting the baskets. The vendor stumbled forward, along with the melons.

Hamada yanked him up by the scruff of his neck. "Where did you take her?" he demanded angrily. "Don't lie. You must be hiding her somewhere."

The other samurai thrust the tip of his sword under the captive's nose.

"Out with it! Where is she?"

The sword blade tapped menacingly against the man's cheek. "How could anybody with a face like yours think of going off with somebody else's woman?"

The vendor, cheeks flushed with anger and fear, shook his head, but then, seeing an opening, shoved one of his captors out of the way, picked up his pole and took a swing at the other one.

"So you want to fight, do you? Careful, Hamada, this guy's not just an ordinary melon vendor."

"What can this ass do?" sneered Hamada, snatching the pole and knocking the vendor to the ground. Straddling him, he used the ropes to tie him to the pole.

A cry like that of a stuck pig went up behind him. Hamada turned his face around, right into a spray of fine red mist. Looking totally dumbfounded, he jumped up, screaming, "Who are you? What—"

The adderlike blade moved directly toward him. Kojirō laughed, and as Hamada shrank back, followed him relentlessly. The two moved in a circle through the grass. When Hamada moved back a foot, Kojirō moved forward the same distance. When Hamada leapt to one side, the Drying Pole followed, pointing unwaveringly at his prospective victim.

The melon vendor cried out in astonishment. "Kojirō! It's me. Save me!"

Hamada blanched with terror and gasped, "Ko-ji-rō!" Then he wheeled around and tried to flee.

"Where do you think you're going?" barked Kojirō. The Drying Pole flashed through the sultry stillness, lopping off Hamada's ear and lodging deep in the flesh under the shoulders. He died on the spot.

Kojirō promptly cut the melon vendor's bonds. Rearranging himself into a proper sitting posture, the man bowed, and stayed bowed, too embarrassed to show his face.

Kojirō wiped and resheathed his sword. Amusement playing faintly around his lips, he said, "What's the matter with you, Matahachi? Don't look so miserable. You're still alive."

"Yes, sir."

"None of this 'yes, sir' business. Look at me. It's been a long time, hasn't it?"

"I'm glad you're well."

"Why wouldn't I be? But I must say you've taken to an unusual trade."

"Let's not talk about it."

"All right. Pick up your melons. Then—I know, why don't you leave them at the Donjiki?" With a loud shout, he summoned the proprietor, who helped them stack the melons behind the blinds.

Kojirō took out his brush and ink and wrote on one of the shoji: "To whom it may concern: I certify that the person who killed the two men lying on this vacant lot was myself, Sasaki Kojirō, a rōnin residing at Tsukino-misaki."

To the proprietor, he said, "This should fix it so no one'll bother you about the killings."

"Thank you, sir."

"Think nothing of it. If friends or relatives of the dead men should come around, please deliver this message for me. Tell them I won't run away. If they want to see me, I'm ready to greet them anytime."

Outside again, he said to Matahachi, "Let's go."

Matahachi walked beside him but would not take his eyes off the ground. Not once since coming to Edo had he held a steady job. Whatever his intention—to become a *shugyōsha* or to go into business—when he found the going rough, he changed jobs. And after Otsū slipped away from him, he felt less and less like working. He'd slept in first one place, then another, sometimes at flop-houses populated by hoodlums. The past few weeks, he had been making his living as a common peddler, trudging from one part of the castle wall to another, hawking watermelons.

Kojirō wasn't particularly interested in what Matahachi had been doing, but he had written the sign at the Donjiki and he might later be questioned about the incident. "Why did those samurai have it in for you?" he asked.

"To tell the truth, it had to do with a woman. . . . "

Kojirō smiled, thinking wherever Matahachi went, there soon arose some difficulty connected with women. Perhaps this was his karma. "Mm," he mumbled. "The great lover in action again, eh?" Then, more loudly, "Who is the woman, and what exactly happened?"

It took some prodding, but eventually Matahachi gave in and told his tale, or part of it. Near the moat, there were dozens of tiny tea shops catering to construction workers and passersby. In one of these there had been a waitress who caught everybody's eyes, enticing men who did not want tea to step in for a cup and men who were not hungry to order bowls of sweet jelly. One regular customer had been Hamada; Matahachi, too, dropped in occasionally.

One day this waitress whispered to him that she needed his help. "That rōnin," she had said. "I don't like him, but every night after the shop closes, the master orders me to go home with him. Won't you let me come and hide in your house? I won't be a burden. I'll cook for you, and mend your clothes."

Since her plea seemed reasonable, Matahachi had agreed. That was all there was to it, he insisted.

Kojirō was unconvinced. "It sounds fishy to me."

"Why?" Matahachi asked.

Kojirō could not decide whether Matahachi was trying to make himself appear innocent or whether he was bragging about an amorous conquest. Without even smiling, he said, "Never mind. It's hot out here under the sun. Let's go to your house, and you can tell me about it in more detail."

Matahachi stopped in his tracks.

"Is there anything wrong with that?" asked Kojirō.

"Well, my place is—it's not the sort of place I'd want to take you to."

Seeing the distressed look in Matahachi's eyes, Kojirō said lightly, "Never mind. But one of these days soon you must come to see me. I'm staying with Iwama Kakubei, about halfway up Isarago Hill."

"I'd like that."

"By the way, did you see the signs posted around the city recently, the ones addressed to Musashi?"

"Yes."

"They said your mother was looking for him too. Why don't you go to see her?"

"Not the way I am now!"

"Idiot. You don't have to put on a great show for your own mother. There's no way of knowing just when she might find Musashi, and if you're not there at the time, you'll lose the chance of a lifetime. You'd regret that, wouldn't you?"

"Yes, I'll have to do something about that soon," Matahachi said noncommittally, thinking resentfully that other people, including the man who had just saved his life, did not understand the feelings between mothers and their offspring.

They parted, Matahachi ambling down a grassy lane, Kojirō ostensibly setting out in the opposite direction. Kojirō soon doubled back and followed Matahachi, taking care to stay out of sight.

Matahachi arrived presently at a motley collection of "long houses," one-story tenements, each containing three or four small apartments under a single roof. Since Edo had grown rapidly and not everybody could be choosy about where he lived, people cleared land as the necessity arose. Streets came into existence afterward, developing naturally from pathways. Drainage, too, came about by accident, as waste water cut its path to the nearest stream. Had it not been for these jerry-built slums, the influx of newcomers could not have been absorbed. The majority of the inhabitants of such places were, of course, workmen.

Near his home, Matahachi was greeted by a neighbor named Umpei, the boss of a crew of well diggers. Umpei was seated cross-legged in a large wooden tub, only his face showing above the rain shutter placed sideways in front of the tub for privacy.

"Good evening," said Matahachi, "I see you're having your bath."

"I'm about to get out," replied the boss genially. "Would you like to use it next?"

"Thanks, but I think Akemi's probably heated water for me."

"You two are very fond of each other, aren't you? Nobody around here seems to know whether you're brother and sister or husband and wife. Which is it?"

Matahachi giggled sheepishly. The appearance of Akemi saved him from having to answer.

She placed a tub under a persimmon tree and brought pailfuls of hot water from the house to fill it. When she was done, she said, "Feel it, Matahachi. See if it's hot enough."

"It's a little too hot."

There was a squeaking of the well pulley, and Matahachi, stripped to his loincloth, brought up a bucket of cold water and poured it into the bath before climbing in himself. "Ah-h-h," he sighed contentedly. "This feels good."

Umpei, wearing a cotton summer kimono, placed a bamboo stool under a gourd trellis and sat down. "Did you sell lots of melons?" he inquired.

"Not many. I never sell very many." Noticing dried blood between his fingers, he hastily wiped it off.

"I don't imagine you would. I still think your life would be easier if you went to work on a well-digging gang."

"You're always saying that. Don't think I'm ungrateful, but if I did that, they wouldn't let me off the castle grounds, would they? That's why Akemi doesn't want me to take the job. She says she'd be lonesome without me."

"Happily married couple, eh? Well, well."

"Ouch!"

"What's the matter?"

"Something fell on my head."

A green persimmon landed on the ground just behind Matahachi.

"Ha, ha! Punishment for bragging about your wife's devotion, that's what it is." Still laughing, Umpei rapped his tannin-coated fan on his knee.

Over sixty years old, with a shaggy, hemplike mane of white hair, Umpei was a man who enjoyed the respect of his neighbors and the admiration of the young people, whom he bigheartedly treated as his own children. Each morning he could be heard chanting *Namu Myōhō Rengekyō*, the sacred invocation of the Nichiren sect.

A native of Itō in Izu Province, he had a sign in front of his house saying: "Idohori no Umpei, Well Digger for the Shōgun's Castle." To build the many wells necessary for the castle involved technical skills beyond those of ordinary laborers. Umpei had been hired as a consultant and recruiter of workers because of his long experience in the gold mines of Izu Peninsula. He enjoyed nothing more than sitting under his beloved gourd trellis, spinning yarns and drinking his nightly cup of cheap but potent *shōchū,* the poor man's sake.

After Matahachi emerged from the bath, Akemi surrounded the washtub with rain shutters and had hers. Later the matter of Umpei's proposal came up once again. Besides having to stay on the castle grounds, the workers were watched very closely, and their families were virtually hostages of the bosses of the areas where they lived. On the other hand, the work was easier than on the outside and paid at least twice as much.

Leaning over a tray on which there was a dish of cold bean curd, garnished with fresh, fragrant basil leaf,

Matahachi said, "I don't want to become a prisoner just to earn a little money. I'm not going to sell melons all my life, but bear with me a little longer, Akemi."

"Umm," she replied between mouthfuls of tea-and-rice gruel. "I'd rather you tried just once to do something really worthwhile, something that would make people take notice."

Though nothing was ever said or done to discourage the idea that she was Matahachi's legal wife, she wasn't about to marry anyone who shilly-shallied the way he did. Fleeing the world of play at Sakaimachi with Matahachi had been only an expedient; he was the perch from which she intended, at the first opportunity, to fly once more into the open sky. But it did not suit her purposes for Matahachi to go off to the castle to work. She felt being left alone would be dangerous; specifically, she was afraid Hamada might find her and force her to live with him.

"Oh, I forgot," said Matahachi, as they finished their frugal meal. He then told her about his experiences that day, adjusting the details in a fashion calculated to please her. By the time he had finished, her face was ashen.

Taking a deep breath, she said, "You saw Kojirō? Did you tell him I was here? You didn't, did you?"

Matahachi took her hand and placed it on his knee. "Of course not. Do you think I'd let that bastard know where you are? He's the kind that never gives up. He'd be after you—"

He broke off with an inarticulate shout and pressed his hand to the side of his face. The green persimmon that smashed against his cheek broke and spattered its whitish meat in Akemi's face.

Outside, in the shadows of a moonlit bamboo grove, a form not unlike that of Kojirō could be seen walking nonchalantly away in the direction of town.

27

Eyes

"*Sensei!*" called Iori, who was not yet tall enough to see over the tall grass. They were on Musashino Plain, which was said to cover ten counties.

"I'm right here," replied Musashi. "What's taking you so long?"

"I guess there's a path, but I keep losing it. How much farther do we have to go?"

"Till we find a good place to live."

"Live? We're going to stay around here?"

"Why shouldn't we?"

Iori gazed up at the sky, thought of its vastness and the emptiness of the land around him and said, "I wonder."

"Think what it'll be like in the fall. Clear, beautiful skies, fresh dew on the grass. Doesn't it make you feel cleaner just thinking about it?"

"Well, maybe, but I'm not against living in the city, like you."

"I'm not, really. In a way, it's nice to be among people, but even with my thick skin I couldn't stand being there when those signs were put up. You saw what they said."

Iori grimaced. "I get mad just thinking about it."

"Why let yourself get angry over that?"

"I couldn't help it. No matter where I went, there wasn't anybody who'd say anything good about you."

"Nothing I could do about that."

"You could have cut down the men spreading the rumors. You could have put up your own signs challenging them."

"There's no point in starting fights you can't win."

"You wouldn't have lost to that scum. You couldn't have."

"No, you're wrong. I would have."

"How?"

"Sheer numbers. If I beat ten, there'd be a hundred more. If I defeated a hundred, there'd be a thousand. There's no possibility of winning in that kind of situation."

"But does that mean you're going to be laughed at for the rest of your life?"

"Of course not. I'm as determined as the next person to have a good name. I owe it to my ancestors. And I intend to become a man who's never laughed at. That's what I came out here to learn."

"We can walk all we want, but I don't think we're going to find any houses. Shouldn't we try to find a temple to stay in again?"

"That's not a bad idea, but what I really want is to find someplace with a lot of trees and build a house of our own."

"It'll be like Hōtengahara again, won't it?"

"No. This time we're not going to farm. I think maybe I'll practice Zen meditation every day. You can read books, and I'll give you some lessons in the sword."

Entering the plain at the village of Kashiwagi, the Kōshū entrance to Edo, they had come down the long slope from Jūnisho Gongen and followed a narrow path that repeatedly threatened to disappear among the waving summer grasses. When they finally reached a pine-covered knoll, Musashi made a quick survey of the terrain and said, "This'll do fine." To him, any place could serve as home—more than that: wherever he happened to be was the universe.

They borrowed tools and hired a laborer at the nearest farmhouse. Musashi's approach to building a house was not at all sophisticated; in fact, he could have learned quite a bit from watching birds build a nest. The result, finished a few days later, was an oddity, less substantial than a hermit's mountain retreat but not so crude as to be described as a shed. The posts were logs with the bark left on, the remainder a rough alliance of boards, bark, bamboo and miscanthus.

Standing back to take a good look, Musashi remarked thoughtfully, "This must be like the houses people lived in back in the age of the gods." The only relief from the primitiveness were scraps of paper lovingly fashioned to make small shoji.

In the days following, the sound of Iori's voice, floating from behind a reed blind as he recited his lessons, rose above the buzz of the cicadas. His training had become very strict in every respect.

With Jōtarō, Musashi had not insisted on discipline, thinking at the time that it was best to let growing boys grow naturally. But with the passage of time, he had observed that, if anything, bad traits tended to develop and good ones to be repressed. Similarly, he had noticed that trees and plants he wanted to grow would not grow, while weed and brush flourished no matter how often he cut them down.

During the hundred years after the Ōnin War, the nation had been like a tangled mass of overgrown hemp plants. Then Nobunaga had cut the plants down, Hideyoshi had bundled them up, and Ieyasu had broken and smoothed the ground to build a new world. As Musashi saw it, warriors who placed a high value only on martial practices and whose most noticeable characteristic was unbounded ambition were no longer the dominant element in society. Sekigahara had put an end to that.

He had come to believe that whether the nation

remained in the hands of the Tokugawas or reverted to the Toyotomis, people in general already knew the direction they wanted to move in: from chaos toward order, from destruction toward construction.

At times, he'd had the feeling that he had been born too late. No sooner had Hideyoshi's glory penetrated into remote rural areas and fired the hearts of boys like Musashi than the possibility of following in Hideyoshi's footsteps evaporated.

So it was his own experience that led to his decision to emphasize discipline in Iori's upbringing. If he was going to create a samurai, he should create one for the coming era, not for the past.

"Iori."

"Yes, sir." The boy was kneeling before Musashi almost before the words were out.

"It's almost sunset. Time for our practice. Bring the swords."

"Yes, sir." When he placed them in front of Musashi, he knelt and formally requested a lesson.

Musashi's sword was long, Iori's short, both wooden practice weapons. Teacher and pupil faced each other in tense silence, swords held at eye level. A rim of sunlight hovered on the horizon. The cryptomeria grove behind the cabin was already sunk in gloom, but if one looked toward the voices of the cicadas, a sliver of moon was visible through the branches.

"Eyes," said Musashi.

Iori opened his eyes wide.

"*My* eyes. Look at them."

Iori did his best, but his eyes seemed to literally bounce away from Musashi's. Instead of glaring, he was being defeated by his opponent's eyes. When he tried again, he was seized by giddiness. His head began to feel as if it were no longer his own. His hands, his feet, his whole body felt wobbly.

"Look at my eyes!" Musashi commanded with great sternness. Iori's look had strayed again. Then, concentrating on his master's eyes, he forgot the sword in his hand. The short length of curved wood seemed to become as heavy as a bar of steel.

"Eyes, eyes!" said Musashi, advancing slightly.

Iori checked the urge to fall back, for which he had been scolded dozens of times. But when he attempted to follow his opponent's lead and move forward, his feet were nailed to the ground. Unable either to advance or to retreat, he could feel his body temperature rise. "What's the matter with me?" The thought exploded like fireworks inside him.

Sensing this burst of mental energy, Musashi yelled, "Charge!" At the same time he lowered his shoulders, dropped back and dodged with the agility of a fish.

With a gasp, Iori sprang forward, spun around—and saw Musashi standing where he himself had been.

Then the confrontation began again, just as before, both teacher and pupil maintaining strict silence.

Before long the grass was soaked with dew, and the eyebrow of a moon hung above the cryptomerias. Each time the wind gusted, the insects stopped singing momentarily. Autumn had come, and the wild flowers, though not spectacular in the daytime, now quivered gracefully, like the feathered robe of a dancing deity.

"Enough," said Musashi, lowering his sword.

As he handed it to Iori, they became conscious of a voice coming from the direction of the grove.

"I wonder who that is," said Musashi.

"Probably a lost traveler wanting to put up for the night."

"Run and see."

As Iori sped around to the other side of the building, Musashi seated himself on the bamboo veranda and gazed out over the plain. The eulalias were tall, their tops fluffy; the light bathing the grass had a peculiar autumn sheen.

When Iori returned, Musashi asked, "A traveler?"

"No, a guest."

"Guest? Here?"

"It's Hōjō Shinzō. He tied his horse up and he's waiting for you in back."

"This house doesn't really have any back or front, but I think it'd be better to receive him here."

Iori ran round the side of the cabin, shouting, "Please come this way."

"This is a pleasure," said Musashi, his eyes expressing his delight at seeing Shinzō completely recovered.

"Sorry to have been out of touch so long. I suppose you live out here to get away from people. I hope you'll forgive me for dropping in unexpectedly like this."

Greetings having been exchanged, Musashi invited Shinzō to join him on the veranda. "How did you find me? I haven't told anyone where I am."

"Zushino Kōsuke. He said you'd finished the Kannon you promised him and sent Iori to deliver it."

"Ha, ha. I suppose Iori let the secret out. It doesn't matter. I'm not old enough to abandon the world and retire. I did think, though, that if I left the scene for a couple of months, the malicious gossip would quiet down. Then there'd be less danger of reprisals against Kōsuke and my other friends."

Shinzō lowered his head. "I owe you an apology— all this trouble because of me."

"Not really. That was a minor thing. The real root of the matter has to do with the relationship between Kojirō and me."

"Did you know he killed Obata Yogorō?"

"No."

"Yogorō, when he heard about me, decided to take revenge himself. He was no match for Kojirō."

"I warned him. . . ." The image of the youthful Yogorō standing in the entrance of his father's house was still vivid in Musashi's mind. "What a pity," he thought to himself.

"I can understand how he felt," continued Shinzō. "The students had all left, and his father had died. He must have thought he was the only one who could do it.

In any case, he appears to have gone to Kojirō's house. Still, no one saw them together; there's no real proof.''

"Mm. Maybe my warning had the opposite effect from what I intended—stirred up his pride so he felt he had to fight. It's a shame.''

"It is. Yogorō was *Sensei's* only blood relation. With his death the House of Obata ceased to exist. However, my father discussed the matter with Lord Munenori, who somehow managed to institute adoption proceedings. I'm to become Kagenori's heir and successor and carry on the Obata name. . . . I'm not sure I'm mature enough yet. I'm afraid I may end up bringing further disgrace to the man. After all, he was the greatest proponent of the Kōshū military tradition.''

"Your father's the Lord of Awa. Isn't the Hōjō military tradition considered to be on a par with the Kōshū School? And your father as great a master as Kagenori?''

"That's what they say. Our ancestors came from Tōtōmi Province. My grandfather served Hōjō Ujitsuna and Hōjō Ujiyasu of Odawara, and my father was selected by Ieyasu himself to succeed them as head of the family.''

"Coming from a famous military family, isn't it unusual for you to have become a disciple of Kagenori's?''

"My father has his disciples, and he's given lectures before the shōgun on military science. But instead of teaching me anything, he told me to go out and learn from somebody else. Find out the hard way! That's the kind of man he is.''

Musashi sensed an element of intrinsic decency, even nobility, in Shinzō's demeanor. And it was probably natural, he thought, for his father, Ujikatsu, was an outstanding general, and his mother was the daughter of Hōjō Ujiyasu.

"I'm afraid I've been talking too much,'' said Shinzō. "Actually, my father sent me out here. Of course, it would have been only proper for him to come and express his gratitude to you in person, but just now he has a guest, who's quite eager to see you. My father told me to bring you back with me. Will you come?" He peered inquiringly into Musashi's face.

"A guest of your father's wants to see me?"

"That's right."

"Who could it be? I know almost no one in Edo."

"A person you've known since you were a boy."

Musashi couldn't imagine who it might be. Matahachi, perhaps? A samurai from Takeyama Castle? A friend of his father's?

Maybe even Otsū . . . But Shinzō refused to divulge his secret. "I was instructed not to tell you who it is. The guest said it would be better to surprise you. Will you come?"

Musashi's curiosity was piqued. He told himself it couldn't be Otsū, but in his heart hoped it was.

"Let's go," he said, rising to his feet. "Iori, don't wait up for me."

Shinzō, pleased that his mission was successful, went behind the house and brought his horse. Saddle and stirrups were dripping with dew. Holding the bit, he offered the horse to Musashi, who proceeded without further ado to mount it.

As they left, Musashi said to Iori, "Take care of yourself. I may not be back until tomorrow." It was not long before he was swallowed up by the evening mist.

Iori sat quietly on the veranda, lost in thought.

"Eyes," he thought. "Eyes." Innumerable times he had been ordered to keep his eyes on his opponent's, but as yet he could neither understand the import of the instruction nor get the idea out of his mind. He gazed vacantly up at the River of Heaven.

What was wrong with him? Why was it that when Musashi stared at him, he couldn't stare straight back? More vexed by his failure than an adult would have been, he was trying very hard to find the explanation when he became conscious of a pair of eyes. They were aimed at him from the branches of a wild grapevine, which twined around a tree in front of the cabin.

"What's that?" he thought.

The brightly shining eyes reminded him strongly of Musashi's eyes during practice sessions.

"Must be a possum." He had seen one several times, eating the wild grapes. The eyes were like agate, the eyes of a fierce hobgoblin.

"Beast!" cried Iori. "You think I don't have any courage, think even you can outstare me. Well, I'll show you! I'm not about to lose to you."

With grim determination, he tensed his elbows and glared back. The possum, whether out of stubbornness or curiosity, made no move to flee. Its eyes took on an even more lustrous brilliance.

The effort so absorbed Iori that he forgot to breathe. He swore again not to lose, not to this lowly beast. After what seemed like hours, he realized with a flash that he had triumphed. The leaves of the grapevine shook and the possum vanished.

"That'll show you!" exulted Iori. He was drenched with sweat, but he felt relieved and refreshed. He only hoped he would be able to repeat the performance the next time he confronted Musashi.

Having lowered a reed blind on the window and snuffed out the lamp, he went to bed. A bluish-white light reflected from the grass outside. He dozed off, but inside his head he seemed to see a tiny spot, shining like a jewel. In time, the spot grew into the vague outline of the possum's face.

Tossing and moaning, he was suddenly overwhelmed by the conviction that there were eyes at the foot of his pallet. He roused himself with difficulty. "Bastard," he cried, reaching for his sword. He took a murderous swing but ended up doing a somersault. The shadow of the possum was a moving spot on the blind. He slashed at it wildly, then ran outside and hacked fiercely at the grapevine. His eyes rose skyward in search of the eyes.

There came into focus, slowly, two large, bluish stars.

28

Four Sages with a Single Light

"Here we are," Shinzō said as they reached the foot of Akagi Hill.

From the flute music, which sounded like the accompaniment to a sacred shrine dance, and the bonfire visible through the woods, Musashi thought a night festival must be in progress. The trip to Ushigome had taken two hours.

On one side was the spacious compound of Akagi Shrine; across the sloping street stood the earthen wall of a large private residence and a gate of magnificent proportions. When they reached the gate, Musashi dismounted and handed the reins to Shinzō, thanking him as he did so.

Shinzō led the horse inside and handed the reins to one of a group of samurai waiting near the entrance with paper lanterns in their hands. They all came forward, welcomed him back and led the way through the trees to a clearing in front of the imposing entrance hall. Inside, servants holding lanterns were lined up on both sides of the hallway.

The chief steward greeted them, saying, "Come in. His lordship is expecting you. I'll show you the way."

"Thank you," replied Musashi. He followed the steward up a stairway and into a waiting room.

The design of the house was unusual; one stairway after another led to a series of apartments, which gave the impression of being stacked one above another all the way up Akagi Hill. As he seated himself, Musashi noted that the room was well up the slope. Beyond a drop at the edge of the garden, he could just make out the northern part of the castle moat and the woods framing the escarpment. He found himself thinking that the view from the room in the daytime must be breathtaking.

Noiselessly, the door in an arched doorway slid open. A beautiful serving girl came gracefully in and placed a tray bearing cakes, tea and tobacco in front of him. Then she slipped out as quietly as she had entered. It seemed as if her colorful kimono and obi had emerged from and melted into the wall itself. A faint fragrance lingered after her, and suddenly Musashi was reminded of the existence of women.

The master of the house appeared shortly after that, attended by a young samurai. Dispensing with formalities, he said, "Good of you to come." In good soldierly fashion, he seated himself cross-legged on a cushion spread by the attendant and said, "From what I hear, my son is much indebted to you. I hope you'll pardon my asking you to come here rather than visiting your house to express my thanks." With his hands resting lightly on the fan in his lap, he inclined his prominent forehead ever so slightly.

"I'm honored to be invited to meet you," said Musashi.

It was not easy to estimate Hōjō Ujikatsu's age. Three front teeth were missing, but his smooth, shiny skin testified to a determination never to grow old. The heavy black mustache, streaked with only a few white hairs, had been allowed to grow out on both sides to conceal any wrinkles resulting from the lack of teeth. Musashi's first impression was of a man who had many children and got along well with young people.

Sensing that his host wouldn't object, Musashi went

straight to the point. "Your son tells me that you have a guest who knows me. Who might that be?"

"Not one but two. You'll see them by and by."

"Two people?"

"Yes. They know each other very well, and both are good friends of mine. I happened to meet them at the castle today. They came back with me, and when Shinzō came in to greet them, we started chatting about you. One of them said he hadn't seen you for a long time and would like to. The other, who knows you only by reputation, expressed the desire to be introduced."

Smiling broadly, Musashi said, "I think I know. One is Takuan Sōhō, isn't it?"

"That's right," exclaimed Lord Ujikatsu, slapping his knee in surprise.

"I haven't seen him since I came east several years ago."

Before Musashi had time to make a guess at who the other man was, his lordship said, "Come with me," and went out into the corridor.

They climbed a short stairway and walked down a long, dark corridor. Rain shutters were in place on one side. Suddenly Musashi lost sight of Lord Ujikatsu. He stopped and listened.

After a few moments, Ujikatsu called, "I'm down here." His voice seemed to come from a well-lit room that was situated across an open space from the corridor.

"I understand," Musashi called back. Instead of heading directly for the light, he stood where he was. The space outside the corridor was openly inviting, but something told him danger lurked in that stretch of darkness.

"What are you waiting for, Musashi? We're over here."

"Coming," answered Musashi. He was in no position to reply otherwise, but his sixth sense had warned him to be on the alert. Stealthily, he turned and walked back about ten paces to a small door, which let out onto the garden. Slipping on a pair of sandals, he made his way around the garden to the veranda of Lord Ujikatsu's parlor.

"Oh, you came that way, did you?" said his lordship, looking around from the other end of the room. He sounded disappointed.

"Takuan!" called Musashi as he entered the room, a radiant smile on his face. The priest, seated in front of the alcove, stood up to greet him. To meet again—and under the roof of Lord Hōjō Ujikatsu—seemed almost too fortuitous. Musashi had trouble convincing himself that it was really happening.

"We'll have to bring each other up to date," said Takuan. "Shall I begin?" He was clad in the plain robes he always wore. No finery, not so much as prayer beads. Yet he seemed mellower than before, more soft-spoken. Just as Musashi's rural upbringing had been leached out of him by strenuous attempts at self-discipline, Takuan, too, seemed to have had the sharper corners rounded off and to have become more deeply endowed with the wisdom of Zen. To be sure, he was no longer a youth. Eleven years older than Musashi, he was now approaching forty.

"Let's see. Kyoto, wasn't it? Ah, I remember. It was shortly before I went back to Tajima. After my mother died, I spent a year in mourning. Then I traveled for a while, spent some time at the Nansōji in Izumi, then at the Daitokuji. Later, I saw a good deal of Lord Karasumaru—composed poetry with him, had tea ceremonies, fended off the cares of this world. Before I knew it, I'd spent three years in Kyoto. Recently I became friendly with Lord Koide of Kishiwada Castle and came with him to have a look at Edo."

"Then you've been here only a short time?"

"Yes. Although I've met Hidetada twice at the Daitokuji and been summoned into Ieyasu's presence a number of times, this is my first trip to Edo. And what about you?"

"I've been here only since the beginning of this summer."

"It seems you've made quite a name for yourself in this part of the country."

Musashi didn't try to justify himself. He hung his head and said, "I suppose you've heard about that."

Takuan stared at him for a few moments, seemingly comparing him with the Takezō of old. "Why worry about that? It'd be strange if a man your age had too good a reputation. So long as you haven't done anything disloyal or ignoble or rebellious, what does it matter? I'm more interested in hearing about your training."

Musashi gave a brief account of his recent experiences and ended by saying, "I'm afraid I'm still immature, imprudent—far from being truly enlightened. The more I travel, the longer the road becomes. I have the feeling I'm climbing an endless mountain path."

"That's the way it has to be," said Takuan, clearly pleased with the youth's integrity and humility. "If a man not yet thirty claims to know the least bit about the Way, it's an unmistakable sign his growth has stopped. Even I still shudder with embarrassment when anyone suggests that an uncouth priest like me could know the ultimate meaning of Zen. It's disconcerting, the way people are always asking to tell me about the Buddhist Law or explain the true teachings. People try to look up to a priest as a living Buddha. Be thankful that others don't overestimate you, that you don't have to pay attention to appearances."

While the two men happily renewed their friendship, servants arrived with food and drink. Presently Takuan said, "Forgive me, your lordship. I'm afraid we're forgetting something. Why don't you call your other guest in?"

Musashi was certain now that he knew who the fourth person was, but elected to remain silent.

Hesitating slightly, Ujikatsu said, "Shall I call him?" Then, to Musashi, "I'll have to admit you saw through our little trick. As the one who planned it, I feel rather ashamed.''

Takuan laughed. "Good for you! I'm glad to see you're up to admitting defeat. But why not? It was only a game to amuse everybody anyway, wasn't it? Certainly nothing for the master of the Hōjō Style to lose face over.''

"Well, no doubt I was defeated," murmured Uji-katsu, reluctance still in his voice. "The truth is that although I've heard what sort of man you are, I had no way of knowing just how well trained and disciplined you are. I thought I'd see for myself, and my other guest agreed to cooperate. When you stopped in the passageway, he was waiting in ambush, ready to draw his sword.'' His lordship seemed to regret having had to put Musashi to the test. "But you perceived you were being lured into a trap and came across the garden." Looking directly at Musashi, he asked, "May I ask why you did that?''

Musashi merely grinned.

Takuan spoke up. "It's the difference, your lordship, between the military strategist and the swordsman.''

"Is it, now?''

"It's a matter of instinctive responses—that of a military scholar, based on intellectual principles, versus that of a man who follows the Way of the Sword, based on the heart. You reasoned that if you led Musashi on, he'd follow. Yet without being able to actually see, or to put his finger on anything definite, Musashi sensed danger and moved to protect himself. His reaction was spontaneous, instinctive.''

"Instinctive?''

"Like a Zen revelation.''

"Do you have premonitions like that?''

"I can't really say.''

"In any case, I've learned a lesson. The average samurai, sensing danger, might have lost his head, or perhaps seized upon the trap as an excuse to display his prowess with the sword. When I saw Musashi go back, put on the sandals and cross the garden, I was deeply impressed.''

Musashi kept his silence, his face revealing no special pleasure at Lord Ujikatsu's words of praise. His thoughts turned to the man still standing outside in the dark, stranded by the victim's failure to fall into the trap.

Addressing his host, he said, "May I request that the Lord of Tajima take his place among us now?''

"What's that?" Ujikatsu was astonished, as was Takuan. "How did you know?''

Moving back to give Yagyū Munenori the place of honor, Musashi said, "Despite the darkness, I felt the presence of peerless swordsmanship. Taking into consideration the other faces present, I don't see how it could be anyone else.''

"You've done it again!" Ujikatsu was amazed.

At a nod from him, Takuan said, "The Lord of Tajima. Quite right." Turning to the door, he called, "Your secret is out, Lord Munenori. Won't you join us?''

There was a loud laugh, and Munenori appeared in the doorway. Instead of arranging himself comfortably in front of the alcove, he knelt in front of Musashi and greeted him as an equal, saying, "My name is Mataemon Munenori. I hope you will remember me.''

"It is an honor to meet you. I am a rōnin from Mimasaka, Miyamoto Musashi by name. I pray for your guidance in the future.''

"Kimura Sukekurō mentioned you to me some months ago, but at the time I was busy because of my father's illness.''

"How is Lord Sekishūsai?''

"Well, he's very old. There's no way of knowing . . .'' After a brief pause, he continued with warm cordiality: "My father told me about you in a letter, and I've heard Takuan speak of you several times. I must say your reaction a few minutes ago was admirable. If you don't mind, I think we should regard the bout you requested as having taken place.

I hope you're not offended by my unorthodox way of carrying it out."

Musashi's impression was of intelligence and maturity quite in accordance with the daimyō's reputation.

"I'm embarrassed by your thoughtfulness," he replied, bowing very low. His show of deference was natural, for Lord Munenori's status was so far above Musashi's as to put him virtually in another world. Though his fief amounted to only fifty thousand bushels, his family had been famous as provincial magistrates since the tenth century. To most people, it would have seemed odd to find one of the shōgun's tutors in the same room with Musashi, let alone talking to him in a friendly, informal fashion. It was a relief to Musashi to note that neither Ujikatsu, a scholar and member of the shōgun's banner guard, nor Takuan, a country priest by origin, felt any constraint because of Munenori's rank.

Warm sake was brought, cups were exchanged, talk and laughter ensued. Differences in age and class were forgotten. Musashi knew he was being accepted in this select circle not because of who he was. He was seeking the Way, just as they were. It was the Way that permitted such free camaraderie.

At one point, Takuan set down his cup and asked Musashi, "What's become of Otsū."

Reddening slightly, Musashi said he hadn't seen or heard anything of her for some time.

"Nothing at all?"

"Nothing."

"That's unfortunate. You can't leave her in the lurch forever, you know. It's not good for you, either."

"By Otsū," asked Munenori, "do you mean the girl who once stayed with my father in Koyagyū?"

"Yes," replied Takuan on Musashi's behalf.

"I know where she is. She went to Koyagyū with my nephew Hyōgo to help nurse my father."

With a noted military scientist and Takuan present, thought Musashi, they could be talking about strategy or discussing Zen. With both Munenori and Musashi present, the subject could have been swords.

With a nod of apology to Musashi, Takuan told the others about Otsū and her relationship with Musashi. "Sooner or later," he concluded, "someone will have to bring the two of you together again, but I fear it's no task for a priest. I ask the assistance of you two gentlemen." What he was actually suggesting was that Ujikatsu and Munenori act as Musashi's guardians.

They seemed willing to accept this role, Munenori observing that Musashi was old enough to have a family and Ujikatsu saying that he had reached a satisfactorily high level of training.

Munenori suggested that one of these days Otsū should be summoned back from Koyagyū and given in marriage to Musashi. Then Musashi could set himself up in Edo, where his house, along with those of Ono Tadaaki and Yagyū Munenori, would form a triumvirate of the sword and usher in a golden age of swordsmanship in the new capital. Both Takuan and Ujikatsu concurred.

Specifically, Lord Ujikatsu, eager to reward Musashi for his kindness to Shinzō, wanted to recommend him as a tutor to the shōgun, an idea the three of them had explored before sending Shinzō for Musashi. And having seen how Musashi reacted to their test, Munenori himself was now ready to give his approval to the plan.

There were difficulties to be overcome, one being that a teacher in the shōgun's household also had to be a member of the honor guard. Since many of its members were faithful vassals of the Tokugawas from the days when Ieyasu had held the Mikawa fief, there was a reluctance to appoint new people, and all candidates were investigated with great thoroughness. However, it was felt that with recommendations from Ujikatsu and Munenori, together with a letter of guarantee from Takuan, Musashi would get by.

The sticky point was his ancestry. There was no written record tracing his ancestry back to Hirata Shōgen of the Akamatsu clan, nor even a genealogical chart to prove he was of good samurai stock. He assuredly had no family connections with the Tokugawas. On the contrary, it was an undeniable fact that as a callow youth of seventeen he had fought against the Tokugawa forces at Sekigahara. Still, there was a chance; other rōnin from former enemy clans had joined the House of Tokugawa after Sekigahara. Even Ono Tadaaki, a rōnin from the Kitabatake clan, which was at present in hiding in Ise Matsuzaka, held an appointment as tutor to the shōgun despite his undesirable connections.

After the three men had again gone over the pros and cons, Takuan said, "All right then, let's recommend him. But perhaps we should find out what he himself thinks about it."

The question was put to Musashi, who replied mildly, "It's kind and generous of you to suggest this, but I'm nothing but an immature young man."

"Don't think of it in that way," said Takuan with an air of candor. "What we're advising you to do is become mature. Will you establish a house of your own, or do you plan to make Otsū go on indefinitely living as she is now?"

Musashi felt hemmed in. Otsū had said she was willing to bear any hardship, but this would in no way lessen Musashi's responsibility for any grief that might befall her. While it was acceptable for a woman to act in accordance with her own feelings, if the outcome was not a happy one, the man would be blamed.

Not that Musashi was unwilling to accept the responsibility. On the whole, he yearned to accept. Otsū had been guided by love, and the onus of that love belonged to him as much as to her. Nevertheless, he felt it was still too early to marry and have a family. The long, hard Way of the Sword stretched before him yet; his desire to follow it was undiminished.

It did not simplify matters that his attitude toward the sword had changed. Since Hōtengahara, the sword of the conqueror and the sword of the killer were things of the past, no longer of any use or meaning.

Nor did being a technician, even one who gave instruc-

tion to men of the shōgun's retinue, excite his interest. The
Way of the Sword, as he had come to see it, must have
specific objectives: to establish order, to protect and refine
the spirit. The Way had to be one men could cherish as they
did their lives, until their dying day. If such a Way existed,
could it not be employed to bring peace to the world and
happiness to all?

When he had answered Sukekurō's letter with a challenge to Lord Munenori, his motive had not been the shallow
urge to score a victory that had led him to challenge
Sekishūsai. Now his wish was to be engaged in the business
of governing. Not on any grand scale, of course; a small,
insignificant fief would suffice for the activities he imagined
would promote the cause of good government.

But he lacked the confidence to express these ideas,
feeling that other swordsmen would dismiss his youthful
ambitions as being absurd. Or, if they took him seriously,
they would feel compelled to warn him: politics leads to
destruction; by going into government he would sully his
beloved sword. They would do this out of genuine concern
for his soul.

He even believed that if he spoke his mind truthfully,
the two warriors and the priest would react either with
laughter or with alarm.

When he did get around to speaking, it was to protest—he was too young, too immature, his training was
inadequate . . .

At length, Takuan cut him off, saying, "Leave it to us."

Lord Ujikatsu added, "We'll see that it turns out all
right for you."

The matter was decided.

Coming in periodically to trim the lamp, Shinzō had
caught the gist of the conversation. He quietly let his father
and the guests know that what he had heard pleased him
immensely.

LOOK FOR

MUSASHI

BOOK V

THE WAY OF LIFE
AND DEATH

The Shōgun is struggling to consolidate his power—and Musashi has been recommended to tutor him in the martial arts. But Japan is torn by new upheavals and deadly internal strife, and when Musashi is denied the appointment he sets off to pursue spiritual enlightenment—only to be slowly and irrevocably drawn into a fatal duel with Sasaki Kojirō, the only man who could possibly defeat him with a sword. The legend of Musashi is spreading across the land and opening the way to a great new age. But while the crowds flock to Musashi, his old friend Matahachi is hired as an assassin—to kill the Shōgun himself!

AN EPIC SAMURAI ADVENTURE

MUSASHI
by Eiji Yoshikawa

MUSASHI is the riveting story of Miyamoto Musashi, the son of a country samurai, who became the greatest swordsman in Japanese history. Left for dead on a battlefield, rescued by a Zen priest, Musashi trained his mind and disciplined his spirit, to embark on a epic journey to become the greatest swordsman in the land.

DON'T MISS MUSASHI—
THE FIVE-BOOK EPIC FROM POCKET BOOKS.